ESCAPEMENT

TOR BOOKS BY JAY LAKE

Mainspring

Escapement

ESCAPEMENT

JAY LAKE

TOR®

A TOM DOHERTY ASSOCIATES BOOK
New York

ESCAPEMENT

Copyright © 2008 by Joseph E. Lake Jr.

A Tor Book
Published by Tom Doherty Associates, LLC
175 Fifth Avenue
New York, NY 10010

www.tor-forge.com

Tor® is a registered trademark of Tom Doherty Associates, LLC.

Library of Congress Cataloging-in-Publication Data
Lake, Jay.
    Escapement / Jay Lake.—1st ed.
        p.   cm.
"A Tom Doherty Associates book."
ISBN-13: 978-0-7653-1709-4
ISBN-10: 0-7653-1709-5
I. Title.
PS3612.A519E83 2008
813'.6—dc22   2008005263

First Edition: June 2008

Printed in the United States of America

0 9 8 7 6 5 4 3 2 1

To Elizabeth Bear and Jeff VanderMeer. In a field overflowing with glorious exemplars, you have also been both spirit guides and dear friends.

ACKNOWLEDGMENTS

This book would not have been possible without the kind assistance of many people too numerous to fully list here. Nonetheless, I shall try, with apologies to whomever I manage to omit from my thank-yous. Much is owed to Kelly Buehler and Daniel Spector, Sarah Bryant, Michael Curry, Anna Hawley, Robin Hill, Sarah Hoyt, Carolyn Lachance and Brian Dewhirst, Ambassador Joseph Lake (aka Dad), Adrienne Loska, Lisa and Angel Mantchev, along with Elisa Aspert, Ruth Nestvold, Luís Rodrigues, Ken Scholes, Jeremy Tolbert, and, of course, my entire LiveJournal community in all their bumptious glory. There are many others I have neglected to name: Do not doubt that you are precious to me as well.

I also want to recognize the Brooklyn Post Office here in Portland, Oregon, as well as the Fireside Coffee Lodge and Lowell's Print-Inn for all their help and support. Special thanks go to Jennifer Jackson, Beth Meacham, Jozelle Dyer, and Eliani Torres for the very existence of this book in its present form, and to Irene Gallo and Stephan Martiniere for making the cover so beautiful that you wanted to pick the book up and take it home. As always, errors and omissions are entirely my own responsibility.

ESCAPEMENT

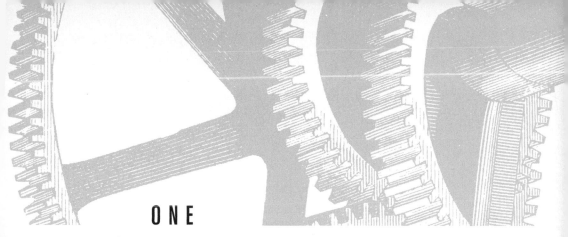

ONE

PAOLINA

The boats had been drawn up in the harbor at Praia Nova when the great waves came two years past. The men of the village generally thought this a blessing, for that circumstance had spared their lives. The women generally thought this a curse for much the same reason. *A Muralha* remained silent and unforgiving as ever, a massive rampart of stone, soil, and strangeness soaring 150 miles high to separate Northern Earth from Southern Earth. In the shadow of the Wall, there was less food than ever until boats could be rebuilt and nets rewoven, but no self-respecting man would go without dinner. So the women quietly starved themselves and their babies to keep the drunken beatings away.

No one starved Paolina Barthes, though. Demon-haunted or touched by God, in either case she had saved Praia Nova after the waves. Still, she was boy-thin and narrow-shouldered, not yet to her monthlies though she wore the black linen dress that all the grown women favored.

The *fidalgos* spent every Friday night in the great hall at the edge of Praia Nova. The building had been erected in an absolute absence of architects or—at least prior to Paolina—engineers, but instead with the dogged determination of the *fidalgos* that they knew best. Generations of pigheadedness had raised a monstrosity of coral cut from the reefs at the foot of *a Muralha,* granite chipped with slow, steady pain from the bones of the Wall itself, marble salvaged in furtive, fearful expeditions to the cities of the enkidus higher up. This resulted in something like a cross between a cathedral and a toolshed. Still, it had survived the quakes that came with the waves, where many of the traditional *adôbe* houses had not.

It was a harlequin of a building as well. The mix of materials and styles across the years made the thing a patchwork, a Josephan coat to shelter the guiding lights of Praia Nova in their wise deliberations.

This night, they were drunk and afraid.

Paolina knew this the way she knew most things. It was obvious from the scents in the air, the rhythm of the glasses pounding the table, the fact that another of Fra Bellico's children had been buried that day in the hard, thin soil on which Praia Nova huddled, 317 steps above the coral jetty and the unforgiving sea.

She walked toward the great hall on the path they called *Rua do Rei*— the King's Street. In truth only four men and one woman in Praia Nova had ever seen a street, and they had no king save the Lord God Almighty. *Rua do Rei* was just wide enough for two goats to pass, and had a rope strung to provide a grip during one of the great Wall storms off the Atlantic. One side opened into a ravine where the villagers threw what little garbage they were not able to intensively and obsessively reuse. The other passed close to a knee of *a Muralha*.

Juan and Portis Mendes had found a boy, but no one had brought him to her. Instead the fools had taken their prize to the *fidalgos*.

He was English, she'd heard, and had not come from the sea like every Praia Novado. Not from the sea at all, but down the eastern path through the countries and kingdoms of *a Muralha* toward mythic *Africa*.

Paolina hated, hated, hated being told things. All they had to do was let her see and she would find a way. When the earthquakes dried the springs that watered Praia Nova, she'd built the pedal-powered pump to raise water from the Westerly Creek down near sea level. When Jorg Penoyer got his leg trapped up on the coal face, she'd figured out the pressure points in the rock and set rope-and-tackle rig to get him out without an amputation. She understood the world, and when the *fidalgos* managed to forget Paolina was a girl, they remembered that.

Even more she hated being told she was merely a girl. Not even a woman yet. God had not put her on this Northern Earth to squeeze out some lout's get like a she-goat every nine months after being topped. Women lived only to serve, while the *pilas* of the men made them Lords of Creation.

To hell with that, Paolina thought.

She stopped outside the great hall and stared up at the sky. The earth's track gleamed, tracing a brass-bright line across the hemisphere of the heavens, that barely bowed outward from *a Muralha*. The Wall itself remained mighty as ever, the world's stone muscle, greater than any imagination could encompass.

Except hers.

Paolina smiled in the evening darkness. God could set His little traps. She would find her way out.

The rising blare of voices called her onward. She marched toward the doors of the great hall, closed now against evening's chill and the untoward attentions of people like her.

Inside, the men did what they usually did, which was pretend not to notice her. Dom Alvaro, Dom Pietro, Fra Bellico, Benni Penoyer, and Dom Mendes were pulled close around a plank table in the main hall, a bottle of *bagaceira* between them drained down to eye-watering vapors and bubbled glass.

The English boy—a young man, really—sat on a bench against the west wall. Half a leering face, broken off some great enkidu carving, was jammed into the stone above him. He was sallow and burned by the sun, with greasy, pale hair and a tired look in his eyes. Their gazes met a moment. There was no spark of recognition, no sense of a kindred spirit close to hand.

Just another man, then, in love with his own *pila,* to whom she was nothing more than furniture.

Still, Paolina wished she'd gotten to him first, before the stranger witnessed the drunken anger of the *fidalgos*. He would think them nothing more than a village of fools. This boy, who must have seen London or Camelot once, now knew her people to be little more than asses braying in an unswept stable at the very edge of the world.

Paolina felt her anger rising again.

"We cannot afford him," shouted Dom Mendes. He was haggard, dusty to the elbows with the work of building new boats. Oh, they had not liked her opinion of that effort. "That old fool who lived among us before the waves came was bad enough, and we dwelt amid plenty then. There are too many mouths now."

"One less today," blubbered Fra Bellico, who had not missed a meal yet though he kept his Bible always close to hand.

"My boys hunt," Mendes hissed.

Penoyer snorted. "Yes, and bring back more mouths." No *fidalgo* he, his grandfather having come off an English boat by way of unsuccessful mutiny. Only quality took the titles of respect in Praia Nova.

Caught between anger and embarrassment, Paolina finally stepped up to their table. She shoved herself between Mendes and Pietro. "Do you suppose he might understand Portuguese?"

Bellico waved a pudgy hand. "He is English. The roast beefs never speak anyone else's tongue, only their own barbarous barf."

"Then I shall speak to him in English," she announced. "Perhaps he brings knowledge or tools with which to feed himself and others."

Penoyer, pale as a grub with hair the color of fireweed flowers, shot her a glare before answering in that language, "No good will come of it, girl."

The boy perked up a bit, then slumped down as the words sank in.

"It can't possibly get any worse," she snapped, also in English.

Let Penoyer explain it to the *fidalgos*.

Paolina stepped around to the boy. "Come with me," she told him, in his language.

He stood and followed her out, without a backward glance. Nothing lost there, she realized. Outside she turned to him. "I am sorry." She paused to frame her next words.

"*Não faz mal,*" he replied, surprising her. *It doesn't matter.*

Despite herself, Paolina giggled. "You understood everything they said?"

"Most of it." English again.

"My mother has bread." It was the kindest thing she knew to do for the boy. She took his hand and tugged him along the path that was King Street, back to the houses of Praia Nova and their quiet, hungry women.

To save the expense of the candle, they ate on the back step of the hut. Paolina's mother washed and swept the stone daily. She'd been sitting quietly, staring out at the moonlit Atlantic when Paolina came for the bread, and did not stir.

So it had been in the years since Paolina's father's boat came back without him. Marc Penoyer had been captain. He and his two brothers had sworn a tale so alike it had to be concocted—even at six, Paolina had known no two people perfectly agreed on anything. People didn't *see* what was in front of them. They saw only what was dear to their hearts.

After that, her mother worked her days and dreamt away the nights. Sometimes she spoke, sometimes she didn't, but Paolina always had at least one dress. She'd never gone an entire day without eating something.

It was the bargain of childhood, she'd supposed. As her cleverness had begun to count for something extra, Paolina had made sure there was always a little flour from the sorry mill above town, always a little dried meat from the line-caught fish the idled boatmen brought in.

The boy asked no questions about her mother, merely gnawing the crust with a gusto that betrayed how long it had been since he'd eaten decently. She'd spared him only two chunks torn from the loaf, and a handful of dried sardinella, but Paolina knew that offering food made her civilized.

He'd seen *London,* a voice within her cried. London. Even Dr. Minor had not been there.

In that moment, she hated *a Muralha,* Praia Nova, and everything else about her life. She stared up at the brass in the sky, wondering how to break it and set free the earth, and herself.

"Thank you," the boy said.

"Hmm?" She swallowed the harder words which lay too close to her tongue.

"Thank you. They were going to throw me out of the village, weren't they?"

"Of course." Despite her anger, Paolina laughed. "You might say or do something dangerous. News of the world helps no one, serving only to make us doubt our traditions. Besides, we are starving."

"So am I."

She looked over at him. The boy wore a leather wrap, something that had been tailored in a sense, but as if sewn by cats who had only seen paintings of real clothing. He had a grubby, torn shirt beneath that, and a pair of canvas trousers that must have once been white. Bare feet, which made her wince.

"Sure you did not walk here along the Wall?" she asked him.

"I fell from a ship."

She resisted the urge to glance toward the ocean far below, but there must have been something in her face. He raised one hand in defense. "An airship. I fell from one of Her Imperial Majesty's airships."

Despite herself, Paolina was impressed. "You look well enough for a man who fell to earth."

"I had a parachute."

She didn't know the word, but she was not going to ask him to explain. It obviously referred to a device for retarding the rate of fall. Cloth or ribbons could do that, though with his weight, it would need a wide spread to provide sufficient surface area for braking. In the back of her mind, she began to work out the formula for the relationship between the size of the cloth and the weight of the load.

"I am Paolina Barthes," she said. "This paradise on Northern Earth is Praia Nova."

He stood and bowed awkwardly. "Clarence Davies, late the loblolly boy aboard Her Imperial Majesty's airship *Bassett.*" After a moment he added, "Very late, for it has been two years since I fell overboard and began my walk along the Wall."

Now she was very impressed. "You survived two years on your own?"

He nodded, still looking both hungry and hunted. It could not have been easy—Praia Nova barely clung to life, and that was with several hundred people who at least theoretically could coordinate defenses and share what they had.

"You must know how to live out there, then," she said.

"Knew how to live aboard *Bassett*." His head drooped lower. "Stay out of Captain Smallwood's way, listen to whatever the doctor mumbles when he ain't drinking, watch out for the clever dicks like Malgus and that boy of his."

"You're not a— clever?" She was disappointed. He was *English*. They were the genius sorcerers who ran the world. Dr. Minor had taught her that, before he'd fled into the wilderness.

She'd learned so much from the old Englishman.

"Just a boy, me," Clarence said. "The officers and the chiefs, they know their business. Al-Wazir, he was a magician, could make a man do anything. Need to, I guess, to work the ropes."

The power of compulsion. That explained a great deal about the British Empire.

The boy went on. "Smallwood, too. The gas division. They walk in poison, you know."

"This *Bassett* was a magnificent ship?"

For the first time, Clarence Davies smiled. "The greatest. Soaring through the clouds on a summer day, looking down on them whales and sharks and fuzzy wuzzies . . ." His head dropped again. "I want to go back to England, though. But 'tis too far to walk."

"You flew through the air to come here, and now you cannot find your way home." Something in Paolina's heart melted, that she had not known was frozen. "They'll grumble for a month, the *fidalgos,* and never come to a decision. So I decide now. I invite you in my mother's name. We will find a boy's family for you to stay with, and I will make sure there is a bit more food."

"I . . . I . . . have nothing to give."

"Nothing is required. Help where you can, lend your muscles, speak to me in English." She smiled, trying to coax another flash of bright teeth out of this Clarence. "There are few enough safe places on *a Muralha.* Stay here a while."

"Thank you." He came to some visible decision, a flash of relief and recognition in his face, then dug deep into an inner pocket of his leather wrap. Clarence shoved a little bag at her. "Here. I don't need this. Ain't wound it in months. Smart, clever girl like you maybe could use it."

The thing was heavy, a hunk of metal or glass. She pulled it out and corrected herself. A hunk of metal *and* glass. Round face, with hours on it like a sundial and a heavy metal rim containing more weight. The face was topped by three metal arrows. There were tinier faces within, with their own calibrations, and a little cutaway showing something behind the face.

She peered close and saw Heaven.

Gears.

It was God's gearing, the mechanisms of the earth and sky captured in the palm of her hand. Light flooded her head for a moment, the dawn of a new awareness. Paolina's stomach knotted in something between fear and fascination. She'd had no idea that a person could fashion a model of the world to carry with him.

"It counts the hours," she whispered, her voice and hands trembling in awe.

"Yes." He touched a little cap extending from one end. "See? It's a stemwinder. A Dent marine chronometer that needs no key."

Her fingers lay on the knurls of the cap. At his nod, Paolina very gently twisted it.

The tiny model of the world within clicked, just as the heavens did at midnight.

This was Creation in the palm of her hand. The English were truly magicians.

Much to her surprise, Paolina began to cry.

Praia Nova had seven books. They were kept in the great hall, in an inner closet with the precious bottles used to contain *bagaceira* when Fra Bellico found the necessaries to distill more, or the wildflower wine the women made when Fra Bellico lacked materials, time, or ambition.

There was half an English Bible, the Old Testament through the middle of Ezekiel. It was water damaged. The New Testament, with its stories of the Romans and their horofixion of Christ, existed in Praia Nova only as a scrawled leather scroll reconstructed from the memories of the various shipwrecked sailors who'd brought their indifferent faiths to the village over the generations. It did not matter what she thought of the prophets or the inept copy work of recent times—the Bible needed no more explanation than a look to the sky.

The other books were a different matter entirely. Her favorite was *Fiéis e Verdadeiros Segredos,* a Portuguese translation of a book that claimed to have originally been published in French, written by a Comte de Saint-Germain. It was a magnificent volume, bound in a slick, smooth leather that she was fairly certain was human skin. The title was stamped into the binding with traces of gold leaf and faded red pigment. There were lurid woodcuts within, lavishly illustrating scenes of debauchery from the ancient days. She'd spent time studying those, but had not yet divined the meaning of most. In any case, Paolina found it difficult to credit what Saint-Germain said of himself and the world. The man, whoever he had truly been, was an extraordinary storyteller at the least. She hoped to meet a Jew one day so that she could pursue some of the questions raised in *Segredos.*

There was also *Archidoxes Magica,* by Paracelsus. It was bound in boards, and quite damaged by damp and age. Furthermore, no one could aid her with the Latin. She had no second text to compare it with in order to puzzle out the language. As a result Paolina had struggled mightily with the book. In *Segredos,* Saint-Germain claimed to have known Paracelsus as an alchemist and physic, but that only told her one thing—fraud or genius, he had seen into the heart of the world.

That inspired her.

Three of the other books were popular texts, two in English, one in Spanish: *The Mystery of Edwin Drood* by Charles Dickens, *Mathias Sandorf* by Jules Verne, and *Cartas Marruecas* by José Cadalso. There was also one volume in an alphabet that looked maddeningly familiar while making no sense at all. Paolina was surprised the last hadn't been burned for fire starter. She'd read through the English works many times, and puzzled through Cadalso twice.

She'd learned how strange the world was, beyond *a Muralha* and the goat-dung paths of Praia Nova. That, and how badly she wished she lived in a part of the Northern Earth where there were printing presses and libraries and bookshops.

Even Dr. Minor's visit to Praia Nova, while immensely improving her English and her knowledge of the world, had only deepened her dissatisfaction.

Now, though, now she had a treasure beyond price. She had a pocket watch. A stemwinding marine chronometer, to be specific.

Neither the Bible nor Saint-Germain had anything to say directly about watches, though both certainly discussed clockwork—albeit somewhat metaphorically in the Bible. Paracelsus was no help at all, and neither was Cadalso. Verne and Dickens, however, seemed fully in command of a world where pocket watches were ordinary.

In the days that followed, she reread both works carefully. The purpose of the watch would have been clear enough even if Davies had not explained it. Paolina was far more interested in the design and construction. She'd never so much as seen a clock. There were obvious inferences to be made about the mechanism from looking at God's design for the universe. He had written His plan in the sky, after all.

What Paolina wanted was a clear set of instructions.

The stemwinder was heavy in the pocket of her homespun smock. She knew it was there the way she knew her heartbeat was there. Wound, it ticked. Ticking, it reflected the world.

Time beats at the heart of everything, she thought.

It was one of those ideas that pricked a spark in her mind, a little flare that staked a claim of importance.

God had made the universe of clockwork. The world ticked and turned. Two years ago, it had stuttered. The great waves and quakes came from deep within, she knew. Midnight had slipped by a few seconds. No one else understood, and there was no point in explaining, but she'd known.

Then the world had been fixed. Whatever time beat at the heart of the earth had been restored. Paolina wished she knew how. A question that ran through all the books (except the Bible, of course) was whether God acted directly in the world, or simply let His handiwork sort itself out.

Something had been sorted out.

And still time beat at the heart of everything. The stemwinder was a model of the universe, no larger than the palm of her hand, no thicker than two of her fingers, and it ticked away the moments and hours just as all of Creation did.

Paolina put it close to her ear, listening with the words of Dickens and Verne and the Old Testament prophets close in her mind. Ezekiel 24:6 suggested itself to her in the gentle ticking deep within. *Woe to the bloody city, to the brasswork in which there is verdigris, and whose verdigris has not gone out of it! Take out of it piece after piece, without making a choice.*

That was clear enough. God was telling her to take the watch apart.

Paolina's most difficult problem was finding a clean, clear workspace. Whatever gears and trains lay within the stemwinder were tiny reflections of the brass in the heavens. She'd need a room sealed from the winds, relatively free of dust and dirt, where the complex work could remain undisturbed in her absence.

The inner room of the great hall, among the books and bottles, would have been ideal. But even Paolina couldn't quite imagine how to get the *fidalgos* to come around to that. They would beat her for a stupid chit and set her to scraping moss off the water stairs if she had the temerity to even ask.

She wandered the village, looking at the houses and storerooms that comprised most of Praia Nova. The ones that were not inhabited were tumbledown. Paolina didn't want to contemplate the patience required to clean up an abandoned hut.

On the Oporto shelf, the second ledge above town, where more of the thin wheat fields ran, she realized she was looking at her answer—the mushroom sheds. They were sealed with lacquered canvas, and they were quiet. It would be a month or more before another set of trays was picked. All she needed was a bit of light.

Best of all, the women of the town ran the sheds. Senhora Armandires was the dame of the mushrooms. Paolina had built a much improved chimney in the woman's house last year, once Senhor Armandires had finally moved out for good and the senhora could make her own choices. The lady would make no objection.

Light was still an issue, but it would take little enough to see the watch. Candle stubs were her friends.

Paolina went off to find Clarence. He could help her drag a table out of one of the abandoned houses and up to the Oporto shelf. And a cloth to cover it.

She would find a way. This was the solving of problems. She was good at that.

During the course of the following days, Paolina opened the back of the stemwinder to observe the delicate movements of the mechanisms within. What she saw nearly turned her away from her project. She lacked the tools to grasp such miniscule things. She might be able to make those, in time, with scraps from the Alcides' smithy. She would need a lens, as well, scarcely possible here in Praia Nova. In any case, this was a task for the slow and patient. She stuck with picks and pries made out of hardwood splinters.

Clarence was something of a help, ghosting about and answering her occasional question. He spent time foraging, too, farther from Praia Nova than most of the locals would go. Of course, he'd walked the Wall for two years—the boy had survived far stranger things than the glittering, scaled cats that occasionally prowled the ledges here, or the bright, frigid rocks that sometimes bounded down from higher up.

He came running in the evening of her fourth day in the mushroom shed. Panting, sweating, as the whites of his eyes gleamed in the light of her little candle stub. "The *fidalgos* are looking for you!" he shouted in Portuguese.

"Someone is always looking for me." A tiny stab of fear stole into her heart.

Davies switched to English. "You have been summoned. Senhora Armandires argues with Fra Bellico down in the village."

Paolina sighed and put down the teakwood picks. She carefully covered the stemwinder with a square of pale silk, part of the bounty harvested from the body of a Chinaman brought up in the nets the year before the big waves. "What does the good father want of me?" She dusted off her hands.

Clarence looked down at his feet a moment. "The *fidalgos* are angry."

The answer was obvious now, but her rising irritation made her unkind. "About what are they angry, Englishman?"

Walking behind her through the canvas flap that was the door, he mumbled some answer she couldn't hear.

"Pardon?" Nasty now.

"That you were given the watch."

"That I was given the watch." Her singsong tones mocked him. What had she ever thought worthy of this idiot boy? "The heavens opened up and spat a watch into my hands, which by the grace of God should have been given to the men of Praia Nova, is that it?"

"I'm sorry," he muttered, but she already raced down the paths toward the shouting.

The *fidalgos* were drunk and angry. The first thing Paolina realized was that they were into the wildflower wine. The *bagaceira* was gone, and Fra Bellico had not found any more of the wild grapes and plums from which to press his pomace and make more. No wonder they were upset, forced to drink a woman's swill.

The five were drawn up to their table again, facing her: Alvaro, Pietro, Bellico, Penoyer, and Mendes, who chewed his moustache and looked thoughtful. The rest merely seemed possessed by the same tired anger that had gripped the men in the village since the fishing fleet had been lost.

They badly missed the seafood trade with the enkidus and the down-trail tribes.

"You!" roared Bellico. "Thieving girl! We should sell you up *a Muralha*."

"I have stolen nothing," said Paolina. "I give you everything and more. What is it you want now?"

"What is our due," Mendes said quietly, casting a sidelong glare at the others. "What the boy mistakenly set in your hand."

"What he *gave* me?" She let her voice seethe with contempt, though in truth these men scared her. Not for who they were, but for what they could do. The *fidalgos* in council, which they were now, were judges and swords of the law in Praia Nova. Never mind that no one owned such a blade.

This was as large a matter as they'd ever broached her over.

"The watch," said Penoyer. He was flush, even in the candlelight, with a graceless air of shame.

"You want me to give you my watch?" As with Clarence, she would make them say it.

"Yes!" It was Bellico again. "The village could do much with that wealth of metal. Trade it, keep it for a treasure. Not let it be greased by the clumsy hands of a youthful *Carapau de Corrida* with more ambition than sense!"

"Fra," said Paolina slowly and deliberately. "If you call me that name again, I shall make sure your still produces nothing but vinegar, and your *pilinha* will burn every morning for the rest of your days."

"She's a witch," muttered Alvaro. "Always was, little chit."

"Enough," said Mendes. He was not the bull among them—that was Fra Bellico—but he was the only *fidalgo* with enough sense that Paolina could consider having respect for him. "It does not matter. What matters is you took an object of great value, easily considered salvage and thus the property of all, and have hidden it away. That should have been the decision of the village."

"You mean your decision." Paolina just couldn't stop herself from speaking. The men didn't merely believe they were entitled—they *were* entitled. This transcended reason.

"Our decision is the decision of village." Mendes leaned forward, the room around him now quiet, the guttering candle filling his eyes with shadowed darkness. "Your decision is not."

And there it was. The truth of the matter. She might as well argue with *a Muralha* as argue with generations of tradition.

"No," Paolina told him. "You cannot have it until I am done."

"You will not obey the decision of the *fidalgos* in council?" Mendes asked. Slowly, carefully.

She was on an edge here. But she simply couldn't give in. If she did it now, she was lost. "No." It was amazing how easy that word was to repeat.

Mendes glanced at Bellico in particular. The father took a deep, shuddering breath, then nodded. "Very well. At fifteen, you are old enough to heed the will of the village or pay the consequences. I only regret we did not take you in hand earlier."

They were getting up from the table, chairs scraping, feet shuffling as the large drunken men encircled her.

Paolina felt a stab of fear. She shrieked when they grabbed her, already clamping her knees together, but the *fidalgos* dragged her to the back room, shoved her in with the books and bottles, and shut the one door in all of Praia Nova that actually had a key.

It took her a while to cry, and longer to begin screaming, but the door remained thick, wooden and locked no matter how she pounded and pleaded. In time, they doused their candle and left. She didn't know whether the wine had run out or they had tired of the noise of her fear.

AL-WAZIR

Threadgill Angus al-Wazir, formerly Ropes Division chief petty officer aboard HIMS *Bassett,* ship lost in service along the Wall, scratched at the starched collar. The civvie shirt cut into his neck like a dock monkey's shiv. "This is worse than a lashing," he muttered, though no one could hear him save the two lobsterbacks standing guard in front of the great double doors outside which he waited.

Royal Marines, in uniforms that could have been paraded in his grandfather's time. Insufficient to fend off a howling mob, and yet too much for the mere keeping of a door, no matter how many admirals and MPs sat on the other side of it.

Some days he almost missed starving on that dhow off the Mauritanian coast under the blazing Atlantic sun. That was an honest fate for a good sailor. Nothing like death by sweat and knife-edged crease.

Civvies, at that. Not even a uniform. He hadn't worn civvies since he'd left short pants. Even on leave, it was a tar's canvas trousers and some old blues.

The room was as bad as the clothing. The lobsterbacks might as well have been furniture, bayonets silvered and polished to shaving-mirror brightness. The walls were done in some strange lumber, in them little panels like pictures in frames except it was all the same wood. A chandelier with far too much cut glass glowed with ill-wired electricks. A big painting of the clockwork two-decker *Vincent Leonard,* that had foundered under Nelson and put an end to those old spring engines. Back to sail, it had been, until they'd worked out the steam. Another big painting of the admiral himself, victorious at Trafalgar with the head of Villeneuve dangling from one hand. The old Froggie's eyes were as surprised as death ever made a man.

Al-Wazir saluted the Frenchman. It had been near the last gasp of their power.

Below the level of the paintings the room grew peculiar—delicate settees covered with paisleys he wouldn't bury a dog in, tiny end tables bearing tinier silver dishes of mints the size of biscuit weevils. Rugs on the floor from somewhere far to the east, with the look of knotting by little fingers. He'd seen enough posh in dockside knocking shops to have an idea. All that bawdy house stuff was just so much tinfoil and chintz imitation of this room, where the Queen herself could have eaten off the parquet flooring had she taken a mind to do so.

Being a chief petty officer, however discharged at the moment, al-Wazir had to admire the obsessive attention to cleanliness. He doubted even the most white-gloved psychotic could have found fault on an inspection here, unless one of the marines had soiled his linens. Knowing that lot, their bladders were at firm attention.

He scratched at his collar again, grinning with evil intent at the unmoving sentries. *He* was out of uniform, he'd by God scratch. Al-Wazir studied them intently. Yes, the one on the left had a bead of sweat on the tip of his nose. He didn't quite have the kidney to give a good ribbing, not when yon doors could open at any moment and his undivided attention be required by Admiralty, but for now he could enjoy another man's discomfort with a genteel incivility.

Al-Wazir waited in an antechamber somewhere within the second floor of the Ripley Building, where Admiralty was housed. He was aware of the irony of finding himself in this elevated estate only after being discharged from the Royal Navy by an examining board at Bristol. The summons to London had been a surprise, to say the least. Al-Wazir had been on a train to Scotland with the last of the Queen's shillings in his pocket. A whey-faced lieutenant with a squad of Royal Marines in sensible woolens and hard hands had pulled him off at Pemberton. It was not arrest this time, as had happened when their dhow had finally creaked into Bristol harbor to the jeers of the dockside idlers. Rather, he was taken aboard a sealed first-class car, alone except for his escorts.

That had been all right with him. Al-Wazir hadn't really been looking forward to seeing his ma anyway. Besides which, he possessed no notion of what to do next out of uniform. Al-Wazir had figured on dying in the air one day, but when *Bassett* had gone down under the combination of monstrous attack and inclement weather, the Lord God Almighty hadn't seen fit to take him with the ship.

So now he was here, scrubbed and shaved and pressed and folded into a black suit and a little seat in a room where Prime Minister Lloyd George had passed him by an hour before.

Quality, his ma always said he was destined to hit quality. She'd just meant it in a different way.

Al-Wazir startled awake when the doors creaked open. A quiet little man in a suit much like al-Wazir's own nodded to him.

The Royal Marines remained a pair of silent logheads. This was no better than being called before the captain on account of some ropes idler going stupid while he wasn't looking. Admiralty, and even the Prime Minister, were nothing more than bigger captains.

So he followed the quiet man into a very large room, where older, heavier men with long muttonchops and red faces sat around a table the size of a longboat, nodding at a bloody huge chart of some islands. It wasn't anywhere al-Wazir had ever been; that was for certain. He adopted the blank look-at-nothing practiced by sailors in the presence of officers since the first reed boats had sculled along the Euphrates.

His escort faded into a number of similar men making notes and riffling through red folders along the dark edges of the room. There were no windows here, just as in the outer room, though a pair of frosted skylights admitted some gray from above. Otherwise the room was lit by electricks in sconces around the walls, giving forth a slightly scorched smell. Where there might have been more paintings of naval history, there were now charts or maps. Al-Wazir would be damned if he was going to stare.

Busy. The room was busy. In some indefinable way, it reminded him of a gun deck just before battle. Men were sweating and the air was thick with tension. Simply because no guns were in evidence did not mean there was no enemy at hand.

"Chief al-Wazir." He was being addressed by a broad-faced man with humor in his eyes, dressed as all of them were here in black. The Prime Minister, in fact—Lloyd George himself.

"Sir, yes sir."

"The man with the interesting name. You would seem to be as Scottish as the next oat-eater from Lanarkshire, I must say." The Welsh in Lloyd George's voice was almost absent, though the humor carried through. "You may think of me as the Member from Caernarfon Boroughs, if that helps. As for the rest of the gentlemen here, they are simply persons committed to the interests of the Crown. Their names and titles should not matter to you."

"Sir, no sir." Though he did wonder why a room full of senior men in the heart of the Admiralty complex should be so empty of uniforms. Including his own.

"Tell me, Chief . . ." Lloyd George's eyes sparkled. "Have you ever heard of the city of Chersonesus Aurea?"

Of all the questions Her Imperial Majesty's Prime Minister might have asked him, that was not one al-Wazir would have imagined in his wildest dreams. "No idea, sir."

"To be expected, I suppose." The PM sounded disappointed. "Neither had any of the rest of us. I daresay you know the Wall, and the Bight of Benin?"

Al-Wazir felt a smile cracking. "Thumping huge bit of rock, sir, far to the south. Been on her a bit, then sailed myself home out of the Bight by way of Dahomey and Mauritania."

"So we have been informed." He walked around al-Wazir, an inspection in all but name. "I shan't apologize for your discharge hearing in Bristol, Chief. Regulations are regulations." Lloyd George reappeared in al-Wazir's line of sight. "But would you be interested in going back to the Wall on Her Imperial Majesty's service?"

"At my rank and grade, sir?" The question slipped out.

"If that is what is required. Or as a civilian— No . . . I think not." Lloyd George nodded at one of the quiet men on the edge of the room. "I expect you'll be a chief petty officer once more by Monday next, if not sooner."

"Sir, yes sir." Al-Wazir could feel his sweat pooling now. He felt much like the marine he'd silently mocked in the antechamber.

"Kitchens," said the PM in a carrying voice. "The other map, please."

One of the quiet little men used a long pole topped by a metal hook to roll up the island chart. A moment later he replaced it with a chart of the Bight of Benin, the bulk of the Wall a dark line brooding at its southern extent.

"Your ship was driven down there, yes?"

"Sir, yes sir. Storm and enemy action."

"I've seen the report of your court-martial. Pity to lose Smallwood and so much of his crew. Experienced hands, the lot."

Al-Wazir held back a shuddering breath. They were long dead now, his old crewmates and charges, and nothing he could do for them or their memory from this distance. "I was rather surprised to make it home alive, sir."

Lloyd George gave him a long look. "I'm sure it's a fascinating tale, Chief, but I don't suppose I'll ever have time for it. However, your recent experiences have granted you the unique qualification of being the Crown's leading expert on survival at the Wall. We lost far too much with Gordon's expedition of 1900."

"*Bassett* foundered in support of that same expedition, sir."

"Of course." The PM seemed slightly surprised. "Yet the holocaust produced you, trained and experienced, annealed in the blazing sun of the tropics."

"Burnt red is more like it, sir." He wasn't sure about the annealed bit.

"There is a town, Acalayong, just above the foot of the Wall at the easternmost verge of the Bight. I would ask you to take ship and go there."

"Sir, if I'm in uniform again, I'm under orders." Al-Wazir could feel the trickle of his sweat burgeoning to rivers. Nervous, he was not nervous. A chief never was. "Her Imperial Majesty's Navy don't ask its sailors what they want to do."

Lloyd George gave him a long, thoughtful look. "In this case, I'd prefer to have your willing agreement, Chief al-Wazir. There's a scientific expedition being mounted, under qualified supervision. I've many men who will follow orders. I'd very much like an experienced man along for whom I can have some hope of personal trust."

"Sir . . ." Al-Wazir swallowed hard. "You do not know me in the least wee bit. I'm a sailor, a Scotsman, and quarter an Arab. Any Englishman will tell you that makes me a liar three times over. You've no cause or call to trust me. Not outside the following of orders."

"I said hope of trust," the PM reminded him. "Neither of us is a fool. We'd both have been cast aside or left for dead long ago if we were. I've good men and true in the expedition, both officially placed and otherwise. But they're each under orders in their way. You, sir . . ." He took a deep breath. "You survived, in a place where most men have perished without a trace. As did your father, it would seem, back in his day. That's a special quality in a man. Quite possibly incongruent with the quality of obedience."

Al-Wazir cut to the obvious point. "So you're not certain this expedition will succeed?"

"No. I'm not." Lloyd George turned toward the map. "I shouldn't think it prudent, or even possible, to claim certainty, no matter what drivel we tell the papers. It is a great hunt we're about, Chief. We're surveying to drive a tunnel through the Wall, to beat the Chinaman at his own game. Because regardless of whether you or I have ever heard of Chersonesus Aurea, the Celestial Emperor most certainly has."

"They're finding a way across the Wall?" al-Wazir asked. Might as well find a way to the moon. There were always stories, to be sure—*Bassett*'s lost navigator Malgus had walked amid some of the tales himself, and his poor, doomed boy Hethor—but it was one thing for some plucky hero to scale God's ramparts and look down on the kingdoms of the Southern Earth. It was far different for Johnnie Chinaman to do the same thing with his wizards and his priests and his coolies and his endless waves of marching yellow soldiers under their banners of heaven.

Al-Wazir found that thought horrifying.

Lloyd George cleared his throat. "Through the Wall, we believe. Which cannot be permitted. Should China gain a foothold on Southern Earth unanswered by Her Imperial Majesty, our game of nations is at an end. There are no higher stakes.

"Her Imperial Majesty is sending a scientific and technical expedition under one of Her German subjects, the engineer Lothar Ottweill. Herr Doctor Professor Ottweill will have full command of the mission. It is my hope that you will accept responsibility for securing their survival. A thousand men and more are nothing but a mote in the grand design of the Wall."

The Wall. He'd hated it, feared it, lived on it, fled from it. It had eaten his da's wit in the years before. The old man was never the same once he'd come back. It had eaten al-Wazir's ship and most of his friends and mates.

It was the only thing besides the thought of serving once more in the air that might truly bring him back to life.

Al-Wazir dropped to one knee. "Sir," he said, fumbling for the words. "For the sake of that, I'll be your man to the Wall and beyond."

"Up." The PM was clearly uncomfortable. It was as if the two of them were alone, in this room of whispers and maps. "Mr. Kitchens will take you in hand. There's much to be learned about Dr. Ottweill and the expedition before you leave. I believe the next sailing is in less than a week."

Al-Wazir stood. Kitchens was there, though he hadn't seen the man move. These dark-suited men were the true heart of the Empire, not the braying asses in Commons nor the bright Lords in their formal estate.

He tried to take comfort from that thought as he was led away from the Prime Minister without a farewell.

CHILDRESS

Librarian Childress sat at her high desk in the Day Missions Library, the Berkeley School of Divinity at Yale University. Her heels hung nine and quarter inches off the floor when she used this stool. The height allowed her to look down at all but the lankest of the Yale boys. That in turn helped keep their worst tendencies at bay.

Most people had the sense to be afraid of an old woman with iron-gray hair and a long ruler.

The day had clicked slowly by, dust roiling in the shafts of golden light from the high windows, the ever-present smell of leather and glue and paper that made up the bellows breath of the library, the footfalls of students and porters, the gleam of the dark, ancient oak shelves under generations of oil.

She loved these autumn days when the semester had begun but the students were not yet consumed with research and the fear of their midterm marks. The trees were just turning outside, while the building within still retained a bit of the warmth of summer.

The clock on the administration building struck the third hour of the afternoon as a woman approached her desk. That was unusual—there were no women at Yale, save for a few specialists such as herself. The porters were ordinarily quite firm about not admitting the weaker sex.

This one was no student. Perhaps forty, with pale brown hair and an unmemorable face, wearing high button shoes and a sage-green silk dress that rustled of crinolines. She had a white sweater shrugged over her shoulders against the possibility of an early autumn chill.

The visitor's steps echoed with a controlled rhythm that set Childress' mind to racing. Her arms seemed a trifle thick, muscled even, through the silk. Her eyes were the same pale green as her dress. They tracked the room briefly, then focused on Childress.

This was a dangerous person, trained to violence in a way that Childress had rarely encountered in men and never in a woman.

"Emily McHenry Childress." Neither question nor greeting. Just a statement.

"You already know." Her voice was so soft that the woman had to strain slightly to hear her.

"As may be." The accent was London with a hint of the Continental beneath it. The woman reached up and touched the edge of Childress' high, narrow desk. Something clicked beneath her palm. "Tonight." Her voice was equally soft. "On the Long Wharf, at dusk."

A feather carved of delicate ivory remained behind when she walked away.

It reminded Childress painfully of a silver feather a boy had brought her some two years earlier. He'd stood here, holding back tears and wondering how it was he'd seen an angel of the Lord when no one else knew or cared. She'd sent him on in the name of the *avebianco*, the white birds.

She'd wondered, ever since the earthquakes stopped and time seemed to settle down once more, when her turn would come. She'd wondered ever since if she would go.

Even without the threat implied by the messenger, Childress knew she would have answered the summons.

Through the course of the afternoon, Childress walked the halls of the Day Missions Library. She made one silent excuse after another as she passed from room to room. Inspection . . . a lost book . . . reinforcement of her *ars memoriae*. Nostalgia, even, for the overwhelmed young woman first hired on sufferance during the labor shortages of the Loggers' Rebellion.

Childress was certain that if she went to Long Wharf at dusk, she would not be returning to the library. The messenger hadn't said so, but it stood to reason that the *avebianco* would hardly have sent someone all the way from Europe to New Haven for a quiet hour over tea and sandwiches. One had to look into the thing to understand it. The true powers in society were almost always invisible, much like God's messenger angels passing on a moonless night—sensed but rarely seen.

The sum of her days thus far had been little more than another round of days. Her greatest deed in life had probably been to send that young man on to Boston. She might as well follow the path and see where it led.

She'd sworn herself to this, after all, when she'd become part of the *avebianco* all those years ago.

Childress went to pack her desk. Though the entire building had in a sense belonged to her, there was little enough that was personally hers. Reverend Doctor Dunleavey was the head of the library, with his fur cap and tassels and seat on the faculty senate, but it had been Childress who sought out new works, accepted bequests and donations, cataloged what came in and what was found moldering in the basement storerooms, shelved and then reshelved books as times changed the needs of the students.

Other clerks had come and gone, pinched men of furtive habits who spent too long looking at the coltish boys playing rugby in the yard outside, and the occasional woman waiting for a proposal to carry them to maternal, married life. She'd remained here, married to the library, girl and woman, for almost four decades.

And still the white birds had held her. Childress remembered when the first feather had come, pressed within a slim volume of anonymous verse that arrived addressed to her. It had carried marks from Strasbourg in Her Imperial Majesty's Germanies. Her sixth year at the library, 1877, and old Master Humberto had finally allowed her the privilege of cataloging new works. In that same month, this had come as if by signal.

Which, of course, it had been.

To be a librarian was to know everything that was known. Not the entire sum of human knowledge literally at the command of one's thoughts—Newton had perhaps been the last to do that. But to know what *could* be known, understand the indices and passwords of all the secrets of Creation. The science of libraries was the science of the truths hidden within the world. She'd even learned the *ars memoriae* as first described by Simonides of Ceos, using the library as a locus to build a memory mansion.

The library and its work were her life, both within and without, but for where God dwelt in her heart. Into this world the white birds had spoken with a bit of doggerel about the vanities of creation and those who stood in the stead of God. Later, there were other books, letters, whispered words. The *avebianco* were in libraries the world over, from the emerald-hatted mandarins of Imperial China, to the rough-hewn keepers of shipping records in African ports, to the university librarians of the British Empire.

Childress looked up to see the head porter watching her. Cletis Barron's long, dark face was infused with concern. "No one said you was going away." His voice was as deep and gentle as a boat's horn on the foggy Sound.

She tried to smile. "No one told me, either."

"Woman put away her nibs and her cutting knife, she ain't coming back."

"I shall miss you," Librarian Childress said firmly.

"We too, ma'am. We too."

With that, he escorted her to the door. When she stepped outside, the evening chill was already descending. She'd forgotten her cloak, but Barron handed it to her. "Go with pride," he said.

She nodded, words flashing away from her like fish before a hand set in a stream, then set her heels to the street and the walk down to the Long Wharf. She wondered as she strode whether the Reverend Doctor Dunleavey would even notice she was gone.

And that, Childress realized with a sad shiver, was perhaps the truest sum of her life.

New Haven was dubiously blessed with shallow anchorages, a problem that had been solved with the Long Wharf. The structure extended from the west side of the harbor well out across the tide flats to where the deepwater channel lay. Six airship towers stood closer in to shore, along the waterfront itself among the dories and skiffs and shallow-draft fishing boats that plied the coast and crossed the Sound. Only at the Long Wharf could steamers and clippers and Royal Navy ships be found.

A few years earlier, a coalition of merchants and shippers had built a great pier out in the middle of the harbor, near the far end of the Long Wharf, to provide greater ease in unloading and transshipment. An effort was in progress even now to reinforce both structures so that railroad trains could reach every portion. This would remove the necessity and expense of horse-drawn drayage from the ships to the freight terminals along the shore itself.

The gulls wheeled in great gray clouds amid the gathering dusk. The scent of their waste filled the air like damp ammonia. *The waterfront is a giant midden,* Childress thought, but without the benefit of tillage being turned so it could rot decently into the ground.

It was simple foolishness to think she'd find someone, anyone, on the Long Wharf. There were hundreds of longshoremen out there even now in the decline of the workday, along with their carts and hand trucks, horses, dogs, sailors both merchant and Naval, errand boys, pickle sellers, women of questionable virtue, customs officers, deputy port-masters and the miscellanea that any great port drew into itself. Childress had known this all along.

She would not find anyone, but they would find her. It was a reasonable presumption that the white birds had a ship tied up among the several dozen vessels moored to the Long Wharf. There they would conduct the business of the secret empire of knowledge.

The *avebianco* all held a common goal—quiet advancement of the Spiritualist cause. The movement went by different names in different places, even within the British Empire, but the purpose was always the same: acknowledge and preserve God's work in the world, while advancing the labors of Man. The Rationalists dismiss that viewpoint as secular spiritualism, while the orthodox laughed them away as feeble in both faith and mind.

It was of no matter to the white birds and their allies. Only a fool could look at the brasswork in the sky and deny God's handiwork. Only an idiot could look at the brasswork in the sky and declare God immaterial. Childress and her sliver of the quiet wisdom of librarians had been content to nudge where nudging was called for, teach where teaching would be heard, and report that which was noteworthy.

This business came back to Hethor and his feather, she knew. That had been a time when the world shook, great waves striking coasts all over Northern Earth. That New England had been spared was nothing short of a miracle, but English and Colonial lives had been lost aplenty elsewhere. The boy had gone seeking William of Ghent and passed out of her view. She'd heard sufficient echo of his later effort to know he'd achieved something.

Success, evidently, as the world seemed to be yet turning, and the horomancers had settled down once more to casting lots and predicting the fevers of children. William of Ghent had left Boston on a mysterious errand, not yet returned to the courts of Empire even now.

She tried not to wonder if her own note to the man in Boston who ran his specials had made things worse for poor Hethor. Phelps was part of the *avebianco,* too, in his way.

As she reflected, her boots echoed down the wooden planks, past bales of cargo netting, cotton and canvas, as well as larger, bulkier containers—hogsheads and tuns and barrels. There was a profusion of practice around her that signaled a vocabulary of action and word. Every craft carried its own cant, librarians and libertines alike.

Men looked at her, too. Wondering. Childress knew that nothing of her appearance telegraphed any sense of belonging here. She was far too old to be a dockside hussy, or even a madam. Her attire, high-necked black in close semblance of widow's weeds for all she'd never married, was far too plain to be a captain's wife or widow-owner. In the rising dark of the evening, the torchlight and great storm lanterns would deepen the lines on her face to those of a children's witch.

It was no surprise at all when the *avebianco* found her. The woman who'd visited her at the library looked out from under a sailor's flat hat, just as Master Boyett of the University of Connecticut libraries stepped around a stack of wide, shallow chests.

"Good evening, Librarian Childress," Boyett said quietly.

She was aware that at least four of the sailors nearby were not moving about at their tasks, but rather focused on her.

Childress let her voice go frosty. Boyett had always been a bit of a sucking grind. "Something of a walk from Storrs, isn't it, Brian? Out for your evening constitutional?"

Boyett moved his hands slightly, the *v*-and-*x* signal of the white birds. "I'm here as witness. . . ."

She took satisfaction that he couldn't quite bring himself to call her by her Christian name. She still had the advantage of him. Her only advantage now, and not one she could see a way to playing. "Witness what? I have been called, I come. Most of us spend our lives watching and waiting without ever serving at all."

The sailor-woman's hand closed on her arm. "Time to go, Librarian." Had Childress not seen this woman in a dress some hours earlier, she would not have questioned that a man stood beside her now.

"Nonsense," Childress answered. "The tide's running for several hours yet. Your sense of the dramatic is overtaking your judgment."

The grip grew tighter. "You will not be baffling me as you have him."

"Then I go. I came, did I not?"

Boyett shuddered. "I'm sorry."

"For what?" she asked, but he did not answer.

Then the woman led her up a gangplank of a fast packet named *Mute Swan,* which shuddered as its engines chuffed somewhere deep within the metal hull. Childress looked back when she reached the top. Boyett stared up after her.

"What did you tell him?" she asked her captor.

"The truth," the woman said. "As for you, you go below now."

Childress looked up at the brass curving in the evening sky, wondering if that poor, lost Hethor had found any reward to go with his success.

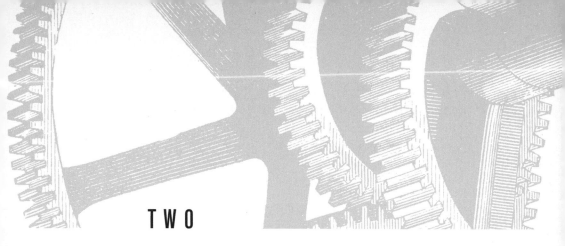

TWO

PAOLINA

Paolina realized that the *fidalgos* were not simply going to let her out. She'd been offered neither food nor water since being pushed into this closet. Sipping at the dregs of wildflower wine and *bagaceira* to stop her thirst was hardly sensible. But they had not returned, nor had they sent one of the women to care for her.

All of this? Over a watch? They were very angry, or very frightened. With these fools, the two were almost the same.

She spent much of her time visualizing the stemwinder, imagining what parts might be needed to ensure its successful continued operation. There would be a way to store energy, of course. A coiled spring was the only reasonable solution for that, given the shape and size of the device. That spring would slowly unwind, driving a series of gears designed to capture its motion and transmit that to the hands. The gearing would be required to adapt to the differing tension of the spring as it uncoiled, so that the rate of motion of the hands did not change.

There would be more, much more, but those were the basics.

And so Creation worked, the planet spinning like the hands of a watch, meshing with the ring of its orbit as it transited through the sky. Everything danced around everything else, advancing in a mechanical sarabande that told the story of God's craftsmanship more eloquently than words in any book could talk of the brass snake that had clacked through Eden or the horofixion of Christ.

It was all *there*. She'd been unfolding the secrets of Earth in the mushroom shed before they'd taken her away. Only the English truly understood God, those wizards of *Bassett* and the Dent watchworks back in the motherland. Clarence Davies might well be an idiot, but he was an idiot sprung from a race of wizards.

Could she build a stemwinder herself, she wondered? Her own model of the universe? Surely not with teak splinters and brittle iron.

Paolina Barthes sat in the damp, breathing darkness and imagined her way toward the doors of knowledge. The world could be solved, and she would solve it. There simply was no other way.

Sometime later she lay slumped and stinking, her mouth dry as rotting canvas. Paolina became aware that a glaring bar of light had fallen across one hand.

"Girl," said someone quietly. The voice still scratched at her ears like tiny claws. "What have they done to you?"

Senhora Armandires, Paolina thought. She let her head loll sideways though the glare hurt her eyes. "Hel . . ."

"No." The woman knelt. "Don't speak." She bent close to touch Paolina's neck. "They are fools and worse, but they are our men. Right now they are also being kept busy." Senhora Armandires propped Paolina's head up and pressed a damp rag to her mouth. "Here, close your jaw."

"Out," Paolina tried to say around the rag. The word was little more than a grunt.

"When I can." The senhora shoved a sack next to her. The rough fiber scraped on Paolina's thigh as coral might, rough enough to draw blood. "Three waterskins and some bread from your mother. Soak it before you eat. Also, that English boy sent some things." Another bag, with the first. "He is frantic for you. It would be sweet if he were not so unsuitable."

She let the rag drop from her mouth. "Get me out," she whispered.

"We will. The *fidalgos* must think it their idea."

"They w-w-want to kill me."

"We all live in this world. They do not mean to kill, only to frighten you into sensibility."

Exhausted, she had no more to say. Senhora Armandires slipped a sliver of mango between Paolina's lips—where had the woman gotten *that*?—smoothed her hair, and kissed her forehead. "Patience and prayer," she said. "Someone will return with more water, but guard what you have."

She nodded, terrified of the darkness that was about to return. When Senhora Armandires shut the door, what remained behind was a familiar, close silence. Not the fear Paolina had dreaded, not at all.

Groping, she found Clarence's bag. It clicked. What had he sent her?

Within she found metal. *Tools.* And shapes. Not the stemwinder, not anything she recognized. But metal.

He'd been raiding then, along *a Muralha,* maybe up to the ruined cities of the enkidus.

"Patience, prayer, and watchmaking," she told the darkness.

She could have loved the boy in that moment, for all that he was the inadvertent architect of much of her troubles. Instead Paolina worked to sort what she had, laying it out on the floor before her knees.

God had created the world in darkness, had He not, before lighting the lamp of the sun? This was a much smaller thing.

Besides, her fevered dreams had given her so much more than she'd had before falling into restless sleep.

Tools, tools and metal. With those, any intelligent woman could remake the world. She could do no less.

A week and more Paolina was in the darkness. Her sense of time was not so perfected, but every day or so one of the older women came to her. It could hardly be a secret they were caring for her, but the men continued to pretend. She knew they had to let her out soon enough—something would go wrong with a well, or a winch would jam too hard, and they'd need her help.

She explored the logic of her tools and the inexorable movement of time. Every click of every second of every day was fodder for her. She'd measured the skies years before, understood perfectly well the dance of sun and moon and planets. It was time now to visualize how God had assembled these things in His work.

All she had to do was copy, not invent.

So in the darkness she cut and scraped and filed. Tiny pieces seemed to hold firm in her fingers, though she knew with the right clamps and stands she could have cut them almost dust-small. The shavings she carefully swept by hand, separate piles for each consistency of metal, in case she needed them for even tinier springs. Likewise the slivers, which could provide a roller for a movement almost too small to see. She could not build those here in the dark, with these tools, but she could anticipate the need and how it would work.

There was frustration, too, as some parts fumbled away from her hand, and others couldn't be made to fit with sufficient smoothness. Wherever and whatever Clarence Davies had traded or stolen for her, he had been a genius unknowing. She kept finding just one more bit of metal, one more fragment to serve as a bearing, one more tip to cut.

It was like being at prayer, save with metal in her hands instead of some scrap of Scripture.

When Senhora Armandires came to let her out, Paolina was ready. She'd repacked Clarence's bag with her bits of tool and machine. Working in the darkness had provided magnificent focus for her imagination, with no diversion of purpose.

Now she needed to be terribly sick awhile, and sleep in honest light. Then she could reopen the bag and see what she had wrought.

Outside, it was as if nothing had changed. Pretense, all pretense, as was much of life in Praia Nova. Walking slowly on Senhora Armandires' arm, Paolina saw the men ignore her, the boys stare at her, and women keep their faces turned away.

"Am I supposed to have learned some lesson?" she asked hoarsely.

"Hush, girl. You need rest in decent shelter. Talking about what happened will only make it worse."

In that moment Paolina knew she was not going to stay in Praia Nova. No matter that she had no airship to carry her away. If the fool boy Clarence could find his path across *a Muralha*, so could she. It was only a matter of determination.

Though not being killed along the way might matter as well, she had to admit.

She spent two days sleeping, waking periodically only to relieve herself and sip a little fish broth.

"They've been casting nets," Senhora Armandires explained at one point.

"From a boat?" Paolina's voice squeaked badly.

"A raft."

"Fools," she muttered, then slipped back into sleep, dreaming of the Atlantic swells that crashed against the base of *a Muralha*.

Waking finally on the third day, Paolina felt almost normal. Her strength seemed to have returned, and her eyes didn't hurt anymore. The senhora sat on the foot of her little cot in the tiny house. "We must speak."

"I listen."

Senhora Armandires picked at her mantilla a little while. Satisfied finally that there were no hidden flaws there, she looked up again at Paolina. In that moment the girl realized how old the senhora was. Not in years, perhaps, but in cares. Her face was seamed with lines. One eye was clouded fog pale. Her hands shook slightly.

A Muralha killed people, quickly or slowly, but still it made martyrs of them all. That Praia Nova was a settlement of refugees and rebels and wreck survivors might give them all a sliver of noble pride, but they were not meant to be here. None of them.

It wasn't just she who should leave.

"The *fidalgos* will not say this. . . ." The senhora paused, looking again into Paolina's eyes for something. "It is so difficult to be a man."

Paolina began to laugh in choking gasps.

"No, no. Attend me. They have so much to live up to, before God and their fathers and one another." Senhora Armandires sounded like she was trying to convince herself. "They will bleed before they show weakness. And apologizing to a woman is weakness. So we must read their words in their acts. The *fidalgos* have forgiven you, and repented of their haste. Do not distress their dignity by raising questions. In public or in private. Please."

"What has broken?"

The senhora's head bowed. She let her breath out in a long, slow sigh, like a lie escaping. "The pump will not work. We are running out of water. Every ounce must now be carried up from below, or foraged from the beck along the enkidus' borders."

"I suppose it is just as well that I did not starve in the dark as they intended."

"Their pride . . . you must always remember and respect their pride."

Never, thought Paolina, but she kept the word within. "I shall fix the pump. Then I shall expect to be left alone."

Senhora Armandires' eyes flashed. "You are still a girl—"

Paolina let some of her anger leak out. "*I* am the only one who can fix the pump. I believe that makes me an honorary man."

The senhora stood, brushed off her mantilla, and made a slight bow. "I am sorry," she said as she retreated from her own house.

Paolina wondered if that was the only honest thing the senhora had said to her today. Though in truth, if Armandires was lying, it was more to herself than to Paolina.

She drew Clarence's bag out. She wasn't quite ready to open it yet. The lumpy, scratchy homespun carried promise, more than anything else she'd known in her life.

Paolina *remembered* seeing how everything worked. If she opened the bag and found she'd been grinding junk to dust in the dark, she would simply throw herself into the sea.

So she hugged it awhile, and rocked, and listened to the sea pound below, and wondered how many men and boys would drown fishing from the raft before they let her help them figure out how to build the boats. Finally she realized that she didn't care anymore.

The next day Paolina was back in the mushroom shed. She had decided to wait until one of the men asked her to fix the pump. *She* had water, after all, in three gourds left her by Senhora Armandires.

It was quiet and dark, but so different from the closet in the great hall. She was here by choice—a vast improvement. No one barred the door. The darkness was different, too, filled with the gentle texture and reek of the mushrooms. The night soil of the village was spread here, used and reused to build a stinking bed on which the little brown buttons grew. Periodically the mushroom beds were turned out into the fields for fertilizer.

In other words, the mushroom shed was like the spring at the heart of the stemwinder, storing energy meted out over time in the form of food for future consumption.

She liked the idea. It gave her a certain sense of sympathetic resonance. She wondered if God had some divine equivalent of a mushroom shed in which He had labored at crafting the clockwork of Creation.

The pieces she'd cut in her blind fever were more difficult to assess. They bore only a passing resemblance to Clarence Davies' English stemwinder, insofar as she'd been able to study it before being hauled away. Paolina figured the watch was unlikely to come back to her now, not while it was still hung on the point of the *fidalgos'* pride.

No matter, she told herself. Her memory would suffice. She set herself to recreating her vision of how the energies of Creation were gathered and stored.

It was not simple. Much like the skies themselves, her course was charted in complex paths and traceries of brasswork. There was a mainspring, but she seemed to have made several other, smaller springs, as well as a profusion of minute gears. They were more crudely cut than the sparkling elements of the original stemwinder, but they were true.

She did not need what the English needed. As Clarence had explained, that was agreement with clocks at an observatory just outside distant London. She required only a model of the world. The heavens themselves gave the time to anyone who knew how to read the signs. It was the rest of the order of Creation with which she was concerned.

Paolina did not want to go to *Bassett*, let alone all the way to England, with empty hands. Those great sorcerers would scarcely hear her suit if she did not bring a journeyman's work with her to prove her worth.

She imagined standing before the Queen and her court of the wise and the magical, showing her own stemwinder, demonstrating to all how she could follow in the footsteps of Dent, Watchmaker to the Queen.

Here, she was little more than a tool for pumps and levers, an otherwise inconvenient girl. There, well . . . how could an empire ruled by a woman not be able to see what she might do?

So long as she could show them.

Paolina bent to her parts—long, narrow levers with serrated catches, beveled wheels, little worm gears, springs and pins. It seemed as if she could build a hundred stemwinders. But she'd had a vision in the dark, and it hadn't vanished completely with her return to the light.

The first problem was a plate or frame on which to build the train of her genius. Her hand slipped back into Clarence's raiding bag, to see what might serve at that size and weight. It would have to be a bit bigger than the Dent stemwinder, as her tools were not sufficiently fine, but it would still be something a girl could carry in her hand.

The following morning, Senhora Armandires had bustled in tense silence before leaving Paolina alone with her thoughts. After eating the senhora's thin gruel, she returned to the mushroom shed, where she found her mother and Clarence Davies waiting together.

Clarence smiled. He seemed to stand a bit taller, be a bit happier. *Perhaps he'd found a place here*, she thought, some purpose or sense of home. Miserable as Praia Nova was, after two years of walking, ordinary people who spoke some English might have seemed to him a gift from God.

Her mother, on the other hand, was bent lower than ever. The years of her father's absence weighed on Senhora Barthes. Still, somehow Paolina had missed the arrival of old age in the droop of her mother's eyes, the wrinkles upon her face marking the scars of time.

"Madre," Paolina began, then stopped herself. It had been Senhora Armandires who'd come to her in the dark, not Senhora Barthes. She nodded at Clarence with a hint a smile. "Senhor Davies."

"Daughter." Her mother's voice was thin and strained as her face. "I am glad to see you well."

Clarence returned her smile.

Paolina wondered what this was about. Surely the freshwater pump, though she'd resolved to make the men ask her. "I am not so well as I might have been otherwise."

"Please." Her mother raised a trembling hand. The woman needed a cane, Paolina realized. Badly so. "Do not speak of what has gone past. You must earn your trust, daughter. There is little water left."

"Let them carry buckets," she said bitterly. "As they would have done in any lifetime except mine." Her anger at being shut away flooded back. "What am I to the *fidalgos*?"

"What are you to the girls who must lift those buckets?" Clarence asked quietly.

It was strange, a man even thinking about the work that women did. As if Clarence had never been told of the natural order of men and women. "I am a girl with a project." She nodded at the mushroom shed behind them. *A girl with different aims, beyond this place.*

The world was so *little* here. *A Muralha* towered above them like the walls of Heaven, the Atlantic spread before them as a moat around God's castle, and yet all the people of Praia Nova could do was live within their tired places, generation after generation.

"I will come fix the pump in three days' time," she said. "Until then, I shall work here in the mushroom shed. In the meantime, I suggest people carry buckets. *Everyone.*"

"They will not like it," her mother whispered. "Please, don't be foolish. They will put you back—"

"No," snapped Paolina. "They will not. Not if they expect me to ever again turn a finger to any need in this village." She pushed between them and bent to pass through the canvas flap that served as the low door to the mushroom shed.

The secret to being a man was simple, she realized. It was nothing more than to act as if the world belonged to you, and everyone owed you duty.

Within, the stemwinder awaited her, taking shape on its frame. It seemed to sparkle in the darkness even before she lit the latest of her candle stubs.

The night of the third day she took her stemwinder with her when she left the mushroom shed. Clarence's stolen scraps were returned to the roughspun carry sack, which she tucked behind one of the beds. She wanted nothing more than her own model of the world and the decent boots she wore.

Outside in the early fall of night, the stemwinder glowed slightly. She'd made a round frame from enkidu metal, and cut a glass face from an old lantern lens. The shell was half again as big as the Dent watch, overfilling her hands. The face was blank, for she already knew the time, but there were four hands. One to measure the time that beat at the heart of everything, one to measure the beating of her own heart, one to measure turning of the earth, and one to measure whatever she set it to. Paolina had built a stem, too, in imitation of the English watch. Hers could be set in four different positions, one to adjust each hand, as well as pulled out to rewind the mainspring coiled within.

When she held it, the enkidu-metal back and cut-glass face were slightly warm, almost velvety—like shaven skin. It seemed to move slightly at her touch, as if she held a compact, contented child.

The new stemwinder, *her* stemwinder, was beautiful. She had enough pride to hope it would prove her credibility to the wizards of England.

"Time to fix the pump," she announced to the gathering darkness.

Praia Nova was quiet. Candles flickered in the great hall. There was the glow of firelight from some homes. The Atlantic brought a wind that smelled of storm. She could see lightning far out to sea, though there were stars immediately to the north.

The pump she'd built was in a little shelter near the top of the water stairs. It was meant to be operated by someone leaning against a post and walking in place. Though no one in the village had ever before heard of a foot pump, it had been perfectly obvious to Paolina that the legs were far more powerful than the arms, and thus much better suited to the work of raising water.

They raised the body off the ground, did they not?

The piping—bamboo sealed with tree gum and rags—let out into a trough. She'd proposed an arrangement of tanks, to store more water over longer periods, but a lack of both interest and materials had led the *fidalgos* to ignore the idea.

Paolina settled into the post and worked the pedals.

They rotated in place, their hammered iron scissor frames still articulating, but no water emerged. Within a couple of steps, the resistance increased. Negative pressure was developing in the line.

There was nothing wrong with the pump. The problem was down below, at Westerly Creek.

With the earthquake drying up the springs here at the village, all the water Praia Nova had left was in the creek. If something happened to that source, the village was dead. You could hardly drink the Atlantic Ocean.

She headed down the water stairs, looking carefully at the bound-together pipe.

The creek met the path at the 212th step. A ledge led away there, too narrow to be of use for a foundation or even permanent storage, but wide enough for a person to walk carefully. The cliffs below Praia Nova were a series of staggered shelves and odd-sized ledges like this one—almost like a wall of decaying bricks, if each brick were the size of a ship.

She was just above the little shale beach and the jetty where the fishing boats tied up. There were two partially built hulls careened over, but no one possessed any real understanding of boat building. The fleet lost in the great waves had been accumulated as runaways, salvage, and wrecks came in, each vessel built from pieces of the previous generation.

The men of Praia Nova were re-creating a misunderstood memory of bastardized boats. Without the proper tools or braces. At the least, it would take a frame to fully support the developing hull, but they'd been unwilling to commit the wood to such an apparently wasteful use.

There was a raft there, too, built from wood stripped from the boat project and covered with reed mats.

She wondered which storm would carry this all away, and leave the men even more angry and purposeless.

The water source was only half a dozen paces from the steps. There was a trough here as well, built long ago to trap enough water for people to fetch it away, as they had done once more of late. She wasn't sure exactly when the pump had stopped working, but the upper trough had been dry.

There was plenty of water—the creek had not stopped. She inspected the assembly that anchored the piping and provided the water intake. She'd crafted a screen of woven bamboo to keep the moss and small rocks out of the pipe, backed by roughspun to filter sand.

It was dark with crud and muck.

Paolina removed the screen and scraped it clear with her fingers. She'd told the *fidalgos* and the women both to have a girl come down every three days with a brush and clean the pipe end. It looked as if no one had done that work in weeks.

The sheer foolishness made her angry. Why couldn't they see these simplest things for themselves?

She replaced the filter and turned to walk back up the stairs and test the pump. Paolina jumped, startled, to find Clarence standing in her path.

"You're leaving, aren't you?"

She'd already decided as much but had not yet put it quite so baldly.

The words stuck a moment, stinging her. "Yes," she finally said. "I want to go to England."

"It's not so bad here, this place. The Wall is . . ."

"Difficult?" She nudged him ahead of her, so they could both climb the water stairs.

"Dangerous." They climbed in the moonlight as distant thunder rumbled. "Lengthy. You don't know."

"I don't," she admitted. "But staying here is wrong for me. I am just a girl, and will never be more."

"No one else I've known could have built this pump."

She laughed. "You are English, from a nation of wizards that rule the world. Even if some of you are crazed."

"*I'm* not one," he complained.

"I might become one." Her voice was little more than a whisper. "I have to try, to find out."

At the top, they tested the pump. The pressure on the pedals felt right. With a few dozen step-strokes, the water ran. She stepped off and let Clarence set his feet on the pedals. Even in the moonlight, the spring water ran black. It could have been lamp oil. Or *bagaceira*. This dark fluid that spat from the bamboo pipe as the pedals squeaked certainly was the lifeblood of Praia Nova.

"It's time to go," she told him.

He reached behind the shelter and handed her a small canvas bag. "Senhora Armandires said you'd want this." His smile was crooked in the moonlight that faded before the coming storm. "A spare dress for traveling, and a little bread, and a steel knife."

It was a wealth, in Praia Nova, especially coming from a woman. "Will you go with me?" She hadn't meant to ask, but his smile sent a pang through her chest.

"N-n-no." Now he was sweating, enough to make her laugh. "The senhora is very kind to me. She's—" He stopped, embarrassed.

Another man, then, topping a woman, though the senhora could have been this boy's mother and more. Paolina didn't know whether to be disappointed or relieved. "Well. Thank you." She waved the bag at him. "For this, and for the metal and tools you brought while I was locked in the great hall."

"It was senhora's doing," he admitted. "She thought you might know what could be done, if you had the right things in your hand."

"East, then," Paolina told him. "To find *Bassett*, or Africa, whichever I come to first."

" 'Ware the spiders." He shuddered as a wet wind gusted, bring the smell of rainwater and lightning. "And the brass men who will bother to talk to you can be trusted. Their word is good, if they give it."

"Spiders. Brass men." The breeze continued to rise, damp and oddly chill. She wanted to be gone before the storm moved in and folded Praia Nova in a blanket of rain and wind and shuttered windows. There were cracks and caves enough anywhere on the ancient, eroded face of *a Muralha*.

"Farewell," he told her.

Their hands met, squeezed a moment. What did she care for him? Senhora Armandires had taken the English boy into her bed. He was sweet, and her figure was full for a woman of age. It was no business of Paolina's—she still hadn't begun her monthlies, what use had she for a man?

She turned and walked away from Clarence, following the path east, out of Praia Nova, into the wilderness of the Wall. The storm would close a curtain behind her that no one in the town of her birth would ever bother to draw open again.

Paolina only wished she'd been able to bid her father good-bye.

The stemwinder was heavy in the pocket of her dress. She slipped a hand in to stroke it. This was hers, her measure of the world. Before she was done, she would measure all of Creation, she swore. No man would ever again hold a hand over her head.

AL-WAZIR

He spent the next several days in Admiralty being led through meeting after meeting by Mr. Kitchens. It was a great and troublesome bore, reminding the chief why he'd never had the slightest interest in officering. Much better to work the decks, where the orders of the day were the work of the day and someone else worried about the politics of empire and the Law of the Sea.

Still, Kitchens and his fellow quiet men treated al-Wazir like something of a toff. A toff in a velvet prison, pointedly discouraged from stepping out to find a smoke or a tot of the good, rough rum he knew he'd find not many streets away. The place always smelled of oil soap and crisp linen and something sour they used to keep down the ants and perhaps cut the smell of piss in the heads. Bad plumbing was the English way, after all.

And so he was seated in a small room, being lectured about the submural tribes on the Gaboon coast by an old fellow of the Royal Society who'd probably never seen a fuzzy wuzzy in his life. Then he was taken to another small room, where three gentlemen from Greenwich talked at length about air masses and wind currents along the Wall. This was a subject with which al-Wazir was intimately familiar, having been Ropes Division Chief on *Bassett* as she'd sailed those airways. Much like the anthrophagist—that's what al-Wazir thought the old fellow had claimed for his title—these climaxologists or whatever they were had no real notion of the worldly facts of their subject.

Walking down yet another carpeted hallway past a painting of storm-tossed ships, he turned to Kitchens and tugged the quiet man to a stop. "It's like blind men talking about the sunset," al-Wazir said, "these old fellows with their papers from the Queen talking about the Wall."

Something almost a smile quirked Kitchens' face. "Of course it is. But these are the experts we have. You will note that the Member from Caernarfon Boroughs has not troubled to send *them* to the waist of the world. There is a reason you have the doing of this task, sir."

"Then why am I frittering my days here?" grumbled al-Wazir.

Kitchens' voice was patient. "Because these are the experts we have. And when Questions are raised in Parliament, or the paper-voice wizards who attend Her Imperial Majesty make their reasonable inquiries, this is what they will desire to hear."

Al-Wazir laughed. "What? That you didn't place the security of the empire in the hands of a drunken sailor of uncertain parentage and a questionable service history?"

"We are quite certain of your parentage, sir," Kitchens replied, brushing al-Wazir's arm free and resuming his pace.

Al-Wazir laughed even harder. "I do believe you've essayed a jest." He followed Kitchens to the next little room. "I didn't think you had it in you."

The morning of the third day, Kitchens attended al-Wazir as he ate kippers and eggs in the little refectory amid the attic rooms where he had been lodged.

"You don't take your mess with me," al-Wazir told him. "I've not even seen you swill water yet." He speared a kipper. "Fish, then?"

"No, thank you." Kitchens opened a red folder and made a note.

Al-Wazir ate the offering himself, watching the quiet man carefully. He wanted something, but more to the point he wanted the chief to speak first. That much was obvious. Al-Wazir obliged. "Am I to make the next sailing to the Wall?"

"If not, there will be more."

That wasn't his purpose, then. Damn, but this was no different from talking to an officer. He went with his own mind this time, instead of trying to second-guess Kitchens'. "When do I get sprung from this place and find out about that Dr. Oddball? Everything here is just frippery for the papers. You said it yourself. This is like any new command—I need to see to the men and the gear. I already know more about the Equatorial Wall and its airs than any of your lot, saving your presence."

"Including my presence, I'm afraid." Kitchens seemed relieved. Something in his stance shifted. So, al-Wazir had asked the right question. "Then as you have asked, I shall transfer you to the Engineering section for their briefings."

"This is another of them formalities for the Parliamentary Questions, ain't it?"

"I'm sure I wouldn't know, sir. Have your bags ready in half an hour. We can place you on the next train to Maidstone, as you have requested."

"Indeed," said al-Wazir. He tucked into the last of his kippers. There didn't seem much point in rushing. Kitchens wouldn't leave without him. His entire kit consisted of a canvas satchel not much larger than a ditty bag. That was mostly secondhand gear given him in Bristol by other sailors to offset his complete destitution debarking from the dhow from Dahomey.

Twenty-five minutes later al-Wazir stepped out of Admiralty into a cool September morning, then boarded a waiting carriage. Somewhat to his surprise, Kitchens climbed in after him to tug the door shut on the first honest sunlight the chief had seen in days.

They boarded a train at Bricklayers' Arms, though to al-Wazir all the stations of London could have been one vast brick-and-glass hall. He'd always been a ropes-and-sails man, first on the water, then in the air. The gasbag division and the engine gang had their own ways, dark and dingy to al-Wazir's thinking.

So it was here, the belowdecks of a great iron ship turned inside out to form the tendons and muscles of the Empire. Steam engines stood naked on wheeled trucks to ride the rails, rather than lurking decently below, where they could be tended by a black gang. The blue sky and green world were hidden behind walls everted to remake the world. Instead of the unpeopled sea and the broad green lands passing below and beside him, here there were crowds everywhere, heads bobbing and nodding, shoulders pressed together tight as any assembly of the deck, faces every color of the Empire, though mostly the honest beefy pink of the home islands.

He walked up two iron steps and into the railroad car. Kitchens followed, reaching forward to direct al-Wazir to a private compartment.

Soon enough they were rumbling through slums filthier and more crowded than the meanest Caribbean port town, along clattering rails where grubby children scavenged for clinkers and metal scrap. "The Battersea Tangle," said Kitchens absently as they rattled past an endless, confusing expanse of rails knotted together worse than any seaweed mat on the Sargasso.

Then it was open lands and village greens and standing lines of oaks and the rolling country of southeast England as they bore on into Kent.

He finally asked the question he'd been wondering about for a while. "Why Maidstone?"

"Where else to find Africa in England?"

Once again, al-Wazir suspected Kitchens of humor.

The Maidstone railway station was so much smaller than the brick caverns of London that it felt almost normal to al-Wazir. Like a dockside without longshoremen or a flint-eyed wharfinger, though there were idlers and strumpets in evidence, even here. Kitchens steered him directly past the porters and the touts to meet a pair of Royal Marines in green woolens. They opened the hatch of an armored steam-powered omnibus.

Inside the light was dim, filled with shifting shadows, much as belowdecks on an iron-hulled steamer.

"Quiet and easy, this monster is," al-Wazir said, poking Kitchens in the side. "No one will notice what you're about, for certain."

Kitchens sniffed. "I am not responsible for security provisions here."

One of the marines up front glanced back, grinning. "Kent ain't exactly brimming with hostiles. We take this'n out twice a day to fetch the mail, truth be told. Gives the old girl a whirl. No one knows the difference."

The difference to al-Wazir was that he saw nothing from inside the omnibus except bits of treetops and sky through the gun slits.

They drove for the better part of an hour, with a slow lurch that spoke of country lanes too narrow for the chuffing, screeching bulk of the vehicle. When they eventually ground to a halt, even Kitchens was sweating despite the cooling weather. The marines threw open the hatch and helped al-Wazir and Kitchens out.

Whatever he had expected from the Kentish countryside, it was not this.

They stood at the edge of an enormous pit that extended an enormous mile or more to the other side. It was a quarry, al-Wazir realized, and a bloody huge one. One end had been expanded, dug deeper into layers of varying colors. Tailings spread across the bed of the excavation. A great quantity of machines and equipment had been erected in the newly opened section.

Al-Wazir tried to sort out what he was seeing. A scaffold covered much of the wall at that end of the quarry. There were rails laid on the floor, in two gauges—one seemed to be a standard English railroading gauge, the other was much wider, with massive sleepers. A huge machine sat at the end of the broad-gauge spur, up against the cliff face. Just beyond it was a tunnel into the rock. Men swarmed over the machine, making repairs or adjustments.

"We calls it the boner," said one of the marines.

"Shut your biscuit hole," the other said.

"Boner" was a good word for it, al-Wazir thought. The machine was perhaps seventy feet long, about fifteen feet in diameter, bearing a bulbous head crisscrossed with studded members. It was basically a giant drill with a rotating nose meant to cut the tunnel before it. The thing rammed into the stone and flayed open a path.

"Her Imperial Majesty's iron dick would be more like it," al-Wazir said with a laugh. He swallowed his humor at the look Kitchens gave him.

They took a lift cage down the cliff face to the quarry floor. There was a village spread about the base of the lift: equipment barns and dormitories and cottages for officers and engineers, along with a dining hall, a gymnasium, and dozens more outbuildings. Descending, al-Wazir got an excellent view of the rooftops.

He hated what he saw. Admiralty's quarters at Ripley Building had at least been blessed with some echo of the majesty of state. Even the Bricklayers' Arms train station had a purpose around which its form had been built. This was just another factory, another mill, at the bottom of a hole.

What he'd gone to sea to avoid.

As they reached the base of the lift, the tunneling machine erupted into a series of loud steam whistle blasts. Moments later a clattering, churning racket echoed through the quarry, though it was soon muted. Now out of his line of sight, al-Wazir presumed that the machine had moved into the tunnel.

"I believe that Herr Doctor Professor Ottweill will be joining us shortly," said Kitchens.

They stood in the stone street at the bottom of the quarry amid tarred shacks in a sun that had become far too hot. Al-Wazir found himself wondering if he should have stayed aboard the little dhow, sailed back to Africa, and made his living among the fuzzy wuzzies.

But he'd taken the Queen's shilling. Her Imperial Majesty had kept him in the air all these years. If she wanted to send him beneath the stones of the Wall, it should be all the same to him.

CHILDRESS

Librarian Childress put to sea aboard SS *Mute Swan* under steam with the late tide from New Haven harbor the night of Wednesday, September 17, 1902. She made a note of it in her *ars memoriae,* as if her departure from everything she'd ever known was little more than a citation in a work of distant history.

Things cataloged, marked down, recorded, didn't have the same edge as what a person felt in her skin. She'd always known this. It was what being a librarian meant to her, and to so many others. Few would choose a life among quiet books and dusty shelves unless they sufficiently abhorred the company of others.

The ship moved smoothly through the gentle swells of Long Island Sound. She stared out the tiny barred porthole. Childress might have been able to toss a coin into the sea, if she'd worked at it a bit. Still, her eyes were free. So she used them.

The full moon painted the Sound silver, while the shoreline bulked blue black. Wooded headlands lent the shadows a darker texture. The towns and waterfronts flickered with light. She'd lived in Connecticut all her life, never going farther than New York City or Providence. Now the *avebianco* was taking her away, quite possibly for the rest of her life.

At least she'd see more of the world.

Later, after Childress had lain down to sleep still dressed in the clothing of her day, the bolt on the outside of her cabin's slid open. The muscled woman looked in. She was once more decently attired, rough clothes for traveling but unmistakably female. Childress knew better than to be fooled by her dress.

"Do you have needs?"

"Civilized discourse, personal freedom, and a decent wardrobe."

"The Mask Poinsard will speak to you of those things tomorrow."

"And for tonight? . . ."

"Sleep," said the muscled woman. "You will be bettered for the time spent."

"And meanwhile we steam into the Atlantic." She hadn't meant to say more, but she did. "Away from my home."

"Your home is the *avebianco*." The muscled woman nodded sharply. "I am Anneke. I will see you in the morning."

The hatch shut. The bolt outside shot home with a click.

Childress settled down, but sleep did not come. Instead she walked through her locus awhile, recalling how she'd come to this pass. Somewhere deep inside her house of memory, sleep claimed her.

Morning brought a shoreline she had no way to identify—more wooded headlands, some water meadows, old piers gone to rotting posts topped with the dying remnants of a crown of summer growth. Logic told her it ought be the coast of Massachusetts, but she had not yet sorted out the speed of the vessel. Nonetheless she dutifully noted the arrangements of the low-hilled peaks lest by some strange chance she ever passed this way by ship again.

Despite Anneke's promise, dawn had come and gone several hours with neither breakfast nor a walk to see the Mask Poinsard. And there would be the crux of this whole business.

To say that the white birds, the *avebianco*, were loosely organized was something of an understatement. They had their signs and symbols, but there was no real arrangement of cells or commanders or revolutionaries. Not such as the Loggers' Rebellion had maintained under Lincoln and Lee. The two farmer-generals had managed to control portions of Virginia, Maryland, and Pennsylvania until General Arbuthnot had put them down with the help of the Sikh divisions.

Unlike those poor doomed rebels, the white birds had never aimed for overt political or economic dominance. Influence, instead. As through the spread and reach of libraries.

But they did have Masks—senior members of the *avebianco*, tapped for advancement within the brotherhood to assume more public roles, in places and times where a direct influence would be important. Masks were such commanders as the white birds had.

Childress was not enough of a fool to believe it ended there. Surely the Masks looked up to other Masks, persons of rank and title invisible to her. People could not be otherwise. Every tribe had a chief, every gang had a boss, every little pack had a leader.

The drawing of the bolt startled Childress from her reverie. The coast outside had become long dunes and a sandspit. Houses dotted the rise above the storm tide line. Near Boston, perhaps?

She turned to meet Anneke.

"The Mask Poinsard will see you now."

"No." Childress might as well make what little point was hers to make. "I require a bath, clean clothing, and a decent meal before I can present myself to a senior member of our brotherhood."

Anneke snorted. "I see you have not spent much time aboard ship." She shrugged. "I can escort you to a lavatory. Do what you will there, but be quick about it."

"And breakfast?"

"Tea and crackers, if you're lucky."

Anneke's patience had limits, then, something that came as no surprise to Childress. Still, she'd won a small battle, simply by standing on propriety. She had no illusions of power—a lifetime as a woman and a librarian had ensured that—but she could show that she, at least, valued herself.

The lav was dreadful small, and reeked of rust and the natural uses to which it was put. The water that dropped from the little pipe overhead was bone-cold. Childress didn't even consider washing her hair. She did undress to her chemise so she could wet her face and hands and dab elsewhere that fear and stress had left their scent. She resolutely pushed aside her feelings of humiliation at being forced to clean herself this way, like a prisoner in a cell.

She was not a prisoner. She was a white bird, under transport now, following a guide she'd agreed to decades before. This was not a sentence. She was not being punished.

Childress didn't believe that for a minute, of course. But it was what she told herself to feel better. Not that it worked, but still she forced the thought. To think on a thing was the first step to creating it.

Anneke banged on the hatch all too soon. "You're late already," she called, voice muffled through the metal.

Childress buttoned herself back into her slip and dress, taking care that the high collar sat properly. She felt shoddy, dusty, and rumpled, but it was the best she had available to her in this moment. She opened the hatch.

Anneke held a mug of tea and two rough slices of coarse brown bread. Childress reflected that if she had ever chanced to learn the arts of men, she might contrive an escape in that moment, tossing the steaming tea in her captor's face and running toward—what? The stern of a ship she didn't know, steaming off an unfamiliar coast?

Instead she took the mug and sipped cautiously. It was a strong dark tea such as the coolies drank in the restaurants in East Haven, where a woman alone might safely dine on exotic foods from the Indian subcontinent. Still, the drink was warm and good and she could taste the stiff infusion, which would set her blood to pumping harder. Childress braced herself against the door and drained the mug as quickly as her tolerance for the heat within would allow. She pocketed one slice of bread as she handed the mug back to Anneke. She gnawed on the other.

Childress felt like a beggar boy going before the truancy bench. This was idiotic. She was an educated woman of spacious intellect and strong will. A single grubby night of confinement and poor nutrition was insufficient to break her spirit.

She gave Anneke a broad smile, letting her eyes twinkle—a look she'd never yet offered to a student, not in thirty-six years at the Divinity School.

"It is now convenient for me to pay a call upon the Mask Poinsard," she said in her most pleasant voice.

Anneke snorted, but led her down the passage, the empty earthenware mug clutched like a club, perhaps in case weapons should suddenly be needed.

The Mask Poinsard waited in a forward cabin above decks. The room was spacious, eight or ten times larger than Childress' tiny lockup, with large windows that overlooked the sea. Chairs that might have come from a faculty club were bolted into place, the deck hidden under maroon carpet.

It looked like a saloon, perhaps, a place intended for gentlemen to meet over cigars and port to discuss finance, horses, and females. In this case, it contained only an ordinary-looking woman. Her dark hair was flecked with gray, over brown eyes in an oval face that might have blended in any English crowd. Where Anneke's dress was much the same as last night, a sort of female compromise to the necessities of labor aboard ship, the Mask Poinsard wore a smart lavender jacket with a flowing skirt to match, a ruffled white blouse, and small black bow. A matching hat waited on a stand beside her chair. Remarkably impractical for shipboard wear. The Mask Poinsard was making a point. Childress wondered to whom the point was addressed.

Somehow she had expected the Mask Poinsard to be a man.

"May I present myself as the Librarian Childress." She stepped through her uncertainty. "Late of the Day Missions Library at Berkeley Divinity School and lifetime resident of New Haven, Connecticut."

"You may address me as the Mask Poinsard. My given name is not of consequence for your purposes." Where Anneke had a broader Continental accent, the Mask Poinsard's accent was pure Received Pronunciation, the English of the court and the bench and all things prestigious.

The clothes, up close, were very finely tailored, with a stitch count too high for Childress to estimate by eye. This woman was very wealthy. But then, she controlled this vessel, for all practical purposes. Possibly through outright ownership.

"Mask Poinsard," Childress said quietly. "I am at your service."

"Indeed." Poinsard settled a bit more deeply into her chair.

Uncomfortable, Childress thought. There was something afoot this woman would prefer not to address. Years in faculty committee meetings had taught her the value of extended silence. She practiced that wisdom.

Eventually the Mask Poinsard stepped into the gap. "We of the *avebianco* do not . . . require oaths." She was picking her words with care. "The vast majority of our members are at best loosely associated with one another or the brotherhood as a whole."

Another pause. Childress smiled brightly and attentively.

"Much as yourself," Poinsard finally said, filling in Childress' line of the playlet in her head.

Childress allowed herself a polite but indistinct murmur.

"Sometimes a member, an affiliate, puts herself forward, inserting herself in the higher business of the brotherhood. Knowingly or otherwise."

This time the pause was accompanied by a sharpened stare. Childress continued to smile in silence, though she was certain her expression was transiting rapidly from attentive to vacuous.

Poinsard took a large shuddering sigh. "You, Librarian Childress, through your actions, began a chain of events which directly brought about the disappearance and presumed death of two individuals critical to the success of our brotherhood's purposes. One, Simeon Malgus, was a key agent in our long-term contests with the Rationalists and their so-called Silent Order of the Second Winding. The other, William of Ghent, stood in the highest councils of the Silent Order." She leaned forward, pointing a finger at Librarian Childress, talking faster now.

Nerves, Childress realized. She steeled herself for what must come next.

Poinsard rushed on. "Through your actions, they were both lost. The Silent Order even now goes to war against the Feathered Masks that sit in our order's high councils. The *avebianco* have made overtures of peace to them—we have, after all, coexisted in compromise for centuries. The price the Silent Order has demanded is that you be bound over for trial by their star chamber."

Ah. This was worse than anything she might have expected. To be brought before the hierarchy of the white birds was one thing. To be cast as a sacrifice to the Rationalists was entirely another.

Childress thought quickly. "Let us have no pretense, Mask. Relying on my loyalty and obedience, you summoned me aboard your ship so you could betray me for the sake of the Feathered Masks and their peace of mind. I am not here to answer for my actions, or as a reward for my steadfastness. I am here to be sacrificed as a pawn to the Rationalists. You waited until we were under way rather than bringing your case on shore in order to ensure that your mission prevailed. The cowardice you have shown in approaching me is despicable. Worse so those who stand above you in condemning me to ease their own fears.

"But," Childress said, "I would have gone willingly, had you only asked." She was mildly surprised to realize that truth. "All that would ever have been required was the statement of need. For I *am* loyal, even now. Not to you, or even to the Feathered Masks. You have shown yourselves as miserable and venal. No, I am loyal to our brotherhood's ideal, that man can make a place among the works of God on his own terms. We are the middle way, neither extreme Spiritualists demanding blind obedience to God's writ, nor Rationalists seeking to expel Him from His creation.

"You, I am afraid, have been driven by your cowardice. You have betrayed me. I will not betray you in turn."

Childress turned and walked toward the door. She had no power here but her dignity. She was secretly pleased to see the startled expression on Anneke's face as the other woman moved to the hatch, looking past Childress for some direction from her mistress.

"Librarian Childress—," the Mask Poinsard began.

Childress smiled, a petty, nasty smile she knew, but Anneke stopped and let her pass. She'd won, not the struggle for life or freedom, but the moral struggle. When Poinsard had spoken, she'd conceded that Childress had stripped away her rationales.

Truth is not for the weak of heart.

Out in the corridor beyond, she made for the open deck. She had no thought of flinging herself into the sea, or embarking on some other Brontë-esque expression of romantic failure. Just a desire rather to stand in open air, embrace the honest wind, and look to her own future without the foolishness of the Mask Poinsard echoing in her ears.

A few moments later Anneke caught up to Childress at the rail. Her broad, strong hand touched the librarian's shaking old one for a moment. Anneke then pressed a warm pastry into Childress' palm. "I am sorry."

"I don't suppose you were meant to hear that. The Mask had a rather different piece of theater in mind."

"Yes . . . well . . ." Anneke's hand brushed Childress' forearm again, more deliberately this time. "I shan't be bolting your door anymore."

"Thank you," Childress said distantly. She realized she was on the starboard rail, looking out into the Atlantic rather than at North America. Not that it mattered now. There was no going back, figuratively or literally. And she'd meant what she said, about loyalty to the ideal of the white birds.

A small moral victory was little comfort, but it was far better than miserable surrender. She smiled again into the wind, listening to Anneke's slow footfalls and wondering how long she'd live once the Mask Poinsard had conveyed her to the waiting hands of the Silent Order.

THREE

PAOLINA

A Muralha was a beast, Paolina soon realized. A great stone beast taller than the sky, with one mighty paw raised to strike down anyone so foolish as to crawl along its face.

Still, it was beautiful. She kept to paths hundreds of yards above the sea to avoid being pressed onto the eroding faces near the water. In this area *a Muralha* still had the same stepped shelves that hosted Praia Nova back to the west. Whatever geology or Divine plan that had made this portion of the Wall had worked with a principle of consistency.

The sea was always below to her left, rarely out of sight in good weather. At night it murmured to her, much as it had at home, simple polysyllabic lullabies in the tongue of wave and water. That eased her mind.

To her right rose the bulk of the Wall. It climbed, rising and sloping away, but still vaulting past her line of sight to create a horizon almost straight above her head. The ledges up there held whole countries of their own—logic alone told her that, but every now and then the thought was reinforced by a glint of metal, or the sight of a streamer of smoke, or some broken piece of wrought stonework fallen from high above to smash at her level.

Clouds, too, up there. She saw layers on layers like stacked wreaths, clinging close to the face of *a Muralha* but never completely obscuring it. Sometimes they would part to show a vision of ever more fields of stone and air. At night, she would watch lightning walk sideways across the face and listen to the rumble of storms so distant, their water never reached her, though it fell for hours at some faraway height.

She had lived with the sheer monstrous size of the thing all her life, but in Praia Nova it had somehow faded into the background. Out here, *a Muralha* filled the sky to overlook the sea like a scaled cat watching a rabbit burrow.

The weather was a bit more troublesome on the trail—the storm that had broken the night she left Praia Nova had been a harbinger of a series of rains. The days were hot, the nights had an edge, there was always wind, and she was wet more often than not.

For a while Paolina amused herself conceiving of possible methods of rainproofing. Simplest would have been some of the coated canvas with which the mushroom sheds had been covered. She could have trimmed it into a cape or jacket and traveled well enough.

There were certainly more fanciful solutions. Tar could be boiled and distillated to elastic components, but that would require far more glassware than she could imagine finding out here. She could conceive of using tree sap, or the skin of marine animals, or some great system of fans to create a bubble of air pressure.

All the speculation was pointless, but it continued her long habits of thought. Paolina wondered how so many people managed to live in the world without any need to understand its workings. God had laid everything before man, a banquet of knowledge. All one had to do was step to the table and sup! Yet so many people sought sleep or wine or foolishness instead of simply opening their eyes.

Not to mention their ears and their minds.

So, soaking wet much of the time, she walked. She camped in darkness, making fire with the little sulfur sticks she'd fabricated the summer before. Those had been laughed at in Praia Nova. Here on an open trail, their value was immeasurable.

The one thing her thoughts shied away from was the sheer distance. The diameter of the earth was obvious enough. It was readily measured from the period of a single day, with elementary analysis of the rotation as measured against the brasswork in the heavens. The track itself rotated around the sun, which introduced subtleties in the mathematics of time, but still it was simple enough.

She assumed at least three thousand miles from Praia Nova to the African coast. There she might hope to find the English at their works. The chances of running into *Bassett* or one of its sister wizard-ships seemed remote, but still she kept her eyes sharply on the sky.

Clarence Davies had walked a good portion of that distance. It had taken him two years, but he'd done it alone. A boy. Dr. Minor had left to follow it farther, though his fate was unknown.

She was a girl, but she was fifteen and nearly a woman. Her legs were long, her arms were strong, and she had no illusions about the sharpness of her wit.

All of which would mean nothing if a scaled cat or a band of enkidu raiders should drop from above.

Paolina took refuge in her stemwinder.

She never removed the device from its little sack unless she was camped securely. She didn't trust herself not to drop it on a trail, or even worse, over some edge as she crossed a precipice. It came out only when the moments were quiet and she had time to consider what the hands told her, what the device meant.

The hand that measured the time that beat at the heart of everything ran true. That was useful, because she had no way to hear such a thing with her own ears or measure with it her own eyes, as she did the next two hands. Any fool could observe the turning of the earth, and any fool could lay a finger on her own pulse to measure the beating of her heart.

The last hand, though—the one she'd built a gear train for and arranged separate springs for—it was taking a measure, too. And she did not know what this hand was measuring.

Paolina decided that was far more interesting than frightening. She spent much of her evenings huddled with the stemwinder in her hand, trying to see further into the world.

Sometimes she succeeded.

A month on the trail, she came down with an ague. Perhaps it was something she ate despite her care with strange berries and pallid roots. Paolina was afraid to simply curl up and sleep out her chills and cramps. She kept moving, stumbling through days that lasted moments, and hours that crawled at the speed of seasons.

The stemwinder was like a compass to her in that time. She would reach, hand grabbing and clawing weakly, until she found the canvas sack within her dress pocket, and clutch it close.

When the path came to a gate, Paolina was surprised. Short men—no, women—with stumpy bodies armor-clad and wearing tusked helmets, surrounded her. They stared. Their spears coursed with a pale green fire so faint as to seem illusory.

One of the weapons nosed close to Paolina's fingers where she clutched the stemwinder. She jerked her right hand up and away from the crackling point before slumping to the stones. A circle of faces closed over her; then she was lifted and carried through a gate. She could see only the arch, decorated high above her head with blue and orange gemstones, intermixed with chunks of quartz and glass. She imagined that was how a jewel box might look from within.

Clearly, the stemwinder was her passport here.

Were these people sorcerers, like the English?

A building, then, the entrance another high bejeweled arch, followed by hallways lined with bulging golden columns beneath clerestory roofs where sunlight glowed through colored panes.

These people loved color.

Paolina tried to focus her thoughts. The gate guards had been so dispassionate, they might well have speared her where she lay but for the stemwinder's presence in her hand. Still, a child could have wrested it from her.

They deposited her in a smaller room with a closer ceiling painted in abstract designs that seemed intended to signify flowers. Another toothy, snouted face pushed through her bearers and leaned over her.

"Are you dying?" the strange woman asked in English.

Paolina chose to lie, for the sake of valor. "I do not believe so." She wanted to ask, *Why English, who are you, where am I?* but the words were too hard. She might not understand the answers anyway.

The woman looked her over. "You carry a gleam."

A gleam. Somehow Paolina knew this woman meant the stemwinder. And the word fit, like glove to hand. "When I am well . . ." She stopped to breathe. "Then I will show you . . . what you wish to know."

That seemed to satisfy the woman, who turned and growled. More ugly little women took her away. She was stripped and bathed, though they kept a wary distance from the stemwinder clutched in her hand.

What had she made?

"Gleam," the ugly woman had said.

Paolina wished she had an English wizard to guide her in the moment, some descendant of Newton or Dee or one of the other wise men of the court of St. James.

She fell asleep while they were spooning a thin vegetable broth into her mouth.

AL-WAZIR

Herr Doctor Professor Lothar Ottweill was the sort of man for whom any self-respecting crew in Her Imperial Majesty's Royal Navy would have found a convenient accident shortly after sailing. As a division chief, al-Wazir would have spent half his time protecting the fool from himself, and the other half beating his men into line so that when the inevitable discipline parade was held, it wasn't *his* division before captain's mast.

For one thing, Ottweill was madder than a St. James hatter. He might as well have been swigging mercury, or one of those strange alchemical mixes the powdersmiths were always on about. Bald as a church pew, the engineer stood about five foot four and didn't weigh upwards of eight stone. He seemed to think he outsized everyone around him. He thought it so thoroughly that almost everyone else was fooled. Even al-Wazir, pushing twenty stone at six foot four, felt an eerie and sickening magic.

That was not the whole of the thing. There had been officers in his career, some martinets, others sensible characters, who'd overcome disadvantages of size with sheer bravado. As much as anything, the problem was the angry, spitting shout in which Ottweill constantly spoke. The tone presumed you were a purblind fool in need of constant oversight.

All the man had on the other side of his balance sheet was sheer, walleyed genius. That and a clear vision of what it would take to tunnel through a hundred miles and more of basal rock to penetrate the Equatorial Wall.

Bloody-mindedness struck al-Wazir as the first requirement for this project of the Prime Minister's. Ottweill had bloody-mindedness woven into the fabric of his body and soul.

Al-Wazir had to admire the man's strength of purpose, in the same way he admired a spectacular storm or an especially wild mad dog. Such respect seemed safer from a distance.

He was beginning to see the essence of Lloyd George's plan in pairing him with Ottweill. The chief realized that he and Kitchens might be the only two men anywhere in the quarry who were not cowed by the good doctor. And al-Wazir was probably the only man on the expedition with enough experience of chain of command combined with sufficient disregard of the same to wrestle with Ottweill.

Literally, if need be.

He wondered how Ottweill had survived long enough in life to achieve a position of this magnitude and responsibility. Of course, officers did it all the time, buffoons and monsters rising to flag rank without ever seeming to be noticed by Admiralty or their fellows.

By fighting dirty, of course.

In the meantime, he listened to the doctor rant about the steam borer, mark four. Watt and Doulton had built the boilers, while most of the construction had been done at Chapman and Furneaux, locomotive builders. Three had been completed, two shipped out for the Wall some months ago by slow boat under heavy escort. The third remained here for final testing and design improvements, with the appropriate parts and amendments to be sent south to the other two units.

All would be an indefinite work in progress, al-Wazir saw.

"Why we are not permitted to weld the operators into their cabins I am not understanding," Ottweill was saying at his usual shout. "Enormous are the efficiencies to be gained. No wastage on egress and support systems. From their bucket they can eat, then shit back into. Three buckets, three days, then—*foo!*—open we cut the cabin and them we replace. Two men, three buckets each, we run three more days. What problem is there here, by damn? Stupid soft *Englanders*. Good Prussian peasant give me. On black bread and beatings they live, in the name of the mother of God."

Al-Wazir looked around. Nine men listened to this briefing. A pair of Fleet Street reporters with their own quiet man to watch them—some counterpart who had exchanged nods of recognition with Kitchens. Two more men in Overseas Civil Service uniform. A pair of Royal Marine sergeants who kept exchanging eye-rolling glances. And of course, himself and Kitchens.

All of them, even the marines, were completely overwhelmed by Ottweill. No one was questioning the man. Yet somehow, the engineer ranted onward through stupidity and thickheadedness to something that actually worked on a rational basis. It was an amazing display.

The chief began to develop a second theory, that Ottweill was in full control of himself and had adopted this approach as the best way to force compliance from the men around him.

Either way, he decided he was amused. Al-Wazir began to chuckle. This earned him first a glance from Kitchens, who smiled another of his elusive smiles, then stares from some of the other attendees, then finally a sputtering and amazed silence from Ottweill.

"No, really," al-Wazir said. "Please, do carry on."

"Do I *entertain* you, you great red jungle ape?"

"Quite a bit, sir." Al-Wazir bit back more.

"Well." Ottweill folded his arms, standing before the unrolled chart of the steam borer. "I am glad to be seeing that my education and credentials and experience have come to serve a useful purpose for Her Imperial Majesty's government."

Kitchens stirred slightly at that, but al-Wazir rose to his feet. With both of them standing, Ottweill came to the second button down on his chest. The little man lost much of his physical authority just standing with the big chief. "I'm told you do," al-Wazir said. He let his voice rumble, as he might talking to a new chum with big ideas about deck discipline. "I am here to help." He added slowly and deliberately, *"Sir."*

"Who is this man?" Ottweill demanded of the rest of the room. "Have him discharged immediately, or no tunnel will there be." He crossed his arms and glared triumphantly.

Kitchens cleared his throat. "Chief Petty Officer Threadgill Angus al-Wazir is in charge of preserving your life on the Wall, Herr Doctor Professor Ottweill, as well as the hundreds of lives of, ah, lesser value. By *direct* appointment of Her Imperial Majesty." Kitchens let it rest a beat, then added, "Sir."

Ottweill visibly swallowed, then stared back up at al-Wazir. "I see," he said. "Your job is the beating of your fellow apes. By brains I shall survive, as I always have. Survive you will by being a bigger savage than the monkeys and the *Schwarzers*. Very well. You may sit down now."

To his own surprise, al-Wazir sat.

Afterward, they took carriages down to the steam borer. Ottweill asked al-Wazir to ride with him in the lead on a little self-propelled vehicle much like a sulky save that it sat two. It was the first time other than visits to the head that al-Wazir been away from Kitchens since leaving Admiralty.

The sulky clattered through the town at the bottom of the quarry. Al-Wazir took the moment to examine his surroundings. The town itself was unremarkable—cheap buildings hastily erected to last a few seasons. In a handful of years, this place would have degraded to a dreadful slum.

He turned his attention to the excavation ahead. In a sense, the quarry was vaguely like the Wall, in that stone towered toward the sky. It was such a *short* towering, though. If he'd never seen the Wall, he might have thought the sides of the quarry high, especially at the deep end where the steam borer was deployed. And of course these walls were fractured, split away by blasting and steam shovels and pickaxes to be hauled to London for foundation and building stone.

The floor of the quarry rose behind him, so that the end that pointed just south of east formed a ramp. This was how the quarrymen had originally dug it down, keeping always an exit behind them. The steam borer had to have come in that way, too, though the great rails did not now extend to the top.

He wondered how they'd gotten it here from the locomotive works. That would have been something to see.

Ottweill slapped the reins and turned to him. "So, you are being Her Imperial's man to watch me. When you would arrive was I wondering."

"Not me," said al-Wazir. "I'm the Wall Johnnie, not the spy."

"Tch." Ottweill shook his head. "With one of those little eels who belong to Lloyd George you come. A political you are, big man."

"As you like it. No one's asked me for reports, and I won't be a rat." Al-Wazir chuckled again. "Seen too many rats in the Navy. They have a way of going overboard in storms."

"Not so many direct appointments of the Queen do we get," muttered Ottweill.

There is money here, al-Wazir thought. All the treasure it took to build the doctor's great machines, ship them to Africa, move a thousand men across half of Northern Earth. Money that flowed to and from Ottweill's word, regardless of who might be playing the purser.

So many dangers. And here he was, thinking like an officer again. Al-Wazir hated that.

The sulky followed a road that cut diagonally back and forth across the downward slope of the quarry to reach the flat at the west end where the steam borer had gone back into its tunnel. A small crowd of men there bent to their tasks. With Ottweill coming, he could understand why they might want to appear busy, though he suspected that with the borer working inside, their purpose was mostly to stand and wait.

They clattered up to a carriage park.

"On the way back we talk," Ottweill said sharply. "In my work you believe, we are to do well. At my work you laugh, I am not caring what Her Imperial Majesty has said about you."

"Oh, I'm Royal Navy." Al-Wazir laid on his best talking-to-officers smile once more. "I can believe in anything I'm told to."

Despite himself, Ottweill snorted.

The official tour walked through the navvies clustered about, awaiting the return of the steam borer. It was obvious to al-Wazir that Ottweill intended a grand entrance for the machine. All these people were standing to in order to show the visitors how elaborate and necessary the care of the mighty device would be.

It was all to prove the need for money, al-Wazir realized.

"The coal gang these are," Ottweill said, pointing to a group of a grubby men with dusty black covering their faces and clothing. "Thirty-two tons of coal they can move into the borer's box in less than twenty minutes."

A few more steps to four thin men and two boys, standing next to a tangle of large tins and narrow hoses. "The oilers. To lube the gearing and drive-lines." Ottweill looked around. "Separate from the cutting face this is, *ja*? A different crew."

And on they went, looking at and occasionally talking to metalwrights, watermen, diggers, jackers, electrickmen, chemists, assayers—an Industrial Revolution's worth of men, al-Wazir realized. It was not so different from the organization of a ship's company at that, with divisions and chiefs and idlers and the various specialists.

Al-Wazir traded glances with Kitchens. He didn't know anything about tunnels or heavy equipment, but he was quite familiar with crewing a complex task. Ottweill, or one of his deputies at least, knew what he was doing.

The three of them ended up standing next to the rails that emerged from the tunnel. These were twice the size of ordinary rails. Up close, al-Wazir could see that a second set of smaller rails ran between the wider spread. He turned to look. The standard gauge rails curved away from the abbreviated steam borer's track to a long shed. A service train, then, to reach the borer, carry supplies and workers.

Of course. Ottweill couldn't possibly plan to constantly back the great monster in and out of a tunnel that would run a hundred miles or more through the base of the Wall.

"Two of these shipped to the Wall?" he asked.

"Yes," murmured Kitchens.

"In case of breakage or other problems." Ottweill seemed almost to vibrate. "For lack of equipment will we not fail."

"Hot there," al-Wazir observed. "Everything rots fast."

"Not once we are inside the Wall."

Something within the tunnel shrieked. A whistle, al-Wazir realized, echoing from inside the digging. The ground began to shudder as the steam borer backed out of the tunnel.

The stern appeared first. It was a wall of black iron, a massive vertical plate emerging so slowly from the tunnel that it seemed to be a moving building—much like standing close to a steel-plated dreadnought just setting out from dock. The butt of the borer was almost vertical, with a large hatch in the center and several smaller hatches. Coal, he figured, and smaller ports for water, lubricant, and possibly a secondary fuel such as bunker oil. Beneath the hatches was a gaping hole where a series of chains or belts could be seen to turn slowly. It was topped by a glass cupola, where an engineer or operator could oversee the monster's backing up.

Once the steam borer emerged into the light of the quarry, it seemed smaller, built almost to human scale. In truth, it was still at least twice the size of any locomotive al-Wazir had ever seen. The body was roughly cylindrical, plated with armor to protect it from falling rock. Walkways clung to the side and top. The thing's great bulk was supported on massive trucks slung beneath, eight-wheeled monsters like those used in shipyards to convey the weight of a fully built hull into the water for the first time.

The rounded length extended fifty feet before the cab appeared. A collar passed around the diameter of the steam borer, glassed in with heavy framed view ports. There was a small hatch that opened onto the walkway—al-Wazir would have been hard-pressed to fit his body through it. Perhaps they used boys to drive the thing.

He could see the point of Ottweill's argument about the welding—space was very constrained, and it would be quite difficult for a boring crew to extract themselves from the machine while it was in the middle of a dig. Which in turn made al-Wazir wonder once more how the tunnel would progress within the Wall.

Forward of the cab was a flanged bit of heavy armored plate, rising like a scoop to face the direction of travel. It must be to catch debris thrown back from the drilling surfaces. The whistle screamed again, close enough that the chief had to cover his ears, as the working end of the steam borer backed out.

That was as vile looking a set of blades as al-Wazir had ever laid eyes on in thirty years of sailing Her Imperial Majesty's air lanes. Three main members spiraled to a point, in a shape like an unopened tulip bud. They were heavily cross-braced, with a great threaded beam at the heart that rotated to propel the members like the blades of a sidewise reaper. Each member was moving slowly enough that al-Wazir could see the bright-edged knobs that lined them, varying from the size of his head to the size of his hands.

It growled as well, a beast meant to chew through the heart of the world.

He had been wrong about the size. As the crews swarmed over the steam borer, he realized once more that it was *big*. A rolling building, a house of cutting designed to rend open the secrets of the Wall.

Taken as a whole, the steam borer looked wrong to al-Wazir, a violation of nature. Like a device meant for painful torture instead of honest combat. In that moment he badly missed the grace and beauty of Her Imperial Majesty's airships.

He looked around. The rest of the inspection party seemed awestruck by the overwhelming power of the machine and the undeniable reality of the tunnel out of which it had backed itself.

"Hardened steel," Ottweill shouted as the boilers vented and the steam borer ground to a halt with a shriek of distressed metal. "Every three days in soft rock repaired the cutting head must be, each day in hard rock. The cutters we change for some rock conditions. Openwork it is so we can extend powder drills and blasting tamps, or men send forward to work a face by hand, without backing out and decommissioning the front end." His voice dropped as the borer sagged into silence, save for the tapping tools of two men opening the hatch to let the crew out. "A string of specially designed goods wagons to accept waste removal, she can tow. An ordinary locomotive in behind we send to take those cars off and then shunt out for dumping."

"You don't back 'er out of a tunnel as long what as you're planning to drive into yon Wall," said one of the marines.

Ottweill shook his head vigorously. "Every five miles of cutting, with traditional equipment we will follow and open up a larger chamber. Back her up we can for servicing there without retreating the breadth of the Wall. Forward bases that also provides for supplies, equipment, and quarters for the men."

Al-Wazir noted the shouting madman had dropped away in the face of the equipment itself. Ottweill was one who needed to be alone with his tools. And the doctor would do anything to protect his mission.

He turned to Kitchens. "I don't know nothing about bloody great rock cutters, but I do know something about men. You've got a problem with that one. He could kill us all for the sake of another mile of stone."

"Consider Ottweill to be one of the hazards of surviving on the Wall."

Al-Wazir nodded, then approached the steam borer. It was huge, hot, and stinking. Men were all over it, opening check panels, pumping in water and oil, inspecting the cutting surfaces. Like crabs on a dead whale.

Save dead whales were not made of black iron and didn't sport teeth fit to chew through stone.

CHILDRESS

She spent the next few days walking the decks, watching America slide by the port rail. Anneke followed at a distance of a few paces. The librarian made no attempt to seek out the Mask Poinsard.

Of necessity she encountered the crew of *Mute Swan* about their duties. Them she watched with more care, as she always studied people.

The Mask Poinsard had taken ship with a polyglot complement; that much was certain. The language of the deck was English, in that the officers made their commands in the Queen's tongue. There were seamen whose accents and words hailed from the Scandinavian protectorates, from the American colonies, from the Caribbean, from Suez, from farthest India.

In effect, the crew was a map of the British Empire.

She'd never taken ship before, and had no standards by which to judge a crew, but living in a port city all her life had led Childress to believe that sailors tended to run together. So while a ship might hail from one port, and her captain and senior officers from another, the crew were all Greek or Arab or Portuguese. Not so here.

She wondered what that meant. Was everyone aboard a white bird? The name of the ship might imply that. In fact, it was a ridiculous piece of allusion, drawing attention to the nature of the vessel's mission for anyone with enough understanding to read the clue.

"Too clever by half," as she'd said of many students who'd passed her desk over the years.

Childress finally concluded the sailors were mostly white birds when she realized how carefully they kept a watch over her. Ordinary deckhands wouldn't have given much thought to her comings and goings so long as she didn't impede their work. Here, in addition to Anneke trailing her like the ghost of an old affair, there was always a man coiling rope or polishing a rail at the corner of her eye.

Some smiled, some did not, but they never left her alone. Were they afraid of her, or afraid *for* her? That probably depended on whether or not they'd yet had the pleasure of meeting the Mask Poinsard. The woman would freeze steam.

But in the meantime she walked alone. Initially this suited her mood perfectly well. After several days, she tired of the game and began to wish once more for at least minimal company.

Childress decided to embrace Anneke first.

She walked along the port rail under a gray sky gravid with rain. The pine-dark forests the past day had given way to open sea on all sides. *Mute Swan* had bent her course more east than north. The weather promised not so much a storm as a rising of the waters, one of those rains where the air and sea seemed to mix without boundary. She'd loved them on the harborside in New Haven. Here in the North Atlantic, the prospect seemed more grim.

At least it was no nor'easter to pitch waves taller than the pilot's cabin of their ship. Those she'd heard talk of in New Haven, the sorts of stories men recounted in low voices that trailed off when they realized a woman was near.

Grim, to match her mood, and the deckhand trailing her right now was a tall Scandinavian fellow of uncertain English from what she'd overheard thus far. It seemed as good a time as any to turn to her governess.

Childress reversed step in one motion, swinging on her heel to head back toward Anneke who followed five or six paces behind. The other woman's green eyes widening a moment.

"You may be my guard," Childress said in her most pleasant voice. "But neither of us serves the other." She extended her arm. "Will you take the air with me?"

Anneke stepped forward, looped her elbow with Childress', then they resumed their walk under the grinning gaze of the big Scandinavian boy. Somewhat to Childress' surprise, Anneke spoke first. "You have upset the Mask Poinsard. She composes messages all day in her cabin and tears them up again, casting the shreds into the sea."

"The Mask Poinsard is welcome to her upset. I am the one being bound over into the hands of our enemies, and for small cause at that." She paused, groping toward the conversation she'd meant to begin. "I beg your pardon, Anneke. It was not my intent to voice complaints to you."

"What then?" Anneke's voice was almost breathless.

"I am very lonely here." Childress knew her voice had dropped into a quiet register where she swallowed her words. "I have lived alone since my mother died, but I have been at the library six days and church the seventh every week for years. I believe the Mask Poinsard meant to lecture me, tutor me even, to bring me to her point of view and show me as a triumph on our arrival in Europe. For the sake of my pride I have cut myself off."

They walked a few paces in silence, crossing over to the opposite rail at the bow. The view to the east and south was nearly as watery and dark as the port side had been, interrupted only by a few bright shafts where the sun pushed through the clouds.

"I do not think you did wrong," Anneke said. "Like you, I am loyal to an idea. The Feathered Masks look at that idea from a different perch. The Mask Poinsard has ambitions to rise to their level some day." She smiled, her face crooking. "Women can do that in the *avebianco*, you know. Rise to the top.

"When I was a girl in Götheborg, I could fence any man in the city to his knees, but it meant nothing. At first they took the matches for the novelty, crossing blades with a pretty chit. But none would fight me twice, and many claimed it was not worth the trouble. Had I been a man, I could have risen to become arms master to the Viceroy of Uppsala. As a woman, I was only an embarrassing curiosity."

"And so the *avebianco*?"

"The Feathered Masks, yes."

Childress shook her head, stepping around a rope coil. They approached the stern and another walk round the rail. The tall Scandinavian still following along. "I had always thought us a loose affiliation of librarians and archivists and common people. Not fighting women and scheming daughters of the quality."

"For the most part, I suppose you are correct." Anneke paused at the taffrail to stare at the churning line of their wake. "People of the book, and people of hope and reason, and people of God, serving a common purpose. But we have our heights and edges, too." She turned to face Childress, her expression set somewhere between fear and need. "You know that I am a Claw? A Claw can never be a Mask. The Feathered Masks will not have blood on their hands."

Childress let the obvious question slide by her. Instead: "It is more clean to order my death with a word than with a fist."

"Yes."

"Anneke . . ."

"Yes?"

"I shall not think of you as a Claw, nor speak of you that way."

Anneke's crooked smile returned. "I thank you. And I . . . I . . ."

"Yes?"

"I . . . never mind." With that, she fled, leaving Childress in the company of the laughing sailor and a pair of narrow-winged white birds that trailed along just behind the vessel.

The next morning a crewman knocked on her cabin door. "Services in ten minutes, ma'am, on the foredeck."

"Thank you," she called.

In the days since her confrontation with the Mask Poinsard, various items of clothing had appeared in her cabin. None had been particularly well fitted or to her taste, but she managed a high-necked velvet dress with a modest bustle.

When Childress slipped out into the passageway, the Mask Poinsard stood waiting.

Today the woman was clad in a cream-colored suit of much the same cut as the previous outfit Childress had seen her wear. Her blouse was pale blue, as were her high-buttoned shoes and her wide-brimmed hat. In short, the Mask Poinsard was dressed more for a smart day in town than Sunday morning services in a shipboard drizzle.

"Ma'am." Childress was cautiously polite.

"I was unsure if you'd have the decency to come to services."

Childress could play that game again. Decades of faculty infighting had left her amply prepared for the barbed remark. "I find your uncertainty to be of no surprise, given your absolute lack of understanding of simple decency."

The Mask Poinsard blinked. "I see we have found the wrong foot with one another again."

"Allow me to be blunt," said Childress, "as time is too short for this dance. If you persist in beginning every mutual encounter with an attempt to put me in my place, I will never bend to you. Sparring is a waste of time for both of us. However, if you wish to engage in the gentle art of conversation, I should find the pastime diverting. In the meantime, I believe I hear the bell ringing to call us to prayer."

They walked, the Mask Poinsard leading, in a frigid, rigid silence that left Childress wondering yet again whether she should hope or despair.

Mute Swan had no chaplain, so perforce the captain, one William Eckhuysen, led the services. Childress was accustomed to the high church splendor of St. John Horofabricus on Crown Street in New Haven, with its racks of votive candles, stained-glass windows in the stations of the horofix, elaborate vestry and sixty-voice choir. It always seemed to her that God abode at His best in the shadows of splendor.

Still, here in the raw weather of the deck with the hands shuffling and yawning, Captain Eckhuysen had a certain passion quite capable of invoking the divine spirit. Childress stood close to Poinsard's elegance and Anneke in her sage-green gown as the crew opened with the Navy hymn. Eckhuysen then read from Paul's letter to the Rhodians, the passages concerning the writ of Holy Spirit in the brasswork of the sky.

" 'For it is given to us as the greatest gift to have proof positive of God's intention, in looking upward in day or night. Lest you doubt, or seek solace in the machinations of Babylon or Egypt, remember where the Lord Jesus laid down His own life, in the slow and inescapable advancement of a man's simple copy of His Father's works.' "

He then looked about the deck, catching the eyes of his officers, passengers, and hands. "The centuries since Our Lord's horofixion have brought change upon change upon change to our world. We sail the boundless oceans on muscles of steam, where once we feared to row far from shore. We walk the lands under the hottest sun of Northern Earth, where once we did not know what lay south of Africa's Mediterranean beaches. The *avebianco* soars over the hearts and minds of men, making free what had before been bound.

"In this, we are following the words of the Apostle Paul. We pursue the slow and inescapable advancement of man's efforts to imitate God. We remake Creation in our own image, over and over, taming lands and seas, wresting knowledge from the fabric of the world around us, always laboring in the light of Christ's gift to us.

"With this in mind, remember what you—"

He was interrupted by the helmsman shouting from the bridge, "Wake ho!"

The words got Captain Eckhuysen's undivided attention. "Which quarter?" he bellowed.

"Trailing portside, just west of north, sir!"

Every man on the ship raced to the port rail, leaving Childress, Anneke, and the Mask Poinsard standing in confusion. "Get to your cabins," Anneke said, but Childress and Poinsard exchanged glances, both shaking their heads. They followed the sailors to the rail.

Almost all the ship's company crowded there, forty officers and men. Fingers stabbed as they pointed out at the choppy water. Childress saw neither ship nor wake, just roughening swells covered with sliding foam. There were no birds in evidence either. She had no idea if that was significant.

Eckhuysen turned and looked up at his bridge again. "Where's it now?"

"Lost it, sir!"

"Emergency stations," Eckhuysen shouted. "Women to the lifeboats. Prepare the rockets. Bosun, open the arms locker immediately!"

With that, the sailors were a whirling riot of motion, racing across the deck, up ladders, down hatches, shouting in half a dozen languages.

"What is it?" the Mask Poinsard asked Anneke, her voice straining over the din. "I see nothing."

"Aft boats." Anneke's voice was grim. She grabbed the Mask Poinsard's arm with one hand, Childress' arm with the other. "We'll want to be in the life rings as well."

Childress resisted the tug. "If we go into the water, there's hardly any hope of rescue *here,* I should think."

The look Anneke shot her was tinged with desperation. "As may be, but it is what I can do. If there were more, believe me, I would do it as well."

"Underwater," Childress said, her voice catching. "They have spied an underwater boat." She cudgeled her memory for the proper term. "*Sous-marin.* There is a submarine nearby."

The Mask Poinsard, unwilling to be budged, hitched herself up slightly. "Her Imperial Majesty's Royal Navy has no submarines."

"No," Anneke said. "But the Chinaman does. Come now, please, ladies."

There was another shout from the pilothouse. All three women looked over the port rail.

A long dark hull was sliding into view above the wave tops. It had a single tower or deckhouse. Sailors poured out of hatches, setting up a gun on the forward deck close to *Mute Swan*.

Above and behind them, there was a loud pop, followed by a whistling screech, as Captain Eckhuysen set off the first of his signal rockets. Childress assumed this would be futile. Even if they were espied, the nearest help would have to come from beyond the horizon's distance.

Men appeared at the rail of *Mute Swan* bearing rifles and pistols. Half a dozen dropped to brace their weapons, half a dozen more standing behind them to present a tight concentration of fire. The rattle of their weapons was painful to Childress' ears, the stink of gunpowder unexpectedly sharp.

The first Chinese shot went wild of the defenders. Instead the wind of it tore at Childress' sleeve as the rail before her shattered. A teakwood splinter eighteen inches long slashed into Anneke's gut like a knife. The woman collapsed to the deck, her green silk gown blooming with blood nearly black.

Childress dropped to her knees next to the stricken woman even as the Mask Poinsard backed away. Anneke stank of blood and bowels and urine. She lifted a hand toward Childress, her fingers twitching as she tried to grab something invisible between them.

"I wanted," Anneke said; then the effort was too much.

The difficult young woman breathed awhile longer as the battle raged. *Mute Swan* bucked and rolled with the impact of Chinese shells. Sailors cursed, while at one point the foghorns blared so long that Childress thought she might be stricken deaf. Still, she knelt on the deck holding Anneke's cooling hand and wondering what it was that the woman had wanted.

To be the best, perhaps. Or even just to be accounted good.

As Chinese sailors swarmed over the rail, small and swarthy and golden-skinned, in their strange blue uniforms, she folded Anneke's hands across her waist and kissed her eyes gently, one and two, before raising her face to greet whatever was to come next.

FOUR

PAOLINA

The one who spoke English came to Paolina at sunrise two days later. None of the others who attended her would admit to understanding the language. In the time she'd been under care, Paolina had tried Portuguese, and her fragmented Spanish, and even attempted a tiny bit of Latin, but received no response.

Now that she was somewhat accustomed to the ways of these people, Paolina recognized the woman as a leading lady of this strange court—her neck was bare. The highest servants wore thin collars of silk, while those of lower rank wore heavier leather bands, or even half helms. Only the great were free to raise their heads unencumbered, it seemed.

On entering Paolina's high chamber with the rain-drenched windows, the woman neither bowed nor turned her head away, but simply said, "I am Karindira. Are you dying?"

"I do not think so." Paolina was fascinated to be pulled back into the same conversation as if no time had passed.

"You carry a gleam." The woman's unblinking black eyes strayed to the stemwinder in Paolina's hand.

"I do." Paolina had been wondering what she would do in this moment. The mechanism had gotten her past the gates, into this palace, and under the care of these strange, squat people. She was unsure that it would be such an easy key to her departure. Not unless she could make something of the gleam.

"Show me, now that you live."

Paolina sat up higher against the pillows at the head of her too-short bed and opened her hand. The blank dial with the four hands faced up. The woman did not move, simply staring at the thing, so Paolina tugged at

the stem until she had it ready to reset the hand measuring the time that
beat at the heart of everything. "See this? Are you certain you want me to
adjust it?"

"No," Karindira said, finally blinking slowly. "Put it away. I know this
for what it is. You carry the gleam. That is enough."

Paolina closed her fingers but kept a good grip on her creation.

"There was another," the woman said. "Two years ago, when the ground
shook, another gleam moved across the Wall. We never saw it."

Even across the many gaps between them, Paolina heard a note of
desperation in the strange woman's voice. "Why do you need to see the
gleam?"

"To know." Karindira glanced away a moment. "We are a city of
women. There has not been a man born or raised here in over a thousand
years. They left in pursuit of another gleam, once. We were bound over to
ourselves to lay nests of girl-children in silent memory of our mothers. We
have been looking for a gleam of our own ever since. Perhaps it will bring
them back. I fear the unbinding."

"As you should," Paolina muttered. "I hail from a village of men. They
are crass and foolish louts who know themselves to be lord of every
woman born, with ears only for decoration to offset their open mouths."

"No matter." Karindira's face settled. "We have made our own way
down the centuries. You carry the first gleam to come to our gates since
then. The temptation is . . . great. . . ."

"I carried the gleam away from my own gates." Paolina clutched the
stemwinder ever more tightly. "I go in search of the English wizards who
understand the true order of the world."

The woman spat on the floor, crudely out of keeping with her otherwise
mannerly behavior. "English. Dog-eaters and monkey-suckers who would
pull down the heavens for their curiosity."

"Yet you speak their tongue. . . ."

"As some among us must, for trade along the Wall. This is not the
language of my nesting clutch."

"*Nem mina*," said Paolina in Portuguese. Then, in English: "But it has
become the language of the order of the world."

The woman smiled, a somewhat appalling sight given her stained
triangular teeth. "We can curse one another in the tongue of those
flatwater barbarians. You will need a week or more to recover properly. I
offer you hospitality until then."

"I will be along my way as soon as I may," Paolina said politely.

"When you are well," Karindira said, "I will show you a thing." She sat on the edge of Paolina's bed. "In the meantime, will you tell me more of men?"

Nine days later Karindira led Paolina down a dank stair in the heart of her palace. "This is a thing of men I will show you. Choose what it will mean to you. I make no urging."

Paolina followed her down a squared-off series of landings around an empty shaft that might have been built for some other purpose, before these wooden steps had been set into place on iron frames. Some of the individual risers were rotten, and the frames creaked beneath her weight, so that her heart raced as she descended. The molder made her eyes and nose run thick.

She did not look forward to making her way back up again.

At the bottom of a long series of flights there was a larger room. A great brass altar or tomb was set in the middle of it, like a metal coffin with a crystal top. There were brass ribbons inset into the floor running east and west from the coffin. Columns loomed around them, broken-off stubs protruding in many places.

"There are weights within the Wall," Karindira said. "Pieces that turn to keep the balance of the world." She patted the brass altar. "This is a cart which moves among the weights. It will take you all around the world and back in a day, should you desire."

Paolina was amazed that such a thing was possible. That the world was filled with the grand mechanisms of God's design was self-evident from any examination of the heavens. That a person might set foot within the mechanism was not so clearly the case.

"How would you control it? How would you know where to stop and exit?"

"These things are not known to me." Karindira shrugged, a remarkable ordinary gesture. "I told you I would show you a thing. I cannot account for it. When the men departed, they took the keys which had been given to us, so they might easily return."

Paolina was sorely tempted. She was clever, more than clever, but this was something she had no basis to understand. She could imagine being trapped in the car, circling beneath the Wall forever, unable to break free or exit until she starved to cobwebbed bones flashing forever in a forest of whirling brass. Still, the possibility of passing so quickly beneath the skin of the world amazed her.

"I would if I could," she told Karindira. "But I cannot see how to control this thing."

Karindira seemed sad a moment. "Then fare well on the trail, Paolina-who-seeks-the-English. I will walk you upward and to the gates. After that, your path is your own."

Traveling to the east gate, Paolina got her first good view of Karindira's city. She'd never seen one before, though certainly Dickens had described London well enough.

This place was no London, but the streets were *stone*. Buildings seemed arranged on top of one another to loom high enough for three and four rows of windows. All of Praia Nova would have fit in one street. Even the walls were overwhelming, blocking out the world outside while hemming the people and their places in close as any fist.

It was so large. She realized that there must be a thousand people there, perhaps two thousand. An almost inconceivable number. Paolina could see the virtue of a place as small as Praia Nova.

She walked some miles from the east gate of Karindira's city before stopping for the night. Paolina pulled herself into a hollow among the ferns and reeds in a wider bamboo forest that dripped even as the sun glinted in the west. It smelled watery, a rich, spongy stink that spoke of life. Monkeys howled nearby, thrashing in the upper reaches of the great stalks, while great moths larger than her face whirred as they displayed the colors of blood and bone.

Had she been given to spiritual fears, this might have been a frightening place. Instead she made a warm and comfortable nest in the underbrush and lay down to sleep again, wondering how it might have gone with her had she boarded Karindira's brass cart. Would she even now be among the English, eating their puddings and drinking their beers and glimpsing the true secrets of the world?

The image of her grinning skull orbiting endlessly in the tunnels beneath the earth was sufficient to discourage that fantasy. Paolina sighed and snugged lower, hiding from the moths that seemed bent on brushing her in their moonlight dances.

And so the trail went for weeks on weeks. She began to understand how Clarence Davies had walked for two years. Every day was the same, though the path might be different and the weather might change and the creatures that roared upon the slopes varied in size and frightening array.

Her confidence grew in her device as the gleam continued to be a passport. Perhaps Clarence's Dent stemwinder had served the same purpose in its way—she did not know. Creatures avoided her when given the chance.

She tried again and again to make the gleam do *something,* anything. Should she be asked again, as Karindira had, Paolina did not intend to be caught out. But she could no more force a flower to grow to fruit, nor a creek to stop running, than she could have halted the progress of the sun in the sky.

In time she found a country of walls, ornate and winding little knee-high labyrinths that seemed to have been built to the scale of marmots or hedgehogs. There was no evidence of structure, really, just miles of the little walls in an endless maze, which Paolina stepped over.

There were bones, too, some so massive as to be beyond improbable. A curve of rib that ran nearly a hundred yards had to be a jest of God, left to tempt the gullible. That, at least, was what Paolina told herself, especially when, crossing a flower meadow filled with glossy broad-leafed plants displaying bright purple blooms, she passed a jaw fragment with embedded teeth that stood taller than she did.

One morning Paolina was camped on the head of a rock knee that gave her a glimpse of the glinting brass at the top of *a Muralha*. She watched it twist and sparkle in the coming sunlight, a warm glint in the predawn gloom that shone briefly bright as a second sun just before the daystar finally appeared.

Onward she walked, losing all consciousness of the time of the journey and immersing herself in the complex nature of *a Muralha*. She developed a theory that the Wall was the true purpose of Creation, while earth and sun existed merely to make the thing possible. God had made a great vertical canvas on which to draw His experiments in broad brushstrokes and fine. How different was she from Karindira's people, really? As alike as cats and dogs, perhaps.

Paolina kept the gleam in her grip. She watched the hands jitter around the face—the heart of the world, the passage of the hours, the measuring of her own blood's beat. The fourth hand continued to defeat her. What had she meant by it, for it? She couldn't quite recall now. No matter what she tried, she could not coax its secrets forth. She would need a wizard, some English sorcerer, to show her the true path.

Then one day she met the brass man.

He stood where a higher path met her trail, right in the middle of the track. She might have mistaken him for a statue, but the rock beneath his feet was worn by generations of travel. Either he'd walked there, or he'd been set long after the trail was made. There was dust and dirt around him to tell the story of his being there awhile, and a scattering of bones alongside the trail.

Had he fought or killed, she wondered? Or were those relics of older combats?

The brass man was slightly over six feet tall. His body was formed of armor—greaves and breastplate and guards, as if he awaited combat with some great and terrible creature. His face was almost the opposite, an eerie beauty oddly marred by its near perfection. His lips were wrought in the ghost of a sneer, though a tiny grate showed where they pursed open. His eyelids were shut.

She stopped in front of him. He was a marvelous work of engineering. Not only was his form nearly perfected, but the joins and solders and borders of his construction had been exquisitely performed.

"You are beautiful," she said in English, tapping his breastplate. "A shame to have made you of metal."

Lately, she'd been more interested in the occasional ordinary human men she met on the trail. The boys who had seemed so dreadful back in Praia Nova were becoming more tantalizing in ways she did not want to analyze too closely.

The banded eyelids slid open. An oiled brass orb with a tiny crystal opening flexed and turned.

"As are you, fair lady."

The voice was pleasant but hollow, as if there were nothing within the armor save dark shadows and empty air. No breathy bellows of lungs, or the clattering echo of clockwork.

"With the manners of a courtier." Paolina was proud of that phrase. It had been in the Spanish letters. She'd never had cause to use it before, in any language.

"Here is where the border lies," he told her. "None may pass beyond without they have a seal."

She looked around. The path ran through a field of low tumbled rocks between which grass sprouted in profusion. There was nothing to mark any one foot of land from another. "Border of what, sir man?"

"The western marches of the Solomnic Kingdom of Ophir."

Paolina had never heard of that. "I seek England," she told him. "I would pass your kingdom in peaceful quiet, looking onward."

He made a hollow ringing noise that might have been laughter. "England is a flatwater pretender to the honest estate of nationhood. You shall not find that demesne of mice and shopmen anywhere within or upon the bounds of the Solomnic Kingdom."

"As may be. If I pass you, what action will you take?"

"I shall perforce detain you until Authority arrives to effect your release."

Paolina considered that. This was a creature of logic, in a self-evident way. She wondered if that logic could be trumped from outside.

"When did Authority last come here?"

There was a long pause. "That is a time most uncertain. Certes, it has been years . . . a century or more."

"So you would seize me and hold me until I starve and crumble to dust, while you shut down once more until someone else comes along?"

Another long pause. "That would seem to be the intent of my direction."

"I have a much better plan," she said brightly. "Convey me to Authority yourself. You will be shut of this dreadful lonely place, and I will be farther along my way to England."

"Authority has instructed me to stand fast."

"To what purpose, if Authority does not return to renew your instructions?" She let her voice grow sly. "Besides, if you take me to them, you can show them your valor and perspicacity in retrieving from the wild a gleam."

"Authority has tendered most specific instructions concerning the matter of gleams."

"Which are?"

Now he sounded very uncertain indeed. "I am to kill any gleams upon first encounter."

AL-WAZIR

The steam borer was even more complex than al-Wazir might have imagined. There was an arrangement beneath the body of the machine to lay the rails on which it rode, advancing them with the cutting face. The standard-gauge rails were also laid in that same process.

A small scar-faced man in a greasy cap, one shoulder higher than the other, explained. He'd mumbled his name so fast, al-Wazir hadn't caught it.

" 'Tis what we calls a soft ride then, sir. She wouldn't stand on 'em for long ere they slipped or gave. No way to set them spikes while the cutter's running. So if the rock's easy, she moves forward fast enough. If the rock's hard, she cuts some, then backs up a wee bit so we can slip for'd and secure the rails by hand."

Not quite the smooth progress Ottweill had outlined in his lecture, but it made sense. "How do you get forward? She fills the tunnel, don't she?"

The scar-faced man grinned, his lips little more than another slash across his face. "Cutter opens up a hole a bit wider'n the body. You sidles along them decks you see down each side, slips around the cab, steps through the blades, and you're in."

"Not much room." He shuddered. "A man would have to be able to abide dark, tight spots with joy in his heart, I'd think."

"Them's as loves the ground loves the ground, over and under. Most of us is miners, sir, out of the Welsh country. The rest is railroad men." He paused, then added darkly, "The first railroads was in the mines, sir. I reckon the last ones will be, too."

"Thank you." Al-Wazir stepped along the side of the steam borer, glad to leave the man's company. He'd take an honest sailor, drunk and stupid, over a tunnel rat any day of his life.

He touched the plated side of the steam borer, just below the walkway supports. It was hot, which surprised him a bit. Much like the gasbag of an airship, the thing got bigger the closer one came to it, until it passed a point of reasonableness and became something like landscape. This was a beast, a land leviathan worthy of some biblical army marching to lay waste to a patriarch's city. Al-Wazir could imagine the Jew-soldiers storming Jericho with one of these machines under their command.

The iron sides seemed to shrug off the concerns of sunlight and open air and the world of men.

"Into the cab would you care to step?" Ottweill asked from just behind al-Wazir's left ear.

The chief jumped. He would have sworn that no one had gotten such a drop on him, man nor boy, since he was old enough to cock a fist. "What, ye wee—" He caught himself and his temper. "No, I don't believe I'd be fittin' in there." A deep, shuddering breath, then.

"That you are afraid, I am sorry." Ottweill shrugged.

Al-Wazir got his voice under control. "I am nae— not afraid. Do not trip me with your words, Doctor. I've been tried by worse than you. In any event, 'tis no matter to me. I don't ever plan to pilot one of them things, and the hatch is a tad small for me."

"Ten thousand, four hundred horsepower, Chief." Ottweill's voice fell. "The largest vehicle ever built to move on land she is, and would put most ships to shame. Do you not long to put your hand on the tiller of such a mighty beast?"

Odd, thought al-Wazir, *that word had come so easily to both of them.* "A fair monster she is, sir, and I admire the work what made her be. I believe in her. But what goes under the Wall is your province, not mine." He tapped his temple. "These eyes will be turned elsewhere while you dig."

"Still, my cutters you will now see." Ottweill clutched his hands in excitement. "They are the greatest expression of my own design skills. There were helpers. Railroad men and fabricators, even marine architects, they were all needed to bring the steam borer to life. The cutting process is mine. Only mine."

Al-Wazir fell in beside Ottweill as they walked to the front of the machine. He noted how the men turned away from the doctor, finding quick business or falling into random, serious talk. "Are you a miner by trade, sir? What are you a doctor professor of?"

"You offend." Ottweill muttered something in German. As they reached the rock shield near the front of the steam borer, he added, "Soil myself with such work would I never. Beneath the dignity of a gentleman this is. Besides, something might happen to my hands. No, good men with good brains must use them. This is as God intended for the order of the world."

Al-Wazir had his own opinion about hard work and clean hands, but he said nothing. Instead he studied the rock shield. There was a little door in the flange, bolted in four places, where the railmen could pass forward to set the spikes as needed.

They stepped around it, close to the cutters.

Nothing served to change his initial impression. There were three main arms, traversing an entwined spiral. The effect was a massive skeletal shape much like the tip of a man's penis. Each was set with alternating large and small teeth, cutting elements in shallow cone shapes that gleamed. The arms were cross-braced and attached to a central rotating shaft that also had a cutting edge at its forefront.

A cock, surely, to tear into the stone of the Wall.

"At six revolutions per minute she rotates," Ottweill said softly. He reached up and touched one of the large teeth. "For the harder rock at the slower speed she runs. Like coring a hole in a board this is not, you know, for all that those fools in the Privy Council can be made to understand anything else. As if a manservant with a hand drill I were."

"Indeed," murmured al-Wazir. Clearly the doctor was his own audience at this point.

"Without driving the borer forward we can still cut," he added. "Forty-four inches of depth standing in place, if the surface is truly difficult and all the power on this shaft we must keep."

Al-Wazir studied the distances between the cutting members and the cross-braces. "Men go in there to spike the rails?"

"Small men," Ottweill said after a moment.

"Everything here is designed for small men." Al-Wazir could not conceal the laughter that rumbled forth. "As if you have a fear of big apes like me."

"Cutting tunnels we are. This is a tight business."

"Tight? Tunnels big enough for railroad trains? Mayhaps. I would not know a coal seam from an inseam, but still . . . sometimes the world has call for a big man."

"And sometimes big men there are." Ottweill's voice was tight. "These men who work the steam borer, a tough gang they are, are they not?"

Al-Wazir stepped away from the cutting members and looked back past the shield. The various crews were standing in little knots, some talking to the other visitors, the others smoking and fiddling away the time until they could get to either serious work or serious loafing.

No different from sailors, really. Pack of puppies. And though they ran small, to fit so many small-man jobs, he didn't doubt for a minute these were men with blades for teeth and boilers for hearts. You didn't work a black job like mining or railroading without being tough. Al-Wazir loved the Royal Navy and Her Imperial Majesty's sailors, air and sea alike, more than he'd ever loved a woman, but he knew it took a special kind of dark soul to do work like this.

"A durable and hardy crew, yes," he said.

"So, any one of them in a standup fight could you take?"

Al-Wazir smiled. "I'm a division chief." His smile faded. "Well, I was, aboard *Bassett*. Ropes I had, and we kept a tight deck. Fifteen years in the air, from the earliest days, twenty on the waves before that. Every time you lift air or raise anchor, there's a new chum or three aboard. More if you've been in home port.

"Some of them have come off another command, some off the merchant service, some dragged out of a dockside crib with whore's drippings still sticky on their thighs. It don't matter. One of them will always want to show he's smarter, stronger, faster, meaner. I wouldn't be a chief, not a good one, if I couldn't take every man who ever came after me." His smile was back now, to fond memories of bare-knuckled fights and midnight tussles. "Didn't always beat them down, because there's other ways to take a man that the captain don't need to have any notice of. But they always knew I could, by the time I was done with them."

"How they account each other let me tell you." Ottweill pointed at a boy. He carried man's height with the thin build and forward-curved shoulders of someone raised on a backcountry farm with too many harvests. "Alrod that is. Her Imperial Majesty's service he joined to escape an oat field in Jutland, I am believing. With the oil crew he now works. He is said to be the toughest man in the gang."

"I could break him." Al-Wazir flexed his fists. "But I wouldn't. Boy who grows up like that probably got beat with a board. He'll not hear anything even if a hand is laid on him, just bend into the blow, then find a way later. Him, you throw over a different way if he makes trouble."

"He's not laid a fist on anyone else, man or boy."

Ah, thought al-Wazir, *there was a purpose to the doctor's rambling.* "What then, what is their test? I've seen jumping and dunking and branding, all manner of rough sport, but you've nothing here but stone and iron."

"Inside the cutters he climbed and rode them for almost ten minutes. When out they pulled him, Alrod desired to ride them into a rock face. No man has ever asked that."

Al-Wazir turned and stared at the front of the steam borer. Despite himself, he was impressed. "Six revolutions per minute? If you clung to the central shaft and had a stomach for it, I could see the thing being done, but that's a lot more kidney than most would have. To want to ride it into a cutting face . . . there's another matter entire. Not enough kidney inside a right whale for any sane man to do that. Alrod's a boy who will get people hurt."

"He's the boy they most respect."

"They'll have to find my respect another way."

Ottweill shook his head, then turned and began walking back along the length of the steam borer. Al-Wazir followed him for a moment before reaching out to touch the doctor's elbow. "Have you ridden the cutters?"

"Of course." Ottweill seemed surprised that al-Wazir even bothered with the question.

Kitchens bade him farewell that evening. "I'm for London again. I believe the Member from Caernarfon Boroughs would prefer you remain attached to the doctor from here on."

"I can see why," said al-Wazir. They walked in the weedy field that ran along the top of the quarry near the lift cage. A trap with a driver awaited Kitchens' pleasure, but the goodman was obviously in no hurry to put away his pipe and newspaper in order to take up the reins.

Somehow al-Wazir didn't think it would matter if the driver were impatient.

"Herr Doctor Professor Ottweill's peculiarities of character are not unknown to Her Imperial Majesty's government. However, the combination of his engineering qualifications and his singular sense of purpose more than offsets the risk that might represent."

"Sir . . ." Al-Wazir stopped. "I don't rightly know whether to speak as a chief petty officer, or a civilian."

"And what would each of those men say?" Kitchens' voice had grown even softer than usual, slipping into a dangerous place.

The quiet man was not someone al-Wazir would care to have to take in a fight. He'd be afraid of razors in the sleeve, or acid thrown in his eyes. "The chief petty officer would say, 'Sir, yes sir,' and follow his orders to the best of his ability."

"I've never heard of a chief yet who didn't know better."

"Of course not. A chief's job is to divine the intent of the order, and make sure the captain gets what he really needs. Which often ain't what he says he wants."

"Of course. And the civilian . . ."

"Oh, he's just wondering who will pay the price when the end comes. Because I've seen officers like him, and sailed under a few."

"Your faith in Her Imperial Majesty's government is duly noted." Kitchens stopped and briefly doffed his bowler. "I am afraid I must be going."

"Me, too."

Kitchens turned to walk through the weeds to the trap, which was now little more than a blocky shadow in the descending darkness, except for the coal of the driver's pipe.

Al-Wazir called after him. "The Wall awaits, amid African swamp and fevered dream. I'll go naewhere else, not now, even with that madman driving the train."

"That is the sum of what has been asked of you."

"I'll make sure the captain gets what he needs."

Stepping into the little carriage, Kitchens surprised al-Wazir by offering to shake his hand. "Be well, Chief," the quiet man said. "It would be a shame for England if you did not return."

CHILDRESS

When the smoke settled and the screaming was done, Childress was surprised to find herself yet alive. Anneke could be no more dead, of course. *Mute Swan* listed to the port so steeply that the debris on the deck had rolled to the scuppers on that side. The ship would doubtless be sinking soon. Three Chinese sailors armed with rifles stood watch over her. The others finished their slaughter of Captain Eckhuysen's company.

She looked out across the water. The Chinese vessel's deck gun was already decommissioned and taken below. Armed sailors kept watch there, too.

The attacking crew moved quickly, as if they expected a threat at any moment. Eckhuysen had sent up rockets, but short of another submarine, there was no ship to be seen between her and the horizon. If any of Her Imperial Majesty's airships were about, they kept their own counsel behind the gray watercolor sky.

Childress sat waiting for the blade or bullet that would claim her life. This wasn't the sacrifice the Mask Poinsard had intended for her, nor their masters. She drew some small, grim satisfaction at the disruption, but that could make no offset to the death of the laughing Scandinavian, Captain Eckhuysen, nor the rest of *Mute Swan*'s *avebianco* crew.

More sailors clambered over the rail, carrying red canisters and lengths of pale gray rope. A squat man bearing nothing but his dignity followed. He turned to approach Childress.

Like his crew, he was Chinese. He was also unmistakably their captain. Her guards straightened to attention as soon as he appeared, acquiring noble, stoic expressions. More than that, he carried command in his stride, the set of his shoulders, the inquiry on his face.

Sailors, she'd learned aboard *Mute Swan*, didn't ask questions. Officers sometimes did.

The Chinese captain approached her, dropping to his heels so their eyes met. He had inquiries to make, she could see that even in the unfamiliar flattened features, but he held them as he studied her.

"Anneke's dead." Childress pointed uselessly at the body beside her.

"My thousand pardons." His English was perfectly good. "If I had been informed you valued her, she would have been spared."

Not from a splinter, Childress thought. Such a strange way to die. Further down inside her head, another voice cried and raged and screamed, but a quiet, sickening peace seemed to have taken hold of her mouth.

"Are you ready?" he asked.

Calm somehow continued to prevail. "Of course I am," she lied.

"Good. We must go soon." The Chinese captain rocked slightly on his heels. "Do you require anything irretrievable to be taken off this ship?"

"Irretrievable? Surely you mean irreplaceable."

He looked thoughtful. "Ah. Yes, la. Irreplacable."

"No . . ." Childress still wondered what this killer Chinese wanted with her. "Nothing not already broken beyond retrieval."

"Replacement, not retrieval."

"Yes."

He rose and offered her his hand. She took it and stood. He walked her down to a point on the rail where they'd slung a rope. There was a drop to the heaving, foaming sea, where a small boat bobbed, tended by two sailors even now staring upward with round blank-eyed expressions on their golden faces.

"If the Mask would care to go first," the captain said softly.

"The Mask—," she began, then stopped with a flash of clear, bitter insight.

It was too much. Laughter bubbled up within. She had not been spared for a purpose at all. Her life in this moment was nothing but error. And when they found Poinsard, the Chinese would put a bullet through her head just as they had with each of Eckhuysen's crew.

Rain and tears and pain and fear mixed together, so that the laughter emerged as a violent upheaval of her gut, disguising all her thoughts and feelings in a sudden vile spew that soaked the captain.

He said something calmly in Chinese, then helped her over the rail and down the rain-slick rope ladder.

The boat below tossed and heaved as the sailors pulled at their oars. The swells rose steadily as the weather worsened. Despite herself, Childress found that she was once more seeing the details around her.

The world had not yet ended. Not for her.

She looked at the captain opposite her in the stern of the little craft. He calmly picked her spew off of his uniform. He was clad in silk in a deeper blue than the roughspun cotton of the ordinary sailors, with tiny fabric closures where she might have expected brass buttons on an English officer's coat. Though it was hard to tell with the mess upon his chest, the silk appeared to be damasked with some complex shape or image. His hat was strange, too, a little round pillbox of a stiffened version of the same silk as his jacket. A small paper scroll, now waterlogged, was tied to the front with red silk thread. Even his shoes seemed to be silk, more like blue gloves for his feet than anything she might ever have expected a man to wear.

A man rough and vile enough to kill an entire ship's company, yet gentle enough to stay both his hand and his words when she embarrassed him in front of his crew. Childress wondered who he was, and what he did here.

Beyond murdering subjects of the English crown, of course.

Her interest vanished with the slap of cold seawater. The ocean was trying to come over the side of the boat now. All she could see was lifting slopes of boiling, chilly gray around her, and a pall of smoke from *Mute Swan* that even the increasing rain had not fully dispelled.

Anneke dead. Eckhuysen dead. The smiling Swede and all the others. That she could begin to smile upon this man who had killed them all revolted her. When they found the Mask Poinsard, Childress, too, would go into the ocean, the accidental deception uncovered.

What if the Mask had died? a dry and logical voice asked. Anneke died by accident. Could Childress, as a Christian and a white bird, hope the woman had met such a fate?

Her resolve crumbled once more into despair. Childress tried to take shelter in prayer, but the water was growing so violent, she could not form the words. Then she was jerked upward by grasping hands. Short unsmiling men lashed to the deck behind them tugged her toward the tower of the submarine. They would push her into the hatches there and take her below, where the guns were kept and all these men must live as they traveled beneath the sea.

She was heartsick enough to ignore her curiosity about what kept the vessel beneath the waves but above the sea floor. They hustled her down a narrow ladder through a tiny hole while the captain shouted over the rising storm.

Within, the passageways were tiny. As the ship rolled, she simply shifted from shouldering one side to shouldering the other. Two sailors clad in the same roughspun blue as their fellows who had assaulted *Mute Swan* led her through three knee-barking hatches before showing her to a tiny cabin. It was only slightly larger than the lav aboard the other ship had been.

Her escorts bowed several times, backing out carefully before swinging the hatch shut. It clicked into place with a hollow, sepulchral clang. The locking lever was on her side.

Not a prison cell, then. Not exactly. Except that this underwater ship was a prison from which she could not escape. Filled with jailors to whom she could not speak, but for the oddly gallant captain.

To stay alive in this undersea prison she must be prepared to play the part of the Mask Poinsard.

"I shall live," she whispered, "and set every inch and noise of this place in my memory, so that someday when I return to honest soil I can tell my story to . . . to . . ."

She was unsure to whom she wished to return. New Haven as she had known it was lost to her. A woman missing even a day of work could expect to never see that employment again. There was always a deserving man with a family to feed. She had no great circle of friends there to welcome her home. The congregation at St. John Horofabricus would see no difference in her going. She was just another aging woman who'd lost her way without ever finding husband and family.

As for Queen and country, living in New Haven, Childress found her loyalty as a British subject a natural position, like breathing. She'd rather return than not, but she did not feel a great pull of patriotism as some claimed.

Which left her with the *avebianco,* who had lately been set to bind her over to the Silent Order.

Tears took Childress in a rush that shocked her. What had she lived for? What had she made her life's purpose? She lay on the narrow bunk and pressed her face into the rough blanket to sob for the first time in decades.

Later Childress arose as if from a tempestuous dream. The submarine had ceased rolling to and fro. She wondered what that might signify. Her head was full of the angry pressure of the recent tears, but her mind seemed clear.

That she was alive was a miracle. No sign from God, for Childress did not credit the Creator with reaching finger by finger into His world, but at least a blessing delivered by the machineries of fate.

She found a tiny metal mirror and looked to see what had become of her face. Even limited by the gleaming disc, the view was not encouraging. The recent battle had left her bruised from blows of which she had no recollection. Several lines of scabs were traced across her forehead. Had one of the splinters that claimed Anneke's life so very nearly missed stealing hers as well?

Childress knew she owed these Chinese nothing but her life. Even that debt was a thing they'd made, a trap for her conscience. But without the cloak of her dignity, she could not face them. They would never believe her the Mask Poinsard unless she had the poise and strength of the Mask. *He* would never believe.

This was not about any captain, Childress told herself sternly.

She set to cleaning as best she could, though that was sadly limited. There were jars on a shelf below the mirror that on examination contained liniments and powders. Not the paint pots of an actress, nor the urns of an apothecary, but something that seemed to somehow split the difference.

So she experimented until she found the right compound of cool smoothness and analgesic tingle. It was a pale green stuff that left a strange tint to her skin, but the balm eased the pain of the cuts and bruises and smoothed the wounded strangeness of her face.

After judicious application of the salve, Childress explored the rest of the tiny cabin. It must be the captain's, she realized. There were two silk jackets clipped behind the door that matched what he had worn out on the ocean. She fingered them. Fine stuff, as good as or better than any bolt she'd seen for sale in New Haven. Not that she'd ever been able to afford such a vainglorious cloth.

The silk was damasked with a pattern of cranes flying under moonlight, recurring roundels with that image repeated across the man so that when he wore it, he would walk in beauty. A subtle, tiny grace amid the humming metal death of this submarine vessel, but one that spoke volumes for what must be behind those black eyes.

Continuing her inspection, Childress found a pair of leather boots beneath the bunk, perhaps for going ashore. There was a modest chest of pale clothing, which she quickly shoved away. What a man wore beneath his trousers was no affair of hers. Three little calotypes, of an elderly couple who must have been his parents, and a girl poised in that cusp of age between childish joy and the serious business of womanhood.

She finally found his books, too. They were in a drawer set into the wall. Two drawers, actually. One had charts and manuals, obviously the documents of the vessel's purpose and voyage. Were she some wily *espion* or saboteur, trained in the traitor's arts and a knowledge of Chinese both, she would have known what to read, what to search through, to ferret out these secrets. It was not difficult to envision the interest that Her Imperial Majesty's admiralty might have in knowing the accuracy of the Chinese charts of the Atlantic.

The other drawer held his personal books. They didn't look much like what lay in her rooms back in New Haven, nor the ones in her library, but she still knew books when they were arrayed before her. Most were bound between thin square boards with silk ties to keep them tight between their covers. Those generally had rice paper over the boards, with some ideogram or other written in a swirling hand. A few others were accordions, folded and pressed tight and kept in place with ribbons. If she were to tug at them, they would pop open and become endlessly long.

Here, where space was at such a horrid premium, even the captain merited a room unthinkably small, he had filled a drawer with books.

Poinsard would have burned them for spite.

A bell clanged distantly, echoing through iron walls. She heard feet pounding. Some new danger was afoot. The thrum of the deck, so pervasive and consistent, she had not truly noticed it before, changed. It deepened, making her feet quiver more.

Childress closed the drawers and stepped to the hatch. She still looked a wreck, far too shameful to have shown her face on the streets of home.

This was not New Haven.

The Mask Poinsard had survived the attack on *Mute Swan*. Emily McHenry Childress had died that day on the Atlantic Ocean. Things could be no different, not until she returned to her liberty among people who spoke her language and lived under the same flag she did.

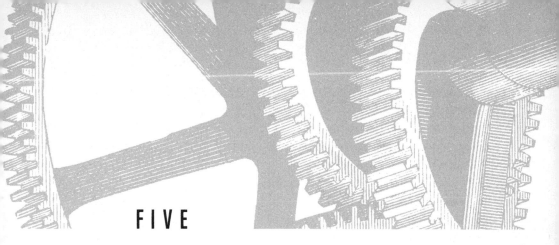

FIVE

PAOLINA

"If you were going to kill me," Paolina said with far more certitude than she felt, "you would have done so already. You have already encountered me. It is too late to kill."

The brass man's eyes flickered. "Authority has not vouchsafed me complete information."

"Authority has forsaken you," she snapped. "Obviously men, the lot of them. You have been left here to rot, except when you wake to kill. Surely whoever built you had intended a higher purpose."

Keep him busy, she thought. *Confuse him. Do not let him awake to his strength or the brutality of his orders.*

"Authority . . ." His voice trailed off. He popped his neck several times. "Will you say a word unto me?"

"Of course." She was relieved to at least have passed beyond the talk of killing. "What word?"

He worked his head back and forth. "I do not hold this word. It is a word I cannot know."

"A word you cannot know . . ." She considered that. "In the numbers that count the beat of the world, there are some things that cannot be counted. I know this is true, but I do not yet know why. Is your word of that nature?"

"Yes." There was relief in his hollow voice.

"So if I say the word to you, what will happen?"

"I am uncertain. I should be released from my bonds. You are correct. I was not . . . made . . . to stand here through the years as the simple papagallo of Authority. My ilk are created beneath the seal in the image of men."

"Like man, made in the image of God," Paolina said.

"Indeed." He cocked his head, staring at her almost sidelong. "There also exists a word to unlock your soul."

"Of course," she told him, though that hadn't been obvious until he'd stated it. "We are all measured by the beat of world. Therefore we can all be rendered into numbers. Within any system of numbers there are always some things which cannot be counted."

"Words which cannot be spoken."

"How would I know your word?" She looked at his face, so handsome and strange and frozen in a moment of casting. "I could speak English and Portuguese and Spanish to you all the day long, but I do not think your word is as simple as 'adumbrate' or 'codicil' or 'polycrastic.' I could talk my voice to dust and not find it." Paolina stretched her finger to the brass man's lip. "You must show me your word, through sign or deed or logic, then I will say it to you."

"But the word is not known to me," he protested.

She laughed. He was such a boy. "Then take me to Authority and we will see what we learn upon the way."

The brass man swiveled almost in place, his feet clattering slightly. "Authority lies to the east."

"By happy chance, I am walking east."

"I shall be forced to slay you in time."

"Of course," she said brightly.

He strode forward, marching at a pace that was almost a trot for her.

Paolina didn't mind. She'd walk as she pleased. Either he'd pursue his purpose and draw ahead of her soon enough, or he'd stop and wait. She would not run at his heels like a dog after a boy.

As evening descended and she looked for a suitable place to bed down off the path, she found the brass man standing next to a jumble of rocks.

"I have cozened the great cats from their den and prepared us a place to abide the night." He pointed the way.

"All this," she asked, "and not even the word from me yet? You are infused with purpose."

"I am infused with Authority." His voice was heavy with dignity. "But Authority is not all things."

"Oh, really?" She stepped into the cleft in the rocks. It stank of scaled cat, to be sure, but he seemed to have torn down several trees to build a nest in there. "What lies beyond Authority?"

His response was chillingly simple. "You do."

"I cannot think so," she murmured, crawling into the leaves.

It wasn't much more than she would have done for herself, save for his comforting bulk between her and whatever might prowl the darkness. Since leaving Karindira's city, Paolina had been less than careful about her risks on the slopes of *a Muralha*. Sleeping in a cat's den guarded by the brass man reminded her once more of what could easily have been her fate.

As the evening went by, she veered between waking and dreamful sleep. The brass man stood still as he had on the path when she first met him, only a shape now where he had been almost real in daylight. She could hear a faint ticking and clicking from within that magnificently armored body.

Pulling the gleam from its case, Paolina hoped for enough starlight to see the hands by. Where the timing that beat at the heart of life was very subtle, wrapped within layers of skin and bone and moving meat, the timing of this metal man was not much different from the stemwinder itself.

Paolina found herself unwilling to experiment. Not without his assent, and even enthusiasm. There was something strangely charming about the brass man. He was more than deadly, to be sure, but he was a person.

She would not be like a man and see others as less than people. If there was one gift to being a woman—well, girl, yet—it was to see others from the bottom looking up, rather than from some high and lordly place.

Still, she studied his shape awhile, wondering what the word was that lay at the heart of him. Also what word it might be that lay at her own heart.

The next morning he walked beside her. This section of *a Muralha* was craggy, tall broken columns of rock hosting isolated, crumbling ledges destined for the sea far below. Someone, presumably the Solomnic Kingdom of Ophir, had built a roadway. In places the inconstant columns had been carved inward to allow the trail to pass. In other places bridges or berms had been built to aid the traveler in crossing the gaps and ravines that punctuated the cliff faces.

The Wall was beautiful in this weather. A floor of clouds swept not far below them, clinging to the ocean's surface to making a sea of variegated white textured with light and shadow. Though the day was sunny, water clung to the cliff face along which she walked, so that Paolina could trail her fingers on the nubbly, mossy texture and lift them away wet with chilly dew that tasted like a midnight storm.

Posts marked the little bridges. Each of those had the device of a six-petaled flower incised upon its top face. She knew that blossom as Solomon's seal.

"Tell me of the kingdom," she finally asked the brass man, who was just then a few paces ahead of her on the narrow track.

"The Solomnic Kingdom of Ophir was established by King Solomon in the light of the days of the First Temple." The brass man's voice seemed to slow, fall into a rhythm. Paolina realized he wasn't explaining, he was reciting. "The mighty king had espied brass in the sky, coruscating from atop the Wall. He did not know the world for what it was, and so he bethought he glimpsed the rivers of gold which had been promised him by the Lord God. At his command a great fleet set forth from the high port at Asiongaber in the lands of the Holy Hour, bound southward where they held that gold must flow because the light of the sun was so much brighter.

"Solomon placed his Admiral Alzabar in command of the fleet, but gave unto him an adjutant who was the first of my kind. This man was hight Brass. Brass had been wrought by Solomon as a teacher and plaything for Rehoboam and others among the best of Solomon's sons. When Rehoboam was grown to his manhood, Solomon had no further need for Brass, and so dispatched him south with the admiral.

"When they came hard upon the coast of Abyssinia, there rose a great storm and a full portion of the fleet was driven ashore. Admiral Alzabar surrendered his life in the catastrophe, as did several of the greatest captains of the fleet. Brass took command and brought them to the Wall. There he played the mercer well, filling the remaining vessels with gold, silver, thyine wood, precious stones, ivory, apes, and peacocks. Brass sent the laden bottoms home to his master and betook his own way into the jungles that lie at the foot of the Wall.

"There Brass rose in might and power, walking among the tribes as a fearsome creature who dispensed justice and death in equal measures, according to how he was met. From him, our kingdom was forged. All who walk in metal are his children."

Paolina waited until it was clear his silence would continue. "What shall I call you, then?"

"Brass. We are all hight Brass."

"Made of metal, do you have a soul?"

He stopped so abruptly, she nearly ran into him. Turning, his strange mechanical eyes met her gaze. "We are children of the holy King Solomon the Wise."

Which did not, she realized, answer the question. But Paolina smiled.

"Of course." She continued, "And Authority. Is that the council of elders among you Brass?"

"Authority is . . . Authority."

The question caused him such obvious distress that she let it lapse.

Eventually the trail brought them to a higher, wider ledge out of the country of the crumbling cliffs. The clouds below were thinning as well. The trail ran through a broad meadow.

The area was wide enough for all the extents of Praia Nova to have been set down within it. It was overlooked by a building, hollow-roofed with gaping windows, stone blackened by fire. The immense structure might have looked at home in Karindira's city, though it was hard to know for certain among the tumbled columns and broken lintels. A great bay in *a Muralha* rose behind it, a place where the Wall had retreated farther from the sea in some ancient catastrophe, leaving rank upon rank of forest and meadow and waterfall and crag. Or perhaps it was just a ravine writ on the scale of all Creation. She could not tell.

Paolina simply stood and stared.

Brass seemed anxious. "Here stands the Armory of Westmost Repose. Beneath the glory of the Wall it wards the paths into the Solomnic Kingdom of Ophir."

Paolina stepped past Brass. Weeds grew among the stones of the plaza before the building, some of them entire bushes larger than she. Whatever had swept the Armory had done so in times long past. "Not in generations," she told him. "How long have you been at the border?"

"I do not know. What is the year?"

She turned to study his handsome, frozen face. "1902 of the Christian Era."

"That is not possible." Now he sounded truly stricken. "I set forth to the armory in Tishrei 5663. I have served here since . . . since . . ." He stopped. "I do not know."

So this place was called Tishrei, but what was 5663? That made no sense as a year, at all. "How can your kind forget?"

"We cannot." Brass began to walk in small circles, one leg jerking with each step. "We are incapable of forgetting. Every memory is recorded in the tiny gears and valves deep within my head. Then that memory is scribed within crystals that are nigh indestructible. When a Brass becomes very aged, he might perchance have his crystals exchanged. This deposits some of his remembrance in the libraries within the Palace of Authority. Still they are his thoughts and deeds and memories." He almost stuttered. "I—I cannot forget."

It was clear that Brass was set to sink into a mechanical equivalent of despair. She pitied him for that, but she also needed his strength and knowledge of affairs along *a Muralha*.

"But you have." Paolina kept her voice reasonable, trying to reach him. "Time beats at your heart, yet you have forgotten it. Your knowledge of the system of the years is wrong. You remember the Armory of Westmost Repose as a great defense, yet it is an old ruin. You do not remember being sent to the border where I found you."

"True," he admitted, stopping his manic pace. His limbs shivered. He was settling into the inanimate object he'd been when she first encountered him.

Paolina had to inspire him. "Then you have forgotten. It is mere reason to accept that. Perhaps your crystals or valves were tampered with. Perhaps your memories were stolen, or removed by Authority for its own purposes. Your thoughts might lie even now in those libraries you speak of, ranked in elegiac array with the mighty deeds of the ancients." She dropped her voice, urging him to believe. "All you can do is go to the Palace of Authority and demand that the theft of your memory be redressed. You are bound there by duty, now, to carry me. You will serve both yourself and your orders if you take us both there."

High overhead some wide-winged bird screamed as Brass stared at her. He remained silent, locked into immobility for seconds that stretched into minutes. She looked back at him, but whatever light had made him Brass, and not simply brass, had faded.

She had failed.

"At least this is a prettier place for you to stand," Paolina told him. If only she could find his word, what he was missing, the inconceivable thought that could not be formed by him. She wondered what that would be. Like a riddle from God. Or in his case, from the first Brass and King Solomon before.

She went to have a closer look at the Armory of Westmost Repose. Layers of stone and forest and meadow rose above the building into the infinite grace of the sky.

In places of beauty like this, she could remember that God had a benevolent purpose for His Creation.

The Armory of Westmost Repose was certainly at rest now. Up close she could see how dark-leafed vines had overtaken the foundations and the rubble of its collapse, so that they clung like a wiry shadow to the building.

This had not been built by whoever had erected the fat-bellied pillars farther east in Karindira's city. Judging from their stubs, these pillars had been wide, squat, and squared off. The building, though quite massive, had been designed with a different sense of how such things should be done—it had been almost crude.

Not precisely an architecture of defense, though. The armory lacked an outer wall. The men of Praia Nova had gone on about a city wall from time to time, agreeing sagely that such a construction made a place a place. Which would have made sense to Paolina if they'd had ten times the manpower available to build it, and possibly any real enemies with which to concern themselves.

Here, though, a wall might have made sense.

Paolina climbed the foundation stones to peer within the broken windows. The roof had collapsed in a number of places, leaving pillars of dusty light to carve the shadows within. There wasn't much to see, only that whatever had lain within was long ago looted or salvaged. Which was to be expected. She'd long ago reasoned that there must be thousands of villages along *a Muralha*, populated by hundreds of races and kinds of thinking beings.

She scrambled back down off the stones to set her face eastward. She was startled to find Brass standing there.

"I have reasoned that you are correct," he said.

Paolina smiled. "About going to the Palace of Authority?"

"Yes. It is a substantial journey from here."

"I know. A boy of my acquaintance took two years to walk from Africa to Praia Nova."

"There may be another method for us to expedite our progress."

"Do the brass cars run here beneath the Armory of Westmost Repose?"

He seemed startled, his eyes clicking. "You know of them?"

"I have seen them in another place. The woman who showed one to me did not know the secret of their direction. I feared to climb in and ride lest I starve along the way, not knowing the proper command to exit."

"This I understand," Brass said. "That was most probably wise of you. But we should pass within, to ascertain if the downward ways are blocked. If they are not, we will discover if the car harbor remains intact. It would turn a journey of months into hours."

Paolina wasn't certain she wanted to come to Authority so quickly. Still, she wanted to get to England with her gleam, and that path lay through

Authority. "I will come. But before we go look, will you accept something from me?"

"What is that?" He seemed suspicious now, and formal as well.

"A name. I would call you something other than Brass. How else will I know you in a city of your people?"

"But we are all called Brass," he protested. "It is the natural order of things. Each kens what he means when we speak to one another."

"Still, I would call you more."

"What would you name me?"

She couldn't tell if he was flattered or annoyed. Nonetheless, she pressed on. "Boaz. It means 'strength.' Boaz was the name of the northern pillar of Solomon's Temple. You are strong, and you are descended from Solomon through the eldest Brass. And besides, it is not so different from your old name, is it?"

"In Solomon's tongue, we are all called *nehosheth*," he said. "Which does not seem much like Boaz, nor does it precisely mean 'Brass.' But I thank you."

"You are welcome. Boaz."

"Indeed." He seemed pleased, though not likely to admit it.

They picked through rubble and the choked canes of old shrubbery to find the passage downward from the heart of the Armory. It was not unlike the shaft beneath Karindira's city, save that there were chains and guides dangling in the center core, while they crept round an outer stair of metalwork affixed to the wall.

"What was this?" Paolina asked, looking up in the vague light of the smoldering torch she carried. Boaz had seemed surprised she would need such a thing. "It looks like a tackle rig."

"There is—" Boaz stopped a moment. "There was an ascender here in another age. The device was lifted and lowered by chains along these tracks. A little floor, in truth. The power to raise the lift was borrowed from deep within the earth, through a system of gears that drew off the endless motions therein."

"Goodness." Paolina would very much have liked to see such a thing. "Like a parasite, robbing the application of force from a larger system with surplus to spare?"

"Yes."

"There must have been such a one beneath the city where I last saw the brass cars. The stair wound around a large shaft there that seemed much too vast for its purpose."

"Precisely." He kept walking.

So did she.

The descent was longer than the shaft in Karindira's city. Of course, they'd come higher up to reach the Armory of Westmost Repose. She presumed that the brass cars ran on a track that was at a constant distance from the center of the earth. Paolina didn't fancy the long walk back up if their efforts proved fruitless.

Boaz pulled ahead of her with his unflagging pace. Where at first he was a pale glint directly in front of her, after a while, he was a corner ahead, then two corners, until he'd gone all the way around. The only reason Paolina knew she was not alone in the shaft was the tapping of Boaz' feet on the metal stairs below.

In time his footfalls changed from an echoing clang to a more muted tap. Paolina had counted him seven landings ahead of her, four landings to a flight, so she took heart from this. When she reached the stone floor, she stopped.

There was still an empty space to her left, where the chains and frames of the ascender continued down. A hissing, clicking echoed from below, just at the edge of her hearing. She thought it must be the turning of the earth. To hear the very sounds of that movement made her flush—Paolina could feel her cheeks reddening.

She had another problem, though. Her smoldering cane torch had become a very poor handful. Darkness opened up before her, where the shaft let out into a larger chamber, as well as to the left where it continued to descend. If this bore any resemblance to the carway beneath Karindira's city, somewhere in the middle of a large room would be a brass car like a large metal coffin with a crystal lid.

But she didn't want to go wandering off into the blackness.

"Boaz," she called. "Boaz?"

There was no answer, only a series of clanging noises.

She stepped out a bit farther into the darkness. "Boaz?" Fear found her now. A pale light flickered ahead. She could see his silhouette moving before it. Even then, Paolina did not walk faster—she was afraid of holes in the floor, or worse.

She made her way to Boaz' side. He stood before a brass car. Its lid was raised to expose the coffin within. The light came from little six-pointed seals along the inside and outside of the car. They glowed with a pale blue flicker.

"The seal does seem to be intact," he said. "We may climb within. I shall then set the carriage to reach one of the carways at Ophir."

"In the Palace of Authority?" For some reason her gut lurched at the thought.

"No . . . ," he said slowly. "Let us go first to the main harbor. We can see how the city stands."

Unlike the Armory of Westmost Repose, hopefully.

He was right. She might have better luck searching for the English if she didn't commence from somewhere deep within Authority's halls.

"Here." He pointed within. "I counsel you to sit to the rear. Lay yourself back on the saddle. I will position myself immediately before you."

The saddle was more of a bench, covered in old and rotting leather. Three small people or two large could fit within, lying on one another's laps. It seemed . . . salacious.

It also seemed rapid.

She climbed in. Boaz settled in before her, careful not to pinch or crush her against the bench. He leaned back and tugged on the crystal and brass lid.

"You may still choose elsewise."

Risk, she thought. *This is risk.* So was every mile walked under the open sky. Paolina tugged the gleam from her pocket. She had to contort a bit to do it, and had she been larger, it would not have been possible.

"Away," she told him.

He touched something, and light blossomed like a private sunrise.

After the initial bright eruption that launched them on their way, the submural transit was shadowed. Oppressively so, in fact, except for the blue glow of the seals within the car. There was barely enough light for her to glimpse towering bands of metal sliding past, smooth cliffs in the shadows. Gears towered the height of mountains, or so it seemed to her. Pillars flashed closer by with a swift whickering.

The saddle beneath her transmitted a series of clicks and bumps as the car slid along. Paolina had no way to judge their progress. She wished for more light, would have prayed for it if she had thought that might help.

All too soon the car clattered to a halt. It slid into a dim room lit by pale seal-light with a sigh of tired metal.

"We are arrived," said Boaz as he opened the canopy.

AL-WAZIR

Herr Doctor Professor Lothar Ottweill and his minions were to take ship at Gosport in Hampshire, across the harbor from Portsmouth. Al-Wazir would have been far happier with a berth aboard one of Her Imperial

Majesty's ships of the air. Their cargo capacity was nominal, due to weight restrictions, and Ottweill wanted to travel with his supply train.

The doctor demanded SS *Great Eastern* carry them to Africa and the Wall, apparently imagining that the largest ship afloat would also be the safest. He and al-Wazir had argued about it several times, both at the quarry near Maidstone and on the rail trip from Maidstone to Gosport.

"I'll be telling you," al-Wazir said to Ottweill as the rails clicked by beneath the floor, "a big iron tub like that'll just pull you down all the faster should a storm come on. If you've got to be stuck on the water, let her be a fast and nimble ship with good trim. Not some madman's great riveted turtle."

"But the space for our equipage and our complement of men," Ottweill had protested. "Unshakable, unsinkable, braving Chinese saboteurs and hostile natives alike."

"Ain't a fuzzy wuzzy born could sink an English ship." Al-Wazir was muttering, his pride stung. "And no ship ever built could be unsinkable, save she sat forever on land like one of them coffin ships of the heathen kings of long ago."

"Neither heathen kings nor English are we, you and I." Ottweill had a sly gleam.

That remark would have given Kitchens a rash. "We serve Her Imperial Majesty, body and soul and shilling."

"Of course we do." Ottweill leaned forward, knees almost touching al-Wazir in the private compartment. "But know that we serve also the Wall. That's why we're both here, my good chief petty officer. Men of vision we both are! We see beyond the lowered eyes of others. If a way we cut through the Wall, our names they shall be teaching to schoolchildren a thousand years from now."

"*Your* name, belike," said al-Wazir gruffly, though he could not turn away the secret smile that tugged at this face. "I'm just an old sailor who knows his way about a bit."

The Wall. It had eaten *Bassett*, Smallwood, and most of the crew. It had broken al-Wazir's da a generation before.

By God, maybe this madman could best it.

And that was the English way, after all. Show Johnnie foreigner a thing or two, run up the flag, and improve the place.

Every day, al-Wazir found a new reason to be glad he was a Scotsman.

Regardless of Ottweill's demands concerning SS *Great Eastern,* Her Imperial Majesty's government had chartered SS *Wallachian Prince* to carry the expedition from Gosport to Acalayong on the Gaboon coast at the easternmost arm of the Bight of Benin, where Africa and the Wall met.

They met *Wallachian Prince* at the docks of Gosport. She was quite a large ship, some four hundred feet stem to stern, iron-built with three massive boilers and triple screws. She had no masts and so could set no canvas if the coal were to run out or she were to be stranded overlong. A large freighter, built to carry machinery across the Atlantic, she was nothing like the ships of al-Wazir's naval career.

When he and Ottweill arrived in another steam omnibus, the pier at Priddy's Hard was crowded with freight, far more than al-Wazir would have expected even that enormous civilian ship to be capable of taking on. Much of it was the sort of heavy dead weight that rendered supercargoes bald and trembling while still in their youth—rails for the narrow- and wide-gauge lines to be laid, metal slugs for fabrication of parts or devices as needed while working at the Wall's face, three small locomotives.

"Is there another ship?" he asked as they stepped off the vehicle. Sailing with that great lot of junk down inside the hull didn't appeal at all.

"No." Ottweill's voice was sharp, his body trembling as they stood out in the sharp September wind. Al-Wazir could tell that the doctor was working up to another explosion. "The troops have their own quarters. Four hundred and seventeen in our company we will have shipping as civilian passengers, in the event that all the men and boys make the dock on time. No second sailing for latecomers will there be. The rest have gone before."

"I was thinking of the materials."

"Oh, that." Ottweill waved a hand. "Trivial. Aboard we tell them to put it, aboard they put it. Sailors you must under—" He cut himself off with a sidelong look at al-Wazir. "*Civilian sailors,* chief petty officer. It is all for the money, with them. Shillings and pounds and debits." He spat. "No vision or purpose they have. Besides, coming down from Kent the other steam borer is. They must load that anyway."

This time al-Wazir exploded instead of the doctor. "Have you gone and lost your bloody mind, you great earwig? Your steam borer weighs ten times what yon locomotives do, and is far too big to be lifted into the hold." How had he missed that detail?

Because he wasn't part of Ottweill's supply train, of course. He merely lived at the end of it. This was like arguing with a purser.

"Look at the ship." Ottweill was clearly confused. "Fit in it all will."

"Not without they cut the deck off first to load it. Then, even if they did, how will you get it offloaded at Acalayong?"

"However they load it here, but in reverse. Not my problem is this."

"We'll be lucky if they have a pier there," said al-Wazir. "Your first project will be building a port to accept this."

"Oh, no," said Ottweill. "A team was sent two years ago just after the great waves, to dredge the river and build the pier. Good roadbed from the waterfront to the Equatorial Wall we should have, and a crane at the dock."

"Then I'll be shutting up. But still, mind you we won't be carrying any of that off the ship by hand." Another thought occurred to him. "How will you be getting the steam borer down here from Kent, anyway?"

"It can be broken into pieces for shipment."

Al-Wazir still did not believe this. "In the two days we have before sailing?"

"If it is late, on another ship we shall have it sent."

He could estimate the odds of *that* happening.

Still, the doctor was sufficiently persistent, not to mention barking mad enough, to get what he wanted.

SS *Wallachian Prince* was loaded without incident within the pair of days before their scheduled sailing, much to al-Wazir's amazement. The supercargoes were busy. They didn't leave room to pack in something the size of the doctor's third steam borer.

Al-Wazir stayed away from that business. It made his air sailor's gut queasy, to see all that heavy gear loaded into something meant to stay afloat. Instead he visited certain shops in Gosport and Portsmouth to make sure he was properly equipped to deal with a thousand restive men.

The fuzzy wuzzies didn't worry him. He wasn't too worried about the stranger things that lived above, either. They were not going up onto the expanses of the Wall, as Gordon's ill-fated expedition had nor as *Bassett* had navigated those heart-aching spaces where God's Creation touched the heavens.

Al-Wazir was worried most about Ottweill's crew, both aboard *Wallachian Prince* and later at the tunnel head. They'd not been picked for their skill at surviving without murder or mayhem. They'd also not been broken down under some chief's lash and barbed tongue until the fight in them had been turned against sea and air and Chinese foe. This crew wasn't prepared for the months and years they'd spend living together in tents at the foot of a place that could turn down the corners of the most stoic and unthinking mind.

So he trusted the manifests to be correct about the rifles and ammunition and hundredweights of salted beef and all the other things pursuers worried themselves into early graves over. Instead al-Wazir bought a selection of coshes and saps, for the men he'd prefer to fight from behind, and some French naughty books to distract the boys, and his own sets of locks and chains to which he'd hold the only key, in case he needed to bind someone to a tree and leave him there beat bloody for a while to think about his purpose in life.

All variations on the sort of gear he'd kept aboard ship over the years, hidden from inspection of course, just as every chief did. For the ones who wouldn't listen when you tried to tell them, and didn't take savage thrashings from their crewmates to heart.

This was different. He wasn't sure he knew how to control so large a group. The ropes division aboard *Bassett* had been small, never more than sixteen common seamen when the ship was at full company. Airships ran with tight crews, under rules that looked far more like the sailing rigs out of his grandfather's time than the orders of the deck on any steamship afloat. There was a reason they were different services within the Royal Navy.

He was going from less than a score of men to something more than a thousand once they were all settled at the Wall.

Al-Wazir would need men to aid him, and need them badly. So he bought bribes as well, tobacco and rum and more of the French items, such as playing cards and little stereoscopes.

Those helpers he'd have to find first, and thrash early, and hope he caught some of the worst troublemakers under his own wing.

Wednesday, September 17, 1902, SS *Wallachian Prince* sailed with the tide, slipping out of Gosport just after the noon hour to make her way into the English Channel, bound for the Wall.

Threadgill Angus al-Wazir, uncomfortable in his civvies, stood near a rail with hundreds of cheering men, watching them bid farewell to England. So far he'd found that not a man among Ottweill's crew had been to the Wall. Only a few of the sailors had even glimpsed it from aboard ship.

Gosport and Portsmouth slipped away. As the deck rolled ever so slightly underneath his feet, al-Wazir found himself wishing mightily to be in the air, in uniform, and in command of his men. This berth was like herding seagulls.

But it was the Wall. No matter who killed whom on the trip south, so long as Ottweill remained alive and intent on his purpose, the ship would arrive, she would be unloaded, and they would be cutting into the heart of the world.

All that being true, he found no little satisfaction that the third steam borer had not arrived in time for loading. Let the other two go on ahead, let them be unshipped by other men. He wouldn't have to look at those giant metal cock-tips waiting to cut into the world. He could just follow them down the tunnel, concerning himself with apes and fuzzy wuzzies and all the foolishness that Ottweill's sailors and railroadmen and engineers could concoct.

And *that* was a chief petty officer's job, after all.

The Channel sparkled in the midday sun, birds following *Wallachian Prince* in a swirling crowd of mindless greed. He was at sea, where he'd started as a boy. The joy of a stout wind and a good bow wave made up for a great deal.

CHILDRESS

The corridor beyond was just as she'd remembered—too narrow, too small, cramped in all dimensions, and damp. There was a sailor at the next hatch, a common seaman from the cut of his clothes. He bowed and scuttled away.

Not knowing what else to do, Childress followed him. She wanted to find the captain. She wanted to know where she was going and why.

China, of course, but even that puzzled her. How had the vessel gotten to the North Atlantic? The only open seaway from the Atlantic to the eastern hemisphere of Northern Earth was through Suez. The Royal Navy would hardly have allowed a Chinese submarine to pass through the canal.

And of course, the Mask Poinsard had to ask the questions, in her manner and form. Not Librarian Childress.

She straightened her back and stepped through the next hatch. She resolved that she would listen closely to the sailors, and see if she could begin to make something of their strange language.

"Please," said the captain, who stood to her right. He was in a room slightly larger than his cabin. A tea service had been set out on a folding bamboo table. "Come in."

She stepped in and accepted the chair he offered. She also noted that a crewman armed with a pistol took station at the door. Did she really present such danger that they'd risk a firearm here? Childress could imagine what shooting the hull might do to the ship. Though perhaps the iron would cause the bullet to ricochet, and kill several of them in one effort.

"He guards me, not you," said the captain quietly. "Without a word of English, unfortunately for him. But I neglect the courtesies. I am Captain Leung Kwak of the Beiyang Navy, serving in the Iron Bamboo fleet. I have the honor of commanding *Five Lucky Winds* for His Celestial Majesty."

Childress answered with a single regal nod, not quite trusting herself to speak. She had to remember how the Mask Poinsard carried her arrogance like another skin. She had to remember this man had just killed everyone around her, for all that they were holding her prisoner. She had to remember this man's golden voice meant nothing.

Leung returned the nod. "And you are the Mask Poinsard, late of the fast packet *Mute Swan*."

This was it, the moment of active deception. She would cast aside Christian virtue and any pretense at being a lady if she answered in the affirmative.

The alternative was inconceivable.

"Yes." Childress kept her voice cold. Though the questions clamored within her, the less said, the better.

This was much, much worse than a faculty meeting. At that thought, part of her wanted to shriek with laughter.

"Were you not . . ." He paused. "Were you not informed of our arrangements?"

The arrangement of slaughter? she wanted to demand. Childress packed that thought away for later consideration when she was alone. "Let us simply say that I am surprised."

Something in his face closed slightly. Enough to set him leaning away from her, all the way at the back of his chair. The disappointment was obvious.

What in God's name was he on about?

"You show remarkable calm for a woman who was not expecting to be taken off."

"A Mask faces much, Captain Leung." She had to cede him some ground in this conversation. "I confess distress at the death of my beloved servant."

He nodded again. "The woman killed by shot with whom you were sitting when I came aboard. I regret her death as an exigency of combat. As for the rest, again, my apologies. We understood that you were to have had your favorites at the bow to be spared. Since no one was present but you and the servant, we followed our part of the bargain through."

They had meant to kill me, Childress thought. The whole scheme became apparent in those few words. The Feathered Masks had bargained Poinsard to the Chinese, allowing Childress and the crew of *Mute Swan* to be killed in a way that left no blame on anyone but the perfidious eastern devils. Perhaps the Silent Order would have been assuaged by her death under such circumstances.

But the Mask Poinsard had not received the proper dispatches. Or she'd been incapacitated too early to execute her wishes. In either case, Childress was chilled to both heart and bone.

"There was miscommunication." She didn't have the heart for the sort of petty gamesmanship that seemed to have delighted the Mask Poinsard, so she left it at that rather than trying to seek rhetorical advantage over the captain.

"Are you still committed to our purpose?"

She could only say yes, and guess her way in from there. "Of course, Captain."

He relaxed. She got the distinct impression that Leung was forcing himself not to glance at the armed sailor standing watch. "Are you familiar with the concept of a political officer, Mask?" he asked in a pleasant tone. "Please, be pleasant and speak with some warmth so we do not appear to be plotting misdeeds."

She tried to smile, but it wouldn't come. "He can scarcely imagine that I harbor the capacity for misdeeds which could disturb such an extraordinary vessel as this, sir."

"You would be amazed. I take it that you do not know of political officers?"

Childress forced a laugh. "No, I am afraid not." Though it was rapidly becoming obvious to her what he meant, she didn't want to give him satisfaction.

"Let us say that while I am in command, I am not fully in control. The Beiyang Navy is a force under much stress, the Iron Bamboo all the more so."

"I am surprised he has not met with an accident," she said sweetly. *That* was pure Poinsard.

"It is difficult for a man to fall overboard from a submarine, madam. And he bravely stayed below during the assault on *Mute Swan* lest there be any unrest among my men."

Childress turned and favored the political officer with a small smile. It was her best talking-to-deans expression. He appeared confused.

"Do not overplay your hand, Mask."

"Of course not."

Leung smiled now as well, this one genuine. "Then know that we embark on a dangerous action. Iron Bamboo ships can pass beneath the ice which caps the Northern Earth. That is a slow, dangerous process, with little tolerance for error of any kind. Even with our air stored in tanks and our electricks properly charged, we must surface at least every three days.

This is late in the year to find air holes along the northernmost portions of our course."

Childress examined her nails a moment, as she imagined Poinsard might do in a time like this. "Should I ask to be put ashore?"

He laughed softly. "You are an amusing woman. Please, confine yourself to my cabin, this wardroom, and the head, which lies beyond. Do not loiter in the passageway. The men will give you the proper respect or their feet will be beaten. All know this, except possibly *him*." Leung's eyes flickered toward the political officer. "I will speak to you when I can. You will be served your meals in here by my steward. Though I have very, very little to offer you, if there is something you desire that can be found aboard *Five Lucky Winds,* I will make it yours."

"Writing material," she said firmly. "A deck of cards if you have one, and reading material in English. Or any European language, I suppose."

"I will see what can be done." Leung rose, bowed from the waist, then shouldered past the political officer.

That one, a little man dressed in seaman's clothes, smiled at her, said, "Hello," and made the sign of the white bird with the hand that did not hold the pistol.

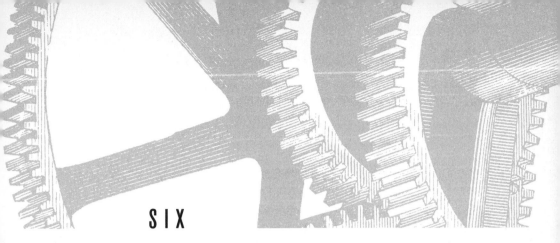

SIX

PAOLINA

She had only thought that Karindira's home was a city. It had been ten, perhaps twenty times the size of Praia Nova, with walls and paved streets and stone houses crowded shoulder to shoulder amid which the little troglodyte women had passed about their errands.

At the time that seemed enormous.

Ophir, though . . . Ophir was a city. Not solely of the Brass, thank God, or she would have been betrayed simply following Boaz through the streets. Even those marvelous mechanical men were but a pale grace note on the symphony that was Ophir.

The city clung—the only word for it—to a vast ledge that projected from a soaring cliff on *a Muralha*'s face. This offered a relatively horizontal surface about a quarter mile deep and several miles long. The buildings ranged in a multitude of styles, from broad-pillared facades reminiscent of the Armory of Westmost Repose to high-porticoed marble structures with peaked roofs and pale fluted columns to catch the sunlight in a bright stone fire to crystal towers with metal skeletons within that glowed like vast mechanical candles. All manner of lesser styles of building were spread among them—shacks of driftwood and salvage lumber, low stone buildings that would have fit in anywhere, odd mismatched structures whose builders had moved on.

The streets were crowded with more people than she'd ever seen. The throngs of Karindira's city paled by comparison, the little tribes and villages through which she'd passed becoming so many shrunken fireside circles in contrast to this mighty reach of Creation.

There were Brass, of course. This was unmistakably their city. Most walked with a swagger far more insolent than Boaz even at his most irritable and uncertain. Others cleared the way, stepping to the side or simply reversing direction. It was as if each Brass were a little moon, drawing tides among the sea of people through which he swam.

But there were others, too. Humans, some pale and fair, others with skin dark as the inside of a cave and ivory eyes gleaming within faces that contained their own shadows. There were near-humans as well, tall hairy men who looked much like the enkidus of Praia Nova with their gaping nostrils and sloping brows; tiny cousins of those, slender apes with intelligent, girlish eyes and narrow faces. She saw thin men brown as carob beans, who wore linen wraps and headdresses clipped on by lapis bands made to look like coiled snakes. They seemed little more than shadows when they turned away. There were several of another race much like Karindira's people, save these had orange skin the color of sunset and eyes that constantly wept black tears. Winged creatures with a rude and savage look to them, mad yellow eyes shifting as they stalked the streets. Even a few other mechanicals not of the Brass race—a giant crystal automaton, thirty feet or more tall, with a barrel-shaped head and flaming eyes, that towed a wagon loaded with mewling kits waving tiny swords and spitting on passersby.

It was a confusion of persons that reminded her once more of the great scope of Creation. Mixed between were a scattering of carts and vehicles, some drawn by men, horses or other creatures, others that creaked and steamed on their own power.

"I do not wish to traffic with Authority yet," Boaz muttered. "There is much here which passes beyond my memory. I would head to the lower city and inquire in certain houses there as to what has transpired."

"How so?" She gawped at the pull and press around her.

"Ophir was never in life this crowded. And mark how many of them are under arms."

She looked. It hadn't occurred to her to wonder at that. Every person seemed to be bearing a sword or spear or firearm, some of familiar make, others of strange device indeed. "Why?"

"I do not know. This disturbs me."

"What of the gleam I carry? Many along *a Muralha* could sense it as I passed. Will it mark me out here?"

Boaz shook his head, shouldering past two mules heavily laden with baskets of oranges. "Half the weapons here are gleamed. Moved by seals or djinns or words, as was the brass car."

They came to a square island in the middle of the road, ringed by an iron fence. It was another stair, she saw, much like the one that had led down the ascender shaft. This stair also followed a shaft, thronged with people of all shapes and sizes, but when Boaz stepped down into it, Paolina saw nothing but air and clouds in the bottom.

Everyone seemed to descending to nowhere.

The crowds in the streets of Ophir were not hurling themselves into the empty air along the face of the Wall. The stairs ran down a hundred yards or so then broke out into an expansive set of metal walkways depending from the *bottom* of the city's ledge.

Paolina realized the city was built on the curl of a wave of stone. An entire second city hung here, dangling over the open air of a lengthy slope to a folded forest far below, just barely visible through the clouds. These buildings were inverted wooden cones, some with truncated tips, others with crystal or glass at their lower ends to provide a view of the long fall. Balconies ringed the cones, with connecting walkways. Foot traffic from the stairwell fanned out among the various levels and catwalks to various destinations.

It was beautiful, in a strange way. The buildings seemed great bats ready to drop away and take flight, the undercity poised to be something other than what it had been made to be.

She and Boaz were soon on a quiet ledge of their own. He stopped to look about, then spoke. "Many of these buildings are contiguous with the lower levels of those above."

"Did you run out of space on the upper surface?"

"Precisely. Some structures are tunneled back into the Wall itself. The Palace of Authority is such a one. But building here granted far more flexibility."

"The cost . . ." Paolina realized she had no idea how the Brass reckoned labor or expense. The design process alone for something like this passed her understanding.

"Pride is the greatest coin in the treasury of Ophir," Boaz replied. "We are King Solomon's children."

He led her on, until they turned into a doorway set in one of the cones. The building's wall loomed forward in a strange forced perspective that caused Paolina to want to bend back—a very bad idea indeed.

Boaz stepped in, Paolina followed. Beyond was a low room crowded with Brass, mostly standing in twos and threes around tall tables. Hoses rose from the table centers to their lips. Some of them twitched and hummed. A few were dented and rusted—something she had not seen on the surface streets of Ophir.

Humans moved among them, tending the hoses and bringing small vials of a dark viscous liquid. A sharp-eyed man, pale as any Praia Novado, watched over the room with a spear in his lap, which crackled with some blue fire.

Boaz made for the overseer.

Paolina followed, afraid to be left alone, but almost as afraid to confront the man.

"Where might I find Anlis?" Boaz asked the man.

"Who?" He leaned forward, a hard expression on his face.

"Anlis. One who oversaw this establishment betimes."

Now the man picked up his spear. "I run this place, and that ain't my name. Been here quite a few years, and Old Golokoshe before me. Anlis weren't his name neither."

"I may have been some time," Boaz said. "I do not intend to offend." Paolina noted that the Brass did not back away as he spoke.

"You want a hose, see the boys. You want to sell her, I'm not buying."

Paolina opened her mouth in startled protest, then shut it almost as quickly. She would learn nothing and gain less by interfering with Boaz' efforts.

Boaz flicked his wrist. Something slid into his palm, though Paolina could not see what. He must have had it stored within. "I have not taken the hose since long before you were alive, man who is not Anlis." He opened his hand to display a jeweled nozzle. "I will give you this in payment for an answer."

"What answer?" the man asked suspiciously.

"What all this crowding and numbers of people means in the city. I request a reasonable response, not some grudging djinn's bargain. Tell me whom we seek to fight and why."

The man took Boaz' nozzle. He examined it critically, then closed his fist over the little device. "There are English on the Wall again. As there were two years ago. This time they have brought machines to tunnel. The oldest Brass have proclaimed this anathema, and so the city fights their redcoats and bluecoats and common men clad in earthen brown."

English! thought Paolina. She was so close to them now. That she might be on the wrong side of their fighting was a small matter, easily disposed of.

"Thank you," said Boaz.

The man laughed, a bitter sound like rain on rust. "You have been among people too long."

Boaz propelled Paolina before him as they exited.

"That is where you people go to get drunk," she said excitedly. "Like the men in the great hall back in Praia Nova. How can you trust them?"

"I cannot. But I espy no reason why he should have lied to us."

"The English." She practically skipped in her glee. "I can take the gleam to them and—"

Boaz took her arm in a tight metal grip. "First we go to the Palace of Authority. There I will discharge my duties. After, if you are once more free to go, you may search out your Englishmen."

"Please. This is more important."

To her shock, his next words came in her voice. " 'All you can do is go to the Palace of Authority and demand that the theft of your memory be redressed. You are bound there by duty, now, to carry me. You will serve both yourself and your orders if you take us both there.' " Then he added in his own voice, "You yourself have reminded me of what is truly important: to serve myself and my orders."

"And if the Solomnic Kingdom of Ophir is indeed at war with the English?" she asked bitterly.

"I will not aid you to seek them out. You are not English, are you?"

"No," she muttered, feeling obscurely disloyal.

"In that case, there is little to fear."

They headed for an undercity entrance to the Palace of Authority. Paolina considered running away, but Boaz could readily outpace her, and he knew this city as well as she knew Praia Nova. She couldn't escape him. Meanwhile, his willingness to listen to her out in the wilds of a Muralha had morphed into a mechanical certitude here in his home city. Ophir had brought him back to whatever it was that being Brass signified to him.

They circled around various cones, occasionally crossing wider gulfs on narrow, swaying bridges. The wind was warm and questing, tugging at her, bringing forest and stone scents from below to mix with the warm miasma of city life. Even though this place had been built by and for Brass, it was teeming with other races—their foods, their clothing, their hygiene, their animals.

Down here, people sat in the doorways and windows, legs dangling over open air. Cats, opossums, and rodents ran along the railings and stabilizing cables, most with little bells on looped collars. Leashed children toddled here and there.

Boaz continued to advance toward the deeply shadowed cliff face at the back of the ledge.

The farther they went, the quieter and colder the walkways became. The cones seemed dedicated to storage or matters of commerce. There were fewer animals, and no children, and the smells became mustier.

He finally stepped onto a cantilevered stone balcony with a triple arch at the back, carved right into the face of the Wall.

"This is the Penitents' Door," he said quietly.

"Is that just a name, or does it mean more?"

"Merely a name." He added vaguely, "There are ceremonies."

Paolina tried the only thing she thought might work at this moment, in this place. "And down here somewhere is your memory?"

Boaz turned to stare at her. "If my crystals were stolen away from me, they would be near to this door. It is my intent to ascertain the current orders concerning gleams and other Wall magic."

"What if you are commanded to kill me?"

"Then we will see." He began to vibrate slightly. "I am Brass, after all."

"You are Boaz, too," she reminded him. "You said that beyond Authority, there was me. Don't forget that."

"Brass does not forget." His voice was sullen now.

"No, but you can have it stricken from you."

With that, Boaz turned on his heel and marched through the center door. Shrugging off one last temptation to run, she followed him into the Palace of Authority.

The entrance hall was dusty and quiet. A faint breeze brushed at them. Pale seal-lights, weak copies of the magic that powered the brass car, cast sufficient glow to see by. There were stone benches carved from the rock of the floor where supplicants might once have sat. A hallway stretched in two directions from behind a lectern, where doors led on deeper into the rock of the Wall.

"This is improper," Boaz said. "There should be busyness afoot here."

"There was no one outside. What were you expecting within?"

He set out walking. They quickly came to a stairway leading both up and down. It wasn't another vacant ascender shaft, just a carved flight. Boaz chose to go up without making any comment. Paolina followed.

The next level had been used for storage. There were wooden boxes filled with scrolls and silk-tied stacks of paper. Old maps and charts were racked in great fanlike frames. Tables and chairs and desks had been stacked.

He led her farther up.

She wondered what had happened. Had his precious Authority somehow collapsed? Or been replaced by some other form of governance?

The next level had more pale flickering lights, along with electricks, and even carpets. There was noise from behind the doors. This was a working hall, not abandoned territory like the floors below. He began walking back the way they had come as if to pass above the Penitents' Door.

Paolina looked at the signs they passed, but she did not recognize the script.

Boaz pushed open the fourth door on their right. She hesitated a moment, then followed him in.

As she entered, Paolina saw two Brass within, standing to each side of Boaz. One touched the back of his neck as the other peered into his eyes with a small instrument. The neck-toucher looked at Paolina and snapped a question in a language she didn't know. She shrugged. He tried another language, then, in oddly accented English, "Is it you that broughting him here?"

"Yes," she said.

"Froming where?"

"The Armory of Westmost Repose."

"Thanking you."

"You're welcome," she said.

The two of them fussed at Boaz a minute or two more, then stepped away.

Paolina summoned her courage. "May I have him back now, please?"

The one who'd spoken to her sounded surprised. "He ising not yours."

"No, no, of course not. He is his own. You are all Brass." She smiled. "But he committed me to aiding him in scouting the English positions. As I am of their race and speak the language, Brass felt I would serve him well. I am enthused to begin our work, yet here you have turned him away."

"He is needing of maintenance." The brass man looked at his colleague. They had a rapid conversation in a burst of clicks and chatters.

"Please," Paolina added. "I would serve Ophir and the eldest Brass."

"Not of you."

"He is." She grasped for something that would make sense to these rude mechanicals. "He . . . he brought me here from the Armory of Westmost Repose. He is to take me before Authority."

Her interlocutor stared at her a moment, in a very human way, then adjusted something in Boaz' neck. "Going then."

"Thank you."

Boaz stirred, an indefinable ghost of life reentering him as it had that day on the trail. Paolina grabbed at his arm. "Come on, Brass. Time for us to do our duty."

She could hear something in him whir, but he turned and walked with her.

"How do we get away from the Palace of Authority," she whispered once they were alone in the hall. "Back as we came?" Up seemed foolish—there were more Brass that way, and people in general.

He led her downward, still unspeaking. They exited via the Penitents' Door and into the cool shadows of the rearmost part of the undercity. Boaz seemed content to remain mute as he took a different way this time, along catwalks and stairways that paralleled the face of *a Muralha*. She remained very conscious of the fact that the Palace of Authority lay just behind the stone to her right.

They came to a point where a stair led farther down. It was cut into the face of the Wall, so that the rock formed a half arch. The steps were staggered, sometimes small and close together, sometimes larger and farther apart. A slow procession of people, both Brass and flesh, headed down. There was no room that she could see for someone to come back up.

Each bore a bundle, some great knot of supplies and gear. The loads were wrapped haphazardly. It was as if every porter had conceived of his own burden and sought out stick by stick what to fill it with. Each trudged staring only at his own feet. None watched their fellows; none looked forward or back.

When she stared along the maze of walkways between the wooden cone-buildings of the undercity, Paolina realized that many of the folk she'd seen before must have been laden for this trail.

To her shock, Boaz grasped Paolina by the waist and hefted her to his shoulders. She was torn between beating at him and grabbing for the gleam, lest its pouch slide free of her dress pocket. She settled for silent protest with gleam safe in hand, though she was furious.

Once he started down the trail, she began to understand why he'd grabbed her. Boaz held Paolina so that her head was on the inside, passing near enough to the stone of the Wall to make her flinch over and over. The other side, though, would have had her head hanging over empty space.

She could not have borne that.

And the trail went on and on. There was a sloping country far below her, woodlots and fields barely visible through a layer of fog. They would be walking downward for miles, it seemed.

Paolina closed her eyes, finally, trusting Boaz not to slam her head into the rock passing so very close. She wondered awhile at why the walkers were all so automated, so quiet and slow, but eventually the lull of his steps and the warmth of the sun sent her slipping into sleep.

AL-WAZIR

Acalayong was a disaster. The port wasn't even a town, just a stinking jungled river mouth with sufficient draft to admit large vessels. Al-Wazir knew as soon as *Wallachian Prince* sailed within sight of the harbor that they were in for some nasty work. One of the specially built freighters that had brought the first two steam borers here to the Wall was in the channel, burnt to the waterline.

As far as he could tell, the borer had been taken off before the burning. He told himself that was a blessing.

The Equatorial Wall loomed south of Acalayong's river, the Mitémélé. Water lapped at a stone bluff that footed a rising plain, which in turn was backed by soaring ribs of rock where the Wall proper vaulted into the sky, blocking the horizon in an immensity of clouded stone. The area at the base lay in deep shadow, something he assumed to be perpetual with the sun directly overhead.

There was a wooden trestle leading out into the channel. A crane stood at the end. It looked like something out of the Middle Ages. *Ivanhoe*, maybe. But this was what the advance engineers had built, at least until someone sank the ship in the river.

Al-Wazir's gaze followed a graded roadbed leading from the trestle upward toward the Wall. The track was very wide as it vanished into the jungle. Somewhere up there, a few miles distant, lost in the glossy green chaos of the tropical forest, were one or both of the steam borers and almost a thousand men, waiting for Ottweill to arrive.

Down here on the river there wasn't an honest English face to be seen. Just a scattering of locals in canoes, and the fire-damaged hulk.

He looked up to the Wall again, realizing the mists he saw were smoke.

Al-Wazir shouted toward the deck from his perch atop the pilothouse. "There's been fighting here on the water, and there's fighting now upon the Wall. Tell Captain Hornsby we'll be going in with Plan Red."

Plan Red was to land all the uniformed forces under arms—a battalion of Royal Marines with a small army detachment—followed by as many of Ottweill's men as could be induced to take up weapons. Under Plan Red, al-Wazir himself was to stay behind and secure the unloading of *Wallachian Prince*. He'd objected strenuously to being left out of the action, but had been overruled.

The ship's crew and a portion of Ottweill's men would remain with him. They would work under the supercargoes to get the ship unloaded as quickly as possible, and the supplies secured once landed. He'd have to lay the rails, too, and get the three little locomotives currently welded to the foredeck laboring to haul those supplies up to the work site.

The fate of Gordon's expedition hung heavy on al-Wazir's mind, but those circumstances had been different. Today they were tackling the Wall on English terms, not following the Wall's own dangerous ways. The ghosties and bright machines that lurked up high could keep right on lurking up there, so long as it wasn't them that had come down to make war on the expedition here.

He put that thought out of his head and went to talk to the first mate about what could be done to clear a way to the pier.

Hornsby and his men had vanished into the jungle, heading toward the Wall. None of the promised runners reappeared.

Ottweill was fit to raise hell and all the dead who lay within. "Splashing about in that miserable river you must stop," he screamed at al-Wazir. Ottweill, the chief, *Prince*'s first mate, and the lead supercargo were meeting in the ward room. It was the fourth day they lay at anchor in the estuary.

Al-Wazir still had blood under his fingernails from Grassi's death by crocodile that afternoon. He was in no mood to hear it. "If you have a better plan, Professor, please share it with us." He slapped the tabletop. "Otherwise I'll drag you down into the river to cut rotten, stinking, fire-hardened wood with the rest of us. Perhaps you'd like to count the leeches? Or carry a rifle and stand chest-deep in the water on crocodile watch."

"You will regret this conduct," Ottweill said stiffly.

"I have no doubt. But only if I first succeed in keeping all of us alive." Al-Wazir knew he should not be bickering with the man who was effectively his captain, not here before their real purpose had even begun to bear fruit. "I regret my conduct, sir," he said heavily, lying himself blue. "I cannot shift the wreck any faster. We already work from first light to total darkness in heat that would boil a chicken. Men are dying in the water."

"Work harder," Ottweill muttered.

"Of course."

And so it went, for days on end.

On the seventh day, Captain Hornsby sent back a detachment with a message. The short column of wounded was led by one of Hornsby's lieutenants, a foppish boy from Kent whose name al-Wazir could never get right.

The young officer was smiling, though he seemed to have bandages in place of one ear, and had walked in with a crutch. "Chief al-Wazir. May I present Captain Hornsby's compliments?"

"Indeed." Al-Wazir was conscious that he stank of Mitémélé bottom mud. It was much like being painted with shit. On the other hand, the lieutenant stank of jungle and gunpowder and old blood.

Sometimes he missed the Royal Navy. "How goes it on the Wall?"

The lieutenant swayed slightly. "The earlier expedition was attacked in force." There was something fixed about his smile. "Almost a hundred dead before they could repel the hostiles. We arrived in time to break a second attack."

"Who is the enemy?" That question might be meaningless on the Wall, but still he had to ask.

"Brass men, sir. Walking statues with spears that throw fire. They have mixed native troops, of all colors and sizes."

"We are victorious?" he prompted.

"Yes. With no damage to the steam borers or essential equipment."

Al-Wazir wondered what constituted nonessential equipment, so far from England and resupply. He was spared the need to ask that question by the arrival of Ottweill from the ship. The chief nodded to the lieutenant, who saluted and turned to tell his tale again while his men stood down to smoke dog-eared butts and stretch out on the planks of the trestle pier.

Back to the river, he thought. The sky was so much cleaner.

Once they'd cleared *Parsifal*'s wreck, *Wallachian Prince* could stand to and be unloaded. That was another sort of work, which fortunately did not require al-Wazir's full attention. He occupied himself with several long, thorough showers and a seventeen-hour slumber in his rack. The cramped cabin was larger than any space he'd ever had to call his own in the Navy, though others grumbled at length about the Spartan accommodations.

There was no question that the ship's crew would be pleased to see the last of Ottweill and his merry band of Wall-drillers.

After that, he watched from the rail as a mountain of gear, supplies, equipment, machinery, rails, and raw material was disgorged from the holds of *Wallachian Prince*. The railroad men had a line laid almost immediately, up and away from the trestle pier before branching into several sidings. They ran one of their locomotives shifting tonnage away from dockside to facilitate continued unloading. Ottweill and his quartermasters worked on the landward side to direct the unloading of that haulage, with an eye toward more efficient reloading and transport to the cutting face later.

It was a masterpiece of coordinated effort. All the slacking layabouts and troublemakers who'd so occupied al-Wazir's time on the long voyage south seemed to have unfolded into as hardworking and clever a bunch of seaman's sons as he'd care to see.

He finally went ashore with the last of the load, eighteen days after landfall in Acalayong. The battle had broken off completely up at the Wall. Hornsby's runners were getting through. The railroad seemed to creep southward whenever he wasn't looking, opening new sidings and cargo dumps, but also developing the mainline that would be required to shift all the goods up to the base encampment.

English industry had asserted itself in the teeth of even the Wall. Al-Wazir began to think that perhaps the Prime Minister's scheme was not so mad as all that.

The cutting face was impressive. The initial teams had surveyed to Ottweill's specifications, following what few maps existed. They'd claimed a great squared-off bay that led some small distance into the Wall. There was no great profit in cutting off a few score yards of the tunnel. Rather, the value was in the sheltered space where the steam borers had been set, the rails laid to drive them up from the river having been pulled up after for reuse inside the tunnel.

A stout wooden stockade had been constructed that bowed outward from the mouth of the stone bay. There was a gatehouse, already being rebuilt in stone, and a palisaded wall, which showed signs of recent heavy fighting. Small breech-loading cannon had been mounted on three towers. As an air sailor, al-Wazir was not one of nature's infantrymen, but he appreciated what he saw.

A trail of wreckage, felled trees, and roughly plowed land led east, marking the direction of the most recent attack by the Wall-dwellers.

The one question no one had answered was the reason for the attack. Not that anyone on the Wall had ever needed a reason, in his experience. Crazed savages and wicked saints, one and all.

Deep within the bay the tracks for the steam borers ran right up to the face. Standard-gauge rails were tucked between them. The machines had been fired every day, their boilers running on wood here rather than coal, but in Ottweill's absence they had not been brought up to meet the Wall. Al-Wazir knew the original plan had called for prospecting for coal, but that was impractical in the face of continued hostilities. Wood they had in plenty, enough to send the borers through the Wall a dozen times over. It would suffice.

Now that the attacks had been beaten back, they were set to begin operations. Ottweill, al-Wazir, and Hornsby had met with the officers of

Wallachian Prince to compose a letter urgently requesting both more civilian workers and soldiers in face of their initial losses. None of them would admit to believing the expedition was in serious peril.

Studying the camp, he looked up from the steam borers to the rising expanse of God's Creation. Al-Wazir had been wrong about at least one thing—sunlight did fall at the foot of the Wall, at least a few hours a day. In that respect, the weather was like home—gloomy and damp, with a bit of brightness in between. Of course, it was 110 degrees here. Not so homelike, that.

But sometimes the Wall sent down a refreshing breeze to break the heat's grip awhile. And when he looked down across the swaying tops of the glossy trees to the brown water of the Mitémélé, he could see the beauty of Africa lying at right angles to the soaring cathedral that was the Wall. Heat to the north, cool shadow above, and those great black steam borers ready to cut in.

Somehow they seemed in scale here. The machine back in the Kentish quarry had been sullen, evil even, in its affect. These seemed so small next to the Wall they were meant to breach that al-Wazir had difficulty seeing them as instruments of destruction.

Ottweill climbed the ladder atop one of his beloved borers. The doctor still favored his tailored suits, which seemed inhumanly hot to al-Wazir, but even Ottweill had given up his necktie.

"Tomorrow against the face we will set the number one borer," he told al-Wazir, patting the iron flank.

"To start cutting?"

"Not yet. Testing we will be. Run the drill up to speed and back down, a final check on the integrity of the rock face we will perform. The rails, too. Everything but the cut. That, for the next day."

"I will be here, on the stockade, watching for hostiles," al-Wazir promised him.

"I had hoped in the cab of number one you might join me. The first part to drive."

Al-Wazir thought about the tiny doorway leading into the armored cab. To ride that coffin into the depths of the earth seemed too far from sailing the sky. "No, I do not believe so. But I am honored, sir."

"Fair enough," said Ottweill. "The limits of his courage every man must know."

It was almost good to see the doctor back in his usual form.

CHILDRESS

She avoided the political officer as much as she could. Staying in her cabin was the simplest solution; nonetheless, Childress was forced at least twice a day to seek a meal in the wardroom. Sometimes the little man was about; sometimes he was not. *Well, they are almost all little men,* she thought. At four feet and eleven inches, Childress was not a woman of any size, but in this company she felt almost tall.

Crammed into the wardroom, where at most four could be seated, a blue-coated steward would bring her meal. It was always a tiny bowl of tea, a tiny bowl of soup, a tiny bowl of rice, and a tiny bowl of something fried and flavored that varied from day to day. All four were always hot, though *Five Lucky Winds* otherwise seemed eternally damp and chilled, cold water beading on her bulkheads and hatches.

The men of the submarine would pass by the door in ones and twos to steal glances when they thought she couldn't see them. Decades of watching over divinity students—as mean-spirited and self-entitled a bunch of miscreants as one could ever hope to meet—had honed her skills of peripheral observation. She knew perfectly well when they slowed their step, and picked it up again.

At least that gave her a chance to listen to their soft chatter.

The peeking only stopped when Captain Leung came to sit with her, or if the political officer were in the passageway outside.

"Are you finding circumstances to your satisfaction, Mask?" he asked, the second day asea.

Childress was now dressed in an old blue uniform. It was extremely undignified, but less so than wearing the bloodied dress in which she'd been captured. The steward had bowed and bobbed and explained something at great length to her in Chinese before taking it away. She hoped the garment would be cleaned and repaired, or failing that, burned, but she had no real way of knowing.

"I should like to have some decent clothing," she said briskly, "as befits my station. And though this native food is charming in its strange little way, a reasonable meal that an Englishwoman might recognize." That was as much like the Mask Poinsard as she could stand to be.

Leung stared at her evenly a bit longer than she might have liked. The political officer hovered at the doorway again. "I am afraid we can accommodate almost none of your wishes," the captain said. He set a stack of books on the table. "Here is a manual for electricks which is written in English. My esteemed engineer would like to have it back at the end of the voyage, as considers it a valued if incomprehensible souvenir. Here is also a Roman devotional, and two postcards from Singapore. That is all the English material aboard my ship."

"I am sure it will keep me sufficiently entertained," Childress said. "May I take these to my cabin?"

"Of course." Leung paused, searching for words, perhaps. "And if you would care to converse, it will always benefit my English to have practice at it."

"Your English is already better than that spoken by most subjects of the Crown," she told him politely. Polite, but true.

Over the next few days they established a habit of him coming to visit her at one of her two meals. Sometimes it was little more than a nod, if he had urgent business elsewhere; sometimes it was a conversation.

"The Feathered Masks have their followers in the Celestial Empire," he told her one morning.

"Of course." Childress was distracted by the damnable little eating sticks. They were more than difficult for picking up rice, but she didn't fancy asking for a fork. "The *avebianco* is everywhere." She thought of the political officer, with his hand sign and his hello. She hadn't yet told Leung about that. She wasn't sure she would.

"Your philosophy appeals to a certain kind of traditionalist."

"I did not think the Chinese held to the supremacy of God the father."

"Not *that* sort of traditionalist." He laughed softly. "To put it in simple terms, the emperor is the Son of Heaven. Heaven's structure can be divined from careful study of the brasswork in the skies. So the nature of Creation guides the emperor, just as the emperor guides his people."

"How do you see Creation?" She was quite curious—God's handiwork was incontrovertible, after all, even if His current state of engagement was subject to theological and practical disputation.

"The world was made," Leung said. "But where you Europeans seem to find one great, overriding presence in a position of responsibility, the Universal Cause, so to speak, we see a balance in the courts of Heaven. So this one made the moon, while that one set the lamps of the stars to wheel in their courses, and this other arranged the faces of day and night so as to favor men."

"Not so different, really." Childress pushed a few shreds of pork around. "You have just named the varying aspects of God. As if each of His hands were a different thing."

"I believe we have a very long way to go before we can properly misunderstand each other," Leung said.

The captain left her with the political officer and his pistol, Childress chasing the last of her brown-fried onions with the useless little sticks.

And so it went for a week. She read and reread about electrickal valves and switches. She studied lives of saints Euphronius, Lupus, Padraig, and Xanthippe, wondering time and again why Fr. Algys B. Huang, SJ, had felt the need to discuss those four saints in particular in his little book. She examined the Singapore postcards until she could recite their respective texts about the wicked imperialist dog Sir Thomas Stamford Raffles and the great prince Parameswara.

Sometimes the ship would change speed or course. Occasionally it would change angle, heading lower or higher in Oceanus' grip. Those moments brought Childress unwelcome fears of attack by British surface raiders or aerial bombardment.

Surely Her Imperial Majesty's Navy even now sought to avenge the insult to *Mute Swan*. Childress had no illusions about her own value. The Mask Poinsard had been a woman of rank, perhaps even a duchess, and thus likely to be sought after on disappearing.

Between reading, sleeping, and brief bouts of terror, Childress ate rice, sipped tea, tipped her soup bowl, and practiced capturing slim bits of food with her little eating sticks. And, of course, spoke to Captain Leung.

"Do your people admit the existence of angels?"

"Angels?" He frowned. "In the sense of messengers of Heaven, certainly."

"No." She was thinking of that poor, lost boy Hethor, who'd gone to wind the mainspring of the world. "The leaders of the hosts of God. They carry swords, to punish or reward."

"There is scant reward to be given with a sword," said Leung. "But no, while Heaven and Northern Earth and Hell are filled with ghosts and demons and mandarins of all orders, there are no angels in the European sense."

"Biblical, actually." Childress wasn't sure what a European angel would be. "The Celestial Hierarchy of Pseudo-Dionysius the Areopagite explains in detail. Ophanim, Thrones, Cherubim . . . more than most will bother to recall these days. But not precisely European." She paused to gather her thoughts. "What I mean to say is that there are orders among the angels, which are described in European theology. Some of them move among men."

"Again, I think we are far from a reasonable misunderstanding of one another." Leung's smile wrinkled his face. "Though surely the Celestial Realms are populated by as many orders of rank as populate the everyday world. The Celestial Kingdom is certainly arrayed much the same."

"*Quod est inferius est sicut quod est superius, et quod est superius est sicut quod est inferius,*" said Childress. *As above, so below.* "Here is my point: Do you recall two summers past, when there were great quakes around the Northern Earth? Waves coursed across the shores of the world, and there was destruction upon the Wall."

"Yes. Our astronomers declared that the time that runs beneath the world was in slippage. Our priests said there was a war in Heaven. Whichever was correct, hostilities did come to an end."

"They came to an end because an angel found a boy named Hethor in New England, and set him to repairing the mainspring of the world."

He chuckled. "I think that explanation would be difficult to tender in the gardens of Soochow."

The next day Leung warned Childress that *Five Lucky Winds* was going beneath the ice. "We may have difficulty with our air. All persons not about urgent business are enjoined to remain in their bunk, breathing quietly."

"What will happen to your boilers?" she asked.

"Their fires are already banked. We run on electricks until we can find a hole to surface. There we will refresh our breathing air and restart the boilers to charge the batteries."

"And so like seals we breathe out the air we have, hoping for a hole in the ice?"

"You have divined the very essence of the Iron Bamboo."

She could swear the captain's voice had a wry tone, though somehow that seemed un-Chinese. "It would appear to be a time for prayer."

"If that is your path. I must warn you that there may be considerable noise, some of it quite odd. The cold and the currents stress the ship unusually."

"I will remain as calm as is given to me to be," Childress said. "And pray for us to find air and light among the ice."

Leung nodded. "You may wish additional blankets."

"Not if they must come from those used by the men."

"Very well." He took his leave of her.

Over the next few days the ship ran deeper, while the noise of the propellers grumbled ever slower. She might have expected them to make quicker time beneath the ice, the faster to reach the other side of the Arctic, but perhaps it was too dangerous to move quickly in these waters.

Five Lucky Winds ran more quietly, too, the electricks not transmitting the same vibrations through the hull that the boilers did.

So they ran silent and they ran deep. The water on the walls grew colder and her breath began to fog. Childress reduced herself to one meal a day. Those were simpler as well, cold rice that grew increasingly tough with each passing day, and stringy pickled meats. The soup vanished and the tea had become tepid.

She did not see the political officer anywhere.

The rest of the time she lay in her bunk. She prayed, though God's deliverance seemed more remote than ever beneath the frozen seawater. It seemed more likely that the divine lurked in sunlight and color and the touch of the breeze, not in chilled metal and deep booming noises that might have come from the mouths of continents.

The transit continued cold, damp, and difficult. Childress breathed shallow and close to the thin pillow to husband the warmth of her breath. She had a chart given to her by a grinning sailor. It showed the coasts of the Arctic Ocean, which she could recognize, though all the notations were in Chinese, which meant nothing to her.

Still, the shapes of the land were some small comfort as the hull groaned and popped.

After three days under the ice, bells rang throughout the ship. She could feel the hull moving upward. Her breath seemed shorter, though Childress told herself sternly that was her imagination. She turned in the chart in her hand, looking at Greenland and Baffin Island and the gold circle marking the north pole, with its dotted black warning not to stray too close.

There was a knock on her door. *Hatch,* she corrected herself. "Come in."

Childress was quite surprised to see Leung when he stepped through. He was dressed in a strange quilted suit.

"Would you care to see the ice?" He offered another quilted suit about her size. She realized that it must serve as armor against the polar cold.

Childress rose stiffly. Leung helped her climb into the suit, right over her clothing. *This is much like setting out in the winters of my childhood,* she thought, strapped into insulating layers in hopes of fending off frostbite. The Chinese tailors seemed to have more skill than her late mother had possessed at keeping the folds and layers of their snowsuits tight. She wondered why they didn't use them for sleeping while traveling beneath the cold Arctic sea.

Childress followed the captain forward, past the wardroom and into a little round chamber. There were lights beyond, in a room full of dials and gauges and great valve wheels, but he shook his head. "Please, do not look."

They climbed a narrow ladder she couldn't recall having come down before. In a small iron room on an upper deck, bright, low light flooded through an open hatch above them.

She climbed out onto a little metal balcony with Captain Leung to behold a world of ice and sky.

And air! So pure, it was like wine from an iced bottle. Childress felt her mind racing as her eyes drank in what lay before her.

It was a frozen sea, but not of swelling waves. More like a landscape— cliffs and crevices and little mountains, all sculpted with the transience of ice. The sun was low on the horizon, in a direction logic told her had to be quite southerly. The pole must lie the other way. She turned and looked across a scape of long shadows and purple darknesses and skyborne brass.

"You cannot see it from here," Leung said. "If we were a hundred miles closer, and the air stayed clear, yes, but we are still too far south." He shrugged, and sounded apologetic. "Our course minimizes transit time."

A whoop interrupted her thirsty view. She turned again to see three crewmen throwing snowballs as they raced across the ice. Captain Leung cleared his throat, but when she glanced at him, he was taking a great interest in the frost on the metal of the submarine's tower.

"It's only a moment in the sun," she told him softly.

"The Beiyang Navy has standards." He looked thoughtful a moment. "Which I do not meet, in truth. I never passed the Eight Legs examination. My poetry fails miserably in any effort to follow classical forms."

"Are those essential to being a ship's captain?"

"Of course." He seemed surprised. "The British have some very peculiar means by which to ascertain if one is a gentleman. We in the Celestial Empire are somewhat more forthright regarding our prejudices. And we have formal evaluations for them."

"So the . . . Eight Legs? What does that mean?"

"A classical test of one's fitness for Confucian thought. Essential for promotion in any service of the Celestial Empire. Due to my deficiencies, I shall never have a flag in the Beiyang Navy."

"Yet they let you go sailing about the Atlantic, rescuing Masks?" Even as she marveled, the question reopened pain she had been resolutely ignoring.

Or maybe it was just the sunlight that brought her back to the deck of *Mute Swan* for a moment.

"It is sometimes surprising how practical admirals can be when awarding independent commands," Leung admitted. "The very same deficiencies of character which will keep me at sea my entire career seem to also suit me to being at sea my entire career."

There was something in the way he said it that pleased her.

Everyone aboard *Mute Swan* had been a conspirator at her death, had they not? She couldn't quite make herself believe that, but it *was* true that Leung had rescued her.

"Would you care to set foot upon the ice?" He was all courtly purpose now.

"I would be delighted."

The captain took her hand and helped her down a short ladder onto the glittering white pack. Up close it was blue and gray and white and clear and all the colors of ice and snow. Also considerably less chilly than she might have believed. Though in shadow or wind, Childress was confident that she would have met an early and difficult end.

They only remained off the ship about ten minutes. She touched it with gloved hands, then with bare fingers, before scraping some ice for a ball of her own. Protruding through the ice beside her, *Five Lucky Winds* loomed like a creature out of time and place.

Some relief valve chuffed within, catching Leung's attention. "Below now."

Childress pointed upward. "Up here, can you deny God?"

"I deny nothing. I merely assert that you are asking the wrong question."

They crossed under the ice in that fashion, surfacing three more times. Childress gratefully took each opportunity she had to walk in the open air. Beneath the ice, she listened to the hull creak and watched the cold condense on the walls. Each time she had to step back within the confines of the submarine, she felt as if she were descending into her own coffin once more.

Still, she had some small time with Leung, which was a relief. Confinement in a prison of language aboard this cramped ship was beginning to wear at her spirit. There was little here to feed her memory or her imagination, which was the worst prison of all.

And then one day she could tell even from within her cabin that *Five Lucky Winds* was cruising on the surface.

Childress tugged out her map of the Arctic. She had reached the Pacific Ocean, or nearly so. They had to be somewhere in the Bering Strait.

That such a thing could be possible amazed her. That she had lived to see it amazed her even more.

SEVEN

PAOLINA

She dreamt of women falling like flowers from the sky. They spun, skirts twirling wide to trail sprays of color like pollen. Paolina jerked awake as Boaz put her down, realizing they *had* been falling. Women, men, Brass—people, tumbling past the endless steps to shatter on the rocks below.

As her spinning head began to clear, she saw they were off the horrible stairs.

"Don't ever do that to—" Boaz waved her to silence. He crouched to stare over a line of rocks. The cold, hard stone of *a Muralha* rose above her, but her back was against a solid surface. There was no trail.

Quiet but seething, she hauled herself over next to Boaz. Her body was oddly stiff. He'd *carried* her like a sack of flour, for hours.

They were on a ledge, though it was more the head of a slope of fallen boulders. The people who'd beetled down from Ophir filed into a clearing among glossy-leaved trees to deposit their burdens before wandering off.

"What is it?" she whispered. She was frightened at the realization of how those people had walked all the miles down the Wall in unending quiet.

"They labor under a seal." Boaz kept his voice low as well. "That was the greatest power the first Brass brought with him to Ophir. He retained some of Solomon's seals in reserve when the original expedition returned to Asiongaber. The seals are the ultimate power in the Solomnic Kingdom of Ophir."

"A spell? A compulsion?"

"Yes."

She thought about that. "Your word, the thing you cannot say, it must be related to the seals."

"I . . . I . . . do not know."

"In other words, you can't say."

Boaz cocked his head to stare at her. His face was brassy and impassive as ever, but there was something of a pleading note in his look. "We are away from Ophir. My loyalty to Authority is not broken, but it has been severely strained on account of my treatment. You strain it further by the moment."

"As may be. It seems to me you strained it yourself more by carrying me down."

"I . . ." He looked thoughtful. "Authority interrupted me. You brought me back to myself for a second time. I seized the moment to carry you free. Even now you are closer to your goal. We are in balance."

She took that in, still ill at ease. "In that case, where are the English?"

"At the far end of *that.*" Boaz nodded toward a trampled trail leading eastward through the jungle that clung to the base of the Wall.

Not far ahead, a flatwater shoreline stretched north and away. This would be the last of the Atlantic Ocean, Paolina realized. "Africa."

"Yes. That is what they call it."

She was ready to join the throng below. "I want to go to them."

He shivered. "An impractical conception. An army gathers here under a seal. Each has brought supplies. Others will come with more."

"You can't move a whole army down a stepway like that," she objected.

"In time, one could. Ophir has other ways down as well. There will be larger things to come, do not fear. This is but one moiety of the effort."

"As far as that goes, do not ever heft me like that again. Not without my permission."

Now his stare was as blank-eyed as any statue. "You are here, are you not? Where you wish to be?"

"Yes," she admitted slowly.

"Then accept your good fortune. Had we come stumbling down that walk at our own pace, we would have been espied and dealt with most straitly. Now that we are off the Wall, we can strike east after sunset."

"Avoiding that sealed army . . ." She peered over the rocks once more.

"They will walk, Brass and flesh, until their feet wear off."

"Who can release them from the seal?"

"One who knows that seal's word."

Paolina thought about that a little bit. "Do you know the words for any of the seals, Boaz?"

"A few," he admitted. "But it is bad enough that I have turned my back on Ophir. I will not betray our armies."

She looked down at the people milling among the trees. "That is no army. They are slaves to the Solomnic seals. This is not the magic of your ancestors, Boaz. This is using citizens of your city like animals."

He was quiet awhile. Then: "You do not know what it means to be Brass. You do not know what has been endured since the oldest Brass came to this place. Do not judge what you do not comprehend."

"I will judge this." Her anger rose. "Every one of those people down there, flesh and metal alike, has a spirit. A soul. That is the seal of God's magic, to make us who we are. Your city has stripped them of the dignity of being themselves and remade them as insects. *That* is not something King Solomon would have wanted, and it is not holy in the eyes of God. Nor is it right in the eyes of man."

"When did you become so concerned with the fate of others? You walked halfway across the Atlantic Wall to get here. How many in their need did you pass up?"

"How many did I *enslave*?" Paolina turned her back. Lacking another purpose in that moment, she tugged the gleam out. She pretended to ignore Boaz, instead concentrating on the stem and the four strange hands.

What would it take, she wondered, to set the fourth to match *his* seal? That was the secret of his word, after all, the name inside the seal. Otherwise he would be just a clever statue filled with gears and springs and joints.

Just as she was nothing more than clever meat, without her mind and spirit at home in her body.

Paolina tugged the stem out to that position. She twirled the setting, trying to visualize what Karindira had turned away from.

Everything in Creation moved in its own time. This was self-evident, given the fundamental order of the world. Solomon's seals were no more than a way of harnessing the energy of that timing and movement—much like settling ropes and weights together to take advantage of the pull of the earth. Of course, it took a very special eye to *see* what the biblical king had seen, to make the seals.

Though Paolina had to admit it was just as likely, or unlikely, that the seals had fallen from his lips as spoken words. *How would I know?*

"I do not know the Adamic tongue," she whispered, "nor what wisdom Solomon had in days of yore. But I know the timing of the world."

She glanced over her shoulder at Boaz. He still crouched, staring down at the sealed army below them. Paolina knew the stairs had to be just to their left and up the Wall. Here, there was quiet.

First he'd carried her; then he berated her. Something in this metal man drew her, but he was a *man* before he was metal.

Paolina drew on her anger to reach into the same dark place within that had helped her create the stemwinder. The gleam, they called it on *a Muralha*. That same strange darkness had kept her always apart and alone at Praia Nova.

The timing of her own heart the easiest. That was simple; it echoed in her temples and fingertips. The hour of the day was not difficult either. The time that beat at the core of all things was harder. She'd first set it back in Praia Nova, when she'd been more certain. It could not be so different now.

She twirled the fourth setting on the gleam, staring now at Boaz. He shifted slightly as he peered down at the sealed army. Since meeting on the trail west of the Armory of Western Repose, she'd come to know him, a step and hour at a time, in a way she hadn't really known anyone before. Boaz had been open to her. He'd *told* her as much. As he had said, *she* lay beyond Authority.

The fourth hand clicked into motion. It began to sweep in a fast stutter, even as Boaz fell as still as the rocks.

She'd drawn the vital essence out of him, drawn it into the gleam. She'd put him under her own seal.

Paolina became frightened.

She waited until dark to do more, her anger melting into her fear. Had she stopped Boaz permanently? What was to become of him? What was to become of her?

Whatever the case was, Brass as well as people of all colors and sizes continued to appear from the steps and move into the darkness of evening. She crouched beside his inert mass to watch. Their burdens had begun to assume sensible form as the sealed army regathered from its wanderings and sorted what had been dumped in great mounts. Pavilions appeared, shelter from the elements. Tools were put to use felling trees as the light faded. Fires began, and the sealed army slowly seemed to awaken to something like normalcy.

Perhaps they do not eat or care properly for themselves under the seal, she thought. Like chickens, the army must be let out to scratch a living and wander a bit before being penned again.

Except the metaphor was backwards. These were hunters of the English. Paolina was confident those mighty wizards could hold back the sealed armies of Ophir, but surely such ancient magic would give even them a challenge. Perhaps *Bassett* was already sailing to meet the attack, carrying the battle to England's enemies.

When the shadows finally merged to a velvety grayness, and only the stars and the brass shone in the sky, she turned once more to Boaz. Paolina held the gleam in her palm, cradled before her. She set the stem to the fourth position again, and stopped the hand that counted Boaz' time.

He jerked to life with a sigh, moving again much as he had in the Palace of Authority.

"Silence," she told him. "Do not cry out. We must go soon."

Boaz rose and followed her to the edge of the ledge. At the eastern end it narrowed to be a part to the long fall of rock and scree dropping to the edge of the jungle that lined the bottommost reaches of *a Muralha*.

Picking her way by the light of the indifferent stars, Paolina led Boaz into the night. They walked slowly and warily above the sealed army rustling in the bed of its camp.

Some hours later, when she was so tired, every step had become a stumble, Paolina began looking for a place to rest. Africa gleamed in the moonlight ahead, though she was not certain of the distance—one mile or five, in either case it was very close. She would reach her goal in the light of the coming day. Somehow she did not think it would be difficult to find the English once she got there.

She stared into a cleft, wondering if it was safe, when Boaz finally spoke again. "Please refrain from once more undertaking that against me." His voice was very soft.

"You carried me down *a Muralha* without my permission," Paolina snapped. Instantly she felt foolish. It was hardly the same.

"That was not death. What you did to me . . . was . . ."

"Different from how you were treated in the Palace of Authority? From where I rescued you?" The whine in her voice was making *her* angry, but Paolina could not seem to stop herself.

"That was a Brass matter," he said. "You stopped me completely."

"And here you are again." Defiance, now. It was as if she had become a man. Paolina tried to break through the fog of her emotions. "I am sorry, Boaz. I thought I could do right . . . no. I knew it was not right. That I thought I could do this thing at all is wrong.

"Listen, this might be the key to your word, that you asked me to say. The word that releases you from the bond of your seal, that makes you your own machine."

"When humans seek to deceive themselves, they are stricken with nerves." He squatted down next to her. "I am Brass. You are flesh. Were I to stop you as you stopped me, you would not restart. Do not mistake what *can* be done with me for what *should* be done with me."

"Even if I find your word that way?" She was genuinely convinced that would be possible.

"Even then. Not unless I ask it of you."

Paolina nodded, then curled in a ball around her hunger and tried to find sleep. Distant thunder woke her repeatedly. She finally realized she was hearing the sounds of gunfire.

AL-WAZIR

He had not been prepared for the horrendous shriek of shattering stone when the steam borer cut into the Wall. It was the howling of every dog he'd ever heard, and it got inside his bones the same way the snap of breaking timbers did at sea.

A cloud of dust immediately obscured al-Wazir's view of the steam borer. It did nothing to dampen the obscene, chattering roar. The men cheered the beginning of the effort to drill through the Wall. All al-Wazir could see now was a looming shadow, a trundling, elongated badger with steam relief valves wailing as the cutter bored on into the stone.

It was a reduced vision of Hell, like peeking at damnation through a keyhole.

As everyone around him continued to cheer, al-Wazir turned toward the jungle. Hornsby's men had cleared a two-hundred-yard field of fire. He and Hornsby had personally whitewashed rocks every ten yards, to provide range for the small-bore artillery and firearms with which the next defense would be mounted. He'd also had the men build wooden platforms in the trees at the edge of the clearing, where scouts or snipers could be positioned. Volunteer squads of Royal Marines and army enlisted ranged the jungle beyond already. Some were on brief patrols, others on long reconnaissance.

It was as much as he knew to defend the diggings. The tactics of weapons and battle were Hornsby's problem. The strategy of what the Wall might bring was his.

Al-Wazir only wished he understood more about the brass men they'd been fighting. The Wall was vast, an entire vertical continent in its own right, but his experience had been that it was sparsely populated. Most denizens fought to defend, not to attack. These brass men had come from *somewhere* to find the English diggings.

In this moment *Bassett* would have been excellently useful. They could have cruised the Wall, safe from the brass men at least, though he did not want to contemplate the winged savages.

Those creatures had finally brought the airship down. Even now, among the swirling dust and howling of the steam borer, he remembered that day two years past as if he'd just lived through it. Smallwood had brought the vessel high, too high, many of the men had said, until the Atlantic stretched away beneath their feet dotted with clouds the size of Ireland, and the horizon had a visible curve. Up there the sky bordered on the violet, and stars could be seen during the day. The deckhands had hated it.

Al-Wazir never did understand what the captain was looking for. What they had *found* was a flight of those damnable winged savages, dark and naked angels without the light of God in their eyes. The beasts had cut at the ropes and savaged the decks and sliced open the gasbag, all the while casting sailors into the air for the long, long fall to distant ground.

He'd led the ropes division in mounting their resistance, with firearms and sword's point, and even bare hands and bloody panic.

It had not been sufficient.

The saving grace was that the bag did not burn. Had the hydrogen caught the flame, *Bassett* would have been nothing but a torch high in the evening sky, shedding embers that had once been men. The air sailor's greatest fear, fire—friend only to the devil and the Chinese. That had been beyond the winged savages' efforts, apparently, or God had been with the few of them who survived both the battle and the miles-long nightmare plunge into the advancing twilight.

The smoke and dust now was close to that memory, the shriek of the borer too much like the screams of men.

Al-Wazir climbed down off his stockade and slipped out into the cleared field of fire. He wanted to be away from the diggings awhile, think his own thoughts in the green light of a jungle evening. He was armed with pistol and machete. Anything big enough to take him on in the face of his weapons wouldn't care what he carried anyway. He was frightened of nothing this evening except memory.

The Wall was a fierce mistress—like a woman, it gave life and it took life away. Sometimes a man wanted time off with a quiet drink and a smooth pair of arms to which he owed nothing.

Al-Wazir had never really had the trick of jungles. The sea in all her moods and mysteries was as familiar as his own bunk. Lanarkshire, for all that it was a distant memory now, had involved open sky, craggy rock, and sheep.

Al-Wazir distinctly remembered sheep. With little fondness, at that.

Still, it was a country he knew. And every port was the same. Airship towers, docks, taverns, knocking shops, slaves, dogs, monkeys, boys, hot pies, and cold women. It didn't manner whether you'd shipped into Nuuk or New Haven or Nouakchott. The weather changed, the skin changed, but the money traps were always the same.

Jungles, though; every time he'd ever set foot in a jungle, it had been a different sort of confusion. Even while unloading *Wallachian Prince* at the dock in Acalayong, going ashore had been like entering a different world with each debarkation.

The ground changed constantly. Where there had been vines, there were moldering leaves, or a bubbling mud pit. Great flowers that stank like rotting meat would be open one day, quivering on the forest floor, and missing the next, as if they'd never been there at all. Stands of trees teeming with barking animals would be quiet as lichyards when he passed them again.

The world moved, surely as the sea, but trees didn't have fins and tails to swim. By God, things that lived on land ought to stay put, honest as houses, until a man learned his way around.

Yet here he was again, walking past the verges of their defense into the glossy-leaved darkness.

Someone had once told him that jungles were the lungs of the world. Al-Wazir had never been sure what that meant, some Johnnie Cleverdick thing, to be sure, but walking here in the dark he could feel it. The air stirred wet and warm as the foetor from a dying man's mouth. Leaves moved both with and against the wind. Things crashed through the branches, many of them from the sound.

The Northern Earth breathed hard here up against the Wall like a tuppeny whore with her shoulders against the alleyback of some sailor's tavern. And there was Ottweill, ramming his will into her. Just as every sailor ever born had done to the poor sisters who'd gone to work beneath their skirts once their men hadn't come home.

Something grabbed at his ankle. Al-Wazir nearly stumbled. He caught himself and reached for his machete, only to realize he'd found a vine.

"Sir?" asked a cautious voice ahead.

"Al-Wazir here," he snapped. He was embarrassed now.

"LaMont and Mitz here, sir." A shape loomed out of the deeper shadow. "Heading in, sir, with your kindness."

"Your patrol was up at dusk, yes?"

"Sir, yes sir." It was LaMont talking, he was pretty sure. Civilians, of all things. A few of them were serving under arms alongside Hornsby's troops. The men were fairies, he'd figured, volunteering to be alone together in the jungle so often. As long as they had sharp eyes and a desire to live to see another sunrise, he couldn't care less.

This wasn't the Royal Navy, after all.

In that moment of relief, al-Wazir realized that some part of him had fallen away with *Bassett*'s long, terrifying tumble down the Wall. He'd asked the Prime Minister for his rank back, and Lloyd George had given it to him, bless the man, but al-Wazir was still in the canvas trousers and cotton shirt of half the laborers in Ottweill's expedition.

There were two uniforms in his kit. He hadn't bothered. Only the Royal Marines would have cared, and them only to the extent of cocking a word, an eye, or maybe even a fist at him. Chief petty officers and Royal Marines were natural enemies, surely as wolves and eagles.

Somewhere along the way the civvies had become natural to him.

"We'll just be getting on then, sir?" LaMont asked, interrupting al-Wazir's thoughts.

"Go," he said.

" 'Ware, sir. There's half an army out here somewhere."

The other one, Mitz, piped up. "They won't be here for a few days, but you might find a scout."

"I'll be back shortly," said al-Wazir. "Tell the gate to watch for me within the hour."

The two of them slipped into the darkness, making less noise than the night itself. *Not like me,* al-Wazir thought. For him it was all crash and stumble.

He had no business being out here, any more than he did riding the steam borer into Ottweill's tunnel. His place was on or behind the stockade, talking to the patrols, watching the Wall, keeping them all alive. Not risking his life wandering in the dark.

Al-Wazir turned and headed back. If he followed the noise, he'd find his way.

The shriek of the steam borer had tapered off. Which only made sense, if the machine were even now beetling into the Wall. The drilling would take years, but not a lifetime. Even if it seemed so at the moment.

Morning brought a buzzing in al-Wazir's teeth, and word of an imminent attack. Hornsby had interviewed two more patrols who'd come in after dawn, and promptly sent a boy for al-Wazir. "Come on, sir," the lad had said. "Captain Hornsby's on about fuzzy wuzzies and marching statues. Talk some sense into him, will you please?"

He went and found the Marine captain sitting on a camp stool in a little white tent. Hornsby wasn't a big fellow, but he had the dried-beef toughness that al-Wazir associated with a certain kind of sailor. The sort of man who'd follow orders for years, never raise a hand or a word, then one day drop out of the rigging with a marlinspike in his hand and murder in his eye.

Al-Wazir would never care to face the wiry officer in a fair fight, either.

"There's a bloody great lot of those brass men forming up less than ten miles east of here," Hornsby told him without preamble. "With a goodly mass of foreigners of various colors and sizes. Like a fewking flower garden, it sounds, but they're tough."

Hornsby having just recently met the enemy in battle, al-Wazir was inclined to trust his judgment. "Do they bear guns against us?"

"Not this time, nor last. But they've some manner of spear which throws lightning. Electricks, Wall magic, it makes me no matter, but it's an evil which can be just as good as a Lee-Enfield in the proper hands. Which the brass men seem to have a bloody lot of."

Al-Wazir turned that over in his head. Had the winged savages possessed such weapons, it would have gone far worse with *Bassett*. "Will those weapons fire our stockade?"

Hornsby frowned. "They don't seem to burn hot, as such. A man which is touched by them is stunned or killed, like someone lightning struck. If there's burns, they're small."

"So the stockade should hold against their fire. Numbers?"

"Perhaps two thousand." Another frown. "Men counting in the dusk then running away will always multiply the number of the enemy. They don't want to be such an idiot in their own minds, you see."

"I know," al-Wazir told him. "I've heard many a sailor tell me of the gang of men that beset him in an alley, only to find later it was two boys and a dog out rolling drunks."

"Ah, yes, much the same phenomenon."

"So do we have some cleverness afoot? Or is it line the walls with men and fire upon them until they drop away?"

"That is where your portion of the plan is at issue, Chief." Hornsby smoothed a crude map he had been developing from the reports of his men. "This is their homeland, these tribes of brass and flesh. No matter how many we drive off, they can lose ten for our one, perhaps a hundred for our one, and return for more of the fight. You are the man charged with seeing us safe upon the Wall. Can you find a way to draw them off, for a long time? If not forever? We did not come armed to go to war, only to fight for what is England's."

"To them, we are here for war," al-Wazir said. "In five years' time the tunnel will be open, and there will be a city growing here. Airships, armies, factories, nannies with children of the quality, sprats the likes of what I once was running the streets with stolen fruit in hand. It takes no great vision to see what will follow us. Someone upon yon Wall, some sergeant or captain of the brass, has looked upon us and thought how he did not want England's foot set so firmly on his porch."

"Do you believe in the mission that we pursue?" asked Hornsby quietly.

"Aye." Or at the least, he believed in the Wall, and the sincerity of Lloyd George.

"Then by all means, man, help me pursue it. Else find a ship to carry you north and follow some other path."

"Of course, sir. I'll find a way through this mess."

He went back up to the stockade and stared west, along the Wall where it extended out to border the Atlantic Ocean. Mists swirled over the dark jungles of morning, while the steam borer still chattered in his bones.

"You are out there," he told the air, already hot though the sun had barely broken over the horizon. "I do not have the guns to stop you. But I am clever, and I have all the treasure of England behind me."

The Wall did not answer, nor did any of the brass who even now must be passing silently among the trees before him.

CHILDRESS

"Tell me more of this boy and the angel," Captain Leung asked her.

She dined with him in the ward room, the old menu restored. The political officer was restored as well, smile and pistol and all.

Childress still wondered what he understood, what he *could* understand. "His name was Hethor," she said slowly. "Heaven had granted him a token."

"A token?" Leung laughed. "A coin of Hell money?"

"No, no." She was almost annoyed. "An angel's feather. Tiny, in silver. A man took it from him."

"Your God does not treat His messengers well," observed Leung.

"That is most certainly not the case. Man mistreats the servants of God. Not the other way about."

"Indeed. So he took this feather in hand and went looking for the spring of the world?"

"The mainspring." She traced rice grains with the eating sticks. That had been growing easier with time. "He looked for the mainspring, passing through one and another of our order before leaving my notice altogether."

"We knew something was wrong," Leung admitted. "We did not know what. As I said, there have been many stories."

"I believe this one is true."

"It still does not make your God true." His voice was calm, quiet.

"No. Not one way or the other. You can deny His workmanship or not as you choose. That is your free will. Still, there is brass in the sky and the world clatters on."

After a while, he said, "Some of the Celestial Emperor's subjects even now search for their own answer."

"Really?" This was a new thread for her mind to pursue.

"South of Singapore. They have found the ancient city of Chersonesus Aurea."

"That is not a Chinese name."

"No," he admitted. "It is not. Once, in the times of antiquity, the city of Chersonesus Aurea had a Golden Bridge that crossed the Wall."

"*Over* the wall?" She tried to imagine the altitude.

"Perhaps it was more of a tunnel," he said with another quick grin. "We work to find or re-create the Golden Bridge."

Childress was horrified. *"Why?"*

Now his voice grew thick, darker, filling with anger as if a rain had come into his heart. "Because of what you British will do to China if we do not. You already box us in from both east and west. Half the Northern Earth acknowledges your suzerainty. You would fly your flags over our cities had you the slightest chance. If you find your way to the lands beyond the Wall, that will be the end of the Celestial Kingdom."

"And you would do no less to Britain?" she asked quietly. "You, who raid into our North Atlantic and drag ships down to their graves."

"For you, Mask Poinsard." His tone was cold. "It was your dealing that brought us here, not mine. The Beiyang Navy gave me orders, but we are not nearly so foolish as to make any habit of savaging British shipping in its home lanes, so very far from a safe port of ours."

She wanted to back away from that line of thought, quickly. "Still, China pushes everywhere."

"If we do not, Britain takes everything without let or hindrance."

They stared at one another awhile. The warmth they'd built between one another slipped too easily away.

She did not want to lose that, did not want to be alone and friendless on this vessel full of men who could kill her at any moment. Childress took a deep shuddering breath. "My apologies, Captain. That is a discussion best left for another time, perhaps never. Still, the Golden Bridge. Do you know what lies beyond the Wall?"

"Of course not. No more than you do."

"My point exactly. Every traveler's tale or saint's myth about the Wall is filled with magic and peril that mounts like waves on the ocean." She paused, picking her words with care. "Have you considered what your Golden Bridge might unleash?"

"It is the Celestial Emperor's Golden Bridge." Leung drummed his fingers on the little table. "And yes, it has occurred to me to wonder exactly that. Any navy officer who has sailed out of the brownwater has seen the sort of monsters which come down off the Wall. Creatures out of legend and beyond. The priests and eunuchs at court do not credit what actually swims the waves and skims the air, though they are willing to count the demons of the underworld as if they were farmers turned out for census."

Inasmuch as the captain's careful English ever did give away the landscape of his thoughts, Childress could hear disgust in his voice. "I am a Spiritualist, sir, as any white toucan is, but I am also an empiricist. Only a blind-eyed Rational Humanist would deny the presence of the divine in our lives. Neither do we concern ourselves overmuch with counting the angelic populations of pinheads. Still, do not discount that which abides in the shadowy realms of belief."

"White toucan?" he asked. "You are the *avebianco,* are you not?"

Childress recognized her mistake. "A New England regionalism. What they call the white bird in the colonies."

"I see. I did not mean to turn away from the discussion, but your choice of words engaged my ear, Mask Poinsard."

She wondered if he'd seen through her deception. There was nothing for it except to carry on. "Call it what you will, we who follow the Feathered Masks do not look to the Wall for salvation. Christ died on the Roman horofix to absolve our sins. Breaching the Wall would release all the unsaved strangeness and magic of the Southern Earth, while also calling down those creatures and races which abide there in the sky. Is the Golden Bridge worth that? Just to steal a march on England?"

Leung seemed glad to return to their sparring. "The executions of your minor prophets are not of concern in the Celestial Kingdom. As it happens, I personally share your concern about the Wall, if only from sheer common sense. There has never been any significant incursion from the Wall into our lands. I would not hope to live to see one arise from our meddling."

"Who could stop the Golden Bridge? The Emperor?"

"The Emperor's word is the word of Heaven. If his will was that every man in the Beiyang Navy fall on his sword, we would fall. However, the Emperor is not given to pronouncements on such matters, as a general rule. The Celestial Kingdom is a complex place."

"Decentralized power," Childress said. "Your admirals and governors hold their own."

"Without ever calling it so, yes." Leung sounded uncomfortable. "We balance the propriety of rank and degree with the reality of distance and the practical application of the mandate of Heaven."

"Truly, you are not so different from the English."

The next day *Five Lucky Winds* made anchorage in a little harbor tucked into an island. A larger landmass loomed in the distance, mountains wreathed in cloud and fog, but here there were craggy hills clothed in towering trees larger than anything Childress had ever seen. Eagles circled above the bay, calling down their dismay at the submarine.

The sailors rowed ashore in two little rafts to dispatch hunting parties and make a camp. Captain Leung had given leave, here where there were no pot shops or women of ease. His men were forced to nature for their pastimes.

"We place a great value on poetry," he told Childress as they stood on the stony beach near the fire a-building. "The worth of a gentleman is often measured in his words, and the calligraphy by which he sets them to the paper."

"Words about mist-covered mountains?"

"Well, yes." He nodded then stepped away to walk the perimeter of the beach camp.

The political officer approached her as soon as Leung had passed beyond earshot. Childress had scarcely been able to avoid him on the submarine. He had his pistol again, and his crooked smile.

"Hello." He showed her the white bird hand sign again.

She couldn't see a graceful way to turn away from him. Or even a graceless way, truth be told. He was armed and she had nowhere to go. "Hello."

"You go Europe."

"Not now." She wondered what this meant.

"Ah, you from Europe."

Another lie. Childress invested all the strength and chill she could find in her voice. "I am the Mask Poinsard."

He laughed. "I watch. I learn. I know." With a slight bow, he wandered away.

Childress stared after him, wondering what that could possibly mean. She turned and looked back out at the bay. The submarine lay at anchor, riding high in the water now. The metal tower rose like a little castle floating on the gray waves.

That the Chinese could build such a vessel, sail it beneath the ice, and sink ships in the Atlantic, probably should have been as frightening to her as that Golden Bridge. But war between nations was simply the way of things. Breaching the Wall, calling down its denizens on the wider horizontal world, was unnatural.

Regardless of the presence or absence of the hand of God in this world, any reasonable person should be able to see the folly of that labor.

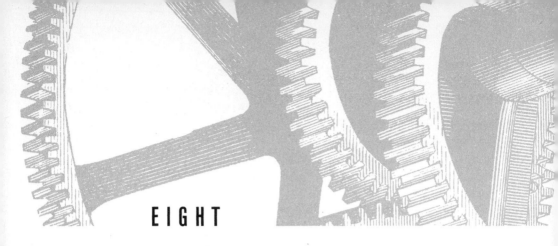

EIGHT

PAOLINA

When Paolina awoke, Boaz was gone. She felt an immediate flood of regret. She had surely used him ill. It did not matter what he had done before, she had betrayed his trust. He was her friend even if his character was essentially male.

She crawled out of her leafy hole. The cracks and booms of the night had dissipated into the undernoise of the jungle—animals, birds, creaking trees, rustling vines. It all moved with a swaying rhythm that comforted her.

The country around Praia Nova had been drier and sparser, but still she knew to avoid things that had too much color, or spines of any kind. Neither the bejeweled frogs nor the quivering flowers were suitable for her attention.

Boaz had been bright and colorful, in his Brass way.

She pushed that thought aside and walked east, along the boundary where the jungle lapped against the rising rock of the Wall. The African coast loomed close, a muddy river draining from farther along the continent's interior.

Closer by she saw signs of fighting—trees knocked down, smoldering ash piles, a mucky furrowed pathway where some portion of the sealed army had come and gone.

She could hear a distant thrumming. A coil of gray smoke or steam rose from behind an outthrust in the irregular pillars that formed the base of the Wall here.

The English?

Paolina's heart raced as she approached their camp.

She clambered over a chunk of boulder fallen from higher up. The rock was growing rougher here, entwined with green tendrils of jungle. Paolina considered heading down the slope toward the army's track, but she had to assume that was under watch by the English.

Coming around the far side of the boulder, she found Boaz. He crouched behind a smaller rock, staring east.

"I thought you had fled," she said.

"Where would I go?" He nodded without turning to look at her. "A barrier lies yonder, a little one of wood."

She positioned herself next to Boaz and peered outward. It wasn't hard to spot—a timbered palisade that extended from the face of the Wall in a bow to meet up with another fold in the stone, protecting a bay hidden from them.

That was where the coil of smoke or dust came from.

There were men along the palisade as well. She could see the heads bobbing as they moved back and forth.

"It's the camp," she said.

"Your goal. Ophir's goal as well."

"Will you come with me?"

"I cannot." He shivered again. "Authority yet commands me."

"What if I knew your word?" she asked.

"Then that would be different."

"It is not written on your forehead." Paolina touched the brass above his eyes. "But I think it is written in your soul."

"I do not posses a soul. I am a machine. A Brass."

"Remember the part of you which fell dark and silent when I used the gleam to control you? The part that awoke angry and resentful, later? That is your soul."

"What does it profit me to have a so—?" Something too fast to see spanged off his forehead, knocking him back against the larger boulder.

She turned toward the English camp as the sound of gunfire found her ears. Another bullet plucked at her dress.

Paolina threw herself to the ground, screaming, "Stop, stop!"

Two more shots hit the stone above her. Splinters of rock sprayed to sting her face and hands. Keeping low, Paolina pulled herself next to Boaz.

He lay flat on his back. His feet twitched slightly, drumming against the mossy muck that filled the little space between the two rocks. He was not dead, nor absent from his own thoughts.

She waited a few moments to see if the shooting had stopped. Then she tucked up against the rock and raised her head.

Two more bullets whined past.

Paolina dropped again. "Stop shooting! Friends! Friends!"

There was no answer from the English defenders. The possibility of *this* happening had never occurred to her. Paolina wondered if she could use the gleam. It had touched Boaz, after all. But she couldn't stop the English defenders. Like her, they were flesh. Flesh could not survive that treatment. Could she somehow disable their guns?

She pulled the gleam free, keeping her head down. Paolina simply didn't see how to set the fourth hand to match anything about the English weapons.

Paolina tugged the winding stem to the fourth setting, twirling it while letting her mind range. The other three hands were moving in their assigned courses. The fourth remained where she had stopped it on removing Boaz from the gleam's thrall.

How to end their shooting and make them take her seriously? Paolina knew she needed a credible threat. Something to make even these rough Englishmen take heed of her.

She looked up at the Wall. What if she pulled rocks down from above? She did not want to kill the camp's defenders, but she did not want them killing her either.

Whatever she did, Paolina knew that she would have to act quickly. They outnumbered her, as well as having a camp full of reinforcements. She focused on the Wall, setting the gleam against the stone.

That had a time, too, a beat that lay within its construction that was close to the time that beat at the heart of the world. It would be easy for the Wall to come apart—it seemed constructed of fracture lines, as if God had assembled it from pieces when He was making the face of the world.

She closed her eyes, listening for the beat and clicking the stem around until the quiver in her hands matched the quiver in the Wall. Sliding the stem back in, she twitched the gleam.

There was an ominous crack from above. Pebbles cascaded downward, followed by the harder echo of large rocks.

"I'll bring it down on your heads if you don't stop and talk to me!"

There was a sudden silence from beyond her sheltering boulder. She hadn't realized how much noise there had been before. The sounds of the Wall giving way had frightened even those animals too stupid to be scared off by the gunfire.

"Are you listening?" She shifted the gleam in her hand. Another cascade of rocks came sliding down.

"Oo's that up 'ere, then?" someone called back.

"A friend." Paolina slowly lifted her head.

A big Englishman in a red coat crouched beside a tree just downslope.

He had a rifle in his hand. She saw another fellow lurking in the rocks twenty or thirty yards back. There must be more, by now.

"No shooting," she said softly. "Talk first."

"Stop it with the Wall, then, missy." The big man kept his rifle close but not aimed directly at her.

"Stopped." She wondered what to say next. "All of you, step out where I can see you."

He grinned. "Begging your pardon, but why should we be doing that?"

"So I won't bring down a piece of the Wall upon your heads. You step out, I'll step out, two of you come for my injured man here. Then we all go talk to the wizards in your camp."

"Wizards, missy?" Another man she hadn't spotted stood up from a shadowed hollow. "You're not from home, are you?"

There were five in all. A couple continued to cast nervous glances up at the Wall. The rest studied her, grinning.

Paolina felt less and less sure of herself. "I need to go to your masters, then, if they are not wizards." Davies had not told her how big and strange these men were. She'd thought them all sweet-faced cherubs as *Bassett*'s boy had been.

These were much more like the *fidalgos* of Praia Nova, oh-so-certain of themselves, no matter their depth of ignorance.

Something scraped behind her. All their eyes shifted, rifles swinging up. "Do not shoot him," she snapped. "Or I will bring it down. He is with me."

" 'E's one of them brassy boldfaces."

"Yes. And he's with me. We bring news of the army you face."

"Oh," said the leader in his red coat. "You're a scout wanting to turn coat."

They all relaxed a bit at that.

"I just want to come home to England," she lied.

Red coat laughed. "We ain't got the Queen stashed away or nothing, but we've brought a bit of England to you."

"That will have to be a beginning, won't it?" She glanced over her shoulder briefly. "This is Boaz. He is also a friend of England."

Boaz said nothing, simply making a shaky bow. She would have to fix him if she could.

"Let's go, then," red coat said. "You other'n, get on your business. We'll take her in."

"First real woman we seen in two months," one of the others snapped. Protesting?

Something was wrong. She heard it in their voices, saw it in their stance. These men weren't drunk, but they might as well have been. They were grinning way too much. Now that they knew she was only a woman, they weren't taking her seriously. Paolina twitched the gleam again, slashing it across the stone in front of her.

A great hunk of Wall rumbled free and fell in a shower of gravel and rock, smashing down on two of the Englishmen. One was killed instantly, crushed in a spray of blood. The other screamed as his groin was pinned beneath a boulder larger than she was.

"You will take me to your camp." She hated the way her voice broke. "Or I'll bring the rest of it down."

"Ho, ho, ho, little chit." Red coat laid his weapon down and held up his hands palm-out, facing her down. He took a step toward her. "You needs to lay off that shite. You kilt Augie."

"You were ready to rush me down. I'll lay it off if you take me in safely. No more of that 'real woman' folderol."

He stopped. "All right." Turning, he shouted to the others. "Put down the weapons, boyos, and shift yon rocks off Bells. We'll need to be carrying him in."

Boaz stepped around Paolina's boulder. "I will ward her." His voice was hollow and loud. "If you wish retribution for the death of your fellow, seek redress from your commanders."

Shortly they were marching in file through the jungle. Red coat's two carried the wounded man in the lead. Boaz followed, then Paolina, then red coat himself. They'd left someone's cloak over Augie's crushed body.

"I'm call't Perks." Red coat was close enough for Paolina to feel the warmth of his body. "A man can't be too careful out here. I hopes you don't mind."

"Not at all," she said pleasantly, gripping the gleam tight and wondering if she could set it to his time. "I shan't apologize for Augie and Bells. I don't have much brief for men who threaten me."

"It weren't noth—," he began, then stopped.

"There's hope for you yet, Perks," she said grudgingly.

"Me ma'am says the same every time she sees me."

There was something plaintive in his voice that brought a swell of pity. She was growing too soft.

Twenty minutes later they filed out into the cleared land before the English stockade. A large red, blue, and white flag twitched over the wooden wall. Gray dust hung in a pall. A chattering thump echoed across the clearing.

Several men on the wall spotted them and quickly rushed to weapon stations. Perks waved his rifle in the air, then stuck his fingers in his mouth to whistle.

The men on the stockade didn't abandon their watch.

Paolina followed Boaz across the open field of churned mud and tree stumps. There were whitewashed rocks every few yards, amid winding paths worn by the passage of patrols. Otherwise the place could have been taken for a wet, mucky desert.

It was quick enough, though. They stood beneath the gates.

"Wotcher got, Perks?" shouted a man from above. He was silhouetted in the morning light.

"Girlie who wants to go to England, traveling with Johnnie Brass."

"Brass boy gave yer some trouble, eh?"

"Nar." Perks laughed, bitter and cold. "She did for Augie and Bells. I figger on letting Hornsby and red Arab handle 'er."

"You marching under their orders?"

"Nar."

The silhouette vanished. Others watched. She saw the dull gleam of guns up there. One man ostentatiously stropped a bayonet.

When the gate creaked open, half a dozen men sprinted out and dropped to their knees to cover her group with rifles. More appeared upon the wall. A small man in a woolen uniform followed the covering party out. He had a pistol at his belt, which remained holstered as he studied her.

"Perks," he finally said, without taking his eyes off Paolina.

"Sir?" Perks' voice lost a great deal of its insouciance.

"Where did you capture the prisoners?"

"Erm . . . guests, sir. Guests they is. We found 'em up along the ridge a mile east."

"I see." He frowned. "Take your man in to hospital."

"She did for Augie," said one of the others sullenly.

The officer—she realized that was what he had to be—sighed. "I am very sorry to hear that. Every man among us is irreplaceable." Still staring at Paolina, he waved them away. "Now off with you lot."

In a moment she and Boaz stood alone with the officer.

"I am Captain Hornsby." One hand strayed to his gun butt. Paolina wondered if he realized he was doing that. Hornsby continued, "Her Imperial Majesty's Royal Marines. Commanding the uniformed forces here, I am afraid."

"I am Paolina Barthes, late of Praia Nova," she responded. "Traveling with Boaz, a Brass of independent loyalties."

"Meaning he is not set to kill me?"

"No," said Boaz, standing just behind her shoulder. "I am not set to kill you."

"Your men, however, were quite set to kill us," Paolina added.

Hornsby cleared his throat. "Ah, well, yes. About that. How *did* you dispatch poor Augustine and wound Bells?"

"By a secret means of my control," she said tartly. "Suffice to say I dropped a rock on him."

"For a woman and a Brass to walk in with Perks and these men requires extraordinary circumstances, given our current intercourse with very nearly all the locals."

She snorted. "I *tried* to approach in the manner of a civilized person. They were too intent on not having seen a woman in some months."

"Bells and Augustine I would not have trusted to leave a pound of fresh liver unmolested. Even so, I should have you confined for trial and execution as an enemy combatant."

Paolina stiffened, but he raised a hand.

"However, very few young women have walked off the Wall to address us in the Queen's English. Not a one thus far, to be precise. And your . . . ah . . . Boaz is the first brass man we have seen who has not essayed to kill us on sight. I am therefore prepared to take civilized self-defense into consideration in this matter and set the death of Augustine aside for future consideration. Bells has only himself to blame for being wounded by an unarmed woman. He will receive no consideration from his fellows or from me."

"I shall not thank you, sir," she said coldly, "but your conclusions are reasonable enough."

"That is excellent." Hornsby took his hand off his gun butt and rubbed his chin. "So, now that we have set that issue to one side, what in the name of all the monkey gods of the Congo are you doing here, and what is it you wish of me?"

"Of you? Nothing, sir. Of England, I wish much."

"Of England . . . Not to be indelicate, madam, but we are quite some distance from England, or truly from much that *is* English. What is it that you imagine England can do for you?"

Paolina took a deep breath. This was her first, and perhaps greatest, chance to make someone in authority see what she could bring to England, and England could bring to her. All the time she'd spent considering this, back in Praia Nova, walking along the trail, dreaming, thinking, planning, it came down to now.

She was standing inside her moment.

"England has the greatest wizards in the world," she told him. "The heirs of Newton. Those who sail *Bassett* through the air. Those who understand the secrets that beat at the heart of the world. Please, sir, I would find my way to England and into their company, that I might learn what your wizards can teach me."

Hornsby's face twitched. She thought at first it was anger that moved him, but when he began to shake and flush, Paolina realized he was laughing at her. He held the outburst of voice within, but finally he took a great gasp. "Girl," he said, still shuddering, "of what do you think the world is made?"

"I think the world is made of men!" Her vision seemed to be reddening. She yanked the gleam out of her pocket. "I think men are imperfect!" Her voice kept rising as she began twisting the stem. "I think—"

Boaz grabbed her arm, yanking hard enough to interrupt her thoughts and words. "Forgive us, Captain. The girl is overwrought at the molestation she received in the hands of your men. I should believe she will be better off with a place to rest and some food and water. Humans require provisioning."

Paolina fought to keep her temper behind her teeth. Boaz was right. She had been on the verge of showing herself either a fool or too dangerous to tolerate. Hornsby had his holster open now, his hand openly on his weapon, but he stared at Boaz. "You speak English, too?"

"It is the *lingua Anglica* of the Wall."

"He is educated," Paolina added, in control of her temper now.

The captain reached a point of decision. She could see it on his face. "I will bring you within our camp," he told them. "You will be kept under guard for your own protection until my counterpart who handles affairs of the Wall can interview you. After that you will either be released or we will discuss further possible course of action. In either case you will be safe from further molestation."

"On your word as an English officer?"

"On my word."

She was insulted and offended, but at the same time, she was gaining what she'd wished—access to the English camp. "Thank you. I have but one question, sir."

"Yes?" He buttoned the flap on his holster.

"Is your counterpart a wizard?"

Hornsby shook his head. "Come within. I will let him explain matters to you. I will say this: He served on the selfsame ship *Bassett* you mentioned. If anyone knows wizards, it would be the chief."

She tried to hide her smile of triumph, but Paolina was sure that the officer marked it as he whistled for the gates to reopen, waiting to lead her into his camp.

They sat inside a steaming hot tent. It was tall, made of pale canvas. There were no cots or bunks. Rather, the interior furnishings consisted of a folding table and six chairs. There were several frames standing in front of cloth walls, each holding cork boards. She was not certain what they were for.

"Here we are." Paolina's nervousness had overcome her excitement. What little patience she'd had was blown out like a candle flame.

"I do not discern what you hope to accomplish next," Boaz told her. "And even less do I see what is in store for me. I am traitor to Authority. I am bound and beholden to you. Will you take ship to England and carry me with you as servant, slave, and bodyguard?"

"You *have* been thinking." She kept her voice soft. "No, my friend, you are not bound to me. Not at all."

"You robbed the light from my eyes, then vouchsafed it to me once more."

"That was wrong of me." Paolina summoned her sense of herself. She had to set this right. "I plead foolishness and ignorance both. I would speak to you your word, the one that stands outside your thoughts, and release you to yourself."

"You cannot speak my word." He was sullen now, sullen as that graceful mechanical voice ever could become. "You do not hold my word, no more than I do."

With a flash of insight, she knew the answer that had nagged at the edge of her thoughts since he'd first explained the problem to her. "No, but I can tell you what your word is."

"Why? Is it written on my forehead?"

"No, my friend." Paolina shook her head and smiled. "It is written *within* your head, in those crystals and valves which make up your thoughts. Consider this: Brass are gifted. You have strength, wit, intelligence, perspicacity, astute judgment. Everything a competent and proper being might want."

"I will not thank you for flattery," Boaz said tightly.

He is so *human,* she thought. "Not flattery. Description. You are all of those things and more. But there is one thing every Brass lacks, from the very first Brass onward through time."

"We lack many things. Souls. Individuality. Free will."

Paolina smiled. "Those things are all part of this. You lack names. Without a name, there is no 'I,' no way for the light behind the eyes to speak to itself without equivocation or confusion."

"Name?" He was incredulous, almost angry. "You think I but lack for a name."

"You are *Brass*. That is who you are in your deepest thoughts. I have named you Boaz to set you apart, and you answer readily enough, but it is not within you yet."

"I am Brass," he said slowly. "It is who I was made to be, it is who I am."

"But when you belong to yourself, you can be whoever you will."

The brass man shook his head, as if trying to force the idea to slide away. "So if you tell me I am Boaz, you are setting me free? It cannot be that simple."

"It is not. The matter isn't whether *I* tell you that you are Boaz; the matter is whether *you* tell you that you are Boaz. Name yourself."

"How?" The anguish was back in his tone.

"Chrism," said a burred, deep voice.

They both turned in surprise to see a large man—almost a giant, topped by red hair shot through with gray—standing at the tent flap.

He grinned. "You want to give a man a name, you give him a chrism. Baptize, like the water of the Lord."

"I . . ." Paolina wasn't sure what to say.

"Never mind that. Yon metal man wants a chrism, he'll be having one." The big man leaned backwards to call to someone outside. "Trucci! Get me a gill of the number two machine oil, from stores. And a decent bowl. Bring it chop-chop!"

He stepped in and dropped the flap behind him. "Chief Petty Officer Threadgill Angus al-Wazir of Her Imperial Majesty's Royal Navy, detached here to see for the safety of the diggings in light of whatever the Wall throws at us." He clapped his hands together, as if he were a great child. "And you would be my visitors, Paolina Barthes and her talking brass man, come to tell me in the Queen's plain English what is happening high above us and why they march against us in their ragtag rows, carrying arms to a fight we never meant to pick."

At last, a wizard, Paolina thought. No man who carried himself so could be any less than a master of his own surrounds and the world at large. "Chief al-Wazir," she said. "I am most pleased to meet you. One of *Bassett*'s wizards, *and* England's ambassador to *a Muralha*. It is as if you have been sent to meet my requirements."

He looked amused. "Hornsby said you was a bit cracked. I don't think he did you justice, lassie, but still it's good to meet you. You can't be all vapors and womanish words, not if you did for two of Perks' men." His smile narrowed. "Don't get me wrong. I've half a dozen outside with rifles and bayonets, should something go terribly awry here between us. I don't reckon on that."

"I am not half the danger you count me," Paolina said.

"Oh yes, you are," al-Wazir and Boaz replied in the same moment.

The two of them locked gazes. The big Scotsman began to laugh, at first a rumbling chuckle, then with a great uproar that brought tears to his bright blue eyes.

A few minutes later they shared a solemn silence that she felt certain was uncharacteristic for al-Wazir. He'd insisted that Boaz kneel—"Only proper way for a man to present hisself before God."—and now stood before the Brass with a little clay bowl of machine oil.

"T'ain't that you rightly need a true christening," al-Wazir rumbled. " 'Sides which, we'd need a wee gown for you, and a parson you could pee on the arm of." He dabbed a finger in the bowl, then traced oil across Boaz' forehead. "Still, in the name of God and man and your own Brass self, take you now this name of—" He stopped and glanced at Paolina.

"Boaz," she said.

"Boaz. To be your own till God should call you home, or you lay yourself down for the long sleep." He wiped his fingers clean on Boaz' shoulder. "There lad, you've been given a proper name."

"Thank you, sir."

Paolina didn't know whether to giggle or to cry.

AL-WAZIR

"It's like this, lassie," al-Wazir said. He found himself spreading his hands, as if there were some part or piece to explain to this little chit of a girl. That wasn't his purpose, and so with a sigh he let his fists fall to his thighs. "I don't know who's been filling your head with what, but neither *Bassett* nor England is as you seem to think."

"Davies," she said. "Clarence Davies, the doctor's boy, told me all."

"Davies?" Al-Wazir had to think that through. "Small lad, pretty sort of face? Never too sure of himself, bit of a bully? He went over the rail, oh, let me see . . . two months before the ship was lost." Memory stirred. "He did have a parachute, as I recall. Where did you say you was from?"

"Praia Nova." She smiled sweetly. "A little port, hundreds of miles west of here, far beyond the western extents of the Solomnic Kingdom of Ophir."

"Long way from the Bight of Benin, then." Al-Wazir tugged at his beard, suddenly conscious that he was a great unwashed bear next to this woman-child. She seemed barely old enough for her skirts, though she carried herself with poise. "Why is it you think a wizard might help you, assuming I would have had one to hand?"

"'Wizard' might not be the right word for what I intend," she said slowly. "Someone learned in the movements and timings which drive the world. Someone who has discerned the hidden cycles behind God's handiwork. Someone who can show me where to look next." She stopped a moment; then her next words came in a rush—a rehearsed plea, if he'd ever heard one from an air sailor brought up on charges. "I have calculated the motions of the planets and the tides. I have found the diameter of the earth, and I believe I know her weight. I can find the timing that counts the heartbeat of Creation. I just don't know what it all *means*, or how to make more of it."

"Ah, missy. Most people never even find the sense in the world's turning, let alone more. You talk like a navigator. Who taught you these things, then? What teacher or wizard was in Praia Nova to open your eyes to that view of the world? Was it perchance a man named Simeon Malgus, lost from *Bassett* as well? Perhaps you are protecting him."

"No one." Paolina glanced at her metal man as if for support. He was strangely beautiful, and all too real looking, like a man who'd been dipped in gold. "No one. I figured it out for myself, even when they told me to stop."

That gave al-Wazir pause. He'd beaten and cajoled and led enough boys to their manhood on decks asea and aloft to have a sense when a young thing was spinning tales. This girl was not. Or at the least, she believed her words, whether they held any truth outside of her own experience.

But what she said made no sense at all. It was the work of years to teach a navigator what he must know, or a cartographer or horomancer or any of the other disciplines that sat in quiet rooms to give the orders that moved men and ships alike. A certain talent or inborn skill was certainly required, but so was a great pass of learning. Al-Wazir himself could read a manifest or a crew list well enough, and he knew how to check a paymaster's book or a quartermaster's receipts, but he'd never been one for the long, deep abstractions that made men like Malgus or Lloyd George.

He'd never heard of a man who raised himself from a pup to the understanding of the world. He'd *certainly* never known of a woman to do any such thing.

"What is the noise that comes at midnight, girl?" he asked gently. This was something that boy Hethor used to be on about.

"The earth touching her track as she turns to go about the sun," Paolina replied promptly.

"And how wide is that track?"

"I believe it to be twenty miles."

That was more than al-Wazir knew, truth be told, but the prompt confidence in her answers would have pleased an officer. Not to mention her direct honesty.

"How do you know that, girl?"

"Over time I measured the angle of the track in the sky at all hours of the day. I then compared my observations, calculating from the differences in size and apparent brightness."

"If you're lying," he said after a moment, "you couldn't prove it by me. Dr. Ottweill might know better, but I don't wish to disturb him with your presence. You're a creature of the Wall, Miss Barthes. Your fate is my decision. As it happens, I don't expect that the good doctor professor will be able to see the sense that lurks in a woman's head, no matter how right she might actually be."

"What does that mean?" she asked suspiciously.

"It means I can't prove you're not another Newton, girlie. It means I don't know what to do with you here. It means that I think you should go to England and talk to a man I know there, to steer you where you might need to be. Most of all, it means that I think your cleverness is probably wasted here upon the Wall."

"The Wall is no wasteland," said the brass man.

Boaz, al-Wazir recalled. "No. It's no wasteland at all. But it *is* a wildland. This girl was born to be a creature of civilization. I seen your lot down here, throwing lightning with spears and burning the life out of honest men. How's your civilization faring, Johnnie Brass?"

"The Solomnic Kingdom of Ophir is an ancient and honorab—," he began, but al-Wazir put up his hand.

"Stop right there, friend Boaz. Have you come to kill me and mine?"

"No. I follow her."

"You're from Ophir. Them as has been attacking us these past months."

"I am a Brass of Ophir."

"Then why are you here?"

"I follow *her*." Boaz' anger and passion seemed to flee him as quick as they had come upon him.

"And would you follow her to England?"

Boaz and Paolina exchanged a long look. Al-Wazir tugged his collar and cursed the heat with a silent inner voice. The silence between them finally broke off.

"He will not go," said Paolina. "We are not so close as you might think."

"I am more of the Wall than she," Boaz added. "I do not concern myself with the doings of some flatwater kingdom. No matter how many ships your queen may have."

"Then will you give me your parole?" al-Wazir asked Boaz. "To remain among us without working against our efforts and our safety, and to raise no hand against England or English forces."

"Am I free to walk away?"

"Not without my permission. If you will not place yourself under my oversight, I cannot allow you to stay here."

Boaz stiffened. Then: "I accept your terms. For her sake only."

"What about me?" Paolina asked. "Am I under parole as well?"

"My girl, I think a truly prudent man would most likely place you in irons." He smiled. Oh, to have had such a girl as a daughter. "Thankfully I am not a truly prudent man. Besides which, if you are half the woman you claim, irons will be of little use in tempering you. You may consider yourself under parole so long as you are willing to give your word on the same terms as friend Boaz here. As you wish to go to England and meet with the great minds of the age, I am not so concerned about your behavior."

"You will send me to England? When?"

"When I can, madam." He felt the urge to bow, but took himself in hand. "I have no scheduled voyages right now, but there will surely be ships or airships calling soon enough. I can arrange a berth, believe me."

Boaz nodded. "And when Paolina departs, what becomes of me?"

"You, Johnnie Brass, will then either walk free into the forests around us, or stay here to help me plot an end to these ridiculous attacks. *Until* she leaves, you are the one best suited to watch over her and secure her safety, day and night. I do not control all of the men in this camp. If you are loyal to her, this is your test."

Boaz nodded. "Thank you, Chief Petty Officer."

Al-Wazir looked Paolina over again. She nodded, but there was nothing demure in the challenge of that direct gaze.

He wondered what Kitchens and Lloyd George would make of this strange girl who'd come off the Wall. It seemed possible she might indeed be a modern-day Newton. He couldn't say what that might mean for England and the world, but he knew it would be worse if she found the Chinese first, or simply made her own way into adulthood with no guiding hand at all.

Al-Wazir sought out Ottweill. The doctor would be at the digging face, of course. Though there had not been a plan to provide quarters hard by the tunnel, al-Wazir had asked a team of men to build Ottweill a little teakwood cabin there. Ready access to the work seemed to stem some of the doctor's tantrums, and kept him close to his beloved machines.

They'd been cutting for eighteen days, and bored almost four hundred yards within the rock. So far they'd found no hard layers that required a change of cutting surface, or a withdraw for traditional blasting. Ottweill had announced the number one borer would back out on the twentieth day and be replaced with the number two. He wished to analyze any metal stress and mechanical failure that might be occurring.

Not that any such thing was expected, of course.

There was a work gang just outside the tunnel. They loaded a short string of flat cars with the additional rail required for operations within. The progress of the borer was slow enough that the crews had been able to practice their various crafts and drills. If the cutting sped up or things went wrong, they would be fully prepared.

Al-Wazir approved.

He tapped Mercks, the stoop-shouldered railroad man he'd first met back in Kent. "Is himself down the hole?" al-Wazir shouted. The vibrating racket from within the Wall was enough to make a man's ears ache if he stood near the tunnel. Al-Wazir wondered how the borer's driving crew withstood it. Even if Ottweill had not meant to hire the deaf, he would soon have them in his employ.

Mercks nodded. "Aye, and shouting about the cutting heads or summat."

Ottweill was almost always shouting about something.

Al-Wazir knew better than to ask a railroad man about the state of the digging. Each crew was vitally jealous of its function, and practiced an aggressive indifference to the work of others.

"You going down the hole soon?"

Another nod. "Aye."

"If the good doctor is in a listening mood, tell him I'm wanting him."

Al-Wazir retired to the little porch of Ottweill's cabin. There were several corkboards propped there, covered with notes and diagrams and lovely shaded drawings of one of the steam borers. They were not Ottweill's hand. Some artistic genius lived among the crews. He'd seen sailors turn out work that could have hung in the National Gallery, save they'd never had the schooling nor the patronage. Few ever knew their worth as artisans, carving and drawing between swarming the lines and brawling over rented jennies in the ports they visited.

Likewise here. Whatever quiet talent had done that would end soon enough with some accident or another.

The rest of the boards told the story of Ottweill's work. Much of it was beyond al-Wazir—numbers and charts showing force and stress and how the machines might work or break, the death of iron and steel and steam. He wondered if the Barthes girl could have made more of it.

It was al-Wazir's firmest ambition not to have her and Ottweill meet. He needed to inform the doctor he had prisoners from the Wall, on parole, but he would present them as turncoats now aiding him in the defense of the camp. He simply didn't want to encounter Ottweill's reaction to a girl of such gifts.

The doctor would at best ignore her. Worse, he might sabotage her, or worst of all, draw her into his own work.

If she was what she seemed to be, Paolina Barthes deserved far more than the digging of holes. He settled in to wait for the doctor, thinking over ways to mask the truth without actually committing insubordination in the process.

Luckily, the better part of a lifetime's service in the Royal Navy had given him extensive practice at such creative reporting.

Ottweill finally emerged from the tunnel so coated with dust that he seemed to be a man of sand and stone, save for the pale circles where his goggles had sheltered his eyes. "You on the porch are being, I see," he said. "No work needing attention there is?"

"Aye, work and more. But sometimes there's 'at which requires even your attention, sir. A patrol brought in two locals off the Wall. Hornsby's seen to 'em and so have I, but I figured you ought to have the saying of it, too."

Ottweill grabbed a rag from a bucket by the porch step and wiped his face. "Of what the saying?"

"I gave 'em a pardon on my parole, in return for they tell us that which we need to be knowing about the Wall, and especially these brass men what march against us."

"You know best, sure I am." Then, in German, *"Unwissender Affe."*

"Indeed, sir." Al-Wazir was just as glad he didn't speak Ottweill's native tongue. Otherwise he was fairly certain he would be forced to take offense. "I'll be seeing to it, then. How goes the tunnel?"

"Deeper, ever deeper." Ottweill bowed from the waist. "And now going I must be."

"Going indeed." Al-Wazir nodded and headed back toward the north end of the camp, where the rows of tents and shacks were that housed everyone but Ottweill.

All he needed now was a ship to get that girl out of here.

CHILDRESS

That night around the fire they roasted a boar some of the men had shot in the woods. Childress didn't know whether pigs were indigenous to the islands of the North Pacific, or if the Chinese had previously introduced them by way of providing resupply.

It did not matter. The meat smelled good.

Other sailors had gathered wild onions and half a dozen more varieties of shoots and herbs. These were chopped fine, along with carrots and peppers from the ship's stores. She'd not seen the galley aboard *Five Lucky Winds*, so the opportunity to watch the cooking process was fascinating.

No English cook would cut her vegetables so fine. And Childress had never seen a pan like the big ones they brought over from the submarine— shallow shields without any flat base, that quivered on the rocks stacked within the fire. Woks.

But two little men, each wizened and folded as tightly as any monkey, were in complete command of their craft. They approached it with a mixture of parsimony and art that she found delightful. Oil was husbanded as shredded pork was mixed in. Some dark sauce sprinkled on as needed, and eventually the vegetables added to the mixture. Childress resolved that if she were able to spend time among the Chinese under ordinary circumstances, she would learn to cook as they did.

The result tasted divine. Their cooking aboard ship was excellent, miles above anything the Royal Navy could ever serve if rumor was to be believed. She would believe this food rivaled the best a duke's yacht might offer. Here outdoors, served steaming hot over rice warmed in a clay pot by the fire, it surpassed any meal she'd eaten in her life.

Even with the leaping glare of the flames, the sky was vivid. Earth's track rose high and bright. The moon's crossed over it. Luna herself was approaching full, a gravid silvered presence along her gleaming track. Her silvered light pressed down upon the waters of the bay without masking the shine of the stars. Stepping away from the fire a moment with a bowl of hot, steaming pork in her hands, Childress traced Venus' orbital track rising in the east. The stars were so bright, she thought she could make out the guttering of their individual lamps. If she knew where to look, she might find the tracks of Mars and maybe even Jupiter.

Was this how God saw the universe? Childress imagined Him looking at His Creation, His view from everywhere at once. What would it be like, having eyes in every ray of light? To even encompass such magnitude was beyond her understanding.

It was like falling into the sky, slipping beneath a pool of water she'd never noticed hanging over her head. Childress had never supposed God listened to her personally, but she knew He listened to the world. How else could things be arrayed, in His Creation?

She began to pray.

"Our Father, who art in Heaven
"Craftsman be thy name
"Thy Kingdom come
"Thy plan be done
"On Earth as it is in Heaven
"Forgive us this day our errors
"As we forgive those who err against us
"Lead us not into imperfection
"And deliver us from chaos
"For thine is the power, and the precision
"For ever and ever, amen."

When her voice trailed off, she stared at the heavens and wondered what was on the other side of the velvet wall of night. Was that where the dreaming mind of God lay?

"It is your religion," said Leung, startling her.

Childress turned, letting a flash of surprised anger roll away from her. "It is not my religion. It is the world."

"No, it is your *view* of the world." He stared up, setting his arm on hers. "In China, we consider the way each person is connected to another to be the heart of who they are. So a son is a son to his father, and a soldier follows his general. Everything in the world is made to fit with everything else. His Celestial Majesty is at the center and head of the order of the world, as the sun is at the center and head of the universe.

"Look." Leung pointed at the thread of Venus. "Everything in the sky relates to everything else. There is a position and an order to the world. In that, we see what is and what must be. A view of the world, much as you have your view."

"Who made your world?" she asked softly.

"It exists. That is enough. People tell stories, but the world has no beginning and no end, any more than the track of its circle around the sun does."

"But the universe is a made thing." She hated the way her voice trembled with her insistence. "The gears are cut. You can see them through the simplest glass, and sometimes when the light is just exactly right."

"So?" Childress could feel Leung's shrug. *Such an English thing for him to do.* He continued: "We are made, as well. Every tree and rock and waterfall is made. It is not so hard to see the world as a garden. You Europeans are so concerned with first causes. It is the order of things which matters, not their origin nor direction."

"Still, we live in the same world." Holding her breath, she stepped closer into his arm.

Leung did not pull away.

When he spoke again, his breath puffed in the chilly air as if he, too, had been holding it in. "You are not the Mask Poinsard, are you?"

A cold stab of fear shivered her heart. Childress almost pulled away from him. She knew she stiffened, and she felt him stiffen in response. There was no point in lying after her body had betrayed the truth.

"No," she said. "Poinsard died with *Mute Swan,* so far as I know."

"Unfortunate."

She wondered what he meant by that, but Leung did not elaborate. After a while, she asked the next question. "What will become of me?"

"That is up to you." Leung hugged her even closer. "I can sail to Tainan with the Mask Poinsard aboard. I do not believe the Beiyang Navy would know any difference. There are some in Nanking who would, eventually, but you could play that face for some time."

"My name is my passport to life and death, in this ocean, far from the protection of my country."

"Yes. We have a school of thought which calls for the rectification of names. That a thing is not in its proper place until it is properly called." He paused, perhaps for a smile. Childress was afraid to look at Leung's face. "In the languages of China, a sound may carry different meanings. Tiger, or bravery, or lake, all in one sound and the tone of its speaking. This is a more careful question than it would be in your language, I think. Still, here is a chance to choose your name. Be who you will. The Mask Poinsard. Or some other woman of valor and thoughtful demeanor and careful wit."

Childress puzzled through his words, trying to unravel both the criticism and the compliment she thought she found there.

"I think he knows," she finally said. "Your political officer."

"Choi?"

She laughed. "You have more than one?"

"No, no." Leung pulled away, distracted. "He speaks English?"

"A little. And he knows something of the *avebianco.* I think he knows who I am. Or more to the point, who I am not."

"I see." Silence awhile, then: "His discretion will be difficult to assure."

Childress chose her next words with care. "Another man would arrange an accident."

"I am not another man. Besides," he admitted, "there would be consequences. He is the only sailor on the ship not under my direct command."

"Practical as well, I see."

"Indeed." Leung hugged her again. "So what would another woman arrange?"

"The Mask Poinsard would cut his throat," Childress said. "Or at least have someone do it for her. Li— Another woman . . ." She cleared her throat. "Another woman would find a way to convince him otherwise."

"By cutting throats to demonstrate her resolve?"

It took Childress a moment to realize that Leung was gently mocking her. "Perhaps." She noticed then that her pork had grown cold. "I think I need the fire."

"All men need the light," he told her. "If only to set borders on the darkness."

Five Lucky Winds sailed at first light. Childress understood they were going to cruise the surface while the weather held, for maintenance and cleaning. She seemed to have more freedom of movement, extending to being abovedeck herself. Shy sailors had shown her various rooms one at a time—bunks in one, a dispensary lined with jars of herbs and snakes, storerooms, big sweating tubes of obscure purpose, a kitchen not much larger than the dispensary, where the two old cooks fit together like monkeys in a puzzle.

Only the bridge and engines remained off-limits.

That was fine with her. She was no spy, trained to see the secrets by the arrangement of dials or the lights of a map table.

Childress spent some time above decks, but if there was any swell at all to the sea, she was distinctly uncomfortable. The submarine was not designed for the convenience of passengers in any case. Still, she craved the sunshine. Every time she saw Leung, there was inquiry in his eyes.

Who was she—the Mask Poinsard, or a woman of valor?

That was the sort of question any good person should ask of herself. The metaphor was usually not quite so literal, however.

When she saw Choi, her thoughts ran a different direction. It was neither in Childress' nature nor within the reach of her arms to cut a

man's throat, but she kept wondering what the political officer would say
to his secret masters when they stepped off the boat in dock at Tainan.

Could she kill a man to save herself?

That she could even ask that question frightened Childress.

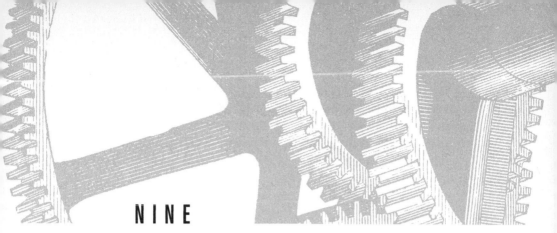

NINE

PAOLINA

After two days, Paolina was bored. She wasn't permitted to wander the camp unescorted, and not at all near the diggings or upon the stockade. The same restrictions applied to Boaz, but he seemed content to sit quietly in their quarters. Of course, she reminded herself, he had stood for years on the trail. Time seemed to flow differently for the Brass.

The men who worked here avoided her. In one sense, this was fine. She had her fill of men in Praia Nova, and didn't have cause to think the workers in al-Wazir's camp would be any more gentle toward women than the *fidalgos* had been. At the same time, they would be *interesting* to talk to.

Wizards or no, these Englishmen tended al-Wazir's great machine clawing ever further into the Wall like some parasite intent on gnawing out the heart of a dog. In between that, they worked in little shops and forges, cared for smaller machines that still stood large as her mother's house while still puffing and screeching, and got drunk. If she had been a boy, Paolina might have thought that a perfect life.

As it was, she wished very much to simply speak to someone. Only al-Wazir and Hornsby would talk to her. She'd tried to explain to the big Englishman about the cars inside the Wall, and what their tunnel would eventually encounter as it bored through, but he'd been too busy to pay proper attention.

No one else came near the tent. She suspected the men of the camp had been threatened with shooting or worse if they bothered her. So she begged for books and was given a set of *Punch* magazines from volumes 117 and 118, dated in the autumn of 1901 and spring of 1902. They apparently were intended to be humorous. The articles provided a window into the life of England even more recent and expansive than that which Dickens had thrown open for her.

She also spent time listening to the chatter of the digging machine, timing how long it ran and paused, and working to deduce the depth of the tunnel from the minutes it took men to walk in and out. There was so much to measure here.

Paolina wondered what al-Wazir would do when his machine broke through to the whirling discs of brass that were set within *a Muralha* as counterweights to balance the spin of the world. Surely he had a plan. An Englishman always did. Dickens and Davies had taught her that. Al-Wazir had done nothing to disabuse her of the notion.

Around noon on her third day, partway through a particularly tendentious January issue, she heard a great shouting outside.

"Do not go without," Boaz said. "You do not understand their ways."

"It is *something*," Paolina argued, though she knew he was right.

"I hold no command over you, but our purpose here was made clear to me."

She settled back with a flash of anger, hating her own bad grace, to read more about some individual named Floyd Gorges, who was supposedly a Minister from Carnivaltown. Paolina hadn't quite worked out how the clerical aspect fit in with the rest of it, but she presumed she'd learn.

More shouting outside tugged at her ear. She ignored it. Likewise she ignored steam whistling and the rattle of gunfire. It was not enough to have been an attack. But when the droning echoed from above, she tossed away the magazine from which she'd been reading the same sentence over and over and over and stormed out.

A great ship of the air was beating down over the camp.

Bassett, she thought, then remembered that al-Wazir had told her the ship was lost. One of its sisters, surely, with the long, bloated bag suspending a boatlike hull beneath. Engines on each side spun propellers, while furled sails hung on spars tucked close in. The bag was covered with netting, with a great version of the British flag was worked into that.

England had come for her!

She raced back inside to tell Boaz.

Paolina spent the rest of the day under guard. The man outside her tent with a gun wouldn't say anything, except to order her back inside. Boaz sat quietly, lost in so thoughtful a mood, he might almost have been stilled once more.

Her mind raced furiously. She could use the gleam somehow, or simply sneak out the back of the tent. She could talk her way out, or scream for help. Plan after plan came to her, all of them pointless.

She was the only woman in the camp, after all. No one would mistake her for anyone else. She could not hope to blend in. She could hardly slip unnoticed aboard the ship of the air, either. It was crewed with officers and men accustomed to fighting, and moored above a camp of armed men.

She was trapped at the pleasure of al-Wazir and Hornsby.

That thought made her very angry. The anger, however, bought her nothing.

Finally she went and knelt beside Boaz.

"Why do you seem so lost, friend?" she asked softly.

He looked at her, his brass eyes dilating. "You shall take ship and leave. I shall remain here in the camp of my enemies, alone and traitor to Authority."

"What of your name?"

"Nothing has changed."

"Were you expecting some stroke from the heavens?" She reached forward and traced the line of his chin. "With people, it never works that way. What becomes new is slower than dawn, slower even than the cycles of the moon. Your name is your answer; it has to be. Otherwise you are only Brass and always Brass. I prefer you Boaz."

He simply stared at her, eyes clicking faintly.

"Lassie," boomed al-Wazir from the tent flap. "I need to be having the talking of you, right now. Me and the good Captain Hornsby await your pleasure."

"Boaz," she said softly. "I'll be back."

Turning away from him, Paolina had to fight not to skip her way to freedom.

Al-Wazir hustled her into another tent. This one was stacked with crates, crowded close and dank in the midday heat, though the canvas walls were flooded with light. Hornsby was there as well. He had no pistol at his belt this time, she noticed. The marine officer stood with a small dark-skinned balding man, with a hooked nose and hooded brown eyes. The stranger wore a blue uniform that didn't match anything she'd seen in the camp thus far. With lots of gold braid.

He was from the airship, of course.

She smiled.

The dark man did not smile back. He looked her up and down, twice, as if he were considering buying her. "No."

"I—," Paolina began, but al-Wazir grabbed her arm hard and jerked it slightly.

"I do not believe this is subject to discussion," Hornsby told the man.

"Of course not." A weary smile quirked his face. "I am captain of my ship, and my word is law. Literally so, here beyond the bounds of the Empire. There is no discussion."

Hornsby exchanged a glance with al-Wazir. Then: "You misunderstand me."

"This business will run back to the highest levels," al-Wazir rumbled.

She realized he was pitching his voice low, even lower than normal. Anger? Intimidation? The giant Englishman was certainly an overwhelming presence.

The chief continued. "If you must, I have letters."

The airship captain raised his hand. "No, no. We do not need to resort to that." He rubbed his eyes, then focused his attention on Paolina once more, this time meeting her gaze as a person rather than simply evaluating her as a thing. "You are a woman, young lady."

"Sir," she said quietly, keenly aware of how much of her future lay in this man's hands at this moment.

"Women do not belong on Her Imperial Majesty's ships of the air. Not for superstition's sake, but practicality. Eighty-seven officers and men will not mix well with one woman."

"Meaning the English Navy are not gentlemen?" She regretted the words as soon as they left her mouth, but al-Wazir snorted, while Hornsby shook his head and laughed out loud.

Even the captain smiled at that. "Touché, mademoiselle. But no, I am afraid not. The officers, naturally. It says so on our commissions. The men are sailors."

"I traveled almost two thousand miles to get here," she told him. "From a village of men, through countries peopled by men, and across a war being fought by them. A ship full of men does not frighten me."

"Then you do not understand men."

Al-Wazir squeezed her arm again, more gently this time. "She needs England, Captain, and England needs her. You can carry her there faster than anything else we can push her to."

The captain nodded, then focused his gaze once more on Paolina. "And *why* does England need you?"

"I am not sure," she admitted. "But I know England is where I will learn about the world. I have already deduced what I can about Creation. I must go to the wizards who studied with Newton and Faraday and Priestley, who can show me what I have not yet seen for myself. I must go where there are more books than the handful in my village. Libraries, sir, real libraries. With learned men."

"And what have you deduced about Creation?"

"What can be seen, of course." She found the question slightly surprising. "The nature of our earth, its diameter and orbital period. The heartbeat of Creation, that timing which regulates all things. The motions of the planets. Something of hydraulics and mechanics."

"The lass is another Newton," al-Wazir rumbled. "As much as my poor self can tell."

"Or me," Hornsby added. "I do not have the wit or education to overmatch her."

The captain studied her awhile. "You hear the beat of the world?"

"Yes." Paolina reached into her dress and pulled out the gleam in its pouch. "I built this to measure the hours and the beat of my own heart and the beat of the world." She showed it to him, clutched tightly in her hand.

Something strange and almost fey closed the captain's face for a moment. "By the horofix," he muttered. Then, more loudly: "I am Captain Hakeem Sayeed, Royal Navy, commanding HIMS *Notus.*" He nodded, a most abbreviated bow. "I will convey you northward with me, and ensure your transport to England. But understand that will be a difficult journey at its best. Ships of the air do not have spacious quarters, and are in no wise designed for the needs or modesties of women. If you create trouble of your own accord, I will set you down wherever we are and carry on without you."

Paolina clutched the gleam closer. "If I create trouble, I deserve no less. I am Paolina Barthes, sir."

"So they tell me." Sayeed's glare swept across at all three of them. "Is she ready to come now? Are you ready to let her go?"

"Yes," said al-Wazir.

Hornsby nodded. "Ottweill is at the digging. Right now is very good."

"But Boaz—," Paolina stopped, interrupting herself. She hadn't said farewell to the Brass. Otherwise, what? She had only her clothes and the gleam. Her few other belongings were meager gleanings of her journey across the face of *a Muralha.* Nothing more. "I am ready."

"Then let it be done quickly." Sayeed led them out.

AL-WAZIR

He watched *Notus* cast off a little over an hour after he sent the girl up. Ottweill had not appeared, but several of Hornsby's men stayed close to the chief, their weapons unslung.

Not until the graceful airship slid over the glossy tops of the jungle to the north did he consider what to do next. Set the metal man free, as a start.

In the tent, Boaz sat on the cot, staring forward.

"Hey, John Brass."

The metal man did not move at all.

"She's gone. Shipped out for England. I come to tell you the gates are open if you wish to leave."

Still no reaction.

He knew a brown study when he saw one, even in a creature such as this.

"You are free to stay," al-Wazir said, "but I cannot promise no one will take a hammer to you if you lay around too long. Fine metalwork there, son."

"A name," Boaz said, finally looking at al-Wazir. "She granted me a name."

That surprised the chief. "Well, and it was me that brought the oil to paint your brow, fool. What, you were John Brass all your days before?"

"Yes. In Ophir, we are all hight Brass."

"So you come down the Wall to fight us for your names?"

"You do not understand."

Al-Wazir sat on the tent floor, deck-style, though it was hot as a bilge pump station in here. "No, I do not. You do. You know more of the Wall than I ever will. So if you're not walking out the gates, I'd be obliged if you'd tell me so, and perhaps stay to lend a hand."

"Might I abide here for her?"

Al-Wazir laughed sadly. "She's nae coming back, son. To think aught else is foolish hope."

"England will spit her out as the tiger rejects carrion."

"I do not know, John Brass. England has eaten half the world, and seems able to digest us all. She swallowed Scotland many years gone without complaint. A Rome for the modern age, save our roads are ships of the sea and air, not stone ribbons for the march of armies."

"Rome was a mere eyeblink. My people recall King Solomon, who was greatest of the kings of old."

"*My* people are ruled by Queen Victoria, who is the greatest of the kings of today."

"I told Paolina once that she would replace Authority for me. I did not understand the truth of what I said. For her, I will stand by you."

Poor bastard. "You're a statue, son. Fallen in love with a chit of a lassie too strange for any man, methinks." He smiled and extended a hand. "I'll take your help and be thankful in the bargain. Walk with me, Boaz, and help me keep England's flag flying here."

The brass man stood and took his hand. Al-Wazir tried to shake, but it was like grasping at a statue. Instead, he just laughed.

Together, they left the tent.

There had been no attacks since the visit of *Notus*. The long patrols reported the brass army still at some miles' distance, but camped and settled, not immediately forming up for skirmishing or all-out attack. The local patrols reported nothing but the usual jungle animals and African strangenesses. The men drilled by division and in firing ranks, so grudgingly that it had made Hornsby angry, but drill they did. Al-Wazir thought they might be able to survive another attack.

The fuzzy wuzzies from the river had even begun to come up to the camp. That convinced al-Wazir that attack was not imminent. The natives who lived in the shadow of the Wall surely knew what signs to watch for, even if he did not.

Hornsby was showing signs of his own. The Marine captain was divided and troubled much as the camp was.

"We cannot be split among ourselves," he muttered. The two of them stood atop the palisade one evening, smoking cigars and staring northward into the African night. Even out of their line of view, the Wall loomed close in their consciousness—it bent the winds and weather as surely as it shadowed the daylight. Better, sometimes, to look for monkeys crashing through the trees and the pale glow of night-blooming flowers.

"I ken," al-Wazir said softly. "A split crew will not pull together when the moment comes. We live and die as one."

"Then you must make it right with the doctor." A long, slow puff, the coal at the tip of the cigar flaring and dying and flaring again. "He still holds hard against you for sending that girl onward."

"Nae." He was surprised to find himself still passionate. "He does not hae the judging of me. I was put here under different authority."

"A ship cannot have two masters."

"This is no ship, if such has escaped your notice." Al-Wazir took a breath around his cigar, reining in the upset that caused his accent to slip back to his Lanarkshire boyhood. "I am sorry. We have no cause for argument, Captain."

"It is nothing," Hornsby told him. Then: "I have always despised mixed commands. If we were all under service discipline, yours or mine, this would not happen."

"Ottweill would never make a flag officer. Summat would have befallen him."

"No, no, not my point." Hornsby chuckled. "Though you have it true enough, to be sure. Just . . . you are not bound by duty to me."

"The Queen's shilling."

"As may be. But neither am I bound to you, as officers are to their men. Ottweill is bound to nothing save his bloody steam borers."

Even now, in the quiet dark of the evening, al-Wazir could hear the thrumming as they cut ever deeper into the Wall. The diggings were deep enough that the first chamber had been blasted out, so some of the equipment and supplies that had been piled about the camp initially had vanished down the tunnel for more convenient access.

He'd considered an attempt to persuade Ottweill to bore a second stub of a tunnel for storage, especially of the ammunition and explosives, but right now it would be fruitless to make any proposition to the doctor. If he were lucky, his thinking would be ignored. Chances were just as good that it would be rejected out of hand and thus all the more difficult to implement later when circumstances had settled.

Ottweill was never a man to go back on his word, no matter how poorly considered his original position.

"Those great machines," al-Wazir began, speaking into the silence that had lengthened with his thoughts. He stopped. "Do you hear aught?"

Hornsby looked around, cocking an ear. There was nothing but the distant rumble of the borer down in its hole. "Quiet here."

"It's never quiet here." The chief glanced up into the sky. Clouds blocked whatever moon there might have been. They had only a sullen silvery glow, faint as a preacher's conscience, to light the night-dark jungle before them.

Where were the howls and crashes and creaks of the African night?

The captain turned and cupped his hands to shout, but he never got to make the noise. A swirl of feathers and a rush of air brought a sword to part his head from his neck. It was a winged savage—naked angel, a brute made in imitation of God's servants, and all too familiar to al-Wazir from his days aboard *Bassett*.

The chief ducked, dropping to the creaking deck of the palisade even as the air rushed in a whir of razor-edged pinions where he had been standing. He slapped his side for the cutlass, which was not there. *Unarmed, by God, caught like a new fish!*

There was nothing for it but to scream his fool head off.

"Attack, attack," al-Wazir shouted. "Ware the air!" It was hard to get the volume in his voice while pressed to the wood.

Wings whirred overhead as he wriggled butt-high next to Hornsby's body. The captain had worn his pistol, as usual, a Webley service revolver. Al-Wazir tugged it free. There was blood on the grips from the fount that had blossomed out of Hornsby's neck.

He'd never liked pistols, but it was something to fight with now.

Rolling over to face up, his hair and back sticky, al-Wazir cocked the pistol and aimed skyward. A shape flew low overhead. He pulled the trigger. It stuck.

The damned thing had a safety catch!

A blade gleamed as another winged savage landed just past his feet. He scrabbled in the dark for the lever, damning Hornsby for being such a cautious man. Something clicked, so he pulled the trigger again.

The revolver made a brief flash of powder as a liquid flower blossomed in the narrow tattooed chest of the killer angel.

The echoing shot seemed to wake the camp as his shouting had not. There were no sentries on the palisade—they must have all been killed as Hornsby was—but men were running from the tents, calling out and screaming. Already other firearms were popping. Keeping a firm grip on his pistol, al-Wazir scrambled for the bronze sword dropped by the winged savage he'd just killed.

Blade in one hand, firearm in the other, he stood to confront the next wave of attacks.

Once the camp was awake, there were so many firearms that the English were a danger to themselves as much as they were the winged savages. Al-Wazir cut down two more attackers as they dove across his wooden wall, then leapt to the ground some dozen feet in order to avoid being swarmed. After that his role seemed to be reduced to shouting his men into orderly lines so their fire could be profitably concentrated instead of spent willy-nilly into the close, hot night.

The camp had ten times the men that *Bassett* had carried. A force of several dozen winged savages had overwhelmed the airship's defenses from all directions. Here with firm ground under English feet, they were much harder pressed. There was a lesson there, but he could not discern it in the heat of affairs.

After a few minutes, someone got to the heavy guns. They began barking into the night. The crash of cannon woke the jungle again—al-Wazir could hear it even while straining and shouting to beat the men into formation as death winged close above their heads.

He heard someone shout, "John Brass!" but he did not know if it was for Boaz, or if there were a second wave of attack coming across the open ground.

The question answered itself when the gates burst inward.

The fight grew worse.

An hour later, al-Wazir found himself directing a group of exhausted men piling shattered logs and railroad ties against the empty gateway. Anything for a defense. Boaz was with them, lifting without complaint thrice what the strongest man could do. The others stared at him, muttering, but they kept to their work.

"You think he's the danger on account of he's Brass!" al-Wazir shouted, suddenly angry. "An if ye ever fought a Welshman, would that make all the taffies your sworn enemies? Fools, one and all." He heaved on the end of a log, turning it as it splintered, until a few of the laborers backed away.

"Just a man," one of them said. "Can tell who he ain't though."

"Of course not." Al-Wazir thrust the log into place unassisted. "Ye great pack of ugsome ninnies. Don't know your own mates."

"Enough," said Boaz quietly. "They've seen their friends fall to Brass who look no different from me."

Al-Wazir nodded, keeping his next words in. After a deep breath, he said, "John Brass here is to lead the crew. I must go count the dead."

He stalked off, angry at himself for so poorly handling his men.

The evening brought no better news. One of the expedition's medicos had been killed in the fight. The other had drunk himself blind in panic. Their boys were sewing up who could be sewn, and handing out opium to those wounded waiting to die. Ottweill worked with them, cleaning injuries and talking quietly to the patients. He acknowledged the chief with a brief nod, devoid of acrimony, and continued with his work.

It was the first time al-Wazir had seen a truly humane side to the man's character.

He squatted on his heels nearby.

"I make it at least seventeen of ours dead," al-Wazir said quietly. "Including Hornsby and Dr. Marino."

"At least six here will not survive." Ottweill's voice was just as calm.

The man whose arm he was tending stiffened, but Ottweill ignored him.

Al-Wazir went on. "We killed over two dozen of the winged savages, and another dozen Brass. Massed fire, for the most part, thanks to the drills the men have been doing."

"Good."

"There is an entire Wall full of them. We could kill a hundred for each man of ours, and still lose the battle in the end."

"That is your problem," Ottweill said coldly. "The hole I shall dig. The Wall you shall secure."

"I could as easily conquer China with my bare hands."

"Then the emperor of Northern Earth you shall be, and a shining hat you will wear."

No, al-Wazir thought, *the doctor has not changed so much after all.*

He went back out to search the darkness for the wounded and the dead, wondering on how he should defend the camp from the air as well as the ground. Al-Wazir resolved to speak closely with Boaz once morning came and people had settled back to their work.

Walking quietly through night's deep shadows, he realized the deep thrumming of the steam borer had never stopped.

CHILDRESS

Steaming across the Pacific was a relief after the panic of her first days aboard *Five Lucky Winds.* The dull, deadly fear of their transit beneath the ice had been little better. Leung kept the vessel surfaced as often as possible. No fear of British airships here, Childress realized.

They made landfall at several more islands. These were ports, of a sort. Leung permitted her to come up to the tower, but not to go ashore. The towns were collections of native huts, with flowers and pigs and children in abundance. There was no stone or steel such as she might have expected to see in a harbor within the British Empire.

Fresh water and food were brought aboard, especially fruit as they followed a heading ever farther south and west. The sailors were granted brief leaves in small groups.

At the third such stop, she turned to Leung as they both stood on the little balcony atop the tower. "May I go ashore?"

"I regret that I must decline you permission." His voice was not unkind.

"I am not a prisoner."

"Not precisely, no. But consider this. The Mask Poinsard would not deign to walk among barefoot fuzzy wuzzies." He paused. "I believe that is the word, yes?" She nodded, and Leung continued. "A woman of valor would keep her strengths hidden against the trials to come. Whichever of those two you are, neither of them needs set foot ashore. Besides, I do not care to explain myself more should rumor travel faster than *Five Lucky Winds* can sail."

"That last would seem to hold as much significance as the other reasons," she said dryly.

"I should hope never to be accused of being an impractical man."

That night Captain Leung joined Childress for a dinner of pork and some stringy, tart fruit in a thicker sauce than usual. It was quite delicious.

She was ready to brace him. She had been thinking long and hard about the choice he'd set upon her, and what the significance might be of what he'd told her concerning the Golden Bridge at Chersonesus Aurea. Praying, too, though the only answers God gave her were those which He had always given her—the voice of her own experience.

She had a question for Leung. A very important question.

Childress began almost diffidently. "Captain." She was conscious that Choi could be lurking outside the door, though he had not shown himself that day.

"I listen."

And now the plunge.

"What precisely was the mission the Mask Poinsard was pursuing?" *The one that required my incidental death.*

"A great . . . sorcerer . . . is expecting her in Tainan. There are other, well, needs." His head flickered into a reflexive bow. "I am not privy to all. Just the requirements of the Admiralty." '

"Ah. Thank you. Again, you have told me much, perhaps more than you should." *Words,* thought Childress. She must needs follow their path carefully. "About those needs." Time for her guess. "Chersonesus Aurea and the project there."

His voice was very tight. "The Feathered Masks are much concerned with that. The Mask Poinsard would have an interest, were she aboard my ship."

Childress felt a sickening lurch in her gut that he spoke so freely of her identity where the political officer might overhear. How had her life come to this?

"I cannot imagine you would raise objection to your own admiralty, nor to your Son of Heaven on his Dragon Throne. Everything under Heaven has a place and a name. You doubly so, for your military oath."

"Indeed." Leung seemed to be sliding down a tunnel now.

Was she getting close? Or straying into danger? Vision bloomed in her head—of Anneke, bleeding out her life, and how close Childress had come to dying at this man's orders. She must carry on.

The Mask Poinsard would have done so. A librarian far from home could do no less than that feral duchess.

"It is possible that there are opinions, thoughts, which occur to a man of sense who has stepped outside the realm of absolute obedience and been required to think for himself, surviving on the high seas and deep beneath the ocean." She thought she saw the merest crack of a smile at that. *Courage,* Childress told herself, and plunged onward. "An outsider, brought before the Beiyang Admiralty, skilled and knowledgeable in esoteric matters, might deliver certain warnings which could not be spoken from within. At least not at first."

"And this is your thought? . . ." He spread his hands, inviting.

"This is the thought of a Mask," she told him, lying as she had never lied before, with cold intent for personal gain. "This is the thought of the Mask Childress, come in place of a weaker woman lost at sea."

"You would school an empire to your will?"

"I school nothing and no one to my will. Only speak what is known, and what seems wise to me. A Golden Bridge would bring dangers to China's doorstep that make the British seem like dogs barking in the night. I'll not pretend to surety here, and hope in turn that such honesty will be my passport to credibility.

"Anyone who claims to know what lies beyond the Wall twists the uncertain truth beyond recognition. Anyone who fears what lies beyond the Wall shows good sense."

Leung rubbed his face as if to wipe away fatigue clouding his thoughts. "Were I the admiral, I might speak thus: So you will raise a fleet and sail against your Queen?"

"No. I am no traitor." *Only a liar,* she thought. *Bearing false witness.* "If I were, you would have no grounds for trust. In this, I serve the interests of noble and peasant alike. No matter that they live under the mandate of Heaven or within the protection of the British crown. We are all children of God—Heaven, if you prefer. What lies beyond the Wall is another Creation."

He stared at her awhile. His eyes were frank but also sparkling. "If I were to wonder why I'd spared one woman and not another, now I would say that the hands of my ancestors guided me. As you tell me, I have no opinions, only orders. Admiral Shang at Tainan is a prideful man. He is not a foolish one. Like me he stands outside certain honors. That is why he dwells in Taiwan, and not closer to the Celestial Court. Unlike me, he can cause ships to move and men to bow."

"You move at least one ship, Captain."

"Yes, but not all my men bow to me."

Never forget the problem of Choi.

He stood, nodding to her. "You have proven to amaze, Mask Childress. May you have a long life and good fortune, with double happiness along the road."

It sounded suspiciously like a farewell, so much so that when he left the wardroom, she stiffened, expecting the political officer with his pistol to enter in Leung's place. Naught came save her own fear and the hard racing of her heart. After a time, Childress removed herself to her cabin to worry whether she had practiced wisdom or committed arrant foolishness this day.

If nothing else, she had traded one difficult lie for another, far more comfortable one. And Leung was now her ally. As much as any man, Chinese or otherwise, could be.

She wondered if his stature as a man somehow canceled the meaning of his being Chinese. Childress had known few enough New Englanders with Leung's grace and courtesy and thoughtful bearing.

Choi presented himself the next morning as she ate cold fish cut together with strips of some pale, fleshy pepper over congealed rice—it was her least favorite of the breakfast preparations. He displayed the hand signal of the white bird once more, then stood close.

"*Ni zao?*" she said, straining to greet him politely in such little Chinese as she'd managed to learn. There were at least two forms spoken here on the ship, much as an English ship might sail with officers of the Queen but men who spoke Greek or Turkish or French or some other subject tongue.

"Hello." His smile was brown-toothed and gapped. Something in it made her sad a moment. Had no one ever cared for this man?

She smiled faintly back and tucked in to the fish with reluctance.

"You declare yourself," Choi added.

This is the hour of truth, she thought. *He is come to brace me in my treachery.*

She resolved that Mask or no Mask, she would be Childress, and true to herself. *Help me now, Lord, as you have perhaps never helped me before.* "I am who I am," she said in English, then flushed at the sheer presumption of the statement.

He cocked his head like a bird examining a cart-flattened cat. "Same Mask, not same woman?"

"I am a white bird, of the Feathered Masks." True enough, taken on its own terms.

"You birds fly far, ah." Choi nodded. "Where Poinsard?" He pronounced the name oddly, *Pu-yin-sar,* but she took his meaning.

"I stand in her stead, carrying the banner of the *avebianco*." Childress thought to try flattery. "You of all people should understand that."

The smile stayed fixed upon his face, seeming more and more the leer of an idiot. "Poinsard she come to bring something. Bird business. Make lucky flight."

"What she brought was me, Mr. Choi. I am the purpose of your voyage."

"You weapon of power?"

Lie for once, lie for always. "I am the Mask Childress. There is no more to know."

"Great Relic you thing, England people. Your little Heaven emperor bring it, ah?" His smile split into a grin that was both feral and simple. "You Great Relic, Poinsard not got sense." Choi nodded. "Emperor know all."

With that he was gone.

Great Relic? The Brass Christ had left seven Great Relics. She had trouble imagining that Choi meant that in its specific, Christian sense. The thought that the Mask Poinsard would be carrying one of the Great Relics with her across the Atlantic seemed inconceivable.

Those artifacts of history were *lost.* She was a divinity school librarian; this was the meat and bread of her work. That poor boy Hethor had come looking for the Key Perilous, one of the seven. Childress believed that he had probably found it. Or the world would have stopped turning, most likely. That left six others.

To find them now . . . History was suspect at such a distance of time and legend. There were very few sources to draw from. Most of them were retellings of retellings. You could look back through time with the eyes of faith and see the Brass Christ broken on the Roman horofix. The line of His saints and martyrs descended from Him on a river of blood and prayer. You could look back through time with the eyes of reason and see fragments of Aramaic and New Testament Greek and Hebrew and Latin and Coptic, and find yourself clutching nothing but hopes and dreams and the distant memory of a mystery.

That was one reason people believed, she'd always thought. It was to explain. The first causes hung heavy in the sky, tons upon tons of brass scribed there by God as He had wrought the world. The line that stretched from those fateful seven days six thousand years earlier through to today's racing life of steam and electricks and the politics of Empire, that line was difficult to understand, except through the lens of faith.

Reason failed all too often, building bridges of footnotes and contradictory assumptions. Faith was a highway for the believer.

Still, the seven Great Relics were a story told again and again and again.

Origen was said to have carried them to the Wall when his years were almost done. Bishop Irenaeus of Barcelona claimed that the pagan priestess Hypatia had magicked them into the stones of Alexandria, and so cursed the city to eternal torment. Joseph of Arimathea brought them to England, at Wearyall Hill on the flooded Somerset Levels where the relics slept in Arthur's seat. There were as many stories as there were tellers who'd thought to bring them to life. Each reflected the author's needs— and patronage—far more than any truth.

Truth shone through, however. Over and over and over it shone through. That was the purpose of the lens of faith, to assemble the scattered light of reason into God's intent, and lay sense upon the world.

Now Choi had brought her a tale that would upset all those ancient meanings. All the stories agreed on at least one point: the seven Great Relics had been taken out of time, removed from the lives of men, much as the Brass Christ Himself had been. The workaday world of sin and flaw and compromise would have tarnished and fractured them—the Sangreal would be only a cup, the Key Perilous only a sliver of metal, and so forth.

That the Mask Poinsard could carry one of the seven Great Relics to the Chinese fleet, and hand it to a difficult little man like Choi, beggared reason. The world simply did not *work* that way.

Perhaps Choi had meant to describe some Chinese thing, something of the Rectification of Names described by Leung, which fit his poor English. She far preferred that thought to the alternative.

Even if he'd been drinking wine from the silvered skull of St. John the Divine, that would not have mattered beside the fact that when they reached the port at Tainan, Choi would go ashore and report to someone, somewhere, that she was not Pu-yin-sar. The charade that had thus far preserved her life would be ended.

Childress took to her bed with an aching head and a shaking heart.

They made landfall a few days later. Childress feared they were coming to Tainan, but Leung took her up to the tower to watch *Five Lucky Winds* come into port. "This is Sendai," he said. "A great port of Manchu-Nihon, and one of the bases of the Beiyang Navy. The Sendai Nihon Regiment is raised here as well. In the mountain wars, those are the most feared of the foreign troops in His Celestial Majesty's armies."

She saw a city with gentle folded hills rising beyond, their heights covered with trees. It had a pretty, sleepy provincialism that spoke of purely local troubles and no recent history of invasion. Temples shone with gold roofs and great pillars, but a good portion of the buildings were low, with long ridgelines and pale walls. Closer to the waterfront the substantial docks were backed by brick warehouses and cargo cranes not much different from what she would have seen in New Haven.

A modest city, backwater of its empire, likely having much in common with her home.

"Will I go ashore here?"

"Too many eyes. Some in the port know you are aboard, or at least that the Mask Poinsard is with me. Far more do not. There would be too much to explain."

"And Choi?"

"His chain is wrapped around a post in Tainan. He might be able to send a wireless from here, were he to go ashore and find his way among the right people."

"Can you keep him on the ship?"

Leung paused before answering. "I am supposed to believe that."

She thought on that some more. "Could you leave him behind, once he went ashore?"

The captain chuckled. "That is not so terrible an answer. But he would definitely find his way to a wireless then."

"Let him. A letter from a distant port will not carry the urgency that a busy man with much to say conveys. We can fight words far more easily than we can fight a witness."

Leung slipped his arm around her shoulder. "*We*, Mask Childress?"

She shrugged him away. "You know what I mean. And Choi . . ." She thought once more over how much to say. "Choi is more dangerous than even you know. He has spoken to me, in English, of the business of our voyage."

"In English." The captain fell very quiet a moment, preternaturally still. "Do you believe he has had understanding of our conversations?"

"Yes." She wondered if she'd just pronounced death on the little man with the gap-toothed smile.

Not that he would do any differently to her.

"Go to your cabin. I will send a man to you. Do not be alone, for a moment."

"A woman—" She broke off, embarrassed.

"Have him stand in the door. He will face away." Leung turned and grabbed her shoulders. "Do not be alone. Not until I tell you that you are safe."

"And you?" she demanded. "What can cause such fright in a man who commands *Five Lucky Winds*?"

"I go to see a spiritual pulmonist. There is always a price, and sometimes it comes from an unexpected direction." The chill in his voice frightened her.

She had to ask him, now that things were suddenly turning dark. "Choi . . . Choi expected Poinsard to be carrying of the seven Great Relics."

"He *told* you that?"

That Leung was unsurprised was important for her to know. "The Golden Bridge," she said. "This is all some magic or plan to cross the Wall. Which will be a terrible thing to have done, indeed."

"Perhaps. That's an issue for another time, however. For now you must go below. Stay. Whatever you hear, save it be my voice, do not answer."

"Are you planning to raise riot?" she asked sarcastically.

"For this, more. Ghosts are always hungry."

"I do not believe in ghosts."

"Go," he said, "and hope your beliefs are sufficient unto the day."

All the clangor and racket of making port was so much thumping through the hull, once Childress was locked in her cabin. To her surprise the man Leung sent was one of the old cooks. He brought no weapons but for a small kitchen knife. The cook also carried a supply of grain and coins, which he busied himself tossing and studying, while she waited and wondered what dark magic would walk out of Sendai port to touch this boat that had become her home.

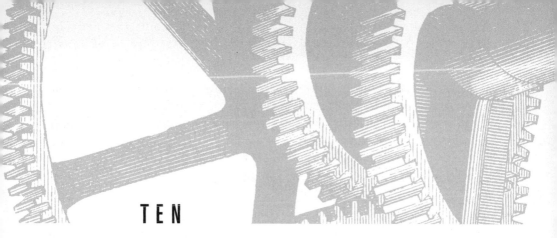

TEN

PAOLINA

HIMS *Notus* ran before the wind with her boilers straining for every ounce of additional speed. Paolina knew that Captain Sayeed was not a cursing man, but if he were, she would have heard some masterful creativity by then.

A Chinese airship pursued them. It was built of a different design—a broader, shallower gasbag, almost a giant kite. The hull below was shallower as well, without the explicitly Naval heritage of *Notus*. The British airship rather resembled a flying boat. The Chinese vessel was a falcon, right down to the hunting eyes painted behind the beaked front of the bag.

So far only the skill of Sayeed and his crew had kept them beyond the range of gunfire. The Chinese had a gradual advantage of speed. Paolina had heard the sailors muttering of stern chases enough to deduce what the obvious eventuality must be.

The eventuality she disliked more revolved around their mutterings of the luck of women and ships.

Still, *Notus* ran.

She wondered why the English wizards had not cast their spells. Were they all as foolish as Clarence Davies?

A Muralha had become a distant black cliff, a permanent shadow on the southern horizon that receded with each passing day. Africa unfolded below them in an endlessly varied sameness of jungle green and river brown interrupted by burn scars and the occasional flashing gap of a lake. This was not a region of high mountains, though she thought she'd glimpsed some in the distance from time to time before their course had bent westward.

Two days they'd been at this game of pursuit, Sayeed apparently intent on not coming to duel. Paolina realized there was little point in seeking advantageous terrain for battle. Not between airships. Whatever the sky brought them, they shared.

What it brought them now was near cloudlessness. High, icy brush-strokes marred the perfect blue of the vault of the heavens, but otherwise they enjoyed a view to the horizon in all directions.

Captain Sayeed was playing for distance, fleeing north and west toward his friends and farther from his foes. She knew nothing of the battle lines between empires, but the sailors had plenty to say about that matter as well.

Bucknell, one of the ship's boys, had been told to stay close to Paolina. The initial thrill of soaring had quickly soured with the realization that Captain Sayeed was not going to relent in his opposition to her presence simply because she'd actually boarded the ship. His men had been in no better mood, growing downright angry since the Chinese had dove into view. Only Bucknell, too young and woolly-minded to share the sailor's fears, seemed to be willing to tolerate her.

He was certainly no wizard. He wasn't even pretty like Davies had been—broad-faced, with lopsided eyes and a scar on the left end of his lips. He looked to have been beaten quite a bit in his young life.

"See, ma'am," he told her now. "We can't not come about, for as we'll present our broadside, he shall have the speed of us and overfly like a pigeon on the wing. Then we'll be a-waddling whilst he turns and turns again and catches the side of us. Ain't long, battles in the air. Someone gets a bag, she's flaming toast a mile high up."

That had been obvious enough. "So we run toward what? I am in no rush to feel the heat of battle, but this seems a long way from British air."

Bucknell's head bobbed. "I'll not have the knowing of that, ma'am. But Captain Sayeed is canny, for all he's a foreign gentleman. *Notus* can outsail the best of them, given the weather and the moment."

"Bound for England, to die in Africa. Not what I'd planned for my epitaph," she mused.

"Chinese never been fighting over Africa before. That's new, ma'am."

"You can keep your new, Mr. Bucknell. I've had quite enough of it myself."

"Ma'am." He smiled vacantly. "Leastwise we don't have a Wall storm coming on."

Paolina knew those well enough. The weather would sometimes get trapped against *a Muralha,* storm violence piling high into that strange zone of air that followed the Equatorial Wall upward into the heavens. Those storms would rage as far up as the wind had strength to blow, and crawl along the Wall until they finally spent themselves.

They were greatly feared in Praia Nova. She did not want to imagine the effect of such weather on an airship. "Surely this far north a Wall storm would not bring us down?"

"They gots arms, ma'am, long as an ocean, where they spreads out and hooks whatever travels in the sky." His head bobbed farther as he fell silent.

She stared after, looking past the rail at the pursuing Chinese to wonder what she might do to bring the enemy airship down. After a time, Paolina's hand strayed to the gleam.

It had engines, after all. Engines beat time surely as clocks or the human heart did.

But the ship had people, too. Men who hunted *Notus,* to be sure, but people all the same.

Paolina wondered if Boaz might have cared to make this trip. She was certain that the Brass would have been indifferent to the Chinese pursuit. He was perfectly capable of standing to fight, but he seemed to lack whatever portion of the heart that drove men to both dread and crave their battles.

Boaz wouldn't have been impressed with flight, either. He was from higher up along *a Muralha* than she—Praia Nova was essentially at sea level. To Boaz, looking down upon the flatwater world was a part of everyday life, not the visceral thrill it seemed to be to the English sailors. And even to her.

She wished she'd been able to better take her leave of him. Al-Wazir would be fair, she knew, but that didn't mean the men in the camp were likely to do the same. There was something sweet and terrible about Boaz.

Even if he'd taken no thrill from the dash through African skies, she would have liked to have had the Brass along.

Paolina waited until the evening. She had not been confined belowdecks, but night's shadows helped her maintain a veil of privacy over what she was attempting with the gleam.

Dark also meant quiet. While there was little to be done about the chuffing of the boilers and the droning of the propellers, conversations on deck were limited by order to command necessary. Sailors moved with a slow, shuffling walk and kept their heads down.

Fear, of course, she thought, staring down at a nighttime Africa. A river braided through the jungle in a dozen or more channels gleaming in starlight. The trees were opening up more now, wider expanses of grassland and clay and sometimes even sand between them. She could see the spark of a few fires dotting the distance. It wasn't hard to imagine herdsmen surrounded by their goats, or a circle of huts about a pit where a fresh kill was cooking. Dark-skinned men living out their lives in the their own world, much as the *fidalgos* and the women of Praia Nova lived out theirs at the foot of *a Muralha* between sea and sky.

Paolina wondered if the people on the ground looked up at the airships and told themselves stories about the people in the sky.

The English wizards were being canny. They must be hiding in the rearcastle, in officer's country. Not showing themselves yet.

She knew a test when she saw it. Paolina was determined to meet the challenge. The gleam lay cool and heavy in her hand. It seemed to have grown weightier with time, though she knew that wasn't possible. It was metal, a made thing.

Even so, standing in the darkness of the deck with the wind of *Notus'* passage tugging at her hair, the gleam was something more.

The hands were barely visible. Their sweep across the blank face plucked at her vision like a bat in the evening sky. She could most easily follow the one that matched her own heartbeat. It seemed to be synchronous with her respiration, as well—six beats for every breath. The other two matched their reference points, insofar as she could tell.

How would I know if I were wrong?

Paolina put that disloyal thought from her mind. It was time to work with the fourth hand again, as she had done with Boaz.

She was just aft of the midmast, near the boom that supported the port engine nacelle. That engine ran with a slight stuttering whine, which bespoke attention required rather soon. Paolina tugged the stem to the fourth position and began to slowly turn it, seeking a setting that matched the beat of the engine.

This was much easier than some of her other efforts had been. Of course, engines were crude and simple compared with brass men, or the labyrinthine ways of breathing, thinking life. She caught the rhythm of the mechanism. Now it was a matter of twisting the stem, and through the gleam the device as a whole, to her will.

Paolina turned the knurled knob backwards, aiming to slow the beat of the engine. The whine dropped away. She turned it forward, pushing the velocity past the current throttle setting. The engine quickly sped up, to the point of shuddering as the airship began to wallow out of her line of travel. She backed it down again.

But her intent was not to disrupt *Notus*. Paolina was merely finding her way. Now for the Chinese, to show the English wizards what she could do.

That will be much harder.

First, she tugged the stem so the fourth hand floated free, disengaging the link between its action and the action of the engines. Even that felt strange to her—even in her thoughts Paolina had skirted the question of how this was possible since making the thing. This was like carrying a tiny sliver of the divine with her, to create and uncreate at will.

What had come upon her in the *fidalgos'* darkness?

She leaned against the rail and looked aftward. The Chinese airship was running astern ten points to port. Their captain had seen fit to hang lanterns—great glowing red cylinders that lit the bottom of his wide, thin gasbag with an eerie light. It was like looking into the fire-hot mouth of a pursuing dragon.

Paolina stared across the darkness. The Chinese mounted their engines within the hull, propellers churning behind. There was no mounting or nacelle. But the engine was in there, kicking over and turning the shaft to wind out the blades that pushed them forward.

There would be pistons. She'd paid attention, even the few days she'd been in al-Wazir's camp, and since boarding here. Men talked about engines all the time. It seemed to be what they did when they didn't have women to push about or wine to drink. Fire and steam and pistons, churning round and about, while mechanics worried over efficiency and insulation and fuel consumption and heat exchange. ·

He had pistons and boilers inside that hull, the Chinese captain did. They sat there like bezoars in the gut of a goat, gleaming hard and bright, hidden jewels in an unholy maw. She strained to see them inside the fire-mouth of the enemy ship.

She was surprised the find the gleam's hand turning. Setting it to match an engine she couldn't see wasn't so different from setting the hand to match one she couldn't touch, right here on *Notus*.

The reach of the gleam had been improving since her first experiments with the fourth hand, but this was so much more.

Life, Paolina thought. *I want to live. I have much to do.*

These men of a distant empire would not take her existence from her.

She found the rhythm of one of the Chinese engines. She slid the stem into place. She slowed the hand at first, until the dragon's mouth shuddered as the enemy airship pitched slightly. Then she sped it up, forcing it to a velocity the Chinese captain had not expected.

The dragon's mouth veered to its left, turning away from the path of pursuit. One of his propellers was moving faster than the other, of course. It was no different from two people crabbing oars in a rowboat.

She pushed the engine farther forward.

"Miss . . . ," someone behind her began. There was the horrendous screech of an exploding boiler, clearly audible even from the already widening distance. The lanterns shook, some of them snuffed out in the moment. The Chinese airship pitched badly as her remaining propeller raced, now driving her too hard the opposite way. A fast-spreading fire guttered.

"His oil is alight," Sayeed said, next to her now. "He will die in moments."

"The gasbag?" She wondered where the captain had come from.

The gleam was hot in her hand, almost squirming. When the Chinese airship did blossom into full flame, it carried the frightening beauty of a deadly flower to fill the sky with light as the crumpling bag fell toward the silver-braided jungle far below.

Sayeed was very close to her now. "You must tell me how you did that. A skill such as yours could unseat empires."

"This is why I was meant to go to England," she told Captain Sayeed over coffee the next morning. Bucknell hovered nearby, bumping elbows with a sour man who Paolina assumed was the captain's steward.

"Your skills are . . . ah . . . more pressing than I might have understood them to be, judging from that enormous Scotsman's garbled descriptions."

They were taking coffee and biscuits on the poop, in the wind of *Notus'* passage. Dawn had brought a rolling brown country of hills interrupted by cliffs and odd little canyons. A country with no memory of the jungle at all.

"Your own wizards . . . ," she began. She stopped at the expression on his face.

"Wizards? My child, what are you on about?"

"You English. Your airships are—" Paolina's face heated with embarrassment. *It had never been true,* she realized. There were not Newtons on every vessel. How could there be?

"Our airships are crewed by men," he said, not unkindly. "The sort who break wind at inopportune moments and don their trousers one leg before the other."

"I thought something else," she muttered.

"We all did, in our way." He added, "That airship burned until we passed over the horizon."

Paolina winced. "I killed them."

"This is what ships do to one another." His voice was gentle counterpoint to the harsh words, yet still strangely distant. "Kill, or be killed. The men who man them are fleas on a dying dog. What interests me far more than the fact that they died is the mechanism of their dying."

She stared silently along *Notus'* sternway and wondered if there was a pall of smoke somewhere to the south that she could see.

"Sometimes an airship dies because of phosphorous shot to the gasbag. Sometimes ordinary shells will pound her stays and rigging until she comes apart. Sometimes small-arms fire will sweep her decks. I think you perhaps see the pattern here, yes?"

"Yes," she mumbled.

"Good." Sayeed pushed on, still polite, still relentless. "Then you see how a prudent and canny airship captain might wonder, in full consideration and gratitude for his good fortune, how another airship came to explode and fall burning to earth. Especially shortly after his own port engine experienced unusual variations in performance."

"It will not happen to *your ship*."

He leaned close. "*What* will not happen to my ship, Miss Barthes?"

"Me." She was surprised to find herself shivering with unshed tears.

"Perhaps you should explain. In detail, preferably."

Paolina glanced around. The deck was wide open, helmsman and master standing nearby, sailors scrambling about their business a few dozen feet away. "Here?"

"It is a small vessel, Miss Barthes. We could go below, but words carry through the walls."

So she told him about the stemwinder, how she had come to build it, and how she had grown to understand the gleam in her travels in pursuit of English wizards to whom she might be apprenticed.

When Paolina was done, Sayeed nodded gravely. "May I see it?"

She stiffened, then opened her mouth to frame some reply when Sayeed raised a hand. "My apologies. I did not mean that as a euphemism for taking the thing in hand. I simply would like to lay my eyes upon your device."

Paolina drew the leather pouch from within the pocket of her dress, then tugged the mechanism out. "Here, sir." She presented it for his inspection while retaining a firm grasp.

Sayeed leaned forward, keeping his hands clasped behind his back. He stared a moment, then looked at her closely. "You have made a thing which measures so closely that its measuring is indistinguishable from what it measures."

It took her a moment to unravel what Sayeed was saying. "Yes, I think so."

"Have you always been interested in measurements?"

She thought back on Davies' original stemwinder, the marine chronograph she'd thought to be copying. "Yes, always, though until I met an Englishman, I had no idea of the extent of your wizardry."

"That is not an English monopoly," Sayeed said dryly. "You may have noted that neither you nor I is English."

"Yet here we are on an English ship, speaking the Queen's tongue."

"One lives in the world one finds." He fell quiet a moment, contemplating something. "There are great and greater clocks, you know. Far more than instruments to measure time. As you have here, but wrought into the architecture of cities."

"How great?" Paolina's heart surged. Clocks were . . . Creation. God had built all the universe as a clock, after all.

"I am thinking of the Schwilgué Clock, in Strasbourg."

"Is that in England?"

"No." Sayeed laughed. "Though the city is ruled well enough from London. No, no, that is in the Germanies."

"What does it measure?"

"Everything. The days, the months, the years, the centuries, sun, moon, tides, all the affairs of God's earth."

She was in love. That was the only word for the warmth that flooded her heart. "That is the sort of genius I came to see, and learn from. True mastery of the magics of Creation."

"I cannot speak of true mastery. Some people say that there are Clockmakers, who came before God, or followed him." Sayeed shrugged. "I follow a different prophet, a man of my people who has given us a different truth. But I know that the Schwilgué Clock is the pinnacle of this road."

She resolved to find her way there. Newton was dead, while the English ships were empty of the wizards she thought she'd been promised. Perhaps she could learn from this great clock instead.

AL-WAZIR

The next day the men of the camp scavenged the corpses of the winged savages looking for clues to what might have brought the feral angels to them. As they worked, the steam borer continued to grind ever deeper in its tunnel.

"*Bassett* never could kill them worth a tinker's damn," al-Wazir told Boaz.

"A ship of the air, with a small company. That would be difficult."

They watched men pile bodies, once the dead had been thoroughly poked and prodded to elicit any lingering response of life. The last few were red-skinned men with needle-filled mouths.

"Be those of your people?"

"No," Boaz said. "They hail from much higher on the Wall. Mutes, of an angry disposition, with little loyalty to any master."

"Then why do they fight for the brass men of Ophir?"

"I do not know."

"Aye. Neither do I. Never the important answers, to be sure." Not even meeting the Prime Minister had changed that.

The work party had a heap of bronze swords, with several iron ones for good measure. All were bloody. There were a few raw or rotting leather harnesses, some with pouches, and a pile of rags that had served as breechclouts.

Little more.

"Ophir is ancient," Boaz explained. "Nearly half the age of the entire world. When King Solomon set his seals to breathe life into the first Brass, the memories of Creation were yet fresh. Asiongaber is as lost to us as Jerusalem itself, but we still remember. A colony, you English might say, from the countries of the past."

"What is the Queen's ambition to your lot? It's not as if we've come to Ophir with sword in hand, or raised our colors upon your land."

"I have not abided in Ophir for well more than a century. I stood senseless upon the western defenses until Paolina found me. I ken not what Authority intends for this age. Still Brass are of the Wall, the Wall is of Brass. We never descend to your flatwater countries, but some of you come to us. Consider that I even speak your tongue, instead of honest Hebrew or the original Adamic. We hear much of English ambition and English pride. You were never ones to grab hold of something and let it go again."

"Aye, and we've spake on this before. Perhaps the Crown is a grasping mistress. To send armies down the Wall, and recruit those filthy winged savages, that steps far beyond mere argument. Is that not true?"

Boaz stepped over a shattered log, then paused to pick up a fragment of metal. "I do not know." He walked onward through the slippery, sticky mud. "Perhaps there are troubles within the city which require distraction. It would not be the first war in history fought to keep the people's thoughts far from home."

Al-Wazir mulled the metal man's words. There was no lack of sense to them. He'd seen much the same thing back in England, time and again. None of which solved his problem. He sighed with frustration. "And so it comes to this. How do I set a stop to them?"

"I think you cannot. Neither vengeance nor justice is afoot here. There is no grievance to be addressed, no reparation to be made. It is simply that England wants one thing and Ophir wants another."

"Desires in dispute." He stopped and turned to look up at the immensity of the Equatorial Wall. Had he been a man given to vertigo, he might have surrendered to it. The height was a magnet, drawing him *upward*, much as the depths below a ship's rail might draw an unwary man to fly the morning sky without benefit of wings.

It wasn't just a Wall around the waist of the world, he realized. It was a Wall that trapped the world. "God has made us in chains," he muttered. "This free will is naught more than a promise of sweets to a bairn, while He bindeth us so."

Boaz' voice was gentle. "You English seek to break those sacred bonds, with your tunnels and your airships."

"Though I am sworn to the Crown, I am no Englishman," al-Wazir said darkly. "I will not break my oath, after all these years, but this is what the busy English have always done since Saxons first came to Albion's shore." He shook his head, trying to clear the mood that clung to him. "No matter now." His voice and thoughts almost properly Naval again. "What you say is that we cannot sue Ophir for some peace, nor reach an accommodation."

"Yes. That is the truth as I comprehend it." Their slow, difficult walk had reached the ragged line where the clearing met the forest. Two shattered brass bodies gleamed in the shadows, riven by shells from the guns on the palisades.

Paolina would have set to examining their interiors, al-Wazir thought. Such a strange little chit, too wise and too weird in the same head.

Al-Wazir toed a chest plate. "Are all Brass brothers to you?"

"Are all men brothers to you?"

"Well . . . no. Not at all. But we are legion, each born of a different woman in a different place. You are fewer, made men of your single city. Stamped from the same mold. Each of these fallen might easily be you."

"When you tear two men apart with sword or shot, what remains of each might as easily be the other."

A roar echoed from behind them. Al-Wazir and Boaz both turned, staring. One of the palisade guns was firing high into the air. Looking up along the angle of the barrel, he saw a flight of winged savages diving fast toward the camp.

"By all that's holy!" he screamed. "I am not with my men!"

Al-Wazir began running across the muddy, churned field toward the camp. His strides were excruciatingly slow as he shouted orders he knew no one would hear yet, Boaz hard on his heels.

They poured from the sky like so many hawks stooping on a vast bury of conies.

Al-Wazir's feet slipped on mud and roots and bones and the blood of armies, too slow, too late, too far to turn back the tide that overwhelmed his duty.

There was no ground assault this time. It was only the air that teemed with death. The cannons on the palisade barked shell after shell, until their operators were slain. Small-arms fire rattled and cracked from the ground, but even as he fought through the broken wrack that blocked the gate, al-Wazir knew the men were not massed for firing.

Boaz shoved past him to shift more of the timber baulks. The gate had not been blocked on their way out.

"I am too *slow*," al-Wazir roared.

By the time they broke through the other side, the winged tide had shifted away again. It was conducted much as the attacks on *Bassett* had been—a strike like lightning on a church steeple, then gone before the thunder could touch a man's ears.

Many of the tents were down. Workmen and soldiers lay sprawled, limbs and heads severed, guts twining on the ground. Fifty or sixty dead, he thought at a glance. Hundreds more shrieked or milled about in panic.

Still the steam borer ground on, down inside the Wall.

"All right, you lot," al-Wazir screamed, "form up now, on your lines in your divisions."

The panic drowned him out.

Boaz jumped up onto a stack of crates and shouted in a voice that threatened to make al-Wazir's ears bleed, ***"Form up, now!"***

The chaos of men swirled into a pattern, but already it was too late. The sky opened up once more with winged savages, silently dropping with feral leers and swinging, bloody swords.

Al-Wazir ran toward the men. They were scattering again. "Massed fire! Massed fire! Get in line, damn your weeping eyes!"

Then it was wings and swords and screaming death once more. He swept up a dropped carbine and fired until the magazine was spent. It was easier to move from dropped weapon to dropped weapon than to reload, though most were slick with blood.

The winged savages flew close. This time they were not so intent on killing the panicked defenders as they were on cutting tents and setting fires.

The attackers were destroying the camp. A thousand men unsupported would not last a week in these jungles.

But there was nothing left to rally, no one left to stand and fight. Al-Wazir had even lost sight of Boaz in the confusion. So the chief strode among the smoke and ruin, firing guns until he ran out of them, then clubbing at the winged savages with an empty carbine until it was splintered and he stood alone under a quiet sky.

It took him a few minutes to understand that the noise of the digging had stopped. The number one steam borer, deep in the Wall already, was silent. The number two was smoldering, damaged but not destroyed.

And he was alone. Utterly alone, save for corpses.

Had the winged savages killed them all?

CHILDRESS

The cook finally abandoned his efforts at divination to stare at her with a flat incuriosity that was almost disturbing. Childress tried smiling at him, but whatever avuncular good humor normally possessed the man was vanished surely as a daisy in winter.

Obviously he believed in ghosts.

Five Lucky Winds had fallen grave-quiet. Even the usual echoing footsteps and pings in the hull were stilled. Childress thought that if she strained her ears, she might be able to hear Sendai's harbor lapping against the waterline of the hull, but even that was most likely her imagination. Whatever the so-called spiritual pulmonist that Leung consulted might be about, the business seemed to involve silence.

When she saw frost patterning the bulkhead above her cabin hatch, Childress began to worry. The cook noticed her staring and turned to look. He grunted, then resumed his casting of auguries.

Childress lay back on her bunk and prayed, silent and wordless contemplation. If there was magic here, it was not her magic. It did not come from or point back to the Bible or Creation as she understood it.

Could a Chinese ghost harm her, who stood outside the Chinese cosmology?

A groaning began. It was a deep metal noise, rather than the sound of a soul in torment. It disturbed Childress from her thoughts of God.

She realized that the sound came from the chill causing the hull metal to contract. Did ghosts walk the boundary between warm and cool? How different was that from walking the boundary between darkness and dawn? Or the half moon, promise of shadow and potential of light bound together in a bisected silver coin.

The cook stiffened, then stood with his hand on the haft of his chopping knife.

Five Lucky Winds groaned again, and began to shiver like a dog. Childress grabbed the edge of her bunk and held on. She was seized by the sudden feeling that she might tip forward and fall downward to the bottom of the harbor. The submarine bucked as a fine shower of rust and dust leaked down from the ceiling and along the joins of the cabin's construction.

When rivets started to pop from the walls like slow, fat bullets, she shrieked.

A moment later, it was done. A distant bell rang, some alarm on the bridge or in the engine room. The frost was gone and the ship rocked slightly, just as it usually did when moored on the surface.

The cook grinned, bowed, swept up his divinatory aids, and left the cabin.

Childress fought tears awhile, wondering what she had done to come to this place so alien.

"We sail soon," Leung said from the doorway. He did not enter her cabin.

"Where is Choi?" The political officer's fate was much on Childress' conscience.

"Asleep in his bunk, I believe."

"Then what was all . . . *that*? . . . Before, when you made me stay here under guard." She brandished a loose rivet.

"A ghost does not touch lightly."

"Choi is still here." She had all but condemned the man to death, to save herself, racked with guilt, and now he was sleeping in his bunk?

Leung nodded. "Patience is the virtue of a gentleman. As well as a woman of valor."

She gathered both her courage and her sense of irritation. "Where to next?"

"Tainan. And Admiral Shang."

The next day, when she saw him again over a breakfast of congealed rice and something she thought might be finely sliced squid, Childress asked once more after Choi.

"I told you, he is asleep in his bunk."

"All the day long?"

"In fact, yes."

"How . . ." She stopped. "The ghosts drew him down into his dreams?"

"Or theirs." Leung picked out a long sliver. "So long as he is not part of ours."

"I sold him to you," she said miserably.

"No, he sold himself, when he chose to work for the Ministry of Correct Thought."

"Are all political officers part of that ministry?"

"Yes." Leung grimaced. "It is where they hold their commissions."

Childress was fascinated. Though Leung talked about the Beiyang Navy, the Celestial Emperor, and the affairs of the Wall, he had said very little about life in the Chinese empire. "This correct thought is the will of your emperor?"

"It is our way. Not so different from what Confucius would have of us, if you consider it."

"In the British Empire, we are at least permitted the luxury of our own thinking."

He laughed softly. "Did you never know someone imprisoned for speaking out against your Queen?"

She turned that over a moment, testing her annoyance. Then: "You understand what I am saying. We do not set spies on ourselves to ferret out what is said and done at every moment in every corner."

"Obedience is a cardinal virtue in China. You English seem to view it as an optional behavior."

"We do not raise ghosts to bedevil our enemies," she said. "Perhaps our need for obedience is less."

His humor vanished into the stiffness of command. "This was all done at your wish. I have had my own accommodation with the political officer for quite some time. He sleeps now to protect you, Mask."

Childress felt a rush of mingled shame and irritation. "I know. I must be stronger. More like the Mask Poinsard, who would have driven the knife home herself. In my heart, I would as soon pretend there was no knife at all, even if it was my word that set the blow in motion."

"In that, you are both human and charming." Despite his words, Leung's eyes were still cold. He took his leave. Childress remained, staring at the last of her squid and wondering how she might have better expressed herself so as not to lose his hard-won respect.

She just could not find easy acceptance in the thought that her words had least plunged Choi into an endless and likely very troubled sleep.

After breakfasting alone the next day, Childress sought out Leung. A sailor blocked her access to the bridge. She looked at him and repeated *"Leung zai nar?"* until he leaned through the hatch and began a lengthy conversation with someone unseen.

A few minutes later, Leung stepped out. "How may I be of service, Mask Childress?"

His tone was still formal and cold, she noted. "I have thought and prayed on this," she said. "I desire that you awaken the political officer. I will not have his death on my conscience."

Leung shook his head. "That is not possible."

"I do not wish him to die."

"He has been slain," Leung said. "His body does not yet understand, but his spirit is gone to the dark country of dreams with little possibility of recall. In time, his breath will fail, or his heart will weaken, or he will simply slip away from starving in his bed."

"I do not want it."

Leung leaned close, almost touching her, his eyes locked on hers. "When I donned a uniform and made my oaths to the Dragon Throne and the Beiyang Admiralty, it meant that I might be called upon to kill, and kill again, in service of my Emperor. On my order your *Mute Swan* sank with all hands save one. The judges of the dead will see this in my tally, and balance their deaths against my oaths. It is what we do, who serve the will and logic of Empire.

"You, Mask Childress, are no different. If you would play this game, then know the price. Else you should have stayed home in New England and tended whatever garden was yours."

He turned without bidding her farewell and pulled the bridge hatch shut behind him.

Back in her cabin, Childress wondered if she *could* have stayed in New England. She had not questioned Anneke's summons at the library that day. A lifetime of obedience—to her mother, to her teachers, to God, to the deans of the university—had moved her. Her only real infraction was allowing herself to be drawn into the *avebianco* without permission.

That was the root of the issue, she realized. Permission. Childress sat on her bunk and stared at the metal wall, thinking on that.

God had not given humanity permission to live in the world. He had supplied instead free will, sending His children into Creation to find their own way. He trusted humanity to return to God on their own. *Some of us have,* Childress told herself, *some of us have not.*

But everything she'd ever done fell within the bounds of permission. She was permitted not to marry, if she served the world of men in some other capacity—librarian, teacher, nurse. All words that meant "mother," without the bother of procreation or parturition.

Permitted work for women. Permitted by the deans to serve their college. Permitted by the widow who ran her rooming house to stay on and on and on, though Childress had long since ceased being the sort of young woman expected to marry away in a year or three. Permitted by the white birds to serve in their loose corps of eyes and ears, writing occasional letters and sending them through the monthly meetings in the basements of fraternal lodges and the upper rooms of restaurants.

She'd had the choice of carrying on her deception or not. Choi held the power of permission over her through his reports to the Ministry of Correct Thought.

That made her angry again. Who was he to hold her fate over her head? But then, who was she to balance her life over his?

The Mask Poinsard would have, without a second thought. The Feathered Masks had balanced their lives over hers, sending Childress to the Silent Order as a sacrifice to keep the peace.

The idea that struggled inside, gnawing at her conscience and attacking her sense of balance and goodwill both, was simple enough.

She was worth more than this.

She was worth more than permission, or the answer to prayer, or the winds of the world. She was her own woman, her own human being.

Silent tears ran down her cheeks as Childress wondered why this was so hard to say to herself. Permission or no, she set about praying for the dead aboard *Mute Swan,* and especially for the lost soul of Choi. God would forgive them their sins, whatever hers might be.

Leung joined her at dinner that night. The meal was stir-fried mushrooms with sliced peppers. She picked at it with her *kwai-tsze,* wishing for a roast chicken with mashed potatoes and corn. This Chinese food was good, even tasty, but lately it seemed to lend her no comfort, only nutrition.

After a little while, she looked up at the captain. "I have taken your words to heart, sir."

"And how would that be?"

"Everything has a price. You made that clear, though I have known it long since. I regret the fate of Choi, but this is my price for continued freedom of action. I am not willing to lay down my life so he might do his job."

He frowned. "I see."

"I . . . I swore no oaths. No oaths of office or fealty, or commission, as you have done. My purposes are different. But they are *mine*."

"Good." Leung's face relaxed a bit.

"And so I have something else to ask. When we reach Tainan, I want to accompany you to report to Admiral Shang. Do not tell my story for me, Captain Leung."

"You would approach the admiral yourself?"

"He is expecting a Mask, bring him a Mask. I will explain what I am about."

"Chersonesus Aurea."

"Yes," Childress replied. "The Golden Bridge. This project is wrong, and it will damage far more than it aids."

"He is expecting a Mask who will speak for the project, bring aid from the Feathered Masks."

"Oh, sir, I will bring him aid. I will aid him in recognizing the madness of opening the Wall. And I will set limits and extents on what the Feathered Masks shall do to assure China's safety in the face of British tests."

"I did not think you had a remit to speak on such things."

She shrugged, smiling. "I do not require permission to speak. Who is to say how Masks succeed one another? I declare myself heir to the Mask Poinsard. She cannot say differently."

Leung smiled back. "You are learning, I believe."

"No, Captain, I already knew what could be. I merely lacked a sense of how to proceed. Something which you have provided to me."

Leung bowed. "Very well. You will accompany me ashore when we make port in Tainan."

ELEVEN

PAOLINA

"Will you take me to Strasbourg?" Paolina asked Captain Sayeed the next day when she met him walking on *Notus'* main deck.

"This is not a passenger vessel, young lady," the captain replied, but he smiled. "Why should I do such a thing?"

"Because you want me to go there." Paolina kept her voice simple, not challenging. She could not storm this man, nor push him. Only ask politely and convince with what logic could be summoned. "Else you would not have told me of the Schwilgué Clock. You are neither a cruel nor a casual man, I believe."

"Your faith stirs my heart. Walk with me."

The two of them mounted the half flight of steps to the poop, then proceeded to the stern rail.

Africa this morning was sere. The jungles of a day or two before had vanished into pounding sunlight, which flooded the land below. Only the shadow of the gasbag and the continued wind of their passage kept the deck from being an oven as well.

"The Wall has already fallen below the horizon," Sayeed said. "Though I imagine it is truly never far from your thoughts."

"No, sir." She stared into the blued south, though there was little enough weather aloft at the moment. "It forms the center and circle of the Earth, dividing the Northern and Southern extents, and defining all that is. Without the Wall, the world would fly free from its path around the sun. We would either die in the fires of daylight or freeze in the crystalline forests of night."

"Well said. Now consider this: The Wall is one of the greatest parts of God's magic. It holds air high above the earth, where elsewhere there is only thin and starveling gas tending toward vacuum. It does as you have said, anchoring and defining our world. At the same time, the Wall is nothing but the stay and support for a giant ring gear that meshes us with the larger fields of Creation. You, my dear girl, carry a piece of clockwork in your pocket which is an echo of that vasty Divine magic. You can call spirits from the timing of the world."

Paolina smiled. "Whether they come is another matter entire."

Sayeed cleared his throat. It was obvious that he was reaching for something he found difficult to say. She stood quietly, wondering what could move the man so.

He finally spoke. "There are . . . schools of thought . . . among the various communities of faith and reason throughout the British Empire." Sayeed stared south, avoiding her eye. "I find my sympathies lie with the Rational Humanists, as one such school is called. A very wise man named William of Ghent provided many of our writings for some years. He believed that the world could not continue to exist without sentient intervention. It is too orderly, too well settled, to have been pushed into motion by some absent God, then allowed to roll forward like a ball bounding down a hill."

"That is one way to see Creation," Paolina said cautiously.

"Indeed. There are others, Spiritualists, who look for God's hand in every shadow. Arrant wish fulfillment, children seeking the safety of an omnipotent father." He snorted. "I have never seen a fingerprint of God's on this world. However Creation was effected, He has found other business to occupy Himself since."

"Indeed." She wondered what point he was reaching toward.

"The Schwilgué Clock . . . in Strasbourg. It was made by men seeking to measure and divide the world all the more closely. Looking for the tracks of the Clockmakers, those who might be God's proxies." He glanced at her, his eyes troubled. "We . . . we believe their presence far more likely than the reassertion of the Divine principle."

"Why are you so nervous?"

"No, not nervous. Though this might be seen by some as blasphemy, it is more fair to say that we pursue a difficult topic." Sayeed was speaking to the distant surface now, refusing once more to face her. "I told you, I follow a different prophet, one who walked the Northern Earth centuries after your celebrated horofixion. A man of my people. The Empire has a rule of tolerance. There is no requirement for me to bow to the Church of England. Our own belief stands outside the Spiritualist canon which is so popular in London, though it aligns well enough with the Rational Humanist creed. Musselmen do not concern themselves so much with the history of Creation as with the perfection of self within the laws of the Prophet."

Paolina found this very strange. She didn't realize there had been other prophets after the Brass Christ. "Is Strasbourg a Musselman city?"

Sayeed laughed. "No, far from it. And they would be most surprised there to even hear you ask the question. But Strasbourg is a Rational Humanist city. Universität Straßburg remains an important center of our thought. So the Schwilgué Clock is there in Strasbourg Cathedral."

Paolina couldn't help but laugh. "The Rational Humanists built their masterwork in a *cathedral*?"

"It has not been so long since Rational Humanism and its antecedents *were* blasphemy," Sayeed said stiffly. "Once we had to work within the churches. Some of us still do. We do not deny God. We simply see Him at a more distant remove than most would credit."

"Indeed. Living on the Wall, I never met God personally, but He was closer there than perhaps He is in the flatwater kingdoms."

"Fair enough." Sayeed fell silent. Below them, a line of animals crossed a sand-colored plain amid far-spaced trees. The animals were big, moving by the thousands to send a plume of red-gold dust to hang in the air at nearly their own altitude. "With your talent and skills, there are men in Strasbourg who would well care to meet you. Modern heirs to Newton, the keepers of the great clock there."

Paolina's heart raced. He spoke of the wizards she'd sought since before leaving Praia Nova! "Them I would meet. Strasbourg is in the British Empire, if not in England. That is indeed my goal."

Sayeed spoke slowly. "I can lay a course more northerly, and cross the French territories rather than the western coast of Andalusia and the Bay of Biscay. Strasbourg is in Alsatia. The Royal Navy has towers there."

She tried to remain calm. "And you would take me?"

"If you wish to go. The Rational Humanists meet there in conclave under the banner of the Silent Order of the Second Winding." His voice became intense, thick with passion. "They will welcome you, with my testimony, and you will be treated with all the respect you have never been properly accorded before."

"Please," Paolina whispered. "Take me there, and show me what I need to know."

"I have already set the course," Sayeed admitted. "I wanted to ensure that you are with me in this."

She wondered what might have transpired had she not been with him. That question was not worth pursuing, Paolina quickly realized.

Not if she was going to see the Schwilgué Clock and those who had mastery of it.

In the days that followed, they crossed a seemingly endless country of sand. Sometimes it was long dunes that stretched across the land as far as the eye could see; other times the stuff spilled over cliffs and dry riverbeds and bluffs of red and gray stone. The trees were gone, as were the animal migrations, the little villages, the braided silver streams.

A terrible country, she thought, and wondered why God had seen fit to include it in His Creation.

Sayeed met with her from time to time, but he avoided the strange passion of their discussion of Strasbourg and the Silent Order. Instead they spoke quietly of the airship's operations, the note of the engines, how the heat affected the gasbag. All the details of the *Notus'* operation seemed overwhelming, yet Sayeed held them in his memory and at the tip of his tongue. He understood his ship the way most people understood their own hands. Maybe better.

Sayeed, al-Wazir, Hornsby—she wished there'd been men like that back in Praia Nova, instead of the petty, venal *fidalgos* with their imaginary empires of manhood and privilege. Men who might have been worthy of their women, and of her.

Of course, there had been that mad Dr. Ottweill, as well, and a camp full of scheming, aggressive laborers and soldiers.

She could admire the good in a few men without foolishly ignoring what made all the rest little better than animals.

These Rational Humanists in Strasbourg promised a much more civilized breed of man. Like Sayeed himself. Paolina was profoundly grateful that she had been able to find this path.

She looked forward to reasonable discourse with reasonable people who could see beyond the walls the world set on the minds of men and women alike.

To Paolina's surprise, the desert sea ended in a real sea. This ocean was the color of glass—nothing like the sullen gray heave of the Atlantic north of Praia Nova. Instead it seemed almost a jewel, some decoration set down by God to make beautiful a corner of His Creation.

"It's the Mediterranean, what is," Bucknell explained, gulping and bobbing. "She's the ocean at the middle of the world."

"Thank you," said Paolina, who knew perfectly well what the Mediterranean Sea was. She just didn't realize *this* was it. There were no charts available to her aboard *Notus,* while her knowledge of the geography of Northern Earth was necessarily limited by her lack of access to maps and globes.

She understood what those were, and what they were for; she'd just never seen one.

There were times when the shame of being a primitive swept over her. She didn't want to speak with Bucknell or anyone else. Rather, she just wanted to grab on to the rail and stare down at that eye-blue sea, pretending she knew everything needful to find her way and place in the world.

"John Chinaman don't sail into the Mediterranean," Bucknell offered. "Hard to pass Suez without the Royal Navy knowing all of it."

"So it's safe?" She stared down at two boats, small things though still big enough to be dragging nets behind like wings beneath the waves.

Where there was water, there were fishermen. The sea was infinite in her bounty. Paolina knew that from Praia Nova. Perhaps they had not felt the great waves here, on this water bounded by desert where the Wall storms did not rule. She wished them the joy of their catch and fair sailing.

"Safe as houses, ma'am." He mused on that a moment, biting his lip where the big raw scar pulsed livid. "If you likes your houses wide as a horizon and filled with sharks, I guess."

Paolina tacked the conversation. The lad was never much good at moving in a straight line for long anyway. "Have you been to Strasbourg, Bucknell?"

"No, no ma'am. *Notus,* she patrols the African coast mostly. Not so much with John Chinaman over the Sahara or the Continent."

"I can see why the Chinese would not patrol the desert," she said dryly. "And I suppose there's no friendly ports of call for them in Europe."

"We has them free cities, ma'am. Even the Queen can't set her flag everywhere she likes."

"Free city?" Paolina didn't mind this kind of ignorance so much—she was merely uninformed, not completely lacking in sense.

Bucknell began to wiggle. She'd observed this was what he did when lip biting did not improve his answers. She hoped the borders of her own knowledge were not so apparent in conversation.

"Where anyone can make a landfall without a permission, I guess," he finally managed. "But things still cost money in them places. Not so free there either. Like wine, and wom—" He stopped himself and blushed a crimson to match the St. George's cross in the British flag. "I means not so much as free for the taking, if you follow the scut of my jibe."

Paolina swallowed a giggle. "I think so. What are some free cities?"

"Oh, Alexandria, Sevastopol, Beirut, Aden, Cotonou. Places on the edge, ma'am. They would never in life make London or Rome or Marseilles a free city."

She'd caught the drift now. "And so the Chinese come and set their anchors for trade in places where the two empires rub together."

He was waxing enthusiastic now. "Aye. They rubs hardest in the east, I always hear tell on the deck. All the American lands keeps John Chinaman and Mother Vicky apart, but Africa and India and them mountain kingdoms where they worships the fat buddy, there's the rub. So we trades in Alexandria, but we fights in Goa. I been drinking with Chinee I knows would be a killing me a week later. Like them what chases us, that Captain Sayeed tricked down?" He stared at her, smiling, as Paolina's heart collapsed. "That was probably one of them cabbage mouth ships they fly. We met them in Cotonou on the way down to the Wall where we found you. Some heathen name of a ship I can't rightly say, sounded like *Shirley Cheese*. But Captain Chinaman and Captain Sayeed stood each other a fine dinner in some fuzzy wuzzy palace, while we 'uns and them 'uns drank that palm tree wine that makes your eyes hurt down on the beach and et roast lizards the size of wolfhounds."

Paolina's sick feeling intensified. Those had not been faceless killers, but men known to Sayeed. *Had he intended to destroy the pursuing airship*, she wondered, *or was it all a feint?*

She was also disturbed to realize that Sayeed had set a course north upon leaving *a Muralha*, outside his patrol orders. She thought she'd been clever, in the matter of Strasbourg, when in fact she'd been asking for something he'd long decided.

Men. Were they all filthy and stupid, lying to her because she was a girl?

"You going to be all right, ma'am?" Bucknell's voice filled with concern.

"Get away." Her tongue felt thick, and she would be damned if she was going to cry here on the open deck in front of the boy and anyone who happened along.

"Yes, ma'am." He bobbed, bowing and stepping away and trying simultaneously to both goggle at her and not look at all. "Should I get Dr. Florin, ma'am? Is it your monthlies?"

Paolina felt a crisp rush of rage overwhelm her confusion. "Get away from me, you stunted lackbrain!"

He got. She went back to watching the water, deeply ashamed of her temper and herself, but not knowing how to repair the damage without looking even more foolish.

Paolina did not see Bucknell for the rest of the day, but Sayeed eventually found her, shortly after she'd messed with the deck division, eating a bowl of beans and a niggardly little chunk of brown bread. She sat on the windward side of a rope locker, watching the horizon's blue deepen toward dusk and smelling the crisp salt air rising from beneath their keel.

"We make port in Marseilles late tonight," he said as he stood over her. "To take on fuel and stores, and grant the men some time."

"Am I going ashore?"

"You are free to do so, though it should be under escort." As she opened her mouth to protest, he raised a hand, palm up. "You are your own woman, but you lack papers. You will find papers can be important, within the boundaries of the Empire. In the company of a ship's officer, you will not be questioned. Alone, I cannot promise your safety or continued freedom."

"I see." She tried to banish the petulance from her voice, but without success. "It is not a free city."

"Nothing is free."

"No." Paolina wondered what manipulation might be under way now.

"Including," Sayeed added, "the services of the boy Bucknell. I set him to serve as your steward because he has a gentle heart, and would protect you from both rumor and the unwise acts of rough and lonely men. Which this vessel is full of, I assure you, just as every ship that has ever sailed since Adam's day. You have sent him away, with a cruelty I would not have expected of you. Do you now prefer to manage the crew on your own, or shall I set another man to your aid? And might he in turn expect the sharp side of your tongue? I've a few older crewmen with wives at home who can turn a hard word like nothing you've imagined, missy."

She was silent a few moments, regret warring with anger. Paolina had never gotten anything yet in this life by yielding to men, so she was not wont to commence doing so now. "Words are strange, Captain," she finally said. "One can lie without ever uttering an untruth. One can deceive while providing even a heart's desire. If I was cruel to Bucknell, I regret it. He had said some things which provoked my fear." She set down her bowl with the last few cooling, gelid beans still clinging to the bottom and clasped her arms around her knees while staring up at Sayeed.

"From the first you set a course north across Africa instead of following your patrol route. All that talk of Strasbourg and the Schwilgué Clock was a mummer's play, to make me feel I'd won something from you. And I learn as well you perhaps did not mean for me to stop our pursuers. Your fear and worry that night make so much more sense to me if I realize you had a lost a friend instead of an enemy. You used that Chinese captain to make an excuse for turning north, and you have meant to carry me to Strasbourg since we left the Wall. Why lie to me?"

"Ah." Sayeed reached down for her bowl with the obsessive tidiness of a sailor. He turned it in his fingers awhile. "I . . . I was not sure of you at first. If I had been wrong, we would have made for England from Marseilles, and none the wiser. As for Captain Yang and his *Shi Hsi-Chi*, the story is more complex than you think, but at heart, you have something of the right of it."

"So you lied to see what I would do." She climbed to her feet. "I killed a ship and dozens of men because I thought I was protecting us."

"It is a risk we all take," he snapped.

"Not at my hands, we do not." She snatched the gleam from her dress. "I did not mean to make a . . . a . . . *gun*! A thing to kill to protect, or be killed protecting. *You* made me a killer, with your lies. And what would you have told me if I had not asked after Strasbourg, sir? If your pretty lures about the Schwilgué Clock had fallen unheeded?"

His voice was cold. "I would have taken you there, if I judged you aright, and let the Silent Order determine what is best for you."

Paolina swallowed the next words that leapt to her tongue. Fighting with the captain would serve her no good at all. Instead she took another path. "I am not a weapon either, sir. I do not want you, or the Silent Order, or anyone determining what is best for me. If I wished to be chattel, I could have stayed in Praia Nova. The *fidalgos* there certainly knew what was best for me. All you had to do was ask them."

"Let me explain something, then." Sayeed, too, sounded as if he were struggling for control. "You are a woman, my dear. In the lands of the Empire, this means that your father, husband, or brother has the final say over your acts. In the absence of family and spouse, responsible men must stand in their place. This is both law and custom. You can argue against it all you want, but if it was freedom of action you desired, perhaps you should have stayed upon the Wall."

"I belong to no man," she blazed.

"All women belong to some man!" he shouted. "It is the natural order of things." With that, Sayeed stormed away.

Paolina sat awhile by the rope locker, sulking and plotting puerile vengeance. She could stop *Notus'* engines, but to what purpose? She could even stop Sayeed's heart, she reckoned, though even in her anger the thought made her ill. He was no worse a man than any other here, tepid endorsement though that was.

She wished she could reach out and give him an awful case of the flux, though. Or cause *him* to bleed and weep four days out of the moon's cycle.

Men were the prime error in God's Creation; that was obvious. If He'd made woman first, He could have stopped there and the world would have been so much better run.

She stayed onboard at Marseilles. *Notus* approached the mooring mast at dawn, a process Paolina watched with fascination. The port had twelve masts near a bustling waterfront crowded with vessels great and small. Many of them set out for the day's fishing even as the airship circled over their heads, setting herself into the wind at the right altitude.

The masts rose from a low hill just to the east of the docks. Their bases were surrounded by a cleared expanse of land which from the air still clearly showed the grid of streets and the outlines of old structures. She wondered if there had been a hydrogen fire, or if the Royal Navy had simply demolished the neighborhood against the threat of one.

The city stretched away in all directions—the waterfront itself, a district of buildings large as anything in Karindira's city or Ophir, miles of smaller establishments.

There were more people here than she'd ever seen in the world. Even Ophir, great and strange as it had been, was not so vast or sprawling. The huge masts where *Notus* came to dock were little more than interruptions in the rolling expanse of people crowded together like swallows in a cliff.

She could *smell* the city from the deck. They were about 150 feet above the hill where the masts were anchored, and perhaps a quarter mile from the edge of the airship reservation. This close, coal and cook fires and food and muck and the swelling scent of a city full of people mingled to a compounded odor the likes of which Paolina had never before experienced. Or even imagined.

The crew warped the airship into place with the aid of men upon the mast. *Notus* came to rest amid four of her fellows, the other seven masts being empty. Though Paolina could see differences in design among the airships, they were all clearly of a type—similar to one another in ways the Chinese she'd destroyed had not been. All flew England's colors as well. No free city here, to be sure.

No one, not Bucknell nor Sayeed nor anyone between them in the ship's company, offered her a chance to go down. She watched as the sailors were told off on their leave rotations to much groaning and shouting and gibing. The ones on discipline, forced to hold back from a city of fine wine and compliant women, bore their punishment with ill grace that the officers ignored and their fellow sailors hooted at.

She was one of those, trapped aboard with the ruffians and the deck watch, and whoever it was that would be aiding the purser in renewing the stores or the engineer in taking on fuel.

The thought of how they might have feted a *man* who'd single-handedly brought down an enemy airship was painful to contemplate. So she spent a while instead deciphering the lay of the streets, how carts and people flowed among the buildings, where commerce must come from and go to. It was a fascinating pursuit—such a great city was a marvel of design and ingenuity, though from the look of it, nearly all accidental. Even that hobby paled after a few hours, and so she went back to her hot little cabin and tried to sleep, wondering how it was that a woman was shrill and thoughtless when she exercised the same power that won accolades for a man.

AL-WAZIR

He stalked through the camp. He didn't know where Boaz was—they'd been separated in the fight. Right now no one was visible, but he realized that there were not enough bodies, either. Many of them were alive, somewhere. He would have noticed the winged savages carrying the workmen away in dozens and scores. The burning steam ram shrieked, some relief valve overwhelmed.

The tunnel. They had to be inside the tunnel. Picking up more firearms as he went, al-Wazir walked toward the cliff face.

Sure enough, there was a barricade at the mouth. A number of winged corpses were scattered outside, with more human remains. There was no one visible at the barricade, but he couldn't see into the shadows. A hundred barrels might be pointed at him now.

"Come on out of there, ye simple-minded liver eaters!" he shouted. "Them boojums be gone, and we've a hell of a lot of work tae do now."

"How is it you're still alive?" The voice sounded like Mercks, the railroad man al-Wazir had met back in Kent. "You been calling them down on us?"

The accusation was so extraordinary that it dumbfounded him. "Are you completely daft, man? I was out here fighting them off. I'm alive because I didn't turn my back and run. That's when they stoop on a man and snatch him up. You fewking rabbits is quivering in your hole now, but you'll have to come out to piss sometime!"

Suddenly tired as he'd ever been, al-Wazir sat on a feathered corpse and began checking the magazines of his armload of weapons. Where he found only a few rounds, he transferred them to other magazines. The two that were mostly full, he set aside.

He looked up when Ottweill approached, trailed by several of his toughs. Mercks' men, to be sure.

"The mission you are failing." Angry, Ottweill's accent was thick. He pointed at the smoldering steam borer. "This cannot be."

"What will ye be having of me, Doctor? I cannot sweep the skies clear. If your men will not drill themselves well enough to recall their orders when battle arrives, there is no fight to be had when the enemy comes."

"That is your concern."

Orders or no, al-Wazir had had enough of the doctor and his tunnel. This occasional, wearing combat would not do. It was like fighting the tide, and he couldn't trust the men at his back. "Then perhaps you should hide in your hole like snakes in a riverbank whilst I go and find proper help. There were never enough men here to fight a war, and a war is what we have. Ophir will strike and strike again. They've made allies of the killers that brought down my ship two years past. I'm man enough to walk under the open sky. You diggers can cower and weep."

"He'll just go and bring more of 'em," said Mercks, hovering at Ottweill's shoulder. "It's how he killed that *Beagle* or *Bassett* or whatever wooden bird he flew."

"Sassenach bastard," al-Wazir said quietly. "If I thought it would do any good, I'd knock out your teeth and feed them to you through your arse so your shit came out chewed tight and you had to suck on your dinner for the rest of your days. But the doctor here is going to need every man jack of you to die for him while I go for help. I shan't deprive him of one more English corpse to decorate his parlor." He stood. "Herr Doctor Professor Ottweill, I'd say it's been good to know ye, but lying's a mortal sin. I shall follow me orders and do what I may to summon aid."

"Go, coward," Ottweill said.

Al-Wazir resisted the urge to shoot the doctor where he stood. Instead he gathered his cartridges and his salvaged carbine and walked back through the smoldering, ruined camp. He would look for Boaz, send the Brass man on his way, then pass the gates and find his own path back down to the dock at Acalayong. The Mitémélé met the Bight of Benin there. He'd come home from the Bight before, by God.

He could do it again.

The river was brown, muddy and lazy as ever. The dock remained unmolested, somewhat to his amazement. Fuzzy wuzzy canoes were drawn up on the far bank in the brown ruck that spread between Acalayong and the water. Al-Wazir walked out along the dock and stared down at the crocodiles lazing among *Parsifal*'s broken ribs.

He wished he'd found Boaz. There had been no sign of the Brass man, neither as metal shards nor walking on two feet. Al-Wazir preferred to think of Boaz wending back even now to his people in their city somewhere up on the Wall.

As for himself, he would need to build a raft. He didn't think he could handle one of the fuzzy wuzzy canoes effectively, and there were no larger boats here. A raft would mean a long, slow sail up the coast until he found an honest ship to carry him home.

Is this my fate? al-Wazir wondered. His da had made a way back from the Wall, those long years ago. Now here he was, possibly the only man in English history to have to find that long way home *twice*.

It was good he did not have a son. The poor lad would be doomed to thrice covering the distance between here and forever.

There was nothing for it but to build a raft, so he did. As he worked, his mind kept straying back to the metal man. Gone now, as everyone was.

Three days later, al-Wazir was testing his little vessel fully loaded in the waters of the Mitémélé when he heard a familiar sound. *Airship*. He scanned the sky with a shading hand to spot the source of the propellers' whine.

What he saw gave him long pause.

Two Chinese airships, their configuration of gasbag and hull unmistakable, cruised in a slow search pattern.

They were flying dogleg turns about two miles apart. The airships weren't working the Wall, which possibly meant they weren't looking for Ottweill's tunnel.

They'd find it soon enough, though, by spotting the dust plume from the excavation. Either that or the dock itself, which would be clearly visible from the air, and just as clearly not a fuzzy wuzzy undertaking.

He set his little sail, laid his paddle into the slow current, and began to steer away from them. No point in inviting attention by remaining near the wreck of *Parsifal* or the dock itself.

The river deposited him into the waiting arms of the sea, where it pooled dark and lazy at the intersection of Africa and the lowest, tumbled foot of the Wall. Al-Wazir let the shore wind push him out past the desultory surf line before he began paddling. The raft handled no better than a floating door might have, but his time was plentiful. He would sail west and north until a ship coming south picked him up, or he paddled all the way back to England.

Al-Wazir watched for an inlet by the failing light of day. Even better, he hoped to spot an island with dryland growth standing permanently above the tide. The moon's track glowed in the sky, lit with the golden fire of sunset, but the sea was already purpling, and he could see a first few stars of evening. The wind was shifting, too, as it always did with nightfall in the tropics.

Al-Wazir had no desire to be on the open water in the dark. Not in this wee unstable rig.

Water exploded next to him. Al-Wazir bit off a curse and looked upward to see one of the Chinese airships several hundred feet above. Sparks flared where grenadoes tumbled down from on high.

He grabbed at the carbine. It was lashed to the mast, wrapped in broad leaves from a fleshy plant growing back along the river. He'd covered the firearm in the fat from a potto he'd killed, in hopes of some protection from the salt air. Several moments passed while he picked at the greasy knots, even as the raft began to buck on the surf it was now passing through with the landward turn of the wind.

The carbine came free at the same time that one of the grenadoes struck the deck. Al-Wazir got the impression of something red and hissing; then a tremendous crash both deafened and wetted him. He tried pulling the trigger. All there was to shoot at were bubbles, and his mouth was filled with salt, and the water boomed like the footsteps of his angry father come home after a long night of drinking.

Daylight brought more than dark dreams of cold hell. Or perhaps the end of dreaming had brought daylight. He was still cold, though, except where he burned like fire.

Something touched him. Al-Wazir tried to push it off, but his arm tingled and dragged. He realized the touch was cold and strong as he was rolled over on his side.

The rush of nausea came as a great surprise. Seawater, bile, blood flooded his nose, his mouth, even up into his head. He seemed in greater danger from drowning of this effluent than he had in the arms of the ocean itself.

Hands pounded his back so hard that a rib cracked with a shooting flare of pain. Al-Wazir burped out a quantity of sand and mud, and another rush of bloody, stinging water, then closed his eyes and gasped awhile.

"I've fresh water upon your being ready for it," said a familiar voice.

Ants, thought al-Wazir, *there are ants upon my body.* He tried to speak, but managed only a wretched croak.

The hands pulled him onto his back and into a pool of stinking, warm fluid, and dribbled something on his face. Fresh, sweet water. Al-Wazir began to sneeze, his nose, so offended by the sand and bile, now fighting back. He could not drink. The sneezing made the injured rib flare and flare again.

Ribs. He was hurt more than there.

Finally he opened his eyes and sobbed.

Boaz—it had to be Boaz, no other Brass would have come to his aid—handed him a rag soaked in water.

Al-Wazir closed his lips around it. He didn't even suck, just let the water drip into his raw, wounded mouth, and from there down his scoured throat.

There was sun in the sky, but it was dappled by green palms wound with vines. He was on land, then. His eyes met Boaz' blank gaze. Al-Wazir wanted to ask, but words weren't in it right then.

Boaz nodded. "You were floating amid the tide, bearing a piece of vine tight clutched in your hands. Had you been asea facedown, you most assuredly would have been long dead."

"Hmm," al-Wazir managed.

"There has been a strange vessel off our shore. In communication with the hostile airships hovering in the heavens above. It surfaces from beneath the waves, then slips once again from sight."

"Ch . . . Chi . . ." He couldn't manage more.

"Sleep. I shall locate some fruit, with ripe, sweet flesh for you."

Al-Wazir meant to protest that, but his body would not cooperate.

"They scan the shoreline." Boaz wiped down one of the Brass lightning spears with a leaf as he spoke. "We shall essay a departure this night. This position is too exposed."

Voice seemed to have returned to al-Wazir, in thin, hoarse measure. He was largely intact as well, with no important limbs or parts missing, though he would swear every portion of his body was bruised, scraped, or sprained. "Chinese," he said. "In the Bight."

"Verily. I would take you back to the Wall, if you could but permit such an expedition."

"England." Too many words at once were difficult.

Boaz checked something at the spear's head. "Not this route, not upon this day. Might you be able to reach England from the Indian coast of Africa?"

"The . . . Wall . . ." Al-Wazir racked his memory. He'd never served on an Indian Ocean station. There much of the simmering conflict between England and China was played out. The Atlantic had always been his haunt. But he knew there was a base at Mogadishu to watch for Chinese attempts along the Wall.

Though the Royal Navy had certainly not lived up to its purposes if two Chinese airships were now cruising the Bight of Benin. Not to mention whatever had been in the water.

Pleased that clarity of thought seemed to have returned, he tried once more for clarity of speech. "Mogadishu. Just north of where the Wall meets the Indian Ocean."

"I can convey you there far more readily and safely than I might be able to escort you north across Africa, let alone travel upon the waters."

"Then let us go." Al-Wazir could not remember having felt so flat and helpless in all his life.

Boaz gathered the chief in his arms as if the big Scotsman were nothing more than a load of firewood. The Brass man turned his footsteps into the green depths of the jungle, away from the edge of sea and sky where death wandered above.

CHILDRESS

Five Lucky Winds steamed into Tainan harbor with sailors ranked along the deck, flags flying from her tower, and staffs mounted at her bow and stern. A red silk dragon snapped in the stiff breeze above a blue ensign. Childress knew the names of none of the sigils, but their intent was clear enough.

We are home, the flags proclaimed. *Victorious and mighty, the sea having bent her back once more to our lash.*

The coast here was flat with hills rising in the land beyond. The harbor was a lagoon, entered through a channel between sand banks. The Beiyang Navy had claimed much of the waterfront.

Sendai had been nothing more than dockside shacks compared with the bustling brawl of Tainan. This could have been Boston, Childress realized. Even to the airship masts, though she would not have recognized the ships themselves that floated there.

More impressive were a series of very large buildings seemingly designed to house grounded airships. The vessels never touched down, so far as she knew—these must be construction facilities.

She could see two other submarines in port, along with a variety of larger, heavier iron ships. Great turreted guns protruded from their decks. The long barrels of the weapons were oddly graceful.

Flags flew everywhere on those ships, and on the shore. People teemed along the docks—not a welcoming party, but simply a thickness of populace she might not have been able to envision without seeing it herself.

Captain Leung swept his hand wide to indicate the extent of the waterfront. "This is the home port of the Beiyang Navy. We were removed from Weihai a decade ago, but have made ourselves stronger in this place."

She was shocked. "Your Emperor expelled his own navy?"

"China has many navies," Leung said. "The Beiyang Navy is the most modern and the proudest. We turn our face to the blue waters of the outside world instead of the brown waters of home.

"Home is more . . . prestigious." They'd discussed this before. She simply hadn't quite realized how literally he'd meant what he'd said about the way affairs were organized in China. The idea of a sovereign nation mounting competing forces to struggle against one another for funds and patronage seemed strange to her, until she considered the regimental system that still formed the backbone of the English army.

But that was men and flags, not these expensive, terrible ships.

Leung spoke up again. "Some battles are still fought by little wooden ships slipping among the islands of the Andaman Sea and such quiet places. That world is largely gone from us, driven away by English aggression and the march of progress. An impudent man might remark that the Imperial Court takes little note of England and even less note of progress. I, however, shall refrain from such untoward observations."

"Indeed," muttered Childress, hiding a smile.

Then *Five Lucky Winds* followed signal flags into her berth, with much shouting and whistling and casting of lines.

There was an odor the likes of which she had never before encountered—bodies and horses and oiled metal and smoke and the salty scent of Chinese cooking, mingled in a scent so strong, it might as well have walked around on two feet, slapping people. Though the docks teemed with people, the wharf at their berth was clear of most traffic. A squad of men in blue uniform stood there, backed by a small mob of people of all ages and genders dressed in loose black clothes.

"Our escort," Leung said, "and the stewards and servants of our sailors."

"Your sailors have stewards?" Somehow she hadn't expected that.

"Yes. Even the least of the men among the Iron Bamboo fleet is great here in Tainan. With nothing to spend their wage on, it is banked. Some may be drawn down to a servant or two to keep their houses and care for their wives and children."

"I cannot imagine a British tar with a manservant at home."

"Then I sorrow for your tars, madam." He bowed. "Please wait here in the tower. I must attend certain formalities."

Leung slipped down the ladder and onto the deck to dismiss the greater part of his crew. An unlucky few remained behind to secure the ship. Looking past the soldiers and servants, Childress could see mechanics and quartermasters waiting beyond a bamboo barrier to approach *Five Lucky Winds* and begin their work as well.

It was a homecoming for everyone but her.

And Choi, said an honest, painful voice inside her head. *Choi, and Anneke, Captain Eckhuysen, the Mask Poinsard, and all the others who'd died aboard* Mute Swan.

Her anger had faded with time and familiarity, but its thin ghost still haunted her.

Leung came for her not long after, as the mechanics and quartermasters flooded past. "I am claiming you as my honored guest," he told her quietly. "The petty officer commanding the detail wishes to bind you, but I have convinced him otherwise by virtue of both my rank and my sheer force of character."

He glowered as he spoke, causing Childress to wonder what else had been said. "The petty officer can scarcely be threatened by one old Englishwoman."

"It is not the woman he would put in chains, Mask Childress. It is all of England, present here only in your slight form."

She smiled, then followed him down the ladderway, out across the deck and up the gangplank to the wharf. There the petty officer glowered his distaste for perfidious Albion but held back an obvious impulse to hard words and harsher orders. That was clear to Childress even across the gaps of language and culture.

Instead he formed his men up before and behind her. They marched Childress out the gate and along the waterfront toward a building with red lacquered pillars fronting a far more utilitarian three stories of windowed stone.

As she'd learned of much of China, the building was a mix of tradition and practicality. The center held to the oldest ways, the edges tried the newest, and the churn between them maintained the Celestial Empire.

She wondered how it was in England, and whether she would ever get to see the differences for herself.

They approached their destination quickly enough. The petty officer seemed ready to march his detail right through the great bronze doors, but Leung halted him with a set of rough-barked orders. With obvious bad grace, the petty officer detached himself from his men and led them inside.

It could have been any lobby in the British empire. The decor differed only in the pattern in the rug and the nature of the paintings on the wall. Electrick fans depending from the high ceilings whicked round and round against the tropical heat. Clerks worked behind little cages like bank tellers. A man at a desk was setting appointments. A number of people, both in and out of uniform, sat on benches like so many tired passengers waiting for a train that might never come.

The three of them marched to a creaking elevator, then rode the wrought-iron cage in silence to the top floor. The petty officer threw open the door and shouted them out. Childress wondered how he'd thought to bring his squad up this little conveyance, which had barely fit the three of them. Perhaps that would only have been a show for the lesser folk in the lobby.

"The Admiral's English is poor," Leung whispered to Childress.

She resisted the urge to shrug. "My Chinese is even more so. We shall find our way."

The petty officer stopped them in front of a set of doors painted red, studded with brass knobs. Some device or sigil had been removed from the center of each upper panel to leave only a blank disk slightly elevated from the wood around it. Childress could see the ghost of an outline, but had no luck in making it out any better.

Their escort knocked twice, sharp, smart raps. He then favored Childress with a narrowed glare intended to melt her.

Someone called indistinctly from within. The petty officer threw open the door and stepped back. The sour, angry expression was still strong upon his face.

She hadn't been sure what to expect from Admiral Shang's office. Certainly *Five Lucky Winds* had not contained a trace of opulence. The submarine was a machine, designed for a machine's purpose, the bodies of men only furthering those ends. Ashore, amid wealth and power, people tended to serve their own purposes, no matter what oaths they'd sworn, no matter what commission they bore.

Except for its size, this office was ordinary. A polished wooden floor that could have been found in half the buildings in New Haven. Square double-hung windows facing the cranes and wharves of Tainan harbor, the noise and bustle and heat echoing in through their raised lower panes. A large desk, carved and ornamented in a style unfamiliar to her, but still unmistakably the lair of a bureaucrat. It might have fit nicely in the dean's office back at Yale.

There were certainly differences in style—instead of portraits of ships or famous dead men, the walls were hung with long, narrow paintings mounted on silk, weighted at the top and bottom to keep them straight. The room smelled of oils she didn't recognize, and incense she'd never encountered before her time aboard *Five Lucky Winds*. The side tables had tea and wine services of curious design.

The only strangeness was the absence of chairs on which guests might find refuge. Admiral Shang apparently believed in holding his meetings standing up. Certainly he was standing now.

She was inexperienced at assessing Asian quality, the countenances and habits of dress of Asian quality, but Shang was a strange man even to her foreign eye. He was taller than any Chinese she'd met thus far.

Tall was only the beginning of it. Shang had hair like brittle straw, which he wore long, and a face as pale as snow. His features were unmistakably Asiatic, but he seemed albino, like the pink-eyed white rabbits one of the children in her neighborhood back in New Haven had raised and sold for the cook pot.

Though she was less equipped to assess Shang's attire, the white brocade robe he wore seemed out of place. There had been very few people on the docks dressed in white. This had all the formality of a bishop's rochet to go with its unusual color. The pale fabric only called out the paste color of his skin.

Of course, she thought, *how would he turn away from it?* Shang had embraced what marked him out, rather than attempting a pointless concealment.

There was also a sharp gleam in those narrowed eyes. He seemed as suspicious as the petty officer. A quick rattle of Chinese, in which she caught a few familiar words—"vessel," "voyage," "Atlantic"?—provoked a long response from Leung. The captain did not seek to placate the admiral, but neither was he overtly confrontational. Rather, their conversation volleyed back and forth for several minutes. Shang's eyes never leaving Childress.

When the give-and-take ceased, Shang bowed low. "Ma sue ka Shi Da Sz, welcome."

She puzzled over that a moment before catching her own name in the strange syllables. "*Hsieh hsieh,* Admiral," she replied, thanking him in Chinese.

Leung took a formal pose, back stiff and chest thrown out. "The admiral bids you greetings here in Tainan. He offers you the hospitality of the Beiyang Navy."

She knew how to decode the hidden warfare behind such politesse. Even across languages, the dance was clear enough. His carefully chosen words signaled that she was being kept here in the naval base. And he decidedly had not mentioned the hospitality of the city or the Celestial Empire as a whole.

"I thank the admiral," Childress said as graciously as she could, speaking slowly in case he understood any of it. "His hospitality is a welcome grace note to the courtesy shown me aboard *Five Lucky Winds.*"

Meaning: I prefer the protection of the captain.

Shang smiled when Leung rattled that off in translation. He responded at some length, with a series of questions and answers.

Eventually Leung cleared his throat. "I am to explain something in my own words, though I still speak for the admiral. Do you understand the intent?"

Childress was fascinated. "Yes."

"It would be normal practice of the Imperial Court at a time such as this to exchange invitations to exquisite services of tea and rice wine. The two parties would pass veiled insults and subtle threats in an attempt to test one another's resources. Each would to compose poems upon the virtues of the season and matters of the heart, until someone tired of the game. Such contests can go on for weeks, even months and years, as the player who yields first loses much advantage. His face is taken away, and he is known for a buffoon and a peasant among his fellows. Even his concubines will laugh behind their fans."

"I have no fan, sir," Childress said.

"Indeed. You are not Chinese, you are of no known nobility, you are perhaps not even human according to the strictures of the Celestial Empire. Admiral Shang, who understands much about the judgments of the color of skin and eye, proposes that we consider the elaborate courtesies to have been rendered. He is even so gracious as to yield the point to you."

Childress swallowed a laugh. "Since such yielding is, after all, wasted on an old woman from the English lands."

"Do not underestimate the power of old women in China," Leung told her, an intense expression on this face. "And as that may be, do you accept Admiral Shang's proposal of courtesies dispensed with?"

"Of course." Childress bowed to the admiral. "And convey to him my admiration for his subtle observation of the forms of civilized discourse."

Some expression flickered on Leung's face that might have been the ghost of laughter. Then he spoke again.

When the admiral answered, Leung froze. The admiral then spoke directly to Childress, in thickly accented but clear English. "Where is the Ma sue ka Pu Yin Sar?"

TWELVE

PAOLINA

Time passed with a slowness that Paolina found excruciating. She toyed with crazed plans once more, bringing down the other airships or somehow reaching out to the city of Marseilles with the power of her gleam. Revenge seemed pointless, even in the privacy of her imagination. All men followed their courses surely as the earth did. To expect Captain Sayeed to relent in his decision to confine her aboard ship was no more sensible than to expect night to fail in coming after day.

Despite her wounded pride and overwhelming boredom, night did follow day, and day came again. By six bells of the second dogwatch, as the curious Naval method of timekeeping had been explained to her, the crew was aboard. Paolina watched from atop a rope locker while the first mate mustered the divisions for a head count.

The captain seemed surprised to have all his men back. She could understand that. They'd just come off a cruise down the Atlantic to the Wall and back, with no company but one another and hostile Chinese airships. The wine and . . . other amusements . . . in port must be irresistible. She'd heard enough English grumbling about the unreliable, incompetent French to understand why the British tars would come back aboard, but the Continental Europeans among the crew were another matter.

They cast off into the chilling air of an October dusk. As *Notus* gained altitude, all Paolina could see were clouds and more clouds, parting to show the brass orbital threads of Luna and Earth and distant Venus.

The lights of Marseilles fell away behind the ship. First the pulsing glow of the central city, as if a furnace powered the metropolis, then the glimmering knots of neighborhoods and outlying villages until there was only the dark countryside below with the occasional light of a shepherd's camp.

There were more people in Marseilles than Paolina had ever thought to exist in the world. Logically the world was capable of containing billions, so long as they had enough to eat and places to sleep. But she'd assumed that cities would be larger versions of Praia Nova, much as Karindira's stone town had been. Even Ophir, for all the proud history proclaimed by Boaz, had still been comprehensible to her.

The teeming sprawl of Marseilles was another matter entirely. Even from the air she'd *smelled* more human beings than she'd ever have known the existence of. She tried to calculate the mileage of all the streets in the city, but gave up when she realized that a thousand miles of pavement would not encompass half of what she could see.

Europeans bred like rabbits in a meadow. The only reason they had not overwhelmed *a Muralha* was sheer distance. Someday this flood of people would lap at the foot of the Wall, then begin to climb. Praia Nova, Ophir, and every village, tribe, and hypogeal monster between the Atlantic surf and the brass track in the frigid air high above would be at risk.

That thought depressed her, immensely.

They sailed almost due north that night, which seemed odd, given Paolina's limited understanding of European geography. She would have expected a more easterly curse. She continued in her strange version of solitary confinement. If she moved about the deck, men sidled away from her. The only exception was if she approached the poop where the officers stood. Invariably some large airman would block her way, looking overboard or aft, anywhere but at her.

She wound up in the bow, watching clouds lit by starshine. Paolina did not need to speak to Captain Sayeed, or Bucknell, or anyone else aboard this accursed ship. They were all men, with the same universal delusions of ownership and importance.

As the night wore on, she found herself wishing she had reached some accommodation with life in Praia Nova. At least there she'd understood what the *fidalgos* were about. These Englishmen of sail and sky seemed more alien than the enkidus or the Brass.

Eventually light stole into the eastern sky. The bright traceries of the outer planets vanished first, taking the slighter lamps of the stars with them. Somewhere during that slowly fading display Paolina realized the strange clouds she'd been watching to the east were in fact mountains. Their white shoulders thrust into the airship's wide sky.

East of north would have taken *Notus* right into those peaks deep in the night. While she had no doubt that Captain Sayeed would fly his ship over *a Muralha* if he felt compelled to do that, she also acknowledged him as a very prudent man.

In some matters, at least.

Sunlight had not made the climb over the eastern mountains, but dawn's brightening lent depth and color to the last of night's shadow play. There were towns below, not large enough to have had electricks against the darkness, where roof tiles glistened with morning dewfall.

It was also cold up here; colder than she'd been before on this voyage. Or really, colder than she'd ever been in her life. Paolina realized she was shivering. Her teeth clicked, and her body seemed oddly numb.

She'd avoided the sailors just as they'd avoided her, but this was too much. She crept to the forecastle and slipped through the hatch to her little cabin. Though she'd slept on deck through most of their African travels, Europe was too cold and damp. Belowdecks there were blankets, and no wind.

She finally fell asleep.

"We's over Strasbourg," Bucknell said, waking her as he leaned through the door without actually setting foot within. He looked sullen, and had a dreadful black eye.

Paolina didn't ask. She didn't want to ask. That would presume she cared for Bucknell and his fate. He was just another Englishman.

"Am I to come on deck?"

"Wouldn't rightly know, ma'am, seein' as *I'm* a stunted lackbrain." He spat on the deck. "Captain might see it amiss if you did not, though."

"Thank you," she said, almost reflexively. Then, on impulse: "Bucknell, I apologize. My difficulties are not your doing, and it was unfair of me to strike at you as if they were."

One hand strayed gingerly to his eye. "'T'were Gunny Rosskamp what struck at me, ma'am. You only did give me the sharp side of your tongue."

"Well, I am sorry for that as well."

Maybe sleep had dulled her edge, or the notion of arriving at a destination so far from the Wall. Whatever Sayeed's machinations, the Schwilgué Clock was here. It counted the unwinding of the heart of destiny, if half of what he'd said about the magnificent thing was true.

She was bound for where she'd set out to be—in the company of wizards, in the presence of great and powerful things beyond what she might ever have found upon the Wall.

Paolina gathered her handful of belongings and stepped into the companionway. Bucknell slouched ahead, leading her back to the main deck as if she'd never found her way there on her own before.

Notus was passing low over a city of spires and thick-walled buildings with red roofs. A cathedral with a single tower dominated a central square, while a complex of large buildings huddled a few blocks away along tree-lined streets. A smaller river met a larger here, and the city was surrounded by the richest, greenest hills she had seen since the jungles at the foot of *a Muralha*. There was a certain twisty charm clear even from the air. The brawling ruckus that had afflicted Marseilles seemed to have passed Strasbourg by. This pretty little city seemed made for the dreams of artists.

There were two masts at the edge of town in the middle of a fenced-off field where sheep grazed. The little base wasn't much—some small buildings of a bunkered, windowless appearance, two large fuel tanks, and a handful of men in dark hats gawping up at the approaching *Notus*.

The group of watchers reminded her of the people of Praia Nova, how the *fidalgos* would stare openmouthed at anything that wasn't part of their everyday lives.

The Silent Order and the Schwilgué Clock; that was what she was here for. The elusive wizards who'd built an empire spanning half the Northern Earth could show her secrets. They would guide her on the road she'd long since tired of building for herself. It didn't matter what Sayeed thought he was doing—she was here.

Paolina wrapped her arms tight against the morning chill and smiled as *Notus'* motors forced the airship downward. The sailors shouted in short, loud codes and cast lines over the rail to secure their arrival.

"I am Karol Lachance," said a gangly Frenchman in black canvas pants, a white linen shirt, and a black leather vest. He wore a small-billed cap over an apparently bald head, with black eyes and a beak of a nose. Paolina couldn't tell Lachance's age, save that he was of middle years.

She and Sayeed had just climbed down the ladder within the mooring mast, and stood in a damp field, which smelled of morning dew and cowpats. The captain shifted uncomfortably. "Where is the Royal Navy station commander?"

Lachance shrugged. "Leftenant Charles was called to Stuttgart two days past. He took his chief with him." His accent was obvious now, different from anything Paolina had heard before.

Captain Sayeed shook his head. "He left a *civilian* in command?"

This time a slow, sharp smile dawned. "I am the Strasbourg harbormaster. This facility belongs to the city, under my care. Your Royal Navy leases it, but this is my field, Captain. And we had no indication you might be coming. *Notus,* she is not on the lists."

Sayeed made a complicated hand sign, to which Lachance did not respond. Paolina wondered if this were her opportunity to break away from Sayeed. She then wondered why she would want to do so. Better to stay with him to the Silent Order. Though she supposed she could find the Schwilgué Clock on her own. A cathedral could not be so hard to locate, after all.

"I must go into the city," the captain said. Paolina assumed he'd considered and rejected several stronger responses.

"Out the gate, to your left," Lachance replied with that same sharp smile.

After a graceless moment, Sayeed walked across the field along a gravel track and past a cart with two harnessed horses. Paolina trailed behind him until they reached the gate and were out on a wider road.

"Your diplomatic skills do you credit, Captain," she said.

He ignored the sarcasm. "This is not right."

"A disaster afoot?"

"No, no. Just poor standards. I might have expected such laxity in some distant port, but not here so close to London."

"They seemed competent enough to me."

Sayeed favored her with a glare. "Lachance does not follow protocol. Neither did the absent Leftenant Charles. Absent good Naval discipline, we are nothing."

"You are men. I am but a woman, and would not know of such things."

After a while Lachance passed them in his wagon. He tipped his hat to Paolina while ignoring Sayeed.

Once again, she had a sense of choice. She elected to continue following the man who would lead her to the Silent Order.

From the ground, Strasbourg was a city of cobbled streets and tall, narrow buildings. There was not as much traffic as she might have imagined, but the hour was early. Had she not seen Marseilles, Paolina would have found this alien and huge, but the place was almost homelike compared with that great Mediterranean hive.

Some buildings flew flags signifying alliances or professions. Others had signboards. She quickly realized that the citizens of Strasbourg lived on the upper floors, while their business stood below. Paolina had never seen a real shop, only knew them from reading Dickens. She was quite curious to look at the windows, or even pass within.

Sayeed set a brisk pace, though. He seemed uninterested in checking that she followed. Paolina realized that the captain understood the invisible cord that bound her surely as she did. The clock, he knew all about the clock.

They found their way to the central square facing the cathedral, a towering square edifice with a single turret rising from the left front. The building was covered with a frenzied ornamentation that struck her as a madman's work, angels and devils and sinners writhing in eye-bending braids of stone. Even the curious buildings of Ophir were far more plain than this cliff of close-carved masonry.

"It is Sunday," Sayeed said, who did not seem to see the wonder before his eyes. "We must await the morning services."

Paolina followed him to a building with several tables out front, chairs upturned. He set two down and they sat. After a little while Paolina realized this was a restaurant, a shop that would sell them food once it opened. Or could, had she any money.

They waited.

The city unfolded as morning passed slowly toward midday. It was one of the most fascinating things she had ever seen, like watching a flower open, petal after petal curling to meet the light. Here each color unfurling was a person bustling into view, throwing open shutters, lowering awnings, unlocking doors, setting out racks and bins and little shelves all around the storefronts of the square.

Bells high atop the cathedral called the times of services, and tolled the hours in between. Other churches of the city echoed the rhythms of the morning, but she noted far more people going about their business than entering or leaving the cathedral.

Horses, dogs, boys, men, women, baskets of fresh-baked bread, barrows full of cheeses and cabbages—all passed her in a parade of color and scent and sound, the unrolling of the scrim of civic life.

This was what had moved Dickens to write of the city and its people. She could only imagine how grand London would be, this small miracle of commerce and society writ large enough to govern an empire.

If she squinted upward, Paolina could even see the track of the earth rising in the sky, a thread to tie this city and its holy cathedral back to Heaven.

Eventually a dumpy woman in a thick black dress trimmed with black lace came out and took down the other chairs. She worked around them—Sayeed paying no attention at all, while the woman ignored Paolina's inquiring looks. Linens appeared on the little iron tables (including theirs), then small dishes filled with sugar and salt and cream. After a while forks and knives as well. Finally, unbidden, a pot of coffee and a basket of rolls for them.

She took one out. It was a flaky half-moon with a fat middle and narrow arms that weighed less than any piece of bread she'd ever touched in her life.

"Crescent roll," Sayeed told her—his first words since they'd sat down. While she'd watched life around the square, he'd stared unendingly at the doors of the cathedral.

Paolina smiled, too happy in the moment to be angry even at this man. "And coffee."

"Mmm." He poured himself a cup of black and sipped at it. "When the next service lets out, we shall approach the cathedral. There will be someone waiting for us. He will take us to the Silent Fathers."

Paolina hoped it might be Lachance. That would be a small humiliation for Sayeed, who had richly earned it.

An onion-seller found them as they approached the cathedral. He wore a rumpled blue garment cut to fit his whole body, not divided into pants and shirt, and carried a basket that reeked of his produce mixed with the scent of damp loam.

The onion-seller made a hand sign, which Sayeed matched. They stood close and murmured to one another, with sidelong glances at Paolina. She smiled again.

Sayeed tugged at her arm. Paolina followed around to an alley beside the cathedral. A man in a long black dress opened a side door at the onion-seller's rhythmic knock. He said something to Sayeed in a language Paolina didn't know, then offered her his hand.

Her last view of Sayeed was the door shutting, the captain's face flushed with frustration.

"You are the girl here about the clock," the priest said.

Surely, she thought, *he has to be a priest.* "How did you know?"

"We are the Silent Order. I could not tell you even if I wished to."

"You are not so silent," she pointed out.

The priest laughed. "No, perhaps not so much."

They stepped from a plain little hall into a great space. The inside of the cathedral was if anything more frenzied and ornamented that the outside. The walls soared toward heaven, supported by a single great pillar. The curious carvings on the face of the building were replicated here, relieved in turn by a riot of colored glass and winged statues and candles and banners, all in dizzying array above a room full of benches that reeked of incense.

It would take hours to sort out everything her eyes could see—much like looking up at *a Muralha* on an exceptionally clear day, where there was more detail than any one person could hope to understand. Paolina felt overwhelmed.

"The clock is this way." The priest tugged at her hand with a dry grip.

She followed him, the gleam so heavy in her pocket that it felt like a boulder dragging her downward.

AL-WAZIR

By the second day, he insisted on walking. Though his pace was poor and his ankles ached abominably, he had no desire to be carried by Boaz across the bottom of Africa like some great, mewling child.

The Brass did not argue. Instead, he outlined what was to come. "We must transit westwards the distance of fifty or sixty miles through this dense jungle scape," he said, "before we may set our faces south and cross the Mitémélé in any hope of secrecy. From there we shall essay the lower reaches of the Wall. There we might hope to continue east with more rapidity and safety than ever we shall find in this rusting misery."

Rusting misery. Stinking misery was more like it, but he had no desire to argue. "Aye," he muttered, "Chinee on the water and in the air. The Englishman's highway is not safe 'til Her Imperial Majesty sends more to sweep them Asiatic leavings off our doorstep. Meanwhile your plan of making for the Horn is better than walking up the fever coast of the Bight of Benin."

"And so we shall proceed." Boaz glanced at al-Wazir's feet. "You shall set our pace, sir."

The first parts of the journey were a confusion of vines and mud and doublings back around obstacle after obstacle while avoiding open stretches. By the second day they had the water on their right, but jungle followed the river inland. Al-Wazir supposed this was a blessing, as it shielded them from the airships he twice more heard pass overhead.

"I cannot conjecture whether they hunt for us," Boaz told him that evening. Al-Wazir ate some sour fruit the Brass had found, and tried to ignore his desire for a fire, even in the night's heat. "But there is a hunt aloft nonetheless. We should not be caught within their wily snares."

"Where's the Royal Navy in all this?"

"Neither of us can say."

So on they walked.

After they crossed the Mitémélé, they angled south and east toward the rising bulk of the Wall. Al-Wazir saw smoke to the west. It might be Ottweill's camp, but he could not find the desire to investigate. All he could do to rescue the men who remained there was press on. He tried not to think about the distance to Mogadishu. Boaz seemed to have methods to move quickly upon the Wall, perhaps in the brass cars the girl had mentioned.

Anything would be better than this damnable jungle.

A Chinese airship found them the next day as they crossed a meadow of waist-high grasses teeming with snakes. Busy looking down, al-Wazir realized their peril only when a rattling crack of small-arms fire got his attention.

It was about a thousand feet above them, trailing their position by a quarter mile. He'd have had the heads of his men for wasting ammunition at that range. Two on foot were not going to escape the attentions of an airship. They could afford to be patient up there.

"Fools."

"We must proceed," Boaz said. "There are larger rocks for shelter ahead."

"Until they land a shore party to flush us out."

"If so, we shall take what steps we may. But there is no purpose in standing here and waiting to be struck down."

"Aye. Ye have the right of that."

Several more volleys were fired as they crossed the open ground, ignoring the danger in favor of quickly making time. Nothing came close to hitting, though al-Wazir felt the familiar prickle of mixed fear and thrill at being the object of such a hunt. Every time *Bassett* had ever fought, he'd had the same sensation.

He'd just never experienced it in combination with the certainty of defeat.

They crouched behind a pair of boulders that formed a vee-shaped gap, like a stone lean-to. "Do ye suppose the Chinee are in the mood for prisoners?"

Spear in hand, Boaz looked over a rim of the rock. "I am in no position to speculate on such, but I rather imagine not. Their behavior of the past few days would seem to indicate frustration."

" 'Tis a bloody pain landing men from an airship when you've got no mooring," al-Wazir offered. His ribs ached abominably.

Boaz shifted, improving his view. "Indeed, one might suppose so, but still they are letting down lines."

Al-Wazir sighed. "We have no guns, we have no knives, and I'm not fit to rassle a sheep. If it were in me to surrender, I'd raise me drawers on a stick and call it done."

"Abide," said Boaz. "Another moment always comes, bringing another opportunity."

"Aye, opportunity it is, ye great, daft bugger."

"We are not taken yet, and we have not begun to fight."

"Indeed, lad, indeed. You'd have made a fine tar."

He rested in the deep shade of the rocks awhile, as Boaz continued to peer out of their shelter.

"Are you yet able to discharge a firearm?" the Brass asked a while later.

"Aye," muttered al-Wazir. "Would that I had one." He was trying to decide if he owed any apologies to God.

"I have formed a plan."

The chief had never suffered from a poverty of imagination, but he would be snookered before he could see how Boaz thought to find a way out of this situation. "Excellent. And what plan would that be?"

"I surmise that the Chinese are hunting you with murderous intent. To the best of my knowledge, they have had no commerce with Ophir up on the Wall. My countenance will likely be of a surprising nature to them. I shall advance upon the party even now being landed by their catenary ropes and seek parley. They are more likely to take me aboard their airship, especially since executing me in the moment is not a meritorious strategy. Unlike you, I cannot be killed by a single well-placed shot."

"Aye. And so ye'd be prisoner aboard yon Chinee airship and I'd be here alone with me busted rib." He chuckled, trying not to laugh. " 'Tis not so troublesome to see what benefit this brings me, but I cannae ken why ye should be so intent on it yourself."

"I shall give to you my spear." Boaz unslung his weapon and began adjusting the rings set into the shaft just behind the wedge-shaped point.

"This is a capital offense in Ophir, to pass such a spear to a native of any sort, but we are not in Ophir now. You shall take aim at the Chinese airship. When the opportune moment presents itself, you shall fire the bolt into the gasbag. Continue firing until the lightning spear is exhausted. With even a minim of luck, we shall see the gasbag ignited."

He handed the spear to al-Wazir, who took it gingerly. These weapons had spouted lightning in the night outside the palisades of Ottweill's camp. He was not so keen to hold one now, for all that it might be a miracle of science from the Wall and worth a pretty penny in London. "Dull-witted sailor that I am, even I can point out several flaws in your plan."

"I possess the strength of four or five of your fellows," Boaz said. "I was able to carry you across difficult terrain. They may bind me or guard me, but it is not unreasonable to assume that I shall be able to break away and find the tiller. I will drive the airship southward and down, so it passes over your position at the lowest altitude possible. Then you will fire upon it."

"While a hundred angry Chinee swarm you, just before a bag of hydrogen explodes above your head." Al-Wazir sat up, gripping the spear more tightly. "And why should you do such a fool thing?"

"I want to see *her* again." Boaz' voice was quiet. "On my own, I shall never find her. Preserving your life is my sole opportunity."

"Best be going, then," said al-Wazir, who knew a suicide mission when he heard one.

Boaz slid around through the rocks and out into the sunlight. A moment later, al-Wazir heard the Brass' voice hailing loudly.

He examined the spear, toying with the three machined rings just below the head. He was unwilling to accidentally eliminate whatever adjustments the Brass had made.

Shouting and the meaty thump of fisticuffs echoed from outside. Boaz was distracting them. He resisted the urge to peek. Let them worry about the Brass. If the airship began to move, he would take his shot. If not, he would wish the brass man farewell and seek a comfortable place to hide, either to heal or to die.

A few minutes later, small-arms fire rattled again. Al-Wazir took that as his cue and painfully pulled himself up to look.

The airship still swung in the wind, keeping station under low engine idle a quarter mile distant and about two hundred feet up. The ropes trailed down, two men ascending in bosun's chairs, when the engines began to growl loudly. Al-Wazir watched in amazed delight as the nose of the airship wobbled, then dipped hard. She began to make headway toward him and the Wall beyond.

He braced the lightning spear, wondering where and how to grab it to fire. Al-Wazir ran his hands up and down the shaft, feeling for a catch or trigger.

He realized he should have asked for more instruction.

The airship wobbled and began to turn across the wind. Al-Wazir realized that if she made that cut, she'd pass no closer than she was right now. He stood and braced himself as the nose swung the other way. Two men tumbled off. The chaos on the deck was audible now.

He'd faced those Brass in combat, and knew how fearsome they were as hand-to-hand fighters. It was hard to imagine what the Chinese captain was about, not to simply have the crew rush the poop and bodily overpower Boaz.

The ship dipped again and the engines suddenly howled. She was almost overhead now. He aimed, fingers on the lowest ring below the spear head in a desperate guess. Twitch, nothing. Turn, nothing.

A pressure caused a bolt of lightning to vomit from the tip, blinding al-Wazir for a moment. When squinting, tear-filled sight returned, he saw part of the gasbag smoldering. Smoke trailing from the port rail amidships.

There was shouting from somewhere nearby on the ground—the last few sailors, chasing their ship and now realizing he must be here.

One thing at a time, al-Wazir told himself. Once he killed them all, God would know His own.

Another shot, this time with his eyes closed at the last moment. He opened them to see a burning man falling almost directly toward him. The wailing scream ended with a wet thump and the mixed smell of blood and shit just on the other side of his sheltering rock.

The airship was almost past. Third time, third time. He aimed once more, fired, and kept his eyes closed for a three count.

Just after he muttered "two," there was a noise too large to really be heard. A pressing wave of dry heat washed over him. Al-Wazir opened his eyes and slid to the top of the rock to gun down whoever was approaching. He tried not to think about the burning hull about to drop upon his head, or wonder where Boaz had gotten to and how the Brass had even intended to survive.

Three sailors were just past arm's length. Al-Wazir streamed the lightning at them, cutting them in smoldering halves even as a chunk of smoking hull the size of a barge smashed down upon them. He dropped and rolled back into the deepest shadow of the rock shelter, waiting for the rest of the fire to rain from the sky.

He was not disappointed.

Al-Wazir unfolded his arms from atop his head and crawled back up to look over the lip of the rock. Shards of burning gasbag lay all over the meadow.

Keeping the spear close to hand, he shuffled out into the smoking field to look for his friend and rescuer. Boaz was facedown, partially wrapped in rope. Al-Wazir poked him gently, then carefully sat next to the brass man. He managed to turn Boaz over. The metal eyes were blank, the head unmoving, but the Brass seemed intact. There were a number of dents and scorches, and he had all his limbs. Nothing was obviously loose.

Al-Wazir tugged at Boaz' shoulders. "Have they knocked your head in, you bloody oaf?"

There was no answer.

He sat there awhile, realizing he had no hope of dragging Boaz back to the rock shelter. Instead al-Wazir struggled to his feet to gather enough scrap to build a little fire. It was not so difficult to light, with all the punky wreckage around still showing ash and coal.

The Chinese, he left dead where they lay. He was injured, and had no shovel besides. And since the Asiatic bastards had tried twice to kill *him*, al-Wazir did not feel moved to spare them any grace now.

Instead he watched the stars come out and tried to keep warm and occasionally touched Boaz for luck.

"It is not meant to be so," Boaz said, around midnight.

Al-Wazir startled awake. He hadn't been asleep, not exactly, but drifting in a painful doze. He rubbed grit from his eyes and looked at the Brass carefully. "You live?"

"I exist, at the least." Boaz sat up with a groan of stressed metal. "I have been better."

"There's plenty who will be looking to see what went a-booming into flame this afternoon. If you can find your way to walking, we ought to be moving on."

"And you?" Boaz asked.

"And me."

Like a pair of crippled lovers, they continued to follow the path that had led them into this meadow, climbing toward the base of the Wall. They had to pass around another hulking section of the Chinese airship, but then there seemed to be no more enemies save the dark of night, fatigue, and the injuries both already bore.

They walked, and walked farther. There was nothing else to do.

CHILDRESS

She stared at Admiral Shang, wondering exactly what he meant by the question about Poinsard. Lacking other wisdom, she settled on directness. "I am present in her stead."

Leung translated.

"Agreements were made," Shang replied in English.

"I shall abide by them." She had no idea what that might mean, but Childress knew she had to maintain control of the conversation or she was lost. "The Golden Bridge at Chersonesus Aurea is a grave danger to the Celestial Kingdom, and indeed, all of Northern Earth. I have been sent in the place of the Mask Poinsard to deliver wisdom she was unwilling to face in her turn."

More translation, followed by another series of questions and response. The captain turned to her. "I am to congratulate you on your promotion. The admiral is familiar with that theory of succession and is impressed that a foreign woman has the face to follow through."

Childress felt a surge of desperation. To thank him now was to further compound the lie, dig herself in where she already had not meant to pass. But she had no choice. She was committed.

"I will not gainsay your conclusions, Admiral Shang. I am here now. The Mask Poinsard is not. I would scarce have made the long and toilsome journey merely to present you with platitudes."

There, she thought, *let him unravel* that. From Leung's vaguely sour expression, she realized the captain was not pleased either. Childress gave the admiral the small smile she normally reserved for wayward students and too-forward tradesmen.

"The admiral apologizes for any misperception," Leung said. "He inquires as to your concerns about the Golden Bridge."

Another gate passed, another brick in the wall of lies. She shook off the guilt. It was time to recapitulate her conversation with Leung. "The Southern Earth is a dark and magical place," Childress began.

When she was done with her discourse, Childress stepped back a pace. The admiral nodded absently. He then began a lengthy, low-voiced conversation with Leung, the two of them ignoring her. Childress wandered over to the nearest window to look down upon the bustle of life in Tainan.

The street before the Beiyang Admiralty was no different from what she'd seen on the way over from *Five Lucky Winds*. This time, though, she had the luxury of observing from a fixed point. She was also in nearly full possession of her sense of nerve. The life of the Tainan docks was spread before her—fruit-sellers, men with the little metal ovens on poles, dogs lounging in the shadows, firecracker-sellers and bicycle-peddlers and hurrying students and sailors and brash women and quiet servants.

The place was less and less different from the New Haven waterfront every time she looked at it. How had she found Tainan so foreign? Even the Chinese seemed normal to her, to the degree that when she saw a tall European in a white linen suit approaching the admiralty building, he looked very strange indeed.

She whirled, looking at Leung in hopes of warning him that something critical might be afoot. The captain and the admiral both glanced over at her sudden movement.

"Someone comes," Childress said. "A tall man, of my people."

Shang just nodded. Leung seemed surprised, then cast a narrow-eyed glance at his admiral. "What have you done?" he asked in English.

Admiral Shang stepped around his desk and sat without answering. He waved Leung to the wall behind him, in the place where an adjutant might stand at his shoulder. Childress stayed by the window, her link to the world of the Chinese. She wondered when she had become afraid of people of her own race.

The visitor was shown in moments later. He was a tall man, with hair even whiter than Shang's, but pale eyes that belied albinism. His skin was faintly flushed with the effort of his recent walk. A brass-tipped cane of some dark wood dangled in one hand.

This man was unmistakably European. Not some sport like Shang, nor a member of a strange race.

Shang spoke in Chinese, from which Childress caught only the interrogative. The tall man nodded, answering likewise.

"She has come in the place of the Mask Poinsard," Leung said into the stretching silence.

"The world is strange, and brings stranger gifts to us all." This time the tall European nodded to Childress. "I am William of Ghent."

The sorcerer! She was found out! There was nothing for it but to play her hand bold as brass, as would a student caught after curfew. She could hope her forwardness would be rewarded. Childress was confident that meek humility never could be.

"I am Emily McHenry Childress, Mask of the *avebianco*, come in place of the Mask Poinsard to speak against the project at the Wall." Something plucked at her memory. "You are dead, I have been told. On good authority." The highest, in fact, as it was this man's supposed death for which her own sacrifice to the Silent Order was penance.

"I would like to say those reports have been exaggerated, but like so many rumors, there is in fact a sad kernel of truth." His expression was almost mournful. "If my passing has given you difficulty, I am at a loss for suitable apologies. I cannot say that I recall our ever meeting before."

"We have not," Childress said. "Though perhaps there are indirect connections." She could not hide the trivial or the historic from this man, not if she hoped to cloak her purposes now. *Please, God,* she prayed, *let one lie be sufficient.*

"Indeed," said William. "Fascinating." He gave her a long stare, piercing her eyes, her thoughts, her heart. "You met him, didn't you?"

"Who?" she asked, though Childress was certain she knew what he meant.

"The boy Hethor."

"Yes. I sent him to you. Perhaps one of my great mistakes. My greatest."

"Madam, if you have lived the sort of life where only one great mistake was possible, I sorrow for you. But in the case of young Hethor, I believe your judgment was proven in the end."

"The world yet turns."

A nod. "And with no thanks to me, I might add. That boy caused many changes before he passed onward."

"He is dead, then?" She felt a surge of sadness for this boy whom she'd met once for an hour.

"Not . . . precisely. No more dead than I am. Suffice it to say he is beyond any concerns of this Northern Earth."

So Hethor had found a life south of the Wall after his great work with the mainspring. That was perhaps not the end she would have prayed for him to find, had she known to hope for his life at all.

"Wherever he is," she said, "I wish him well."

"As do I, madam, as do I." William twisted his cane in his hand. "We each touched something beyond ourselves."

"It is my hope, sir, to find the opportunity to continue to reach beyond myself."

"Indeed." Another long, slow stare. "And with that reach, how is your grasp, *Mask*?"

"Sufficient unto the needs of the day, sir."

With a laugh, William turned to Admiral Shang and began a torrent of Chinese. He nodded occasionally toward Childress.

She could not tell if this was a blessing or a death warrant. Both men kept their faces impassive, even as the two of them argued back and forth, tall men in white carrying on like ghosts of barristers brought back to argue one final case.

When they were done, William turned to her once more and bowed low, sweeping wide with his cane. "By strong words and stout heart you have earned whatever freedom of action remains to you, madam. Build from it as you see fit, with my own goodwill." He favored Leung with a nod, then left.

In the silence that followed, Childress kept glancing down at the street. William of Ghent emerged shortly from the Beiyang Admiralty, then began walking away. For all his height and the color of his clothes, he was quickly lost in the crowd. The swirl of bright noise swallowed him as a heron might swallow a frog.

When she turned back again, Shang was watching her speculatively. Leung began to speak. "I am to tell you that the admiral does not agree with your assessment of the Golden Bridge. However, the foreign sorcerer's endorsement of you carries great weight here in Tainan. It will even provide an echo of favor in the Imperial Court. As you have failed to bring the Great Relic promised by Poinsard, your role in the project can proceed no further."

She had a quick flash of thought that if Poinsard had possessed a Great Relic, it was now in the cold depths of the Atlantic, thanks to Leung's attack.

"To salvage some of what has been lost, the admiral will dispatch you to Chersonesus Aurea to meet with the priests and academicians gathered there. You may present your own case. They will judge the worth of what you bring and balance it against the loss of Poinsard's mission."

"And thus," she said, not caring if she interrupted, "the admiral is free of responsibility for my fate. William of Ghent is not angered, the Imperial Court will not be required to take notice, the Golden Bridge will be advanced in some fashion, if only in the aversion of negative result. I am once more pawn in someone else's game."

"You understand the stakes for which all are playing, Mask Childress," Leung said seriously. She realized he was speaking for himself now. "Your life is the only chitty you have with which to buy the seat you have already claimed at this table. Do not bemoan your pawnhood, any more than I bemoan my service to Admiral Shang, or he decries his own subordination to the Celestial Empire."

"I understand." She suppressed a sigh, instead standing tall and proud. "Believe me, this is not easy. I was never born or bred to the politics of power."

"You are a mask," said Shang unexpectedly. "Wear your power like skin."

She bowed to him, much as William of Ghent had bowed to her. "My thanks, Admiral. I will not betray your trust."

Leung began to speak, but Shang waved him off, laughing. "No trust, devil woman," he said in English. "Only curiosity. Now go."

The captain escorted her out. Childress did not trust herself to exchange a final word with the admiral.

THIRTEEN

PAOLINA

The Schwilgué Clock filled her vision like sunrise after an endless night. The device towered above Paolina, tall in proportion to the front of Strasbourg Cathedral, and ornamented with the same strange frenzy that had possessed the original builders. Where her case for the stemwinder was a simple shell, this was a wooden paean to the joy and skill of the clock's creator.

Two little balconies at the top held carved and painted figures that were meant to move at some impulse from the works within. Below them was a series of faces, each measuring a different aspect of the work of God's Creation. One showed the position of the sun, another the position of Luna and the planets, another the hours of the day as reckoned by men. Smaller hands followed other patterns. She was certain one marked the time that beat at the heart of the world, synchronous with the smallest hand on her gleam. The mechanisms inside must be as fascinating as the clockwork that drove the Earth. Paolina could not know the meaning of them all, not without instruction and careful study, but she loved each of them already.

A great face in the middle of the clock's case was painted with mystic sigils. That had to be the sport, the spare hand that could be set, like the fourth hand of her gleam, to match the will and word of the maker.

This work of wonder and might drowned her poor little gleam in the brilliant light of its presence. "By all the monsters of *a Muralha*," she whispered, "it must be a perfect model of the world."

"What do you see?" The priest's voice was low and urgent.

"What anyone with eyes would see," she answered slowly. "An image of Creation wrought by a master's hand. With this clock, one might decipher all secrets, and set all wrongs to right."

Someone behind her clapped slowly.

Paolina turned to see that a dozen men had filed in behind her. Among them was the onion-seller from the square outside, though Captain Sayeed was not with him. There were others in various elegant costumes she did not recognize.

The clapper left off. He was a man in pale robes trimmed with purple, and a tall hat shaped like an unopened lily. The cut of his clothes was much like the priest who had escorted her in, save far richer. A high priest, then—a bishop?

"We have awaited you down the centuries, Clockmistress," he said in careful, patient cadence. "Be welcome to this, the heart of the Silent Order of the Second Winding, and to our clock, which marks the measures of the world."

"But I—," Paolina began, then stopped. "You are not the builders?"

There was a murmur of polite laughter, though a few exchanged harder looks.

"No, no," said the bishop. "We are the high council. Guardians of the work and the purpose. Tools are meant for the hands of . . . others . . . such as yourself. See how you found your way to us?"

"Not to *you*," she replied, "but to this clock. The Schwilgué Clock is a masterwork. I would learn from him who built it."

"Then you are late in asking," said a man in a smartly cut burgundy coat. "Jean-Baptiste Schwilgué was laid to rest almost fifty years gone. You are the first since fit to take up his tools and his purposes."

"*Our* purposes," the bishop added.

Where were the English sorcerers that Sayeed had promised her? Since leaving Praia Nova, she'd been looking for the ones who could teach her more. These were not learned men—they were *fidalgos,* just like at home, but in the larger world with more power. They saw her as no more than a tool to be set in their service.

By God, she thought, *if I would not serve the* doms *of my home, why would I serve these English* fidalgos? *They are no better.*

Her hand closed on the gleam, fingers sliding out the stem. The priest beside her grabbed at her arm. Paolina shrieked and flinched. He struck her a hard slap with his free hand and snatched the gleam away, even as the Schwilgué Clock began to ring out the noon hour.

It was a symphony, a cacophony, the figures dancing and clacking, chimes shivering, a trumpet blowing, while the great bells in the tower above commenced their tolling. The bishop and his cronies stepped toward her, walking along the pews, cutting off her avenues of flight.

Paolina elbowed the priest in the gut. He tumbled to the floor, still clutching the gleam. Instead of pummeling him, Paolina stepped backwards to the face of the master clock and began to set the mystic hand. If she could find the rhythm that it matched, she could control that rhythm. That was her power.

The high council of the Silent Order knew that, too, for they stopped their advance. The bishop spread his arms, shouting over the racket of the hour, "Come, let us not be at odds now."

Paolina could not concentrate amid cacophony and threat. She shouted, then launched herself toward the bishop. He had not expected so direct an attack. She took him in the chest, knocked him flat, and grabbed up his staff to lay into the man behind him. A moment later she leapt over the pews, stepping from top rail to top rail as they scrambled after her.

The main doors were clear, her pursuers shouting as the bells died. Paolina burst screaming into the light.

Karol Lachance waited at the bottom of the steps, smoking a cigarette as he sat in his wagon. He nodded at her.

Not knowing what else to do, she raced down the steps, hurled the bishop's staff aside, and leapt over the sidewall of the wagon. Amid the clutter there, Paolina wrapped herself in canvas and began shivering with fright. Karol clucked his team into motion as shouting men erupted somewhere behind her.

She watched the sunlight glow through the sheet across her face as they made their unhurried way along the streets of Strasbourg. There was quickly enough a hue and cry of thief, rioter, mountebank. Bells and whistles carried the message, but Lachance drove on. Twice she heard him speaking in French—to policemen?—but with an easy familiarity and a chuckle that seemed sufficient to whatever was being asked.

Eventually the wagon settled to a steadier pace. There was no noise of people or city, just the quiet susurrus of the countryside, until something big and slow rumbled overhead.

Notus, she realized.

Paolina continued to lie hidden as Lachance drove them on, away from Strasbourg and the Schwilgué Clock. A cold feeling stole into her then, along with a hard-breathing panic.

They were heading away from the gleam.

The English had betrayed her completely. She'd lost the stemwinder she had worked so hard to build. Paolina began to cry, weeping in great, long shudders, biting her arm to hide her sobs.

Lachance threw off the canvas. "You must come now."

Shuddering, Paolina slid off the wagon's back. They were next to a field of long brown grass that had been cut and stacked. Trees rose beyond the stubble. The sky seemed shallower, more pale. No airships lurked overhead.

She stared at him. "Now what?"

The Frenchman shrugged. "You are shut of the cathedral and her silent mice, yes?"

"Yes. The Queen can have her own." Paolina added bitterly, "I never should have left *a Muralha*."

"I am sorry?"

"The Wall. I never should have left the Wall."

"Then go back to the Wall."

"Who are you to care?" she demanded.

"Just a bird," Lachance said. "A white bird far from home." He opened his vest and took out a fat envelope of waxy brown paper. "A few maps, and some funds."

"From whom?"

"White birds who do not want to see you trapped by those silent, orderly mice."

Pride warred with practicality. She was deep within the British Empire and very far from home. While she trusted his birds no more than Sayeed's silent mice, whatever Lachance was giving her was more than she had now. "I lost the gleam," she blurted as she took the packet.

Lachance smiled sadly. "I will see what I can do to recover your property. If the bishop and his mice took it, your gleam will not pass readily into my hands, I am afraid." He paused a moment. "If I may ask, why do you travel as a girl? Slim as you are, you could wear trousers and pass for a young man. People would devil you much less if you did so."

"I . . ." It wasn't as if Paolina didn't understand that to be a possibility. "Men are . . . men." The venom in her voice surprised her. "I don't want to be one, even for moment."

"Ah. My apologies. I should not have disturbed you with the question." He pointed southward. "Erstein is beyond that rise. Follow the road, it will lead you to Colmar, then Mulhouse. As I take it you do not wish to continue onward to England, from there you may head south, perhaps by railway carriage. God be with you."

"Thank you," Paolina said automatically.

He climbed onto his cart, clucked to his team, turned in a circle, and drove slowly away without a backward glance.

This is it? she thought. She waited until his dust trail settled, then found a quiet spot beneath a tree to examine the packet he'd given her. There was three hundred English pounds, with several maps of Europe and the

Mediterranean folded around them. Paolina had no idea what that amount of money represented, but it seemed quite a bit.

She tucked the funds away and studied the maps. There was no reason not to go to Marseilles, she realized. Sailing from that great port around the western coast of Africa would get her home fastest, but she didn't want to be anywhere near *Notus'* patrol route. Maybe once in Marseilles, she could find another way to Africa and the Wall.

There was a train from Colmar to Mulhouse. A local, she was told, once the station clerk found someone with decent English to speak with her. Tickets were four pence.

The price confirmed that three hundred pounds was quite a bit of money. She felt odd even presenting a ten-pound note. Odder yet when her change was given in livres and centimes, apparently French pounds.

The helpful citizen also was forced to explain about boarding, clearly baffled at how she could be such a bumpkin as not to understand trains and tickets.

Paolina ate a meal of potato cakes mixed with onions while she waited. The train eventually arrived in a startle of screeching and steam. She could see the kinship the locomotive's rods and flywheels had with the movements in the clock that was the world. That comforted her somewhat.

On board, a conductor helped Paolina to her proper compartment. It was strange, passing down the lacquered wooden hall on footworn carpet, half-familiar from her time aboard *Notus,* yet as alien as anything else in the English world.

Her bench seat was easy on her feet. Next to her, two swarthy men carried on an earnest conversation in some language she'd never heard. Paolina watched the French countryside roll by. It was chilly in the carriage. She wondered if she would move south fast enough to not require a heavy coat.

Paolina had no belongings at all, now, save money and maps. She would need a few other things. Whatever train might carry her away from Mulhouse would surely allow enough time for shopping.

And so it went that day. Mulhouse was not so large as Strasbourg. Had Paolina been about a normal errand, she certainly could have boarded the train to Marseilles back where she had started. Europe was crossed by lines and lines and lines, iron tributaries that flowed into streams and rivers of rail, all of it tying Europe together into one tightly laced whole under the watchful eye of British governors and tax collectors and stationmasters.

There was time to shop. She thought about what Lachance had said, whether to buy clothes fit for a boy. She could claim to be shopping for a brother. But to play a man . . . They were deceitful, brutal, and careless. What if she *liked* it?

Instead Paolina bought a decent dress of muslin and velvet with a pretty cutaway jacket over the bodice, yet somewhat practical. She could not find anyone to consider selling her the heavy workboots she craved, and so had to settle for the pointed toes of women's footwear, though she insisted on a low heel against all fashionable advice.

After that, a leather satchel—"Unfit for a lady, mademoiselle"—with some vegetables and bread and three dark sausages. She was ready for the train.

When Paolina changed trains in Lyon that night for the Marseilles line, there were boys on the platform shouting something about Strasbourg in both French and English. She paid three centimes for a thick bundle of printed paper, which turned out to be the wrong language. Still, the headline was clear enough.

CATHÉDRALE DE STRASBOURG DÉTRUITE!!!

Paolina scanned the text, seeing references to the Schwilgué Clock, and dozens of familiar and half-familiar words; *ville, prêtre, restaurant.* She wandered around the platform until she found two ladies speaking to one another in English. Pale, dark haired, freckled, they were probably sisters. They were dressed as she was—not of the quality, but not workers either.

Like the *fidalgos,* Paolina realized. She was thinking just like the *fidalgos.* The thought made her tremble with a disgusted anger.

"Excuse me." Both women smiled blankly at her. "I do not know French. Is it possible that you can tell me what this says?"

One of the women glanced at the paper. "Everyone is speaking of that," she said, not unkindly. "There was a terrible explosion at Strasbourg Cathedral this afternoon. Sabotage by Chinese irregulars, the newspaper is reporting. It caused a great fire in the town."

"Oh . . ." Paolina felt ill.

"Have you relatives there?" asked the other woman. "Here, let me help you to this bench."

"My, my . . . cousin," she stammered. The bishop would be dead, and the priest, and all those men. They'd done something stupidly improvident with the gleam. Lachance was dead too, if he had gone back to the square to watch for the gleam as she'd asked him to.

How much worse could it have been? That thought froze her blood.

The women fussed over Paolina as she sat, introducing themselves as Bonnie and Grace Jones, sisters traveling on a small income from their grandfather's estate, and how was she, and what else might she need?

When the Marseilles train began boarding, the sisters Jones helped her to the conductor, explaining in hushed tones that Paolina had been stricken with grief for a relative. Eventually the train pulled away through the endless miles of shadowed houses and narrow, grimy yards that seemed to comprise Lyon, but she was no longer so enchanted with cities.

Arriving the next day, she found Marseilles no cause for rejoicing either. The railway station, *la Gare St. Charles,* let her out into a morning square filled with rushing Frenchmen. She didn't know the language, the people were indifferent, the city overwhelming. These flatwater lands were ever so much stranger than the Wall.

Paolina set out to find streets that sloped away from her, until she could catch a view of the Mediterranean and make her way to the docks. She tried not to wonder about agents of the British Crown on her trail. There must be, of course, but would they have pursued her here?

At waterfront, she found a quiet place to sit and watch awhile, to understand the profound busyness that seemed to overwhelm everyone around her. They swirled and ran and shouted and carried burdens much as they had outside the train station. There were more languages spoken by the water, with sailors and women of loose virtue mixed among the suited English bureaucrats and the gray-trousered French errand boys.

The maps had suggested Suez to her, and a trip down to the port at Mogadishu, near the Wall. The dockside was complicated and confusing. She could scarcely wander the docks, asking at gangplanks where each ship might be bound. Paolina was most reluctant to commit her name and face to anyone here, lest the British learn where she had gone next—she would need to find a tout to help her book passage.

She finally hailed one of the errand boys. He was a dark-eyed lad with curls the color of old honey. He wore a bloused white shirt that had been drenched in some nose-wrinkling perfume.

"*Bonjour, mademoiselle, ce qui serait que désirez-vous aujourd'hui?*"

"English, please," Paolina stammered.

"You gots." He grinned, showing brown stained teeth. "What you want?"

Paolina handed him a ten-centime coin. "I will pay you a livre to find me three ships bound for Suez and the Indian Ocean."

"One livre for each ship, yes?"

"One livre for all," she said. *Hold firm*, Paolina told herself, *or this boy will take you all too easily.*

He shrugged, flipped her coin, and slipped away.

She waited perched on a rain barrel for several hours, but the honey-haired boy did not return. Disappointed, Paolina went to buy meat from a seller with a cart, then retreated to her spot once more. Should she try another boy, or begin walking and trust to luck?

It was too hard to say. If she could just be on her way, that would be one thing. The trains were little help—the agent in Mulhouse had only had tickets as far as Dubrovnik when she inquired about crossing Europe by rail. And while she would contemplate walking a quarter way around the world along the Wall, Paolina was hardly likely to walk from France to the equator. Not with both the British Empire and the Sahara in the way.

It would have to be a ship.

And luck would not do it in this sprawling place.

Finally she flagged another boy and asked him the same thing. This time she promised two livres. She was smarter now, tearing both bills in half and giving him the same end of each of the two. His English was not so good, and he looked at her strangely, but he nodded and scuttled off.

In less than an hour, this second boy—not half so cute but twice as honest as the first—was back. "I have found the ship, yes."

"Three ships," Paolina told him. The day was growing late, and she wasn't willing to take up residence in Marseilles. Having passage out would let her take leave of France, so close to treacherous England.

"Ship. Leave tomorrow, she is."

Paolina gave up and followed him into the crowds of late afternoon.

The vessel was an iron monster, with two smokestacks, four deck cranes, and a rusting white superstructure over her riveted black hull. The name on the hull was *Star of Gambia*, out of Liverpool.

"Aboard," said the boy. "See mate, Monsieur Johsen." He stuck out his hand.

It was not the sort of ship Paolina had hoped for, but there were at least sixty ships along this dock. She could hardly go wandering in hopes of finding a solution.

"Where is Johsen?"

"Aboard. Money, please."

Paolina handed the boy her torn bills. She grabbed the frayed rope that served as a rail and trudged up the steep, creaking gangplank to the ship itself.

She must hope and pray that *Star of Gambia* was more lucky for her than *Notus* had been, and that she could stay well away from the clutches of the Silent Order and the treacherous British Crown they served. Spitting over the rail into the stinking tidewater below, Paolina cursed Newton and all his descendants, wishing that England had never found the key to the world's power.

AL-WAZIR

In two days they climbed, slow, aching, and painful, to a sort of highway that ran several miles above the African jungle, still on the lower reaches of the Wall. It was a true road, al-Wazir realized, with bridges and embankments, even if much of the right-of-way had decayed or been neglected.

He let Boaz lead. That bothered al-Wazir at first, but he soon realized that allowing himself to be upset by the metal man's help was foolish. The pall of smoke still visible in the west told him all he needed to know about how Ottweill was faring. The recent unpleasantness with the Chinese airship told him all he needed to know about how *he* would fare without Boaz' help.

The lightning spear was dead now, too, though they took turns carrying it.

"Some creatures of this wild may be sufficiently intelligent to be frightened by it," said Boaz. "Should we hap upon a cache of supplies to replenish it, we shall, but many will recognize a weapon of Ophir no matter whose hands carry it."

The second night they camped in a wider place, which had once been a way station. A cliff towered behind them, with some shallow rooms carved into it. There were dry troughs out front, along with several stone tables. All was sere and abandoned, centuries of disuse obvious.

"What was this built for?" al-Wazir asked.

Boaz moved about, setting some gathered wood for a fire. "Ophir was first settled by migration from the eastern coast of this continent. At times within the curtain of our history, there was intercourse across the full expanse, for trade and society. This route extended from Ophir back to the Indian Ocean."

"What about them brass cars the lassie spoke of?"

"Those run to the Indian Ocean as well," Boaz told him. "And beyond, around the world and back. But they may be boarded or left only in special places. At this moment I would not care to place myself so close to Ophir's hand, lest they summon me home by means of the seals which power and control the cars."

Seals. The proclamations of their king? He was tired and discouraged. "We could travel by foot for months to make our distance. If only we could take to the air."

"My people have had some commerce with the winged savages," Boaz said. "But I should not think to travel with them, even under the direst of straits."

"Indeed." Al-Wazir shuddered at the thought of treating with the vicious creatures, and wondered at the sanity of the Brass. He spent much of that evening with his back to the fire, looking north into the African night, wondering what had become of, well, everything.

They paced themselves over the next few days, walking enough to make decent progress while not straining al-Wazir's injuries. The rocky cliffs where they'd joined the highway eventually gave way to long, steeped vine-shrouded slopes wreathed in pale yellow mists. The road there had been hacked into the angle of the Wall, though vines now fell across it. They stank of rotting meat. Al-Wazir could not see why or from what.

" 'T'would be far better not to abide here for sleep," Boaz advised him. "Neither to drink nor sup from what might be found. There should be burn scars ahead, where we might secure safe rest."

"Aye." Al-Wazir saw the Brass' point. Sleeping in this stench would go to his head at the least. There were creatures slithering among the vines above and below the roads. He never saw them as more than a flash of scale or a ripple of dark, muscled skin. That was enough to convince him that he did not want to see more.

When they came to a cleared area, marked by the fall of rocks and gravel and a wide black burn scar, he was relieved. They were clear of the dangerous vines. Boaz declined to hunt, so there was no food that night, but al-Wazir found a trickle of runoff from higher up to slake his thirst. The yellow mists closed in with the dusk, and he never slept easily, but he at least found some rest.

The afternoon of the next day they finally left the country of the vines, passing on to a place where the long stalks petered out to be replaced with a more complex ecology of bushes and grasses and stunted trees. He was hard-pressed to tell which competing set of plants was winning the struggle, but at least here there were little rodents like fat squirrels, which could be caught and cooked.

Africa below them was changing as well. It lifted from flat coastal jungle to higher and higher ridges. The Ophir road was at sufficient altitude to grant a long view. They walked at ten or fifteen thousand feet, al-Wazir realized.

There was a great deal of Africa below him.

Another day brought them to an area where the highway was in repair, albeit more crudely executed than the original construction. Following that awhile, amid signs of occasional traffic here, al-Wazir and Boaz came to a great gate that had been built across the road. The south side was anchored in a rising knee of the Wall. The north side overhung a drop. A rushing noise and water spraying from behind suggested a fall beyond the gate.

Al-Wazir studied the fortification with Boaz. "Excellent place to block an advance."

It was a square-cornered tower built from a mix of large flat stones and smaller bricks. The gateway itself was arched, and lined with more bricks of finer quality. The gates were timbered and studded with dark metal.

He saw no arrow slits nor murder holes, and nothing except the roof itself that could serve as a firing point. No guards visible to the eye. Just a gate blocking the road.

"Whom does it keep out?" al-Wazir asked. "Besides us."

"Perhaps better to inquire as to whom it keeps in."

Al-Wazir stepped forward and used the butt of the lightning spear to bang on the metal-shod wood. A knocker, for an unreasonably large door.

The noise boomed, echoing briefly, but there was no answer beyond that.

After a few moments he knocked again.

More quiet.

Al-Wazir squatted in the narrow shade of the arch. "Now what?"

"We find a way past it," Boaz said. "The Wall lies steep here, and we would be hard-pressed to climb far, but I believe that if we were to follow back the trail a quarter mile or so and ascend with great care, we might gain the advantage of this rock knee which anchors the gate. We can see what lies beyond."

The climb was difficult. Al-Wazir had one bad, frightening slip that left him dangling over a bulge that would have dropped him hundreds of feet. There was nothing for it but to haul himself up and keep going. When next he achieved a solid resting place, he shivered awhile before carrying on.

They eventually found themselves atop the knee, above the gatehouse. The roof of the structure was flat, with a wall that looked to be waist-high. There was no obvious way on or off—no stairs or ladders from within, for example.

Behind was a wooden bridge built into the piers of a long-vanished stone bridge. The waterfall tumbled beneath it into the same distance that had threatened to swallow al-Wazir.

There was no way down off the back of the knee that he could see. He turned and gazed up the Wall. The rushing creek ran through a deep channel down a steep slope. That would be hellish to cross, and the higher they might try to climb, the steeper things became.

"We will have to go back down," he said.

"No." Boaz walked to the edge of the knee, swaying slightly as he looked at the gatehouse. "If we climb to the top of the structure, we can secure a passage down the back."

"It's a straight drop to yon roof," al-Wazir protested, "and there's no way of knowing what's behind it. I don't fancy a leap from the top. Thirty feet if it's an inch. I'm not crafted for such a tumble."

"Our alternative is go far west along the Wall and climb up or down, trying to pass at a different level."

Al-Wazir sighed. "Days of walking, with no certainty." It wasn't *that* far down to the roof of the gatehouse, was it?

They climbed very slowly down the curve of the knee.

When Boaz slipped and fell, al-Wazir froze. He heard a resounding crash but could only angle his head slightly to look down. The metal man was prone on the roof of the gatehouse. Not sundered into pieces, but not moving either.

Slowly, he told himself. Slow, slow, slow.

It took him half an hour to make the last thirty feet. When his feet reached stone, his fingers were bloody and his arms shook so badly, he had to sit and rest them. He had no idea how he'd kept hold of the lightning spear.

Boaz lay unmoving, staring blankly at the sky.

Al-Wazir remembered how Boaz had recovered from the crash of the Chinee airship. He waited quietly beside his friend.

Darkness brought a chill that was odd this low on the Wall in al-Wazir's experience. The chief watched the stars emerge from day's bright cloak, and traced the brass in the sky as if he were a navigator. Boaz began to shiver.

"I'm here, friend," he said, and laid a hand on the metal man's chest.

After a few minutes of uncoordinated movement, Boaz sat up. "I fare not well. An armorer would be appropriate to my condition."

"I have no arms or armorer. All we can do is push onward."

When the two of them approached the lip of the roof and looked eastward, there was a squad of men upon the wooden bridge. They wore armor in a bright metal color—brass or possibly gold—apparently in imitation of the Brass of Ophir.

"Sweet Jesus and the twelve," al-Wazir cursed.

Boaz raised a hand, giving a jerky wave.

All fourteen below raised their hands and echoed his wave.

"Have you a ladder?" the Brass man called.

Below, they swarmed into action.

CHILDRESS

The noxious petty officer was gone from both the hallway and the lobby. Apparently they were free. Walking down the front steps, Leung took her arm in his. It was only a sensible escort, she knew, but still the firmness of his touch sent a chill through her.

"You are on parole to me now," he said. "Answerable on your honor to me, as I am answerable on my honor for any untoward actions you take."

"I understand." At least she thought she did.

"I tell you one more thing. Then we find a place for you while my ship is cared for and my men take their shore leave."

"What is that?" The two of them pushed now through the same crowds that had swallowed William of Ghent—swarms of small, busy men of yellow and brown complexion, with their animals and their carts and their enormous loads like beetles on the backs of ants.

"The admiral and the foreign sorcerer . . ." His voice trailed off, as if he were searching for other words. "They are feared for many reasons. Power, strength, the ruthless quality of vision each possesses. But understand something else. In China, white is always the color of death. Funerals are masked and garbed in white. Ghosts come white in the darkness. To both be so tall and so white, it would be like wearing horns in an English church. Calling up visions of a demon."

"Dead men afoot in the world?"

"Yes. Both of them waken fears of dreaming death in most of my people."

"I see." In English tradition, white signified purity and possibly strength. William's clothes had seemed a fashion choice suited to his unusual coloration, nothing more. As for Shang . . . there was a man who

acted the part of a ghost, and dressed it. He kept an entire navy full of ships
and men in line partly by playing on their fear.

That was either admirable or despicable, she was not sure which. She
had to concede the genius of the role.

They pushed through a large set of iron gates into the chaos of a public
street outside the docks. What she had before thought a confusing,
brawling mess had been parade-ground order compared with the near riot
out here. In addition to the ubiquitous loads and their bearers, firecrackers
and gongs echoed, children ran screaming, palanquins forced through
crowds on the backs of sweating, hairless fat men while servants cried
their right of way with whips and knives, a basket of snakes wriggled at
her elbow—it went on and on, overwhelming.

She realized Leung was yelling in her ear.

"What?" Childress asked.

"Be thankful this is not a festival day," he repeated. "The street becomes
too crowded."

All Childress could do was laugh and follow him into the life of Tainan.
The crowds' crackling energy buoyed her in a way she had not felt since
before leaving New Haven. *Long* before leaving New Haven.

This was what she was born to do—push through sunlight and color on
a foreign street while plotting to save the world from its foolish masters. It
might be a short life ahead of her, but Childress found herself more pleased
than ever she could remember being.

A few days later, Captain Leung caught up to Childress as she walked
down by the harbor. He was forced to push through the crowd of children
and beggars who followed her about. She had not minded, not at all.

Neither his uniform nor the pistol he wore today seemed to have any
discouraging effect on her mob of admirers.

He glanced about. "*Five Lucky Winds* is almost ready to sail."

"Then it is good that I am ready as well."

He smiled. "Indeed. I could hardly hold back a vessel for the sake of an
errant woman."

Childress followed him, still pressed about by a throng of murmuring
Chinese, mostly the very young and the very old. There were no walls or
gates to separate the naval base from the city. They simply passed down to
the military docks where a pair of armed sailors allowed Leung and
Childress onto the pier. They stopped the rest of the crowd with glowering
threats.

She looked out across the water. *Five Lucky Winds* was tied up at the next pier. A very shallow chop slapped against the curving hull as the submarine rode low in the water. Full, then, of fuel, provisions, ballast, whatever one packed into a such a vessel. Birds swooped, turning and screaming, to follow some shoal of garbage floating across the bay. The sun sparkled on the low ridges of the waves, a bright, cryptic script written and rewritten in every breath of the wind. Out here the tide-and-sea smell competed with the overwhelming human riot of Tainan along the shore. That scent had become almost familiar to her now.

They cast off before dawn, moving slowly out into the straits. Though she was still not allowed in the bridge or engine room, there was otherwise little pretense of Childress being a prisoner. Some of the crew had changed, recruits or replacements stepping in, but most knew her well enough to have greeted her with a certain proprietary affection at the final muster the evening before.

Even the new political officer seemed to defer to her. Feng was a thin, nervous man who appeared to be afraid of Childress. She suspected that Admiral Shang had exercised some informal influence on Feng's final briefings before he came aboard.

Now she sat in the little wardroom and studied a Chinese chart of the Asian coastline. Though she'd learned some of the tongue sailing from the Atlantic, Childress knew she'd never understand the written language. The thousands of little word-houses just didn't cross-reference to their spoken equivalents in her head.

Unlike the charts of the previous voyage, here she had little familiarity to help interpret what she saw. The Atlantic and even Arctic coasts had been at the edge of her awareness all her life—maps in the newspapers, charts posted in restaurants, broadsheets discussing this expedition or that battle. The Pacific might as well have been the moon for all she knew about it.

Still, a map was a map. Leung had shown her roughly their intended course. Being aboard a submarine necessarily limited her opportunities for sightseeing—there was no rail to stand and gaze over—but she could still imagine. Without known enemies in these waters, *Five Lucky Winds* would often as not run surfaced through the South China Sea. She could spend time in the tower.

I am alive, Childress told herself, tracing routes upon the map and wondering what each island and shoreline might offer her. *I live.*

The guilt and fears of the past, even—or especially—the death of *Mute Swan*, seemed to have faded into just another pattern in her thoughts. There was much to sorrow for. Still, to be voyaging here instead of dying in some European dungeon at the whim of the Silent Order was a great gift, not to be denied.

FOURTEEN

PAOLINA

Star of Gambia steamed out of Marseilles bound for Messina, Kalamata, Tyre, and then the Suez Canal and points beyond. Ilona Bartholomew, who still thought of herself as Paolina Barthes, was aboard as a paying second-class passenger—forty-seven pounds passage, plus five pounds the purser demanded for "expediting fees." Unworldly as she was, even Paolina knew a bribe when she saw one. There was little enough she could do about it save smile, pay, and be very grateful for the modest amount of the graft.

Even now in October the memory of summer lay over the Mediterranean. The wind off the coast was warm and quiet, and the water was a lazy, peaceful blue. Paolina had never experienced winter, but she'd read about it in Dickens, and heard tales of snow and ice passed down from various of Praia Nova's settlers. While she had a strong sense of intellectual curiosity about the sky opening up with frozen water, she had no real desire to experience that intersection of chilled air and precipitation.

As far as she was concerned, God had meant the days to be equal the whole year round, and nights always warm. That was how it was upon *a Muralha*. All the way down to her bones, that was how Paolina expected it to be.

The freighter had to have been built to be dilapidated from the first. The crew was a mix of Africans, Arabs, and southern Europeans—much darker skinned than Sayeed's crew, where the captain himself had been the swarthiest man. They didn't seem so horrified of having her aboard, either. There were three other female passengers, while two of the officers had wives, or at least women, traveling with them.

She was the only woman voyaging alone. Somehow that hadn't mattered up on the Wall, where her worries revolved far more around finding food, or not becoming food in her turn. Out in the countries of Northern Earth, propriety seemed to count for more than any measure of sense. It was as if the *fidalgos* ran the world.

Paolina was beginning to appreciate that the old men who controlled Praia Nova had come by their attitudes honestly. Which only deepened her bitterness at them.

Her efforts to reach England had ended in miserable failure. She never did meet the English wizards she'd believed to be there. At this point she was fairly certain they no longer walked the Northern Earth. Certainly those agents of the Queen in Strasbourg were custodians of the Schwilgué Clock, neither its masters nor even its honest servants.

Worse, she had lost the gleam. She wondered over and over whether she was responsible for the disaster in Strasbourg. She told herself that the Silent Order had taken the gleam from her by force. They had misused it.

Yet the logic of *that* felt cheap and self-serving. Had she not built the thing, brought it into the world, it would never have been available to the bishop and his men.

What if they had set their ambitions even larger? How many would have died? How much of the Northern Earth would have perished?

Shying away from that thought, she also very much hoped that Lachance had not been struck down in the disaster.

In no wise was this an outcome worthy of the trouble and pain she'd experienced to get here. Paolina watched the ship's wake and wondered what she should have done differently. The English were afraid of the Chinese, but if she somehow went to them instead, they would see only a European girl and likely treat her no better than the English had.

It was *a Muralha* for her. With some indecent luck, that would mean a chance to locate Boaz. Maybe she would just climb until she found a friendly country, away from the flatwater world of English and men alike.

Star of Gambia was seven days from Marseilles to Messina, then on to Kalamata. Paolina took her meals at the passengers' mess. She spoke little. That seemed to suit her fellow travelers, though the women glanced at her from time to time. The men ignored her in preference for a game of cards that had begun before leaving Marseilles and never really seemed to end.

She wasn't sure what stakes they gambled for, and didn't feel a need to find out. Paolina spent as much time as possible out upon the deck taking the weather. She'd liked the open air aboard *Notus*, and had grown up outside at Praia Nova besides. The crew ignored her, chattering of their own pursuits in strange languages.

Every time she walked the deck, she saw a dozen repairs or improvements she could make if she had time and leave to do the work. From poor rigging in the deck cranes to balky hinges on certain hatches, the ship spoke to her. Cried, even. Mindful of what would be said if she so much as ventured a suggestion, Paolina shoved the thoughts away as best she could.

Heading for Tyre, the ship encountered what the mess steward said was the first bad storm of the season. The passengers were seated for dinner amid clattering plates and sliding silverware when he came from the galley with a sorrowful expression upon his face.

"Friends," the steward said—he always called the passengers friends, as if delighted to see them—"regretting the cook cannot finish service for you. Biscuits and wine you may take to your staterooms. My sorrow is vain and blushing great."

Paolina wondered what language lay hidden below the odd contours of his English. She smiled as she stood. "I shall excuse myself before the walk back to my cabin becomes life-threatening."

"Here, friend." The steward shoved a napkin full of hard rolls into her hand. "Staying calm and quiet until the weather is blessing some other land."

"Indeed." She nodded her head. "Thank you."

"Do you wish to be walked there, miss?" asked one of the married men—Blanchard, a Scotsman on his way to some engineering project in India. The dangers there seemed to be equally from rebellious sepoy, hungry tiger, and wide-ranging Chinese, at least judging from his tales.

"No, no thank you, sir."

She didn't have to pass across open deck to reach her cabin, but the walkway was exposed on the port side. Even that brief exposure had become more dangerous than she might have thought. The Mediterranean roiled, the sea's beautiful eye-blue lost now to a baleful dark color barely removed from black. Waves were high and heavy, thrashing *Star of Guinea* hard. The wind was horrid, snatching at her like angry hands as it carried a mix of salt spray and horizontal rain to soak Paolina in the few dozen steps she passed.

She was very grateful for the railing as the ship pitched and rolled on the rough water.

Back in her cabin, Paolina wrung out her clothes and considered the storm. She'd seen Atlantic storms all her life in Praia Nova—huge, monstrous beasts of weather that spanned the horizon, walking on legs of lightning, making the air so thin, her head ached, threatening to drown the boats and men of her little village. But she'd never been on the ocean when one of those moving walls of water hit. The women of Praia Nova were not allowed on boats save by dire necessity. There had never been a maritime necessity so dire as to require female assistance in *her* lifetime.

She pinned her soaked clothes up to one of the pipes that crossed the low ceiling of her cabin, then huddled in the tiny bed, hanging on to the low rail as the vessel continued to roll.

Would the gleam have somehow been able to calm the storm? She couldn't envision how. There was no engine, not like an airship. There was no center to disturb. Rather, all the world's weather was a giant engine the size of the Northern Earth itself, with invisible parts moving and sliding against one another. Paolina would no more know where and how to reach into such complexity than she would know how to touch Venus in her orbit.

Still, she suspected the gleam could have done something here. Create an artificial calm, or buoy the ship, or serve as a barrier against the worst of the waves.

This was the *Mediterranean*, at that. A shallow sea constrained by land on all sides. One of the great Atlantic storms would be many times as fierce as this misery.

That didn't matter. She had lost the gleam. Though she'd pushed the thought aside recently with *The Adventures of Huckleberry Finn in Haiti*, it always hung at the back of her mind like a wounded animal, or an angry child.

"I built this thing," she told the swaying cabin. "It killed, then killed again. Chinese, the people of Strasbourg." It did not matter that the Silent Order had raised their hands against her—she might as well have handed them a primed grenadoe and run away laughing.

With the power she had give them, the Silent Order could slay the world.

The electricks illuminating her cabin flickered twice, then cast her into darkness. She was just as glad not to be on deck in a storm by night. Instead Paolina pulled her blankets close and resolved never to build another stemwinder. The burning wreck of the Chinese airship melded in her thoughts with a tower of smoke over the rubble of Strasbourg Cathedral.

It was too much for her, and far too much for the world.

That night she dreamt of an army of Brass marching across Europe, driving everyone before them into some cold Northern sea, leaving behind all the towns and cities as empty as old husks. Only she could stop them, armed with a Dent marine chronometer. Even so, Paolina could not find the desire to stand between the subjects of the British Crown and all the massed might of *a Muralha*.

Star of Guinea experienced a boiler malfunction during the storm. The captain, addressing the passengers, didn't seem to feel the need to offer detailed explanations, but the gist of his remarks was that they would be three days overdue into Tyre at less than half steam.

"We are not in any danger," Captain Dagleish stated, standing before them in the passengers' mess. His uniform had been pressed, but the whites were stained and one cuff raveled—nothing like the seemingly casual precision to which Paolina had become accustomed aboard *Notus*. He required a shave, as well.

Dagleish cleared his throat and continued. "In any case, your bookings are not committed to a particular schedule. Unfortunately, there is no way to send word ahead unless we are overtaken by a vessel moving at full steam. In that eventuality, rest assured we shall exchange all appropriate signals."

"So we shall be posted as missing?" asked Blanchard, the Indian-bound engineer.

"Three days is not sufficient to raise an alarm." The captain's voice was confident. "This is one of the most traveled sea lanes in the world. It is far more likely that our word will be passed in advance. We should be only a few days lying in for repairs there as well."

There were more questions, largely of the nonsensical variety, which the captain answered with impaired grace. Upon his departure a light luncheon was served—salad made from tired, wilted greens, accompanied by stale bread.

That did not bode well for whatever might next come their way.

That afternoon Paolina stood at the stern rail and watched their wake. It looked no different from before—the ship's screws were working in unison despite the missing boiler. She could detect no change in the rhythms of the noise, while the volume of smoke from the two narrow stacks seemed unchanged.

Blanchard and his wife, whose name was Winona, approached her at the rail.

"M-m-my husband," the wife began, stammering and blushing until her voice trailed off into an incoherent mumble.

Paolina looked over her shoulder at Blanchard. He blushed as well. "Perhaps your husband wishes to speak to me without impropriety?" It seemed the sort of thing that informed the literature of England.

"Yes." Mrs. Blanchard subsided completely, stepping partway behind Mr. Blanchard as if for shelter.

"You have my attention, sir," Paolina said into the awkward silence that followed.

"Ah, indeed." He cleared his throat. "I have, ah, marked that you are perhaps a more complex young woman than a casual observer might be led to believe."

At least Blanchard was approaching her with dignity and politeness, not the usual rough assumption of privilege that every man she'd met seemed to carry. *With the possible exception of Lachance,* she amended her thought. "It is my experience that most people are more complex than one might believe."

"Indeed. You seem uncommonly observant. I have caught sight of you counting the braces that support the bridge. Something I myself have done, as a practice of my engineer's curiosity. It is not the sort of thing I might expect of a female."

"And you have approached me to discuss my unexpected hobbies?"

"No, no, miss. My apologies." He glanced around, strangely wary. "Rather, this: I imagine you have observed there is nothing wrong with this vessel. Besides that, Tyre has no yards. It would be difficult to lay over there for repairs.

"Some other game is afoot. And when I look about me to see who might be the object of such a game, my eyes inevitably come to rest on you."

Behind him, Winona Blanchard was staring at her with a thoughtful expression. Not at all the simpering twit the woman had seemed a moment before.

Paolina began to wonder which of the Blanchards had in fact thought to approach her. She resolved to speak to Blanchard *uxor* at an opportune quiet moment. The woman might be a friend, but she might just as well be an agent of the Silent Order. As Captain Sayeed had been.

Her own secrecy was already compromised simply by the fact of this conversation. Paolina glanced across the open water toward the several miles to shore. Too far to swim should she desire a rapid escape.

"I am sure I do not know what game might be afoot," Paolina said. "I travel on an allowance from my father's estate, to meet my uncle in Mogadishu. He will provide me with suitable sponsorship into society."

Blanchard's eyes narrowed. "A rather mean society they have in such a distant and forsaken city, I should think."

"And a rather mean allowance it is that I have." She spun a tale comprising her recent reading and her observations of the English character. "I could scarcely stay home and live till the money ran out, only to become a drab or worse, toiling in the kitchen of one of my former neighbors. I should not think my meager funds could provide a proper coming out into society, especially in the absence of the guiding hand of a thoughtful man for my protection."

He considered that a moment. "And where would you have had this coming out?"

She wanted to dodge the question, desperately, but it was a most logical and simple one. *Where are you from?* Blanchard was well traveled. What answer could she make that he would not immediately see through?

"Strasbourg," Paolina blurted.

"Ah." Blanchard smiled. *"Nous sommes tous les fils de Charlemagne."*

"I must think on this slowing of our vessel, sir," she said stiffly, avoiding the strange look in his eye. "I cannot be sure it is to do with me, but many things are possible."

Paolina turned away from the rail, trying not to flee in her foolish panic. She had handled that very poorly.

Later, when Mrs. Blanchard rapped on the door of her stateroom, Paolina feigned sleep. She could not hide for more than a few hours, but she would have to emerge bearing a tale that was not quite so foolish.

No, I am not really from Strasbourg, but if I told you the truth, we would both be in peril. That had the advantage of a certain species of veracity, but wouldn't serve for other, more obvious reasons.

My father brought me there in his service for the railways. A plausible explanation for her ignorance of the language, but it simply begged the original question all over again.

I was born and raised beyond the borders of the Empire, and all of this is strange to me. True in both word and intent, but such an explanation would betray her to even more questions she could not answer honestly.

Instead she rested until her limbs began to tingle from inaction, while her imagination continued to fail her. Paolina finally rose and stepped outside to a Mediterranean sunset. All the colors of the fire's paintbox bloomed off the starboard rail.

Which meant that the ship was steaming nearly due south rather than the south of east heading required to make Tyre. *Star of Gambia* had turned without any mention to the passengers. She also seemed to be making headway at full speed.

Paolina looked back toward the Anatolian shore. Could she swim that? Not now, not with miles of water between her and her destination.

Instead she scanned for fishing boats or other vessels, someone she could plausibly hope to be picked up by if she dropped over the rail. This evening the Mediterranean, one of the heaviest traveled seas in the world, was as quiet and empty as a teacup.

Where were they going and why?

AL-WAZIR

As evening descended, Al-Wazir and Boaz marched up the road in company with the bright-armored men. At close range, their impersonation of the Brass was far more obvious. Even the weapons these soldiers bore were copies—fat-headed spears with metal collars in imitation of Ophir's might.

Half a dozen Royal Marines would have pushed this formation to bloody hash, he thought.

They were not exactly prisoners. It was something more akin traveling under escort. The squad had made no effort to relieve al-Wazir and Boaz of their possessions, most especially not the lightning spear. They kept a respectful distance, leading before and following behind, but not forcing any compliance to orders.

His greatest wish was for food and rest as they marched into the darkness of evening. A glow ahead promised at least settlement. If the current goodwill held up, al-Wazir could find what he wanted there.

Boaz was more of a worry. The metal man walked with a pace that was excruciatingly slow for him, limping and clattering. Al-Wazir would have offered to help, but he could not fathom what assistance would be useful.

"Are you capable of self-repair?" he asked quietly.

"It is not within my abilities to restore parts with severe torsional damage." Boaz clanked onward a few steps. "My seal is possessed of great power, but some injuries even the Solomnic magics cannot touch. I am in need of the attentions of a smith of good training and steady hand."

"Aye. I figure it would be like having some bugger reach inside me flesh to set a bone."

The Brass gave a rattling snort. "An apt comparison, Chief."

They approached the distant glow with rising hope, at least on al-Wazir's part. These strange, silent men had fashioned elaborate armor in imitation of the Brass. Surely their smiths were capable with a hammer, and bore a steady hand.

There was nothing for it but to walk onward and trust to hope and Divine Providence.

The road bent around a towering pillar of rock under brilliant starshine tinged with the sheen of brasslight. The original architects had carved a near-tunnel here, so that dank rock swept over al-Wazir's head to obscure the glow before them. He could still see the miles of Africa scattered to his left. Here, deep within the continent, there were no fires nor lights to mark the night. He saw only the shadowed texture of trees and open grasslands. Even here, several miles up the Wall, a scent of distant redrock hills cut through the water-and-stone smell of the road.

Somewhere nearby a larger fall rushed. It was bigger and bolder than what had tumbled behind the gatehouse. He could see a glittering mist hanging in the open air. The sound had been rising for a while, a distant susurrus that grew to an urgent whisper, now building to wet thunder.

The little column passed the outer edge of the curve. Al-Wazir drifted to a stop. The waterfall was easily the largest he'd seen in his life. Their roadway broke off not far ahead—this had not been so great a cataract when Ophir had built this road, he realized—though a bridge of chains and ropes and wood extended out across the water to a rocky outcropping surrounded by ever more tumbling water.

Even in the dim light of night, Al-Wazir could see that knees and columns and shelves stretched through the middle of the fall. These vertical islands interrupted the cascade at irregular intervals. Some were not much larger than tree stumps; others could have hosted a cathedral. Each exposed rock supported a structure, but the buildings themselves were a mix of architectures that dazzled al-Wazir's eye even by the starlight.

Some were little more than piles of stone, gnarled structures that might have grown up out of the rocks of the falls on some mystical night long ago. Others looked as if they'd been brought from distant parts of the Wall—blocky buildings oddly melded to a pair of close-set outcroppings; a graceful tower with a outward curve like half an arch; a crystal shell that hummed, audible even over the roar of the falls.

All were lit by fire, lamps, torches—the glow he had seen earlier, magnified by reflection among the mists. Shadows moved within and among them as people followed rope bridges or iron stairs or stone pathways that slipped behind the rushing waters. The city, grafted from the debris of half a dozen empires, thronged with life.

This was a place that admitted no mistakes. Slip once and you would end your life tumbling downward amid tons of water. No one could err twice.

Al-Wazir wondered what these people saw in Ophir that they felt the need to imitate. This was a place of power and beauty almost beyond imagining.

A respectful hand gently tugged him into motion once more. The soldier's face was averted. The chief followed his escorts onto the first of the bridges. Walking out over the falls, he realized that the air immediately above the water was much colder, with a sharp, chill mineral smell. He also saw these people had arranged a whole web or array of bridges, lines, and cables that spread back and forth across their waterborne city like the web of some mechanical spider of Dr. Ottweill's deepest dreaming.

He hoped fervently not to have to cross one of those cables by hand. It smacked of the worst of *Bassett*'s landings, such as the vertical city where they had lost so much.

They crossed two more bridges, with short walks around rock walls and a narrow-porched building with windows the proportion of church tapers. Finally they came to a larger apron of stone. A metal hut sat there, with windows glowing. The soldiers marched within. Al-Wazir followed.

Inside was lit by electricks. It seemed little more than a small railway carriage, but lacking wheels or rails to run upon. After all had entered, the last slammed the door shut. The car swayed and creaked and made an alarming twanging noise for a moment before settling into a herky-jerky motion. *Funicular,* al-Wazir realized. This was a cable car to take them farther up the Wall, judging from the motion. He could not see outside from within the well-lit press of bodies. His stomach lurched at the thought of the maintenance in this place—how would they fight rust with the whole city soaked worse than a ship at sea?

He looked to Boaz. The Brass swayed slightly, upright but seemingly dazed. Whatever degree of motion and focus lent him illusion of life was fading once more.

The car finally clanged to a halt. They stepped out into a great hall lit by fitful electricks. A hole in the floor behind them had admitted the funicular car, while a gigantic iron wheel turned on a tower above to wind the cable in and out. An engine hissed and chugged nearby, lending motive force to the transport. The falls were more muted here. He wondered if they had gone into the face of the Wall itself.

Except for the machinery, this could almost have been one of the great cathedrals of Europe. Pillars supported a high vaulted ceiling. The floor was a pattern of stones and tiles with symbols painted or glazed into place. Between the pillars were niches with statuary of long, narrow-bodied fish leaping upward in endless pilgrimage.

There were carvings on the pillars, too. Al-Wazir quickly realized they were twisted, violent images, difficult to focus on in the wet shadows of this place. Which might be for the best, given that some of them featured tentacles and worse.

Another misappropriated building? How did they do that?

More muddling of soldiers, then they swept across the great space to a doorway that lay in shadow. The escorts stood aside there. It was clear enough where the newcomers were to go next.

Boaz was utterly silent, though he still walked when al-Wazir did. Whatever might be done for the Brass man would be done here. They approached the doorway. It was fifteen feet high, with double doors each four feet across. The carvings on the door were both fascinating and repulsive—images of squids and snakes and men locked in bitter battle and passionate embrace at the same time. They almost squirmed. Not a cathedral at all, but a temple of a different race.

Reluctantly, al-Wazir set his hand upon the door and tugged it open.

The space beyond was larger even than the funicular landing. They must have passed within the living rock. Anything was possible in the immensity of the Wall.

It was darker, too, lacking the electricks of the outer chamber, though a few rushlights guttered. A great, rank smell forced al-Wazir to open his mouth to breathe, lest his nose be overwhelmed.

"Be glad you are Brass," he whispered to Boaz.

Something splashed with the sound of a pond's worth of water slopping. It was big, it was in the center of the room, and it was *above* al-Wazir.

He advanced slowly. There was a vague sheen, though he could not at first discern what it was. Al-Wazir got an impression of mass, the reverse of the sense of emptiness that he might have expected in a vast unlit space.

Another splash, then a voice that boomed so low, it was almost impossible to hear, echoed in a tongue he did not ken. Al-Wazir's bones vibrated with the sound.

"Begging your pardon," al-Wazir said, "but I am not understanding you."

There was a silence that seemed ready to burst, then: "A seal has been brought before me."

For a single, manic moment al-Wazir was distracted by the sailor's meaning of the word, before he realized what this creature was speaking of. "He is damaged and does not function well."

Another long pause. "The seal is too powerful to be broken."

"Nae," al-Wazir said. " 'Tis his body. He has need of a righteous good armorer."

His eyes were adjusting to the darkness. Al-Wazir saw a giant tank of water, glass-walled above him. Something substantial shifted back and forth within it.

"He could be torn down and his seal taken for other use."

"I do not think this will be the case," al-Wazir said calmly.

There was a long, slow burbling noise, which he finally interpreted as laughter. "You will not allow it?"

"No. I will not allow it."

In the silence that followed, he realized that a pale patch in the darkness before and above him was an eye the size of his chest. He was being studied.

Al-Wazir stared back, seeing almost nothing, but pretending to be unafraid.

"That spear is empty," the voice said. "Something my servants did not understand."

"You don't know that," al-Wazir told him. "You only believe." This was like talking to some big brute of a recruit, freshly taken into service, who thought he didn't have to take orders from any man he could thrash bare-knuckled. The point wasn't to thrash them back, because no one could beat all comers. The point was to think past their thrashing. Then, if needed, take two or three friends, find the cocky bastard in a quiet corner, and stomp him shiteless, of course. "If you have an armorer with the training and tools to help him, please send us there. Otherwise we shall head onward and eastward."

Another slow, glass-bending chuckle. "Into the house of the sun?"

"Into the house of our desires. Following no one's hearts but our own."

"You are not of the Wall. Why do you traverse it like an insect on a mirror?"

"Why do you hang here in a vat of water suspended amid a fall which should carry you down off these slopes and eventually home to the sea?"

Another splash, followed by a long groan. "Take him out. Tell the peltast he is to see the smiths on Gullie Isle."

"And then we will be free to go." He stated it rather than asking it, pretending to confidence he did not feel.

"And then you will see me once more."

Al-Wazir bowed. He then tugged at Boaz so that the Brass man would follow him out.

Gullie Isle was two funicular rides and another series of bridges away from the cathedral. The peltast, who never did say a word, left them there with a nod. Three sleepy men in linen gowns emerged from a beehive-shaped hut covered with slime and mold. One carried a torch, which gusted in the thundering wind of the waterfall.

"Are you the smiths?" al-Wazir asked.

The torch-holder stared incuriously at him while the other two approached Boaz. They circled, fingers sliding over the dented decorative work upon his chest, brushing his fingertips, flickering over his face.

Al-Wazir couldn't think what to say. He was here for these men to help Boaz. He could hardly object to their examining him, even if the methods were strange.

Instead he settled for studying the smiths. They were cut from much the same mold as the peltast and his troops. Not twins, but they could all have been brothers. Short, bandy-legged, with silver eyes and pale hair. Also like the peltast, not much given to words, though the peltast had certainly seemed to understand what it was al-Wazir had told him back at the cathedral.

Their silence was strange, as was their lack of protest at being called out in middle of the night. He'd never met an expert who wanted to leave a warm bed to help anyone in need. Yet here they were, their nightshirts soaking in the spray, working in the light of their fellow's torch.

Eventually he wandered into the hut and stretched out on a pallet. There was little enough point trying to oversee a process he didn't understand, and he was long past the point of trust.

Morning brought a flood of rainbows, sunrise filtered through the mists hanging in the air outside. The colors danced on al-Wazir's face as he awoke. He stepped out onto the ledge into a flood of light and hue.

There was a beauty by day completely different from the lambent glow of the previous night. The ragged array of buildings, all the more visible and stranger in the sunlight, was wrapped in colored mist. Everything about him gleamed.

There was no sign of Boaz or the smiths.

Turning his back on beauty, al-Wazir went inside to find something to eat. There was not much—a sack of dried beans, a bowl of lichen, which he wasn't sure had been intended for food, and a string of dried, salted fish. He ate several fish whole. They tasted terrible, but then, most food did at sea. This city was little more than a giant ship tied to the face of the Wall.

Al-Wazir was unwilling to casually set out across the byways of this place. There was too much he didn't understand about the paths, and he feared becoming irreparably lost. So he idled awhile, figuring that the smiths would return to their hive-home eventually, with or without Boaz. The rainbows faded with the rising sun. He was treated to a magnificent view northward when the wind shifted and moved the mists away.

No one came. He remained alone, looking down on hawks and cranes in the air far below, wondering what had become of Boaz.

CHILDRESS

They made a brief landing in the Qun Dao islands. These were an unremarkable assortment of low, scrubby sandbars and coral reefs in the middle of the South China Sea. There was a small base there, and even an airship mast, though only a pair of aging sailing craft seemed to be on hand, along with a bored and weathered detachment of sailors.

For the first time in her life, Childress could see the Wall. It was little more than a dark line on the horizon, but it was definitely *there*, a ridge cutting off the southward edge of the circle of sea around the islands. The Wall was everything, in a sense—brace to hold the world's ring gear, and the most direct evidence of the planned nature of divine Creation. The Wall marked the edge of the world and beginning of Heaven. She stared at it awhile, willing detail to come into focus. It was a thousand miles or more south of their position, and resolutely remained nothing more than a stroke on the horizon—a glowering storm of stone destined never to break into rain.

Childress turned away from the pull of the Wall to watch from the submarine's tower as Leung went ashore accompanied only by Feng. The captain forced the political officer to row. On the short, rough beach, Leung conferred with a slouching sailor, then walked to a small collection of buildings. Feng was led off in another direction, presumably to a briefing.

The two sailors on watch with her chatted softly. She followed a little of their talk. They seemed to think this was an awful place to be posted, the junk heap of the Beiyang Navy. An English sailor might have said armpit, or named a more objectionable body part. They joked about the food and the lack of women, until one of them, a boy named Pao, realized she was listening.

After that they stood in embarrassed silence, which lasted until Leung emerged from one of the buildings and trudged back to his boat. The captain rowed himself back to his ship.

She climbed down the tower and met him at the hatch. No one seemed to mind, not anymore. "What did you learn?" Childress asked, ignoring Feng's absence.

"That there is nothing here fit for a man."

"Not about the islands," she said. "When you spoke to Admiral Shang."

He looked surprised.

"Why else would you stop here, save to make a communication? That airship mast would make an excellent tower for wireless, if the Beiyang Navy in fact has wireless. If not, I imagine there might be a telegraph cable here. There are certainly telegraph cables between Boston and London." *Communication for both him and Feng,* she thought, but did not say.

Leung shook his head. "Your cleverness will trip you someday."

"It already has, Captain. Time and again."

"Indeed." He stood looking thoughtful. "I am told that shortly after we sailed, William of Ghent booked passage on a merchant vessel bound for Manchu-Nihon, Hawa'ii, and Mei Guo."

"He was awaiting my departure. Did he in fact board that vessel?"

Leung gave her another surprised look. "The admiral could not be certain."

"How can one be uncertain about a man the color of death?"

"I do not know," he said distantly. He shouted up at the sailors to come below. "We sail now, madam."

"Without Feng?"

"It would be unheard of for me to hold back a vessel for the sake of an errant sailor."

FIFTEEN

PAOLINA

Star of Gambia steamed through the night. Paolina slept little, often checking their heading by the stars and the orbital tracks visible in the night sky. The ship continued on a southerly heading.

She considered rousting one of the crew, but couldn't see them answering any question she might ask. Even if she still had the gleam, Paolina couldn't see how it would help. They were sailing to the edge of the maps Lachance had given her.

How helpless everyone was, who placed trust in people around them. A passenger relied on the ship's captain knowing his way. The captain relied on his officers and crew. One bad seed, one British agent, could send everyone aboard to their deaths.

Life was simpler back at *a Muralha.* There she only had to worry about the *fidalgos,* and someday being forced to marry. No one tried to kill her.

At least not until they had locked her into their storeroom and left her to starve. Even then, the bastards must have known that the women of Praia Nova would help her.

Around four in the morning, Paolina gave up her efforts at rest. Instead she dressed as warmly as she could and found her way to the deck.

The purser leaned against the rail, smoking a cigarette.

"I was a wondering when you will appear." She had come to recognize his accent as Italian.

"I saw no point in coming to ask questions."

"Often there is no point in a questions." His hand slid into a bird shape. Then he flickered his fingers and the sign vanished. "Still, sometimes a thing she changes."

"Like how?"

"We get a word from a passing ship, yes? Royal Navy task force in Tyre harbor. Already captain make difficult decision. Now we head for Alexandria."

Paolina couldn't decide whether to panic or feel relieved. "What does this have to do with me?"

"Me, I don't a know. I don't a want to know. Captain, he get messages. He listen, he think. White birds come and go." The steward took a long draft. "You see many white birds? *Avebianci?*"

"Only gulls," she said slowly. She knew that wasn't what he meant. Lachance had mentioned white birds, back in Strasbourg. Money and power. Mysterious societies. Just like those who had tried to take her in Strasbourg.

They were all servants of the Queen. She did not want to admit knowing anything of them to this man. Especially with the power of the gleam evident in the smoking ruins of Strasbourg.

Still, the steward was helping her. At no small risk to himself, given the example of Lachance. An eddy stirred Paolina's conscience.

"Ah, well. At Alexandria we change some cargoes. Owners lose money, bad for captain. But some better than British to search. Then . . . Suez. You go south."

"You know where I am heading. I bought my ticket from you."

"Of course you buy a ticket from me. I am purser." He grinned, his teeth faintly orange in the glow of his cigarette. "We take you into Indian Ocean, maybe you find your way from there, hey? But when we get to Alexandria, smart girl maybe a hide in her cabin, no go ashore, no answer a door until ship sail again."

"I'll consider it." Her voice was cold, hiding her worry.

He flipped his cigarette overboard. "You smart girl, be a smart." With that he was off into the darkness.

She stood awhile, watching the bright stars over the dark water. *Monsters, there were monsters in every deep.*

The ship reached a scrubby, desolate shore by morning. There she turned eastward again. Half a mile of open water stretched between their line of travel and the desultory beach. Looking off the starboard rail, Paolina saw a line of dunes standing back from the beach, featuring only more scrub and sand. A tall brown storm loomed in the distance—sand or dust, nothing to do with water at all.

It was not a land she thought she could love.

They were already passing little wooden fishing boats out with the dawn. There was other traffic on the water. The sea lanes led *somewhere* here. Paolina could not imagine the Royal Navy being absent from Alexandria, but perhaps the detachment here was not on the same mission as the vessels sent to Tyre in anticipation of their arrival.

After a while there were people wandering along the shoreline, a few groves of struggling trees, even villages. Some of the fishing boats seemed to find their home ports here, amid thin men in grubby white robes and naked children.

There was also a haze in the sky ahead—the city of Alexandria.

She was very much of two minds regarding the purser's warning. On the one hand, Paolina wanted nothing more than to get off the *Star of Gambia*. On the other, she could hardly walk the length of Africa to *a Muralha*. She knew even less of that continent than she did of Europe, except that the land was a many-miled desolation.

What language did they speak in Alexandria? Alexandrene?

Paolina retreated to her cabin, resolved not to go ashore at first, but reserving the privilege of doing so after the ship had docked and the passengers disembarked.

Watching from her cabin porthole, she could see a strange city indeed. *Star of Gambia* was moored in a narrowing harbor sheltered from the Mediterranean by a long westward-running spit. The ship was close in to Alexandria, which might just have well been up on the Wall somewhere. It seemed to combine ancient buildings of mud and sandstone with the newest marble palaces of commerce so beloved of the English. Though she saw only a narrow section of the city while hiding in her cabin, it was enough to show her how much life there was here and how complicated it must be.

There were vultures that crowded rooftops and lazed in the sky above. They seemed to overpower even the endlessly omnipresent gulls that had haunted every port and coast she'd seen, from Praia Nova onward.

Paolina lay in her bunk and thought about what it would mean to step ashore here. This city was larger than Marseilles. She would be so very lost, with even less notion of where and how she should go. How did people find *themselves* in a place like this, let alone anyone else? How many people could crowd together? Where France had been verdant and even lush, this north coast of Africa lived and died by what water could be found. Everyone lived here because of the river, she presumed.

It was like the Wall, she realized. The land focused the way people lived. They didn't understand that in Europe. The British had too much— surrounded by water and food and wealth, they did not know how others struggled to live within boundaries far larger than they themselves were. These Alexandrenes would understand.

With that thought, she finally fell into sleep.

Paolina woke in the steep, rich light of the late afternoon. It was gold in this place on this day, flowing from the sky to cast coppered shadows and touching everything, no matter how rusted or weathered, with a blessing of the eye. Even the air seemed to have been distilled to a breathy wine.

She stood, stretched, and stepped to the porthole once more. The city beyond was still raucous, a thousand times too many people crammed along a slow, muddy river that took much and gave little back except life-sustaining water. Whistles shrieked, cranes groaned along the docks, and even through the dogged glass of her little window she could smell the conurbation.

Each place had boasted a different scent—first Strasbourg, then Marseilles and Kalamata, now Alexandria—every city making its own fires, cooking its own meats and spices, steam cars and electrick plants and the mass of bodies and animals combining in a unique recipe. She watched the slow light lacquer all of it, shit and shining palaces alike, into the dying glory of the day.

To go out or not? Paolina hated letting the purser and the captain control her fate. She had money, but at best she'd book passage on another ship. The only airships that flew south of here were Royal Navy; she was certain of that. And she didn't think there were railways through Africa. Though it shared an ocean with Europe, the both of them nestled together on Northern Earth, Africa might as well have been on the moon from what she had seen aboard *Notus*.

Star of Gambia had not betrayed her. Not yet at any rate. She sensed no great love of the British Crown from those aboard the ship. The truth of their turn away from Tyre was vague, but there had been no search of the ship here in port at Alexandria either.

Paolina controlled her fate simply by sitting still. The lack of positive action rankled her. Despite the haunting dread of what she'd done to Strasbourg, she was beginning to feel tempted to build another stemwinder. It was the only assertive power she *had*, the only way she could avoid being more than a mere woman.

She'd sworn off the horror, though. Even the sense of power was an illusion. The collapse of the Chinese airship loomed large in her mind, for all that Captain Sayeed had been operating under false pretenses at that moment. So she sat and watched night take the ancient city, wondering when they would serve her dinner.

———

The mess steward brought her a bowl of fish stew later in the evening. "Friend," he said, apparently delighted to see her. "Here is having warm food, and to apologize for the mess being so closed."

"Where are all the other passengers?"

He set the bowl down, tugged a napkin from his apron, and shrugged. "Much commotion on docks there is being earlier. Crew stay quiet." He laid out a spoon, a tiny butter jar, and a roundel of some thin, slightly puffy bread. "To eat now, and practice calm."

"Do you know when we might sail again?"

Another shrug. "I am bringing food, not orders from the bridge." He bowed and left her with the fragrant, spicy bowl.

Paolina ate regardless. Even in good times there had never been quite enough at Praia Nova, not for women and girls when the men needed their strength. Whatever she received to eat was so much blessing to her. Afterwards she ventured out to the rail. In the dark she'd be less visible to anyone passing by along the docks. Someone watching with intent would already know she was here, just by observing the mess steward.

As chaotic and overwhelming as Alexandria had seemed by day, it was even less inviting by night. Shadows lay deep, quarters of the city devoid of light. The constellation of sound and smell had acquired a wild undercurrent of menace. At this time waiting seemed less of a frustration and more of a gift—she did not have to descend into that blackness.

The wind brought her a snatch of music, some reedy instrument wailing in the night. It seemed to call to Paolina, telling her she could just go ashore, take up the garments of a woman of the city, and become someone else. Everything that she had done, everything that she had become, would be lost like that music on the wind. The thought of escape tore at her heart, bringing tears to her eyes.

"I am not special," she whispered. "I am just a girl."

She knew better.

Whatever lay within her head and hands, that helped her build the gleam and spot half a hundred other problems here aboard *Star of Gambia* would not go away simply because she decided to sell eggs in the marketplace. The Silent Order would still be seeking her. The Royal Navy would not soon forget, even if they stood down the search that had driven the ship away from Tyre. That search would be renewed once Captain Sayeed made his reports, let alone whatever that scoundrel al-Wazir might send along from his post at *a Muralha*. The big Scotsman had given her to Sayeed in the first place, after all.

No, she could hide awhile, change her name, take a different garb, but Paolina knew her patience for men like the *fidalgos* of Praia Nova was thin. She was certain the Northern Earth was full of *fidalgos* by whatever name. But still the thought of slipping into the night-ridden city whispered disloyal within her head.

Better to head back to the Wall and lose herself in the vertical kingdoms and long silences that overlooked the Northern Earth than to hide here awaiting discovery or betrayal.

That decision made, she watched the shore awhile. The music still carried, but the spell had broken. Eventually Paolina found the steward again. He was smoking a cigarette once more.

"You stay," he said, though she thought he meant it as a question.

"Yes. The city . . ."

He chuckled softly. "I know you now. Girl from the Wall, yes?"

She felt a cold stiffening in her heart. "Perhaps."

"No big a cities on the Wall? My mamma, she tell me empires there, filled with saints and martyrs dying for the Brass Christ."

"Well, I suppose there are empires," Paolina said. "But there are empires everywhere."

"True, true." He flipped the cigarette overboard again. "British officers come inspect ship tomorrow, ye? You want to hide, you want to be someone else? You choice. They a catch you being Wall girl, no one here help you."

"I . . . I would prefer to be someone else." Hiding seemed too much. She'd hated cowering in the back of Lachance's wagon. Besides, she'd decided to carry forward. She would carry forward.

"Good. Then you mute girl, wash dishes for mess steward. Wear a skinny clothes, all a dirty, yes? Hide behind him, act like he your man. You love him, you say nothing. Mess steward, he, a . . . *leccaculo*. Not the eye for beauty of the woman, *capisce*? What kind of girl have man like that, a? You love him like scared, no say a word."

"I believe I can act scared," Paolina told the steward.

"Good. Be big mess, dawn. *Capisci*?"

"Big mess, at dawn. Yes." She resisted the urge to thank him. Paolina realized once again that she should never have left *a Muralha* behind in the first place.

Morning found her in the passengers' mess wearing a torn-down dress and barefooted. She'd walked the decks several times before dawn, rubbing against stacks and vents to acquire convincing grime.

The mess steward smiled but said nothing. They spent the morning working in silence, pulling out every plate and knife and fork and carafe in the passengers' mess. She cleaned each piece, then slowly restored order. Somewhere during the course of her efforts the hatch to the outside banged. Paolina was polishing a punch bowl and did not look up.

Whoever it was did not trouble her.

A bit after the noon bell, *Star of Gambia* let out a long blast on her whistle. With much shouting out on deck, the vessel began to make way. Paolina was washing knives, and still did not look up.

There was no hiding or pretense of love or fear. Merely a day of hard, distracting work that would have been quite ordinary in Praia Nova. There were more forks here than in the whole village. No one in her town had so much as heard of a punch bowl. She didn't mind the sense of accomplishment in so thorough a cleaning, and the mess steward made no attempt to take advantage of his supposed role, so it was all well enough.

When Paolina stepped outside, they were passing very close to dunes. A few men on camels watched from shore, rifles slung on their shoulders.

"Suez," said the steward. "We go to Indian Ocean now."

It was the first time he'd spoken to her all day.

Unsure who might be listening, Paolina nodded. She watched the desert sail by and wondered where all the passengers had gone. Questions seemed so dangerous now.

The banks of the canal were shallow. A broad, slow waterway carried *Star of Gambia* and half a dozen other ships through the desert. A few places along the shore were planted with strange rough-crowned trees, but otherwise this was more desolate than even the Mediterranean near Alexandria. She found much to admire in the shades of sand and the colors of the rock and the way the light played across the rough ground. This was a country of a stark, severe beauty she'd never encountered on *a Muralha*.

After idling in a wide, shallow lake awhile so that a line of ships might pass heading north to the Mediterranean, *Star of Gambia* entered another stretch of canal. Paolina found shade and watched their progress through the day, until they came to a wider stretch of lapis-colored water where the little wooden boats crowded one another.

The sea. The Indian Ocean.

She realized she'd been alone all day, without taking mess or encountering any of the other passengers. Even the few crew she'd seen had kept their distance.

Everyone aboard *Star of Gambia* knew who she was now. Not by name, but as the object of the British searches. The focus of the ship's diversion. Paolina hugged herself briefly. It did not matter. There were few betrayals left. She merely had to stay aboard as the ship steamed west of south toward Mogadishu; then she would be almost back to *a Muralha*. Far, far from home, but it was her native place.

The British and their dogs in the Silent Order would never find her there.

As she retreated to her cabin, Paolina wondered what her life would have been like if she'd followed the music ashore back in Alexandria and cast away her name. She had no notion, none at all. That thought brought tears to her eyes.

AL-WAZIR

Midday passed without any sign of Boaz or the smiths. Al-Wazir continued to study the walkways and trams of this waterfall city, letting himself get soaked to the skin as he paced the ledge.

There was no point in leaving. He wouldn't know where to go, wouldn't know where to look.

He searched the hut three times. Perhaps he'd missed a trapdoor or secret exit to a workroom somewhere within the living rock of the Wall. There was nothing that he could find. So he walked the ledge some more and stared up and down.

Once again he was struck by the impressive beauty and bizarre engineering of the city. Water foamed and roared and fell like a sea upon the move. Cables stretched between the larger buildings and major islands, sometimes braced on great towers to hold up the midpoint of their spans. The metal trams trundled along irregularly. He realized after a while that they must not be a service, like the omnibuses of English cities, but rather transport that ran at someone's whim. People walked the bridges, climbed stairs and ladders, moved about on balconies. Few wore the brass armor he'd seen the day before. This was not a city of soldiers.

No one came to his ledge. No one bore Boaz amid their number. No one even stopped to look at him.

He wondered, too, what he had met splashing the night before. It was big, with vasty, pale eyes—a thing that wanted to live in darkness.

As afternoon passed, al-Wazir realized that he could not remain idle. He and Boaz needed to be eastward bound. He stepped onto the bridge they crossed last night. The treadway was slick, the guide cables crusted with moss, but it was not much worse than working the ropes of an airship in heavy weather.

Still, somehow this was different, crawling across the stone face of the Wall.

Halfway over the bridge, he turned and looked back at the beehive hut. Almost directly below the small building was a cave mouth visible only from out here. Something flashed within.

"Devil take me," he shouted. "And all of you as well." Al-Wazir realized he must have been above Boaz' head all morning.

He walked carefully back, scanning the cliff face for a downward path or ladder. It wasn't hard to see from out here, behind a boulder he had passed a dozen times in his morning's pacing.

Off the bridge, on surer footing, he scrambled behind the boulder and downward.

The cave was indeed a smithy. There were a pair of forges, bellows, racks of tools, anvils, benches, pigs of iron, copper, brass, and bronze—everything that someone with the right skills might need.

Boaz lay on one of the benches, torn down like an engine under repair. His arms and legs had been removed. His chest gaped open. Two of the smiths worked on a leg at a nearby table. The third examined small parts through a lens bolted into a frame.

None of them looked at al-Wazir as he entered their kingdom. Torn between worry and fear, he approached Boaz.

The open chest revealed not a hollow, as he almost expected, but rather a compacted arrangement of clockwork—gears, wheels, escapements. The mechanisms drew the eye into a web of brass built as tightly and closely as any engine. It was a forest of parts, as obscenely compelling as the torn-open chest of a man of flesh. Al-Wazir had seen enough casualties to know the look of liver and lights when they came spilling out. This had the same eerie fascination, though without the blood.

He reached forward to touch a large wheel with detents along its face.

Boaz' eyes popped open.

Al-Wazir jerked his hand back, startled. He felt more than a little embarrassed as well. There was a half-heard hiss as the Brass man tried to speak, his head twitching and clicking.

"No," al-Wazir said. "Quiet. They will repair you."

He glanced once more at the cavity, wondering where the seal might be—in Boaz' head? In that laid-open chest? It didn't seem that the magic had yet been stolen away. Otherwise Boaz would be nothing more than silent metal already, rather than a man straining without breath to speak.

Al-Wazir went to watch the smiths. They continued to ignore him. The two with the leg were repairing Boaz' knee, extending and tightening the joint while adjusting a complex of springs and guys within. The third worked on some small mechanism that must have come from within the laid-open gut.

Al-Wazir knew he should stay away. This was dangerous, delicate effort. So he climbed back up to the hut. There he laid a fire and cooked a pot of beans. When that was done he filled a clay bowl and carried it back down to the cave.

This time Boaz had his legs reattached, though his chest still lay open. Now his arms remained separated. Al-Wazir put the steaming food down on a bench. These people were silent, eerily so, but he was willing to presume that their noses were in working order.

Soon enough they came one by one to eat. The shy smiles and quick glances he received by way of thanks were the first acknowledgments he'd had from the people of this city.

"Does no one here talk save your king?" he asked aloud. There was no response.

He had purchased some goodwill for his efforts, and perhaps earned a place at Boaz' side. With that thought, al-Wazir found his way back to the metal man.

"How are you?"

Boaz blinked at him but did not try to speak this time.

"We must go soon. This place is being kind to us, but it is more than passing strange."

Another blink.

"I will not take you until these smiths are done, or they prove hostile."

Boaz managed to turn his head, his neck clicking and whirring, to look toward where one of the smiths was eating the last of the beans.

"Exactly." Al-Wazir touched the Brass man's forehead. "I'll watch out. We'll leave soon. East, my friend, we must head east."

That evening they closed Boaz' chest. One smith tapped him gently on the forehead. The metal man sat up with a swift jerk. The Brass opened his mouth and began to speak in a tongue al-Wazir did not recognize, babbling for several minutes. Eventually Boaz stopped, then stared at his hands.

"I am better than I might have thought possible," he said in English. He carefully climbed off the bench to stand, then addressed the smiths in the other, strange language.

They nodded. One answered in a slow, soft voice. Boaz glanced at al-Wazir, whose hackles were beginning to rise, then back at the smiths.

"I owe a debt," he explained to al-Wazir. "This city is held in dire thrall. They would have me set them free."

"In thrall to what?" Al-Wazir thought he already knew the answer.

"They are under the aegis of the Inhlanzi King."

"We met him."

"I do not remember. I recall little of what has transpired since I was taken aboard the Chinese airship."

"As when Ophir erased your memory crystals?"

"Yes."

"You do not remember what you are about, but now we will seek out the Inhlanzi King and do exactly what, laddie?"

"We shall cast him down from his high seat."

"Ah. Fair enough." *Deranged, actually.* Crazed, cracked, and doomed. Now was the time to depart. But he couldn't leave Boaz. He took a deep, shuddering sigh. He'd been a dead man since departing Ottweill's camp, properly speaking. Why find concern now? "We owe them your life."

Boaz gave him a long look. "I do. Your debt is different."

Al-Wazir refused to consider it further. "How do we do this thing?"

"We will find a way."

Without a word to the smiths, they climbed back up top. Al-Wazir shouldered his empty spear and followed Boaz as they headed out across the slick bridge.

Twenty minutes later, clinging to a rope, al-Wazir said, "For a lad who don't know where he's been, you surely do seem to know where you're going."

"The smith gave me a path."

Eventually they were in a true byway. This was a dank stairwell, rotten with moss and mold, water flowing in a little rill down the center of the steps through a soft-walled channel it had cut for itself. Al-Wazir trudged behind Boaz, thinking on their errand. There were dozens of ways to kill a man, but this king was no man.

He hoped.

He wondered, too, what this path was that the smith had given Boaz. Secret markers were well and fine, but al-Wazir worried that they had somehow built a new layer into the Brass man's thoughts. Could Boaz be trusted now? Could Boaz trust himself?

Doctors, at least, only cut into a man and sewed him up again. They didn't stir his brains like a drunken clockmaker at an admiral's watch.

When they reached a narrow door on a small landing, Boaz turned to him. "You are not compelled to follow me within."

"That's what you think, laddie," al-Wazir muttered. "Someone's got to pull your clanking Brass arse out of this foolishness."

"For that, I am grateful. Still, if you wish to remain here, I—"

"Shut up and keep moving!"

"After this, I am not so certain," warned Boaz.

"Is anyone ever certain before battle? I dinna think so, but for the foolish and the dead. I am no fool and you are no longer dead."

Boaz tried to tug the latch, but the door would not budge. He shook it several times to no avail. "We go," he said, and yanked the door off its hinges.

They dashed into the high chamber where al-Wazir had heard the splashing the day before. It was lit now by shafts of daylight from high above. A giant slab-sided glass tank stood on eight great iron legs in the center of the room. Something huge and silver flashed within as a wall of scales slid by.

"The Inhlanzi King," said Boaz.

That gave al-Wazir a moment's pause. He'd certainly been on the Wall enough to realize what *could* be here. It was a different world from Lanarkshire or the Royal Navy.

Two of the brass-armored soldiers ran toward them, bringing al-Wazir's brief reverie to an end. The attackers' spears were braced as they moved in eerie silence. No one here spoke. No one at all.

He raised the Ophir spear and stepped to meet them, trusting Boaz to know what must be done next.

The soldiers closed head on, running side by side. They had raised no alarm that he could see, unless they'd banged on the doors connecting to the outer chamber before charging him.

It was as if they wanted to fail. . . .

He swung the Ophir spear butt-first and stepped around the charge to slam one of the soldiers in the side of the head. The man dropped like a poled ox, his own spear clattering across the damp flagstones of the floor. The other defender turned, but instead of engaging at close quarters, he simply charged again with his spear fixed in his hands.

Al-Wazir tripped him.

The solder went down on his hands and knees with a great whoof of air, falling like a child.

They were definitely fighting to lose.

Just to keep himself out of trouble, al-Wazir gave the second defender a good kick in the ribs. He then raced to catch up to Boaz.

The Brass man stood beneath the wall of the tank and stared upward into the murky waters.

"What are ye going to do, laddie?" al-Wazir gasped.

"I wish to breach the vessel above us. Once spilled upon the floor, the Inhlanzi King should be easier to dispatch."

"Yon fish is the size of a whale. Not so easy to chop off his head."

Above them this morning were no rolling eyes or great breathy voices—just that silver body obscured by water and the depth of time that clung to anything grown so huge. They looked around while the fish circled overhead. The room was possessed of the same frenetic eye-bending architecture as the outer chamber, but there was virtually no furniture.

There was, however, a set of pipes leading out one wall to connect to the Inhlanzi King's vat. They were about eight feet off the ground, supported by narrow columns of iron with wide, flat bases bolted to the floor.

"If we take one of these down," al-Wazir said, " 't'will cause the pipe to buckle. That may give us something stout enough to whack at the glass of the tank."

Boaz grabbed at the top of the iron column and gave it a hard shake. The support groaned and the pipes above gurgled, but it did not show sign of breaking free.

Al-Wazir grasped it as well, and threw his back into the next tug. Something popped with a shower of rust, but again the column just shook.

The great double doors banged open as a squad of the brass-armored soldiers poured in. Some of them were armed with swords as well as spears.

"I reckon our moment is nigh," al-Wazir said.

"We shall see," muttered Boaz. They gave the column another concerted pull, al-Wazir grabbing it high up to put his weight into the effort. His ribs stabbed within his chest. There was another popping noise and one of the pipes began shuddering. The king splashed in his tank, while the soldiers were nearly upon them.

He didn't even have the spear in his hands, just a grip on this stupid iron column.

"Fewk that!" screamed al-Wazir, and jumped upward to grab at the shuddering pipe as Boaz yanked once more on the support.

All gave way with a slow, groaning grace. A stream of water shot out of the rupturing pipe, under much more pressure than al-Wazir had expected. Metal shrieked anew. Column and pipe both bent as Boaz tugged. The monster thrashed. The soldiers surrounded them with blades and spears at the ready just when al-Wazir fell to the ground, clinging to the pipe, which now spat water like shot from a cannon. The stream drove back some of the soldiers, while others danced around it, seeking footing.

"They fight to lose!" al-Wazir hissed at Boaz.

The Brass man ignored him and the soldiers both, instead charging toward the Inhlanzi King's tank with the seven-foot stub of the iron column. The other pipe had broken now as well. Dark, stinking water erupted from it.

Al-Wazir tugged at his pipe end in an effort to aim the water. It was the only weapon he had. The captain of the squad seemed determined to close on him, but the others were hanging back or milling as if to pursue Boaz. The chief dropped the pipe and launched himself, fists swinging directly at the officer.

He counted on the others continuing their strange, slow mutiny.

The Scotsman and the soldier hit the floor together to slide on wet stone, just as there was an enormous crack loud as if someone had broken open the sky. They both looked up to see a craze spreading across the glass face above them.

Boaz danced back with the column and made another run, leaping to drive it into the smashed glass.

This time the tank ruptured. It spewed a waterfall of filth that completely obscured the Brass man. The soldiers scrambled away as the tide surged toward them, while their captain and al-Wazir both scrabbled to follow.

The Inhlanzi King was coming out of his water bed.

Whatever he is, 'tis more than some fewking great African fish, al-Wazir thought. *Eel, perhaps. Or just monster.*

The king poured forth, scaly and long, uncoiling to show a mouth taller than al-Wazir, filled with needle teeth the size of a man's arm. The upper body hit the stones with a jarring wet noise. He thrashed even as more of his body rode the sluicing water out of his tank.

Boaz rose from the filthy flood and stabbed one baleful eye with the stub of the iron column. At that all the soldiers roared as one and charged their king. Al-Wazir found himself sitting alone in several inches of rank water as his erstwhile enemies set blade to flesh, tearing into the scales and muscle of those long, thrashing flanks.

There was a great deal of killing to be done. The soldiers did it with a great deal of screaming, hacking, and cutting and sometimes dying, even as more and more of their fellows ran in shouting to join in the feast of blades. The water drained away, thickening with gelid silver-blue blood as it vanished.

CHILDRESS

They weathered two storms between the islands and Singapore. As usual, *Five Lucky Winds* submerged and rode out the worst of the violence beneath the waves. The hull still rocked and the water still boomed, but there was nothing like the violence of a boat upon the water driven by wind and rain. Childress sat in her cabin in those long, noisy hours and refined her arguments against the Golden Bridge. If they made their way to Chersonesus Aurea, which still seemed like a substantial assumption to her, logic would be her greatest and only weapon.

Leung brought them to the surface several hours outside of Singapore. He found Childress in her cabin. "Would you accompany me to the tower?"

She set aside a chart she'd been studying simply for the sake of knowing something about the landforms. "Of course."

Childress followed Leung up the ladder to the deck hatch. They climbed onward up damp rungs to the little cupola at the top of the tower. He helped her into the light.

It was hot. The air seemed practically liquid, and the sun pressed on Childress like a fist.

Ignoring that, she looked around. A low tropical coast, thick with verdant green and a startling array of colors. The water was a muddy yellow brown, smelling of salt and flood. She turned to look the other way.

The Wall loomed.

It consumed her vision. What had been a glowering line on the horizon at the Qun Dao Islands was an immense presence extending so far into the heavens, she had to lay her head all the way back on her shoulders to see it. The Wall was covered with countries—forests and mountains and tumbling rivers, all written sideways, with their own storms and clouds moving among them like the layers in a pastry. High up, where the sun caught a bright rim, frost perhaps, she thought she saw the gleam of brass.

"Oh, goodness."

"Your Wall," he told her. "It stands over Singapore like a rebuke from Heaven."

"*My* Wall?" She laughed. "God's Wall. Or Heaven's, if you prefer. Whatever would the rebuke be?"

He smiled. "Something against overreaching, I should think."

"Indeed." She stared at its mottled vastness awhile. "May I stay here?"

"Of course."

Singapore was a busier port even than Tainan. The scene was busy enough to distract her from the mind-numbing Wall as *Five Lucky Winds* entered the harbor.

The Wall still loomed close, fog-shrouded below and gleaming above with the emerald of bright growth, but the logic of the maps she'd been studying was clear enough. Any trade that passed between the Indian Ocean and the South China Sea flowed here. The British had been here as well, the easternmost extent of empire before the Chinese had driven them out not so long ago.

They moved up a narrow inlet packed with ships and boats and rafts and people. The passage was wide enough for a vessel larger than the submarine, but Childress thought that a person could probably walk across the water from deck to deck virtually everywhere else along the waterway.

Buildings crowded alongside the port, some obviously British, others with a more Asian feel. None were as large as the new iron-skeletoned towers that had been rising in Boston and New York City. Rather, these were broad, solid trading houses, banks, bourses, exchanges, and warehouses.

This city bought and sold, sold and bought. Childress imagined it mattered little to the inhabitants what flag flew above the customshouses.

Even ashore amid the surging chatter of crowds, there was an orderliness that had not prevailed in Tainan or Sendai. This was a city that kept itself a certain way, not surrendering to the riot that sailors brought with them.

It was also hot, soaking her with sweat even through the homespun blues she had adopted on this voyage. Who knew her here, after all? She would likely be arrested if she strolled the streets of New Haven in trousers and jacket such as these, but the crew had taken her for their own now. No one ashore here had firm opinions about the attire and comportment of a good Christian woman from New England.

Childress laughed softly and smiled up at the Wall, which hung over everything here like the palm of God's hand. The sun beat down on her head, the air was thick enough to slice with a butterknife, and the water around her smelled like an old bilge. She was close to whatever this journey would bring to her.

"Chersonesus Aurea, I am here," she said, addressing her words to the imposing presence that was the Wall.

So much for the Mask Poinsard and her Great Relic, Childress thought. *I will do more for those who planned to let my throat be slit than they ever would have accomplished for themselves.*

The surge of pride both thrilled her and shamed her. Childress accepted the two impulses as one, and watched to see where the pilot officer standing nearby would dock the ship.

"Now that you've received Admiral Shang's approval," Leung told her, "you are permitted to debark on your parole. You will return to the ship as if you were a ship's officer under orders."

"I should expect no less." In truth, Childress was surprised, but she saw no point in elaborating.

He coughed, then smiled. "That means, should you elect to go ashore, you may leave the dock and move about on your own. This is perhaps the only port in the Celestial Empire where that would be a useful freedom to you. Singapore was in English hands until only a generation ago. It is still a common language here."

"Is that why you speak English so well?"

"Thank you." His head bobbed in a bow. "My parents are Singapore Chinese. It was a language at our dinner table. I pursued my education in English. There are engineering and scientific journals from your kingdom which have much to teach us, when the Celestial Empire can deign to admit those publications."

She patted the metal of the tower. "Your engineering seems quite adept to me."

"Again, my thanks." He stared down at the wharf, where a detail of sailors from *Five Lucky Winds* was already being sent out. "Our peoples pursue different questions, though. We find different answers."

"Much as with God."

"Indeed."

She walked along a narrow street crowded with faces of a dozen shades and colors. If there had been English here recently, there would still be churches. Possibly Church of England, possibly Romish or Lutheran, but churches. Childress didn't actually know whether the Chinese empire practiced tolerance as a formal policy. From what Leung said, China seemed to lack the obsession with a single path to righteousness that gripped so many in the European world. Tolerance or no, the churches within the British Empire fought one another like aging tomcats. Each was jealous of the faithful of the others.

Many folds in the way was a phrase that had stuck in her memory.

The shore was no cooler than the ship had been. Worse, because the breeze out on the open water was blocked by the buildings of the city. All that pace of life was mixed together in a swirling maelstrom of scent.

She walked past narrow shops hung with blind-eyed ducks and haunches of stringy pink meat she preferred not to contemplate too carefully. Others sold mountains of red paper in many forms—envelopes, posters, folded into strange shapes, mounted as lanterns. Still more featured clothing, tools, jars that swam with pickled animals and tinctures of strange plants. There were more and more beyond, teahouses and little cook fires crammed into doorways.

For all its orderliness, Singapore was as jumbled and crowded as Tainan. Here there was the chatter of a dozen languages besides Chinese, and the dress of many clans and nations.

She wandered awhile, preferring not to ask directions. As there were many older women here, Childress did not feel conspicuous for her age or gender. She was the only European she saw. People did not stare, though. They just kept pressing past, on their own errands. Many rode in little two-wheeled carts pulled by running men dressed in almost nothing.

Her patience was rewarded when she came to a small mission building. It was a church, complete with a cross atop the roof, though the signboard was in Chinese.

Childress slipped through the open door and stood for a few minutes at the back. It looked Papist to her—there was a table full of candles in the vestibule, and large paintings of the Virgin Mary and a thorn-crowned Christ. Both seemed more Asian than the pale faces of traditional European religious art.

She smiled at that.

The pews were mostly empty, with a few people at prayer. A short man in a black cassock moved back and forth at the altar. There was no evidence of a pending service, nor of much else in progress. She slipped into a pew and knelt on the padded bench to pray awhile.

God did not speak to her, but then He never did. Still, praying in a church had always seemed to her to be more to the point than private prayer. He was certainly infinite in His attentions, by definition, but Childress could never escape the notion that God was very busy. Like the dean of an endlessly large college, perhaps—an image that always made her smile. She supposed it was sacrilegious if not outright blasphemous.

It pleased Childress to imagine the Brass Christ laughing at the thought.

When she stood from her contemplations, she saw the priest waiting for her in the aisle. His skin was the color of polished oak but his nose could have come from the Mediterranean. Some race unknown to her, though she'd seen dozens of his fellows in the streets outside.

"Father," Childress said politely.

"Madam," he said. She noted his English seemed to have no accent.

The priest continued: "Are you of the Roman rite?"

"No, no." She dropped her chin. "I am a communicant of the Church of England. But I have not had the opportunity to pray in the house of God for some months."

She could hear the smile in his voice, though the priest's face remained serious enough. "Everyone arrives in Singapore via a long sea voyage. And there are sadly few chaplains aboard the ships which call here in these days of Chinese hegemony." He bowed his head, a chin bob that matched hers. "Welcome, and return to this house of God as it suits you. All Christians are brothers here."

"Thank you, Father." Childress regretted that she had no offering to leave.

"Go with God, my child."

This, from a man less than half her age. "And you."

Outside, another dark-skinned man clothed only in a soiled length of cloth wrapped about his privates waved her toward a waiting cart—one of those runners she'd seen earlier, drawing passengers about Singapore.

"No, no," she began. Someone stepped close behind her, grabbed her arm tightly, and whispered, "Get in the rickshaw."

Her heart felt cold and heavy. There was no one nearby from *Five Lucky Winds*. The priest would remember her, and surely some of the passersby could say they'd seen the European woman.

She stepped into the seat. The runner grabbed the handles as the other man slid in beside her. He was brown, too, and nondescript— middle-aged, wearing the same silk clothes cut Chinese-style as half the people on the street. But not Chinese himself. Some other Asian race, one among the thousands on thousands of people in this city. Only his eyes betrayed more. They were bright, gleaming like knives, and showed her no mercy.

He made the sign of the *avebianco*. "You are the Mask come among us, yes?"

The house of her lies had just caught fire, Childress realized. She could not deny herself now.

"Yes," she said. "I am the Mask Childress." That could hardly be kept a secret. "I am unaccustomed to being abducted on the street."

The knife-sharp eyes flashed, somewhere between anger and amusement. "I could not come to your ship, no."

"I suppose not." *Poinsard, be Poinsard,* she told herself. Childress tried to borrow some of that woman's brittle fearsomeness. *Let him approach you with whatever his petition is.* The Mask Poinsard would definitely have seen it as such, she knew.

They rolled through the streets. Their driver trotted and sang in some language that didn't seem to include the concept of key in its musical tradition. Childress watched the buildings go by, waiting for whatever would come next.

She was not disappointed.

He made the bird sign again. He was nervous. *Good, let him be.* This man had taken a woman alone for a ride in a strange city—he could share her fear.

"Malaya Chinthé," he finally said, almost muttering the words.

"Indeed." She had no idea what he was talking about, but Childress would not give him the satisfaction of asking. In this moment her power lay most in silence and the presumption of authority.

"The red folder, yes?"

This time Childress just stared him down with her best speaking-to-idiots expression.

He sighed and looked away a moment. They were passing a grove of tall trees with long, dangling branches, something like a willow crossbred with a watersnake. When he turned back, the knives were in his eyes once more.

"We hear new word. Fire is higher now."

"I have been at sea," she told him.

"Yes. Silent Order is in a state of panic. Ships come and go from Phu Ket, airships also. Even wireless is not quiet."

"Have we moved against them in my absence?"

"No, no. There is a weapon afoot. A shaman attacked them in their European heart."

She digested that a moment. "Who?"

"I not know. Your people not say. Only to watch for something called the Gleam, yes. Also that the Silent Order are looking for a European girl. Great many reward offered, even."

Interesting, Childress thought. *Very interesting.* "Girl, not a woman? Young?"

His smile cracked into being a moment. "Not the Mask, no."

"And you?" She asked the same way the dean might have.

"Red folder, red folder. All same. But today I must find you, tell you about girl." He leaned closer. "Like Golden Bridge, on two legs. London worries."

"That project is its own problem." She looked at him carefully. "Is the girl coming here?"

"Why? How? European problem, white man make, white man fix."

"Fair enough." She realized the rickshaw was approaching the docks. *Five Lucky Winds* was somewhere near, though in the jumble of vessels it was difficult to discern.

"You go. I go. Never see, yes?" He smiled again, this time without the slightest shred of humor. "Watch for girl. She come this way, I think we all hear the fires."

The rickshaw creaked to a halt as someone behind yelled. She slipped over the side. When she looked back, he was already gone, out the other side and into the crowd. Only the grubby, nearly nude driver remained. He grinned at Childress briefly before running again, keeping his rickshaw just ahead of a straining oxcart.

She looked up and down the docks as traffic flowed around her. Three sailors from *Five Lucky Winds* were approaching as well—Ming, who was something like a petty officer, along with Little Chen and Gray Chen. The Chens each carried a pair of roasted ducks.

Childress hailed them, surprising the sailors considerably. She felt better heading back to the ship in their company. Any further untoward surprises would be witnessed, at the least.

The news given by the man from the Malaya Chinthé had been interesting, but she had no way of knowing who he really was. Another Chinese political officer, an agent of the Silent Order, or someone else entirely. She glanced up at the Wall. Did people there come down and mix on the streets here, sending their agents and spies?

She didn't miss New Haven, but life certainly was simpler there.

Childress found herself grinning as she reboarded the submarine.

SIXTEEN

PAOLINA

The voyage south of the Suez Canal was pleasant by Paolina's recent standards. Spending her days staring at glass-green water, and taking mess with the few passengers still aboard, was a simple pleasure.

The mess steward was kind to her. The rest of the crew continued to avoid her. She was still on the run, and the British certainly had ample Naval forces here along the Horn of Africa that they could search *Star of Gambia* if they so wished. Still, being out of the Mediterranean and away from the long shadow cast by Europe and that sad continent's British masters did much to ease her mind.

The ship passed south through the Red Sea. Amid those shallow, gleaming waters, thick with salt and touched with sand, Paolina got a glimpse of the Wall. Nearing her goal was heartening. She stood at the rail and stared at the thickening horizon even as the African shoreline slipped by. She fancied she could see the gleam of the gearing, and even some sense of texture from the countries and kingdoms in their vertical array.

Star of Gambia called at Port Sudan, where Paolina once more remained aboard. She walked along the rail and looked out at hills brown as toast, covered with modest whitewashed buildings. Paolina saw a city much like Praia Nova might have become if it had ever found a chance to grow beyond a refugee settlement at the edge of the world.

There were two airship masts here, but no Royal Navy vessels were in port. She saw soldiers marching along the dock, but they did not appear to be a serious effort at, well, anything.

Men like the *fidalgos* doubtless dwelt in those pale little buildings. There they waited for boiled grapes or stewed lamb or whatever they ate in a place like this, raising their sons to expect the attentions of women, and their daughters to bow in fear to God and the hard hands of their fathers and husbands. As in Alexandria, Paolina once more felt tempted to cast off her name and go among the people of the city. She would tell those women what they could be, show them that there was a world outside the walls of the houses of their men.

It was a pleasant and pointless fantasy. Even if she were foolish enough to try, she would not last. The only question was whether the British would find her before the locals killed her.

Living as these women did, as women did anywhere in Northern Earth, had passed beyond her tolerance. The wild lands and strange creatures and mechanical men of *a Muralha* were far more to her taste than a life mandated by tradition.

That was when Paolina realized she would not be returning to Praia Nova. Ophir, possibly, to find Boaz, if no other plan presented itself along the way, but she had no need to take up the chains of her childhood once more.

Just after dawn they passed a narrow strait that the mess steward informed her was the Bab el Mandeb Sound. There was a large island to the portside, and a group of smaller islands to the starboard. Two British warships rode at anchor to watch over the traffic sailing from the Red Sea into the Gulf of Aden. Paolina returned to her cabin once she saw them.

When they called at Djibouti to discharge cargo, she saw little that was different from Port Sudan. More sand and fewer hills, and a landscape painted ocher and gold instead of brown and tan. The wind came up while they were in port, and the one airship at mast cast off and lifted away even while the sky tinged from pale blue to pale tan to a deepening brown.

The wind began worrying at the ship's superstructure, a low moaning whistle combined with the hiss of dust like someone running sandpaper across the paint. Paolina had never seen such weather—they had nothing like it in Praia Nova. A storm of dust. It was already seeping in around the hatch coaming and settling in corners of her cabin.

She wondered if there was some further shelter she should take.

Star of Gambia cast off in the afternoon, about the time she lost sight of the city from her porthole. The air outside was whipping and screaming now, sand pouring along the walls and decks of the ship like a rough, hot rain. Paolina was fairly certain that going outside now would be risky if not fatal.

At least the British wouldn't be looking for her or anyone else in this mess.

The ship's progress seemed retarded by the storm. Paolina could feel how the vessel rode heavy and low in the water. The wind was out of one of the aft quarters. Perhaps the captain had them moving underspeed for safety. Even away from Djibouti and out in open water, the air was thick and violent with sand. Lightning crackled in the orange-brown sky amid a sourceless, featureless daylight that felt as if God had pulled a caul over the mouth of the world.

Star of Gambia rocked, too, rolling in the water as she advanced eastward through the Gulf of Aden. Paolina decided there was no point in worrying. She lay on her bunk and tried to calculate how much sand could be carried on the wind, what weight of the world's surface was even now borne aloft in this crippling grind.

They steamed on.

The storm finally died as the sun went down. Somewhere close to midnight Paolina ventured out of her cabin.

The rails were scarred by gleaming silver streaks visible in the moonlight where the sand had abraded the white paint. Likewise the decks. A torn awning flapped the wind of their passage, though she could not see where. The engines muttered, the boilers gurgled, but otherwise the ship could have been carrying the dead.

She headed to the passenger's mess, hoping for something cold to have been left out—roast bird or bread and dates, at the least. They'd always had plain fare that varied in tempo with their travels. Apples and olives in the Mediterranean, now dates and figs and flatter breads, with less and less cheese as the ship had steamed south and east.

Paolina was not disappointed. A tray had been bolted into a framework. It still held a few round, flat breads and a cracked jar of something that smelled like liver.

She didn't care. Paolina smeared two of the breads with the pasty spread and went back out on deck to eat and watch the night pass by.

In the wake of the storm, everything seemed visible. Not even the moon was sufficient to drown out the brasslight. Paolina thought she could see the flicker in the distant lamps of the stars. Paolina turned her gaze southward and stared toward the Wall.

Out in darkness, the stars didn't quite touch the horizon. The storm was gone, and nothing rose in the air between her and *a Muralha* save a bit of Africa close by.

She swallowed her liver paste, then raised a hand with the other bread still clutched to honor history. "I come," Paolina told the Wall. "Returning, never to leave you again."

The purser failed to materialize this night.

Their course took the ship around the Horn of Africa, past Cape Guardafui and into the Indian Ocean. The land remained arid as they steamed south. There was more plant life than she'd seen along the Red Sea. Paolina's sense that she was going home quickened her pulse, lending her an excitement she hadn't felt earlier. She found herself pacing the decks. She mostly spoke to the two Germans who were traveling to Mogadishu to take up work as doctors, but even exchanged a few words with the crew.

She'd been aboard *Star of Gambia* for over three weeks. The ship was starting to feel like home. The rust and paint smells, the pulsing of the deck as the vessel rode the waters, the whistle blasts and ringing bells from the bridge. She could understand why a man might take to sea—see the world and carry his home with him, on such a ship.

Still, the end was coming. Her own passage was finished at Mogadishu. From there she would travel down the coast to Kismaayo at the base of *a Muralha*. Each day the Wall grew larger, more distinct. Where others aboard the ship tended to look away—finding business belowdecks, within a cabin or on the starboard rail—Paolina was drawn more and more to it. Each detail that appeared only fed her hunger to be home.

Every mile of open sea was a mile farther away from England, a mile closer to her goal. Like the seabirds that followed the ship crying, she was ready to fly home in full voice.

When they steamed into Mogadishu, she was surprised at how small the city was. This was the main port of British East Africa. There wasn't a harbor to speak of, just a shallow bay to provide anchorage. Cargo would have to be lightered ashore.

She could judge the importance of this port by the dozen airship masts on bluffs east and north of the city. Three airships were moored, while the substantial cluster of buildings near the masts attested to a strong and active British presence.

"Chinese," said one of the Germans, stepping up next to her at the stern rail. He was Herr Minke, a medical resident studying under Dr. Albertus, his fellow traveler. "They fly the zeppelins along the Wall. The Crown must answer them."

"I have seen a Chinese airship," she said sadly. *Killed it, too.*

Paolina turned and looked south. They were close enough for terrain to be visible—scree and slopes and forests, and higher up fields of snow and ice, all punctuated by the horizontal weather that always possessed the Wall. The threads of roads, too, if you knew how to interpret what you saw. Even settled plateaus with towns and cities

The flatwater world laid sideways would never be so beautiful, she thought.

"It is a struggle." Minke's words tore her away from thoughts of home. "The Chinese are said to be terrible."

"They die the same as anyone else."

He looked at her strangely, then moved on.

Paolina watched as *Star of Gambia* made anchorage at a buoy, following a signal gun and flags from the shore.

She would debark here and find a boat to take her south to Kismaayo. Walking the last miles over this grim, rocky coast seemed pointless. She still held the funds Lachance had given her, and would make use of them until she was safely upon *a Muralha*. Once there, even if she were eaten by a scaled cat, at least she would be where she belonged.

The Queen of England could burn in all of Satan's Hells at once for whatever Paolina cared.

Going ashore in a launch was simple enough. She gathered her few things in her small leather satchel, tucked the balance of her funds within the bodice of the traveling dress she'd bought in France, and clambered down a rope ladder that had been let over a break in the railing.

The water was gray today, an odd color for the Indian Ocean. Though the swells were low, the boat pitched as they headed for shore. She sat with the Germans in the stern watching a whey-faced officer she'd never seen before call terse instructions to the six men rowing.

Pulling up to the little dock will be rough, she thought.

The sailors knew their business. The boat tucked in as the portside oars lifted. The officer heaved up a rope while idlers on the dock tossed down two more ropes. There was one long, slow crunching scrape; then they were tied up.

"Welcome ashore, miss." The officer offered to assist Paolina up the slime-crusted ladder.

"No thank you." She didn't really want his pale, pudgy hands touching her. Instead she hooked the bag over one arm and scrambled up.

A man reached down and helped her off the ladder. Paolina looked up to thank him and realized she was staring at a British officer. Pale eyes, straw-colored hair, skin burned red, in the blues of the Royal Navy.

"Ah," she said.

"Welcome to Mogadishu, Miss Barthes," he said.

She swung the grip into his crotch and kicked him in the shin, then ran down the dock, toward the shoreline and the quiet city beyond even as the shouting rose behind her.

Mogadishu wasn't any bigger than Djibouti had been, but there was more to the city—trees, bushes, alleys. Places she could run to. The land was still dry, but not so sere as farther north. The Wall pushed enough rain toward the African coast to keep it green.

There didn't seem to be a hot pursuit—no whistles or pounding feet—but she knew better than to look back until she'd found the security of a warm, green shadow. A fitful wind was rising off the ocean, blowing hot and wet, making her hiding place beneath a thorn tree very uncomfortable indeed.

No British behind her. No sailors. The few natives who'd stared at her as she ran had not followed to investigate.

She could hardly blend in here. These people were dark-skinned, the color of carob beans. There couldn't be a dozen pale-skinned women in this city. Though she hated Europe with a passion, Paolina still looked European and always would.

Would the gleam have been able to turn me dark?

It was a silly idea, and pointless besides. Still, she wondered how she was going to get to Kismaayo if everyone was looking for a European girl.

Steal one of the native robes, for a start. They wore long, pale linen wraps, some with hoods and veils. If she were to wrap herself in one of those, she might pass.

Paolina had planned to take a boat down the coast. She could have hired one of the little fishing vessels. Not now, though, or possibly ever.

She considered walking. Miles of desolate African coast worried her. Perhaps she could hire a guide. That would be less obvious than walking the docks looking for a boat.

With that thought, Paolina headed farther into the landward side of the town. She walked with her head tucked down, moving slowly. Only a blind man would fail to note her passing, but she could at least move among the poor. They tended to be busy at their own concerns. Also, the British were less likely to be waiting for her away from the waterfront. She'd strike around to the southwest end of the city and see what she could see. With luck she'd find a railroad line or roadway.

If she encountered someone along the way who might be able to help her, so much the better. At least she could find a robe. Paolina hated the thought of stealing from people who had so very little. She didn't see what else she could do. If she stopped to bargain, she would only be remembered all the more.

If she must, she would walk the miles of thorn trees and stinking brush on her own. *A Muralha* was too close for her to fail now.

AL-WAZIR

The squad commander turned out to be a very worried man named Davile. Like most of his fellows he was of dark-colored skin, almost purple. Legs still freshly soaked in blood of his god-king, he led al-Wazir and Boaz along a swaying bridge, shouting unintelligibly over the roar of the great waterfall that surrounded his city. All three of them limped and stumbled, worn from the fight, though with no serious wounds that al-Wazir could see.

They moved along quickly. Al-Wazir was glad enough of that. The orderly motions of the city had stopped with the death of its terrible king. Smoke rose now from some buildings, while people moved in muttering crowds accompanied by the flash of weapons.

A spell had been lifted.

He followed the soldier through a curtain of spray and into another cave tunnel.

Davile turned and said something urgent, slashing his hands back and forward for emphasis.

"East," said al-Wazir, pointing in that direction. "We must go."

Boaz tried another language, which got Davile's attention. The two of them spoke for several minutes.

"He informs me that we will be escorted to the border and given assistance to be about our journey."

"While they have a riot here?"

"I do not know." As they walked, Boaz asked Davile several more questions eliciting short answers that obviously made the man uncomfortable.

Al-Wazir let the two get a bit ahead of him. He turned and looked back toward the cave mouth.

What remained of Davile's squad followed them.

So it wasn't just an escort. They were being cast out. Regicides, to be sure, but something more was happening here. Something Davile didn't want them to see.

He caught up to Boaz. "They are at war with one another, yon angry little men."

"I am aware of their distress," Boaz said quietly. "I think our interests are best served by an immediate departure."

"Aye." Al-Wazir felt frustrated, but this was not his city. These were not his people. That their king's blood was still drying on his arms bore consideration as well. Someone with a serious objection to the royal succession might raise questions.

They came to another cave that glowed with electricks. A number of large machines bulked around it, reminiscent of railroad locomotives or even Ottweill's steam borer. The place had the air of purposeful activity abandoned, with tools discarded on the floor and papers scattered. The engineers here had either fled or marched to their version of civil war.

Davile stopped in front of a half globe mounted on an axle between two enormous wheels at least twelve feet in diameter. The bowl of the hull was propped against a laddered framework. A shaft rose from the floor to penetrate the metal housing at its bottom. The soldier waved them upward, speaking urgently.

Boaz nodded, tested the first rung, then climbed to the scaffold and into the bowl. Al-Wazir followed.

It was padded within, as a coach might be, featuring a circular bench that could seat three or four, depending on their size. The Brass man already had his hand on a tiller bar, which had a grip switch at each end. There were several more controls mounted on the thick column of the bar.

"*Oinos, dwo, treyes!*" shouted their guide. He then did something that caused the frame to fall away. The half globe ticked like a great clock before lurching into motion. Al-Wazir watched nervously as Boaz tried the tiller bar. When the Brass man twisted it first one way then the other, the ticking changed.

Steering was by varying the speed of one wheel or the other, then. What al-Wazir couldn't understand was how their globe stayed arse-side down.

Not that it mattered now. They picked up speed, bursting out of a draped doorway he hadn't realized was there and nearly striking a retaining wall just beyond—that would have sent them hurtling right over the edge and down the waterfall. Boaz fought the tiller to the right, experimenting with the grip switches, and got the conveyance aimed down a road heading east.

It was the old Ophir road, the section kept in repair by Davile's people.

They clicked along, picking up a bit more speed before passing through an open gate that was slammed shut behind them by another group of brass-armored soldiers. The road took a wide sweep to the south past another outcrop. The waterfall city was behind them.

Al-Wazir examined the vehicle they were bowling along in. "Did those people build this?"

"No more than they constructed their architecture, I should think." Boaz watched the road ahead carefully. They were moving at a breakneck pace of at least twenty-five miles per hour.

"Like England, where everything is taken from someone else."

Boaz gave him a quick glance. "All is taken from God. In the end all is returned to Him."

"Heh. Strange thing for John Brass to say."

"I, who have a seal of Solomon burning inside my head, am no stranger to the powers of God. Nor is any thinking creature that walks beneath the brasslight of a moonless night."

They fell into silence, al-Wazir still clutching the still-bloody Ophir spear, Boaz driving their cart. The ticking noise that emanated from the heart of the rounded body of the conveyance showed no signs of abating. Al-Wazir wasn't sure how they would stop this thing, nor how it might be restarted again, but he was pleased to accept that they were advancing more than a day's travel in each hour. This racing machine sliced away at the block of time it would take them to cross Africa from west to east.

All they had to fear was the road turning too rough for the high wheels rumbling to each side of them.

Eventually even the exhilaration of the cart's speed waned. A hard rainfall did nothing to improve al-Wazir's mood, especially when they discovered there was no apparent provision to drain the footwell of the riding cab and so were forced to endure a layer of grimy water slopping about as they continued to be propelled along their way. The water did nothing to stem the ticking heart of the car, though. That was a blessing.

They were moving sufficiently fast that the African terrain to their north changed visibly with their progress, much as it would seem to from an airship. The land to their left had risen into high hills as if the continent had sought to claw up the Wall before being rebuked by God. Jungles steamed, filled with the bright specks of birds and the threads of watercourses.

Al-Wazir saw no cities or towns, just the center of a vast fecundity that moved by with the precision of all Creation.

They drove into the night. Boaz did not tire, al-Wazir knew that, but still he felt guilty about lifting his feet to the curved bench and dozing as they traveled. It was no restful sleep—the great wheels transmitted every bump and crack in the road. There was no way to get comfortable in any case. If he'd been a small man, he might have curled like a dog, but the cart was no larger than a banquette.

Still, he had dreams of fish that swam among the lamps of the stars and spoke to him in the voices of the dead. Al-Wazir strained to hear their counsel, only to find it was nothing but bitter grudges and prophecies of things past.

Life is backwards, he thought, and woke with those words echoing in his head.

The road held out through the next day as well. Al-Wazir found this surprising.

"We have not passed another town or city," he said to Boaz. "Are Davile's people able to keep the right of way up this far west? There have been hundreds of miles of road by now, surely."

"There were cities," Boaz said shortly. "Above and below us. Though many avail themselves of the Ophir road, few dare build directly upon the right of way for fear that the armies might someday return."

After a little while, al-Wazir asked, "Will they?"

Boaz shook his head. "That is not for me to say."

"No, I suppose not."

In the course of the day, the jungles of Africa thinned to endless pale grasslands, sometimes covered with beasts in herds that stretched for miles. Al-Wazir wondered how many millions of sheep could graze there.

Eventually his attention returned to Boaz. "Surely even you tire of driving this cart?"

"Of course. But I wish to follow Miss Barthes. We have gained two months of walking already, though I fear we will lose our road soon. Have you not felt more and more of the roughness over which we travel?"

"Yes."

"We are at or past the reach of civilized repair. We shall be compelled to dismount shortly."

Al-Wazir patted the rim of the cab. "This cart has made better time than even an airship would. Like a railroad across Africa. Certainly Ottweill's men could lay track all down the Ophir road well enough."

"Indeed. I should hope that never comes to pass."

The chief fell silent. He was unwilling to speak against the Queen's interests, but at the same time unable to disagree with the Brass man.

He studied the distance ahead instead. There was a sullen gray glower at the edge of the world, under fast, ragged clouds.

"I believe we approach our goal, laddie," al-Wazir said.

"Was there ever doubt?"

The end to their swift passage came soon enough. The road was increasingly rubbled. There was a landslide visible a few miles ahead that spilled over to block the trackway completely. A man could climb the rock well enough, but the cart would be battered to destruction in moments.

"Seems a shame to just leave it in the road," al-Wazir said.

Boaz slowed them, studying what lay ahead. "There is no going forward."

"Aye, I see that. Yet . . ." He could get used to the convenience of this mad conveyance.

Still ticking, they rumbled to a slow walking pace. Al-Wazir looked ahead to spy more details. A trail led across the rubbled fall on the downhill side of the blocked roadbed. That meant that people passed this way reasonably often. As he'd assumed, the cart would never fit.

They came to a shuddering halt with an increase in the ticking noise from below.

Al-Wazir hoisted himself over the side. It was a good seven feet to the ground, perhaps more. He slipped over and dropped to the stones as the cart rolled back about a foot. Boaz adjusted the tiller then followed.

"That tears it," al-Wazir said. "I do not think we can so easy find our way back into that beastie."

"Sad to abandon such a machine, but we have no capacity to rewind the flywheel in any case."

They turned and surveyed the road ahead, looking for trails that might lead downward toward the coast. The Wall had a sharp downhill slope, rather than the round-shouldered cliffs they'd passed earlier. It was spotted with tufts of some sedged grass and the odd clump of dark, wiry bushes, all growing out of a field of rocks somewhere between scree and boulders.

Not inviting terrain, but certainly passable.

" 'Tis a rail line," al-Wazir hissed.

They crouched amid a stand of thornbushes just north of a miserable little port town huddled against the base of the Wall, enduring a driving rain that had come on at dusk. He was wet and miserable.

No time for that. There was work to be done. He and Boaz stared at the gleaming tracks.

Boaz leaned close. "Should you not go down and locate the Royal Navy officer in command here?"

"Maybe." Al-Wazir was distinctly unsure. "If that is Mogadishu." They'd caught glimpses of a larger city on their way down the Wall. "But I see no airship masts here."

In any case, he'd much rather get the lay of things first. *If* Ottweill had somehow managed to contact London since al-Wazir's departure, he could well be under a charge for desertion.

Better to find a few other old tars in a dockside bar and sniff out the rumors. With luck, he'd meet someone he'd served with who could inquire for him. This dreadful little town—Kismaayo?—was too small to wander into safely without being the instant center of attention.

"How far up the coast do you reckon 'tis to Mogadishu?"

"Fifty miles, perhaps?" Al-Wazir could hear the shrug in the Brass man's voice. "At the other end of these tracks, in any case."

A steam whistle wailed down in the town, audible even over the hiss of the rain.

"Here comes transport," al-Wazir said.

The locomotive finally rattled past with its short string of goods wagons clanking and swaying. The two of them sprinted along the clinkers bedding the track and grabbed on to the ladders of a boxcar. Crouched above the couplings of the rolling stock, the rain was no kinder than it had been down in the thornbushes. At least they was heading for a town big enough to hide in.

And al-Wazir was off the Wall.

Even his smile ached.

CHILDRESS

Five Lucky Winds cruised slowly on the surface amid the narrow channels and protruding reefs of the Kepualuan Riau. A number of the crew were assembled on the flat deck—there would be no submerging in these shallow, uncertain waters, and Leung had wanted his men readily available. The Kepualuan Riau were an array of tiny islands crowded with dark, vine-wrapped jungle for which the sea seemed little more than random bordering. The Wall towered just south, rising up right out of the midst of the chain.

There was nothing around them that could be mistaken for human settlement, either contemporary or out of antiquity.

"Chersonesus Aurea is here?" Childress was atop the tower with Leung and his navigator. The captain was dressed very formally in a

Western-style naval uniform, his buttons polished bright as little fires. She continued, "I should think they might have kept it where it could be found again."

"It was lost for twice a thousand years," Leung told her. "This is not a simple matter, even now."

"Surely their own supply convoys can find them."

"We are not their own supply convoys."

The submarine moved along at a fraction of her normal speed. She eased between green shadows while great, flat fish disturbed the sand as they fled from the vessel's passing. Childress stared upward for the most part. This close to the Wall, it had grown to an immensity that defied her ability to take in the view.

The thing had been easier to see even from Singapore, not too many miles northward. This was like studying the architecture of a church by pressing one's nose against a pillar.

The navigator consulted a little green-bound book and muttered quietly in Chinese. Leung relayed an order down a speaking tube. *Five Lucky Winds* slowed to a controlled drift. A desultory wind plucked at them, carrying the mixed scents of salt and jungle, while birds called in an endless oratory of feeding and mating. They might as well have sailed off the edge of the map.

She tore her regard from the Wall and cupped a hand over her eyes to sweep the nearby islands. They were close to their destination. They had to be or the ship would not have slowed, but Leung did not need more questions from her.

Childress finally realized she was looking at the tip of a mast rather than at a treetop. It rose over the emerald fold of a low hill on a largish islet. She plucked at Leung's sleeve and pointed. He grinned and called down new orders.

Even then, they might not have found the harbor without knowing exactly where to look. It was a narrow channel between two outcrops of jungle standing like green fortresses, so that the harbor mouth seemed little more than an outlet of a creek. *Five Lucky Winds* moved dead slow through a fluttering, screaming riot of birds the color of every flower Childress had ever seen. They took off in cloud dense as the smoke of a coal fire to circle in the air above the vessel.

The trees around them echoed with the calls of something larger and slower that seemed intent on tracking their progress. The channel churned from the action of their screws, bubbling behind them with a dank eruption that belied the sunlit sea just beyond.

A curve to the left, a curve to the right, and then they were in the harbor proper. It was a long oval surrounded by a jungled ridge broken only by the narrow cleft through which they'd just steamed. She imagined that if seen from a height, the bay would resemble a great comma. The city rose at the back of the harbor, extending in both directions. It was mostly pale stone wrapped in vines or crumbled to flower-covered rubble. She could make out buildings amid the greenery, rising like old memories not quite yet faded to nothingness.

An area the equivalent of several city blocks had been cleared close to the water, and a stone jetty restored. There a large steamer and two small junks were tied up. Wooden buildings had been placed among the ruins—they were plain and cheap looking, not at all like the adorned architecture of Singapore and Tainan, and even less like the overgrown structures surrounding them.

Leung brought the submarine to a halt in the middle of the harbor. He ordered his men to open a deck hatch and tug out their launch. Childress actually followed most of what was being said.

"Too shallow?" she asked him.

"We will turn the ship in place," he replied. "Most easy to make our departure at need. I do not trust that tie-up."

She was no sailor, but she'd been aboard *Five Lucky Winds* long enough to mark on the captain's unusual caution.

"Take me ashore."

He glanced at her, his eyes narrowing.

"These are your people," she said. "What is there to fear? I understand there are political intrigues afoot, but you all serve the Celestial Emperor. We are not walking into the den of your enemies. Take me with you and let me play the Mask Childress. They will not know me from the Mask Poinsard, one way or the other. We will both learn more from presenting the unexpected."

Now Leung looked amused. "You do not trust the Golden Bridge. Should you be permitted here?"

"Oh, no, you misunderstand me." She covered his hand with hers a moment. "I do trust the Golden Bridge. China does not fail. I have learned this. Though success take a thousand years, China does not fail. When the Golden Bridge is opened once more, I do not trust what lies beyond."

He made a small noise, though she could not tell if it was agreement, disagreement, or merely acknowledgement.

When Leung climbed down to take his launch to shore, he invited her with him. By the time they were on the dark waters of the bay, the birds had finally settled again. The trees were full of whooping, calling color bright as morning.

There was a delegation on the dock when the sailors rowed them to the ladder. None wore the uniforms of the Beiyang Navy, Childress noted, though she also knew that some Chinese took traditional dress despite their role. Admiral Shang, for example, though he had not been precisely traditional.

These men were turned out in a finery beyond what she'd encountered on the streets here in Asia. All wore silk cheongsams, most of a rich azure with a surcoat of red belted over and small red hats with several colors of beads upon their crowns.

Very traditional or very formal, she was not sure which. Both, most likely.

Leung climbed up onto the dock, then immediately bowed low. Childress followed. She was conscious of being the focus of all their attention. Surely because she was English, but also because she was a woman? Instead of bowing, she dipped her chin, then briefly made the sign of the white bird with her hands.

Though the welcoming party did not break composure, she could see a stir.

These men were very well trained, she thought. Perhaps some of them had the fortune to have dealings with the Imperial Court. Or misfortune, judging from the way Leung sometimes spoke of his rulers.

Instead of launching into a speech as she'd expected, Leung produced a sealed envelope from his tunic. The back was coated with a large glob of green wax. It featured several red stamps, their square imprints filled with some design she couldn't make out. The captain handed it to the man closest to him, a pudgy young fellow so pale as to barely seem Asian but for the cast of his eyes.

The man tore open the envelope, studied the paper within, then turned and bowed to a much older man, speaking quietly and at some length. The old man nodded before stepping forward to face Childress.

"You are the Englishwoman," he said in Mandarin Chinese—the dialect she'd been learning.

Childress knew her accent was terrible, but she could give a creditable answer. "Yes, Honored One."

"Eh." He turned and walked away. All his fellow mandarins followed save the pale man who'd received Leung's missive—he remained, a tall parrot in his cheongsam of yellow over green.

"Cataloger Wang informs me that he does not speak English," Leung said after a moment. "He has instructed me to inform you that his fine ears will not hear the coarse accents of a ghost-face from beyond the horizon."

Childress smiled sweetly at Wang, leaned forward, and said very quietly, "Boo."

Wang's eyes flickered.

"I believe we understand each other." She folded her hands in the sign of the *avebianco*. As if called by her, a whirring flight of pale birds skimmed out of the trees to pass just over their heads. They skimmed *Five Lucky Winds'* tower and circled out across the little bay.

Behind her, Leung chuckled.

Wang said something fast. Childress caught the word for "Englishman."

"*Dwei le,*" she murmured. *Indeed.*

That seemed to settle the issue. Wang whirled and led them down the dock. Leung saluted his ship, then turned to follow the cataloger. Childress trailed behind them both, wondering precisely what was taking place in this strange, glorious place.

Wang and Leung did not head for the wooden buildings as she had expected. Instead they followed a trail that led out of the clearing and up into the ruined city. Pillars lay broken on the ground, overgrown with clinging vines and flowers the color of a dog's tongue. Sweeping wide flights of stairs rose into stands of glossy-leaved bushes that rustled with movement running contrary to the direction of the wind. Monkeys—she hoped they were monkeys—howled and boomed in the foliage above their heads.

Some of the pillars had gold banding. Chersonesus Aurea had been quite literally lost, if no one had looted the precious metals in all the years since the place had fallen. She wondered what catastrophe had swept here. Not fire, surely. The pillars and standing walls did not appear to have been blackened, nor shattered by heat. Plague, or some disaster of political economy that cut off the trade routes and flow of goods. This place had never been supported by self-sufficient agriculture.

The trail crested a rise beyond which some of the trees had been felled to grant a view of the valley. The rest of the city was visible before her. At the shallow bottom, the buildings stood in a dark lake surrounded by waist-high grass. Buildings stood in widening concentric circles from that point, rising with the line of the hills. The structures were taken over by trees where they were increasingly distant from the water's edge.

It is a map of a civilization, she thought, *rising from the muck and climbing to the heights, only to finally be overcome by the forces of nature.* Shattered and broken, the forms of the city were still visible. Statues glinted with gold and jewels where they had fallen in the crossroads.

The strangest thing was that this place appeared to have been built by Greeks, here so very far from the city-states of the Peloponnesus. She knew there had been colonies distant from the great centers of that ancient world in Sicily and Rhodes and even the Exuin Sea. But here, in an island chain tucked between the Malay Peninsula and the Equatorial Wall?

God's world was filled with strange magics indeed.

Cataloger Wang stopped in front of a marble palace. Much of its facade was intact. He drew himself up and seemed ready to make a declamation. Instead he glared at Childress, stared at Leung, shook his head, and led them inside.

Within was a library.

Those words were inadequate to the task of describing what she saw.

A library was a repository for knowledge. A biblotheque. Some of that knowledge was in the form of books, other portions in the minds of the librarians themselves, still more as indices, catalogs, maps, files, displays.

This place was more than a repository. It was the mother of knowledge, the omphalos of human thought. She could have fallen to her knees and prayed, except for what that would likely mean to Wang. She did not need the cataloger's affection, but she did require his respect.

Childress reminded herself that the Mask Poinsard would not have been impressed by mere books.

The center of the palace was a vast dome with vaulted ribs bearing its weight. Below the dome was a pit with slanting walls that descended into the ground. This was lined with shelves and scrolleries arrayed in shallow spirals.

This place must have been built by men who understood the *ars memoriae.* The architecture was perfect for that.

Those days were long gone. Now stinking water stood about twenty-five feet below the rim of the pit. Ramps and furnishings went on into the depths. What remained above the water was crammed with documents, books, bindings, scrolls, plaques—words on all kinds of paper, leather, and wood, thousands on thousands of individual volumes.

Below the water . . . She shied away from the thought, but it was undeniable. Below the water, past the depth of visibility, rotted the corpses of many thousands more volumes. Flecks of paper floated on the surface of the hideous pond like so many water lilies.

She wondered how deep the hole went, why someone would be moved to build such an impractical library, how many books had drowned like hostage children chained to the watergates of some medieval port.

It even *smelled* like books—an almost overwhelming itchy scent of leather and paper wafting over the rotten-pond stink.

Dozens of Wang's fellows worked among the volumes. Some moved slowly up and down the spiral ramps. Others were seated on stools studying the bindings and shelf tags and scroll ends.

Wang the Cataloger, indeed, she thought with a smile. This was a life work for a hundred librarians. An entire guild could spend decades here. It was far too easy to mourn what had been lost. Salvaging what remained might assuage those wounds.

Leung asked Wang something. There was another short, fast exchange.

"I am to tell you," Leung said, "that women are not permitted among the books. You will please stay above the rails here, and not move about the premises unescorted."

"Am I soiled?" she asked pleasantly. "Unclean? Or do they fear my wicked English wizardry?"

"These are the rules here. I cannot say."

"Ask Cataloger Wang how long those rules have stood. Were women forbidden before I passed through his doorway? Or is it the case that he has created this rule now, then endowed it with the appearance of authority by claiming some canon of conduct?"

The captain visibly swallowed a grin. There was another exchange in Chinese, which ended with Leung nodding. "He says you are a bothersome woman and are to stay behind the rail."

"I may be a bothersome woman, but I am also the Mask Childress. Cataloger Wang is free to attempt a restriction of my movements, should he wish." She didn't feel nearly so brave or powerful as that statement, but she didn't know what else to do. If she bowed to Wang's foolish hatreds, she would not readily recover any authority here.

The Mask Poinsard would have skinned this foolish little popinjay. That was not her way, but it was a good thought to strengthen her resolve.

"I believe he takes your point," said Leung.

She did stay behind the rail that ran about the top of the pit. The area had perhaps served as a reading room once, though there was now scant evidence one way or the other. The Chinese had set up a number of wooden tables with stools spread between them. Material brought up from below was stacked across these like drifts from a paper store. More of

Wang's fellows carefully examined the finds. They made notes on small sheaves of paper each carried in his arms.

They were all men; that was certainly true. There was indeed no place for women here.

She moved quietly, looking at what was spread here.

None of the material visible to her was in Chinese. She saw Greek, Sanskrit, Arabic, Roman lettering, and several scripts she did not recognize. A cold, tense excitement stole across her heart. This had once been a repository of books from across the ancient world. Anything might be here, from the lost classics of Homer to the greatest alchemical treatises of the Middle Ages.

Childress had never been one to blindly believe in ancient wisdom. The world demonstrably grew better educated and more clever with time. But so much had been lost along the way, buried in the grave of years. Here was a chance to exhume some of that missing knowledge.

All of it in Chinese hands, all of it somehow in service of the Golden Bridge.

She finally stopped next to an old man studying a scroll. The script was vertical squiggles that meant nothing to her. Nothing she had ever seen, that much was certain. There were several illuminated ornaments on the section he held open, seemingly random abstractions that might be stars or flowers or bonfires.

"Ni hao ma?" *Are you well?*—a polite greeting among strangers.

He looked at her and smiled, gap-toothed, the lines around his eyes drawing tight as any net. "Wo hen hao. Ni ma?" *I am well. And you?*

"Wo hen hao, hseih hseih." *I am also well, thank you.*

He said something she didn't quite follow. When Childress looked at him blankly, he tried again.

She realized he was asking her a question in her language. "Your words are English?"

"Ah, yes. I am English." The accent was thick.

A nod this time. The gapped smile grew wider. He tapped his finger above the scroll, not quite touching it. "Taelsaem. Magic from Africa."

Now that she had the trick of his accent, she could follow him. "Yes."

His hands slipped into the sign of the *avebianco*. "You the Mask we promised?"

"Yes." She made the lie true by telling it over and over. "I am the Mask you were promised."

SEVENTEEN

PAOLINA

She found an abandoned hut. The roof leaked with the rain that drove Mogadishu into the evening, and goats had apparently used it last before her, but much of Paolina's childhood had been spent among leaking roofs and goats. Neither water nor the caprine stench held much concern for her now. Paolina made a place for herself amid rotten straw. Wrapped in her stolen robe, she slept far more soundly than she might have thought possible.

Waking before dawn, she stepped back outside. This city slept at night, without the electricks of a Marseilles or even an Alexandria. There was no harbor light, nor even torches in the streets. It could have been Praia Nova writ just a bit larger.

Perhaps, she realized, the world was not the bigger and better place she'd hoped. Just little villages of men piled one upon the other in ever-larger arrays. That Mogadishu was a small place didn't bode well for her chances to find aid. Seeking out the Chinese in an effort to balance England's mighty and barbaric reach would be pointless. She would just be a different kind of prisoner. It was the Wall for her.

She followed a dirt trail until she found a railroad track. The line led south and west toward the Wall. It connected Mogadishu and Kismaayo, then. She wondered what might be traded up from a nothing town so close to the Wall. Precious metals from the African interior, perhaps.

Paolina began following the line. She walked on the wooden sleepers to keep the worst of the muck out of her shoes, and avoid the slippery, wet clinkers.

She'd been picking her steps for less than ten minutes when something huge wailed in the darkness ahead. The noise startled her for a heart-hammering moment, until Paolina realized that it must be the train heading north on a night run from Kismaayo.

Scrambling down the bank, she huddled beneath a dripping thorn tree and waited for it to go by.

The locomotive moved slowly past her at little more than a walking speed. Paolina wondered if it had traveled at that pace all night for fear of animals on the track or washouts in the right of way. It looked smaller than the locomotives she'd glimpsed in al-Wazir's camp at the Wall, back where she'd first found the English.

The train clanking along behind consisted of a series of short, almost square cars riding high on large wheels, with one axle at each end. The cars were wood, nothing so much as large crates. Metal bumpers kept them from smashing together if the couplings flexed too far.

What they were carrying she couldn't imagine.

Something that glittered clung to the back of the last car. Paolina stared as it passed away from her, trying to sort precisely what she had seen.

A Brass man, she was sure of it.

What Brass would be down here among the English?

Boaz, she thought. *I have just seen Boaz pass me by!*

Never mind that such a chance meeting bordered on the impossible. It was *him.* Paolina scrambled up the bank, slipping and sliding and bashing her knees against the cinders, then began to run behind the train back toward Mogadishu.

It moved faster than she had realized, for she could not catch up as Boaz' faint glimmer faded ahead of her.

Still, Paolina trotted toward Mogadishu. She would follow the train into its station and find him there. With Boaz at her side, she could go home.

She reached the station as dawn was breaking. The train stood there, locomotive chuffing in the last of night's cool air. There was no sign of Boaz nor anything else she might have mistaken for him. Which made sense. He wasn't going to cling to the goods wagons on the chance she might happen along. So far as the Brass man knew, Paolina was in England.

She stood next to the shack that served as Mogadishu's depot and looked around. Where would he have gone? That depended on why he came here, of course. He must have left the company of the English back at

Ottweill's camp. He wasn't looking for her, or he would have gone up Africa's west coast.

Paolina found herself disappointed at that realization.

Still, he wouldn't have come to Mogadishu clinging to the back of a railroad car if he were traveling openly. And Boaz was far more difficult to conceal than she was.

So he would be looking for a native robe to wrap himself in, just as she had. Then he might stand a chance of passing unnoticed. He would also likely be seeking passage away from here. She couldn't guess where he might beg or steal clothing, but the only place to find a ship was down at the waterfront.

Tugging her robe close, Paolina headed the short distance to the docks. She tried to walk with the same slow, deferential pace the women here did, though it pained her spirit to make the effort.

Star of Gambia still rode at anchor, a barge lightering cargo. *Perhaps the train is here to haul the goods south to Kismaayo,* she thought. Two other ships were in port, both far smaller than *Star*—coastal traders, maybe. The fishing fleet was already out under the ragged red sky.

There seemed to be no Royal Navy vessels in the harbor this morning, though she was very conscious of the British officer who'd tried to arrest her the day before.

Paolina shuffled with her head down, her grip bag tucked beneath her robe. Just another woman on her way to buy the morning's first catch. Boaz would be trying for *Star of Gambia,* so she headed for the jetty where the launch had tied up the day before.

A few laborers in their loincloths and head scarves shivered as they waited for work. They whistled and chattered to one another in a high-pitched tongue that seemed filled with laughter. She saw no Europeans yet, though another cluster of locals stood where the jetty met the shore, consulting a sheaf of papers. They were robed, men of higher status and purpose than their cousins lounging nearby. Customs officers?

Or a Brass man asking a broker for passage.

Paolina walked slowly toward them, keeping the same woman's shuffle she'd been practicing. It was not so different from the way the women of Praia Nova never met a man's eye. She would be invisible unless she spoke to them.

Wandering past, she could hear English. Not all locals, or they would be speaking the local language. There was a burred response in a familiar accent. Despite herself, Paolina looked up to meet the pale gray eyes of the giant Scotsman, Threadgill Angus al-Wazir.

The damnable English have brought him here to catch me!

Paolina shivered as she tried to stop herself from running away. *Keep walking, don't recognize him,* she told herself. *Shuffle.*

"Girl." His voice followed her softly as a scaled cat after a coney.

Shaking, she kept walking, trying to not even twitch at the sound of him.

"Paolina?"

She couldn't help herself. Once more, she ran.

Mogadishu was not a large town. This time they did give chase, shouting for her to stop, to wait, to talk. She raced along the waterfront, turned at a crumbling plaster facade of some trading office, and sprinted up the muddy alley beside it, pushing through a flock of sheep just shaking off their night's sleep. A woman stepped out of a door in a mud-brick wall, carrying a shallow metal pan of water to toss away. She nearly caught Paolina with it, mouth open to say something. A moment later Paolina heard the pan clatter against the ground. The woman shouted something.

The chief was considerably taller and longer of leg than Paolina, but fear lent her speed. She would *not* go back to the Silent Order, to the Queen's minions, to have them use her like another tool to keep their clock. She would *not* kill again.

Running, Paolina hated her fear, hated her panic, hated that the world forced her to those thoughts.

She turned onto another street, this one leading past the railroad depot. More people were out here than before—men in their white robes, women shuffling along in their dark cloths. No one was running but her. No one was fleeing but her. All around men turned to look. The women kept moving.

The worst happened. Hands reached for her beneath dark faces filled with concern. This was not a place where women ran. Property did not flee its master, after all. She turned, dodged, heard a whistle, then was tripped to fall headlong on the muddy street. Her grip bag skittering away even as people grabbed her arms and legs and shouted at her in their no-longer laughing language, the threats and demands and fear audible in the tone of their words.

"*Liberar-me!*" she shrieked in Portuguese.

A great, meaty paw grabbed at her shoulder. "For the fewking love of

God, woman," al-Wazir rasped, "shut your bleeding gob right fewking *now*."

AL-WAZIR

Al-Wazir grabbed Paolina Barthes away from the three men who'd pinned her. "Thank you, gentlemen," he growled in the voice normally reserved for drunken idlers who'd missed a muster. They backed away, smiling and chaffering in their fuzzy wuzzy way.

The bigger problem was the whistles. Two local men in blue uniforms—bobbies, of all things, for the love of fewking God!—were striding forward with purpose. He wouldn't be able to bluff them down, nor turn and walk away. Once they took notice, coppers never did let a man pass by quiet-like with his own business in hand.

"Go," said Boaz, interrupting al-Wazir's panicked thoughts. "I will have intercourse with them."

Al-Wazir nearly laughed at that, but the moment was slipping badly. "Come on, girl."

She was shivering, but she'd stopped trying to fight him. He wished he could get her bag and whatever she was carrying in it, but the gear lay in the wrong direction. "Steady," he said. "Steady on. I hope your magic pocket watch ain't in yon bag."

Paolina's breath shuddered.

Behind him he could hear Boaz' voice raised, and a widespread gasp. The Brass man had thrown back the hood and veil of his robe, then.

"That'll keep them," he said, "but we must go to ground quick before they recover."

"I know a place," she whispered. Paolina led him toward the tracks and the little clumps of huts strung along the edge of town.

The two of them sat quietly in a ruined hut. The interior reeked of goat dung and muddy rain, but they were off the street in some measure of safety. Paolina continued to shiver. Holding back tears, he reckoned, though al-Wazir's experience of women was limited to his mam and various port whores—generally not the crying sort.

He left her alone to gather her dignity and watched the muddy track outside from the shadows of the hut's doorway.

Part of the depot was visible beyond a low stand of spike-leaved trees. The train stood there, silent now, waiting for its cargo. There was no hue and cry rising from the street where he'd left Boaz, but al-Wazir couldn't imagine any copper ever born, not even a fuzzy wuzzy, letting someone like the Brass man go without taking him in to the sergeants.

Bobbie sergeants were like Naval petty officers—no one, not the commanders nor the men, so much as took a shit without a petty officer to tell him where to go and what to do when he got there. Even *marines* had sergeants.

"How long do we wait?" he asked as he turned back to look at the girl. He didn't think they could stay in the hut much longer.

Paolina sniffed and raised her head from her hands. *She really is a pretty girl,* al-Wazir thought, *for such a little chit with such large ideas.* He wondered what had happened to her since leaving Ottweill's camp aboard *Notus*.

"What do you care? You do the Queen's work, just as they do."

"Aye, and I'm sworn to my commission in the Royal Navy. But I'm no footman for yon fuzzy wuzzy coppers."

"So take me wherever it is you are supposed to deliver me." She glared at him. "Was my entire flight no more than an arrangement?"

Al-Wazir felt his temper stirring at her feistiness. "I've no notion of what you're on about, lassie. Boaz and me was coming off the Wall for to head to England and catch up to you. That you should present yourself here is more than passing strange. How ye got to this place at all is a complete mystery to me."

"Your people have been chasing me since Strasbourg."

That startled him. "And what were you doing in Strasbourg, lassie? Captain Sayeed was to take you to Bristol, and send you on to London from there."

"Captain Sayeed was one of your Silent Order men," she said bitterly.

He wasn't certain what a Silent Order man was. There were secret societies all across the British Empire. The Masons were perhaps the most notorious, and some whispered of Bavarian light bringers and the Brotherhood of the Rosy Cross. "Lassie, I swear on my mother's name that I kenned nothing of what Sayeed wanted for you in Strasbourg. It was ever and only my intention to send you home."

A herd of goats drove by, the clattering of their dull bells and their bleating stopping conversation. Al-Wazir watched the heaving, furred backs and wondered what he should do with the girl now. He'd been looking for someone to give him the true lay of the coast when she'd happened by. Whether or not he was under charges, she was certainly all sorts of trouble on two feet at this point.

"It's time we get you back on the Wall, girlie," he said as the last of the goats passed.

"I don't believe you." She was stubborn and angry.

"You ought to place your trust in him." Boaz, cloaked and veiled in native garb, bent to look into the hut. "The chief is a good man, one blessed with more than his measure of nature's grace. In the event, we should be away ere more trouble dogs our steps."

"To *a Muralha*?" she whispered.

The longing in her voice tore at al-Wazir's heart. "To the Wall, even now."

The chief crouched and stepped out through the hut's doorway. Paolina followed him, wiping her arm across her face. He looked up and down the track that passed between these ragged huts.

Women and children moved about, some staring frankly at the three of them, but there was nothing else close by.

Then he realized that some of the children were looking up and pointing. Al-Wazir looked up as well. An airship was descending above them, hard and fast, ropes already dropping.

A Chinese airship.

Sirens wailed across Mogadishu from the British base upon the hill.

"*Run!*" he shouted as he grabbed at Paolina's shoulder, but three Chinamen dropped from the sky like silk-clad stones to take him down, even as gunfire began to pop above him.

He fought like a dog, with more of his heart in it than even a drunken marine, but there were so many of the Chinee, and the fuzzy wuzzies soon fled the scene. Large guns boomed as the town rose to battle. They didn't help al-Wazir as more and more of the screaming blue-clad men dropped on him.

Even Boaz struggled beneath the wave of their assault. The Brass crushed a man's skull, shouting at al-Wazir just as a rifle butt caught the chief in the nadgers. His vision turned the color of blood while his gut dropped like a runaway cargo hoist. The butt reversed to a bayonet, which he somehow blocked with one hand even as he vomited against the pain, trying to choke it back and rise for another swing of his fist, but someone lashed a rope around his ankles and he was lifted away.

His left hand hurt like fire where he'd blocked the knife. He couldn't close his fist for one last shot, because it didn't seem to be there anymore.

Upside down, in the air, swinging dead weight on a line, he vomited again. Al-Wazir grabbed his left wrist with his right hand, squeezing tight as he could to stop the spray of bleeding. He spun above Mogadishu, above a knot of blue-clad men still fighting Boaz, above the scattered thorn trees and kraals and huts at the edge, his view expanding as they rose to include the harbor and two airships casting off from masts on the hill while the third began to burn and he thought, *My God, the hydrogen will blow and she's still at the mast,* then he was spinning in the air over the ocean and where had the time gone, chopped away with his hand and something burned bright and loud on the brow of the land beyond and there was the Wall and his body was being dragged screaming across the water until hard faces and pinching hands pulled him over a railing and slapped, slapped, slapped him.

He woke to a splash of warm water—no, piss—across his face. Al-Wazir coughed and spat and tried to curse, but he hurt too damned much. Mostly all he could do was draw breath and try to ignore the taste in his mouth.

He blinked away the sting of the urine. A short Chinese man bent over him, frowning seriously. *Officer.* Something in the look of the man, even wearing blue pajamas.

"You wish the girl, yes?"

He tried to sort through that sentence. "The girl?" al-Wazir finally managed. "Aye. She's wi' me." He wasn't tied down, just flat on a deck with a gasbag bellying low above him. Familiar territory, this, albeit with the details rather different. The freedom of being untied was meaningless given that he could barely move.

There was something wrong with his hands, too. That thought, and the memories of pain it brought flooding back, distracted al-Wazir so badly, he missed his interrogator's next words.

His lapse was corrected with a swift boot to the ribs.

Al-Wazir let out a wordless cry of agony. Something was broken there.

"Chinese airships are bad for my health," he muttered.

"Tell me," the officer said quietly.

"Tell you what, you flat-faced bast—?"

Another kick cut him off. "We talk later."

He found himself staring up at the gasbag, wondering how he would survive this. Boaz was lost to him. Paolina was imprisoned somewhere aboard this vessel. They were . . . where?

Over the Indian Ocean, surely. He couldn't imagine a Chinese captain heading *into* British territory with prisoners on his deck.

Hand, whispered a voice inside his head. *Look to your hand.*

Politics and tactics fled as al-Wazir tilted his gaze to the right. His hand lay flat on the deck, at the end of an arm that might as well have been flaccid, it seemed so limp and powerless. Four fingers and a thumb, skin scraped to potted meat but still attached.

He was forced to rock his head back and forth before he could flip his gaze to the left. Another flat, useless arm. Another swollen wrist, this one bound in rags that had been smeared with some dark, greasy oil. Nothing but a messy stain upon the deck where fingers and thumb and palm should be.

Breath shuddered in his chest. Some fool was keening in pain and panic, using *his* voice, the sound rolling in *his* chest. Al-Wazir tried to flex the missing fingers, closing a fist that wasn't there, as if by some sympathetic magic he could restore what had been taken from him. Though he could swear he felt the grain of the deck under the back of his hand, it wasn't there.

The chill that had been pressing at the edge of his consciousness for a while began to take him over. It was snowing in his soul now. His thoughts were slowing as well. The sharp taste of Chinese piss on his lips not even a distraction. The feeling of his left hand on the deck was nothing more than an illusion. He tried to focus on the gasbag above his head, but it was foreign, distant, different. Not him or his.

Where had *Bassett* got to, anyway? It wasn't like Captain Smallwood to leave an injured man on the deck, exposed to the elements, the victim of ridicule from his crew.

He had to summon the Ropes Division, call the men to attention and work to save the ship from neglect. Al-Wazir struggled to sit up on his elbows. The ship needed him. The captain needed him. England needed him.

A woman's face swam overhead. The Queen? No, no, a girl he'd met. Who had brought a port whore aboard *his* ship? Al-Wazir snarled at her, or tried to. His lips had become little more than canvas rolls.

She turned and yelled. Hands plucked at him awhile. He sank deeper into the country of dreams, lowered by a net from a ship that sailed the sky.

Al-Wazir found himself in Lanarkshire, except that it was Lanarkshire-in-Africa. The hills were coated with broad-leaved plants through which monkeys scampered. Instead of sheep there were miniature elephants grazing in what openscape remained. Rocks the size of houses and houses the size of rocks mixed together, as if God had muddled two sets of playthings and left both behind on the carpet of His Caledonian nursery floor.

He wandered clad only in his grandfather's last threadbare burnoose, the one the old man had been buried in. Araby or no, Granda Faisal had spent all of young Threadgill's life wearing canvas trousers and swearing at the Inland Revenue. Al-Wazir wondered how he'd come by the garment. It was a white faded to the color of wound stains on linen. He didn't know whose sword had cut the bloody rents in the thing through which the light was leaking.

The sun was rising inside him, he realized. *That* explained the warmth in his belly, and why the day was dying outside as the parrots of Lanarkshire rose screeching into the evening sky like so many faded orchids dropping toward the absent moon.

"No," said his mother, rest her soul.

No, he was dead, not her. Or at least Granda Faisal, that everyone hereabouts called Frazzle, was dead. Everyone?

"No," she said again, but in the voice of someone else he thought he knew.

"Know what?" Al-Wazir opened his eyes to see Paolina Barthes crouched close above him. She seemed to be weeping.

"No, don't leave me alone here," she whispered.

"You're not alone, lassie." He shook off the last vision of screaming parrots. "Not while me or the Brass fool walks this Northern Earth."

Piss-soaked shirt and all, she leaned over and hugged him like a child might do. Awkwardly, al-Wazir closed his arms over her shoulder, patting her with one hand while fearing the other.

CHILDRESS

Tan the Archivist was happy enough to have her sit at his table awhile. He seemed to be pleased at a chance to practice his English. "Cataloger Wang look for Great Relic." He cackled. "You great surprise, not so much Great Relic, yes?"

"Yes," she said with a smile.

Sitting in this sunken library at the bottom of the Northern Earth was not so bad, Childress decided. The wealth of the world's knowledge might be half-drowned beneath her feet, but the other half bulked comfortingly close. She felt the pull of it.

They didn't *need* a Great Relic here. This place was almost a Great Relic of its own.

She tried for a polite sally. "Are you expert in African scrolls?"

"Africa?" Another cackle. "Much wisdom there, different kind, yes? Names not so much matching."

Names? Childress had to work through that a moment. She tried Leung's Confucian term, in her poor Chinese. *"Zheng ming."* Rectification of Names.

Tan grinned. *"Well spoken."*

"So what are you searching for within African scrolls?" It wasn't a subtle line of questioning, but their mutual language barrier did not admit much delicacy.

"Eh . . ." He traced his right index finger over the taelsaem, tip hovering just above the illuminations without quite touching the scroll itself. "Other wisdoms. This library, library of libraries, yes?"

"Yes . . ." She knew it for a depository library.

"You Mask, ah, you know this. Truth hide inside truth, inside truth. Like ducks inside eggs inside ducks."

"Of course," she lied.

"So we open truth one at time."

"And a Great Relic would be a . . . shortcut . . . to the truth."

"Shortcut? Too small?"

"No, no." She tried not to laugh. "A path less distant and more swift."

Another cackle. "Truth is winding path. Everyone know that." He bent back to his taelsaem. After a few minutes of silence, Childress rose and began wandering farther along the gallery.

It took her only a moment to notice that Cataloger Wang was following her around the rim. Like her, he was unsubtle, merely hanging back far enough that she could not turn to confront him. Childress settled for a big smile and a cheerful wave—very un-Chinese, and very un-Poinsard for that matter, but it made her feel better to twit the man.

She looked over the shoulders of other archivists as they pursued errands similar to Tan's. What they were doing with the texts was not obvious. Like Tan, these were skimming rather than reading closely, at a pace that seemed highly unlikely to support significant comprehension of these dead and ancient tongues. They made a few notes as they went.

This was not a translation project. Far from it.

Nor, did she think, were they about the business of summarizing the material. Again, the reading went too fast, while the note-taking was too sparse.

Like boys scavenging a gutter for coins early on a Sunday morning, she realized. They were *hunting* for something.

With that notion in mind, she looked more closely at the next reader she came to. This was a young man clad in a cheongsam of the same blue as the crewmen wore aboard *Five Lucky Winds*. Low status, she presumed. He pored over an unfolding book written in some south Asian script, where the letters depended from a top bar that was periodically interrupted. It had been block printed in orange ink on muslin, which was then lacquered to the boards, which had been sewn together to make the folds of the book.

As Tan had done, this reader skimmed his text. Again, too fast for comprehension unless he were possessed of a native fluency. She watched him go down one page, then down the next. He stopped and scanned his way back up two or three lines. He scribbled a series of notes in the Chinese script she'd made very little progress in mastering, then tapped his teeth a few times.

Without ever looking up at her, he went back to scanning his text.

Cataloger Wang drifted next to her.

"Have you found wisdom yet?" he asked in Chinese.

"Wisdom lies in the search, not the finding," she replied in English.

"Of course."

When she glanced over at him, Wang's face was a profile in blandness.

"Most of these readers are idiots savants, aren't they?" She caught herself, and added in Chinese, *"They are persons with skill in only one area."*

Cataloger Wang was no more subtle in word than deed. *"Your skills are in what area?"*

"This," she said simply. In English: "My skills tell me you are hunting the jungles of the word."

Wang leaned over and patted the shoulder of the young man who sat next to them. *"Come take tea with me, Mask."* This time, he sounded almost pleasant.

Watching the tense, round-faced Wang carefully make tea in a little porcelain pot, Childress reflected that she was certain he spoke English. Or at least understood her language. She'd approached the limits of her Chinese with him already, and even outdid herself.

Yet he'd asked her to tea alone.

His office was a room off the circular gallery, one of perhaps two dozen. Just as with the gallery outside, it was difficult to tell what this chamber had been originally intended for. Reading room, repository, living quarters, or even an office, but his desk and cabinets and pigeonholed shelving full of scrolls told of its current uses.

There was a little charcoal fire in a brazier shaped like a sitting dog. Or possibly lion, she couldn't quite tell. Either way, it had one paw on a large ball, while the fire smoldered within its open jaws and a brass pot steamed and perked upon its flat head. The flanks were painted in bright shades of blue and green, with silver tracings, so it seemed as if the lion-dog might have been intended to come from the sea.

Either way, its jaws were black with soot or by design, the eyes flickered with the fire within. The pot rattled with more and more intensity until

Wang grabbed a silk rag and took it off the fire to pour the water into a more decorative porcelain teapot. This one was round, and somewhat fattened at the center. A pale blue painting of bamboo and clouds circled its waist.

Wang measured tea leaves out of a small metal container to shake them into the bottom of two small cups, which matched their pot. He poured water over each of them with a delicacy that surprised Childress. The scent steaming up from the cups was rich, dark, and earthy. This was the smell of which ordinary New England tea was just a ghost.

He handed Childress her tea with a grave smile, then wrapped his hands around his own cup. She found it too hot to the touch for that, and so set the tea down for a moment to cool. Wang sipped and stared at her.

And so we drink tea, she thought. Some form of the same substance, by much the same name, had its own rituals half a world away in the country of her birth. Here in Wang's office, it seemed nigh magical.

She finally picked hers up and sipped. It was as hot and thick as she might have expected, and bitter enough for her to feel her teeth. She drank it slowly as she matched stares with Wang over the rims of their cups.

This was as deadly serious as any face-off between cats in the alley or lords in the gallery of some royal court. She didn't understand what stakes they played for, but the game was of great value to Cataloger Wang.

Childress finally set her cup down in a single graceful motion onto the small table that stood between them. He matched her gesture, then took up her cup to stare within at the bitter leaves pooling amid the brown water in the bottom.

Childress stilled the reflexive motion of her hand for the other cup. This was his game; she would let him play it.

Wang stared into her leaves for a time, then looked up at her.

"So close to the Wall," he said, "the spirits are strong."

In English, she realized. *"What do they tell you?"* Childress replied in Chinese.

"You carry power and the burden of time upon your shoulders. Words flow. You have seen the Golden Bridge."

Quite good English, at that. She leaned forward. "You are not building any bridge here, are you?"

"There are bridges and there are bridges." He set the cup down in a precise motion and sketched an arc in the air. "Bridges of air, bridges of rainfall, bridges of birds. Bridges of thought and deed and obligation."

"Bridges of words."

That smile again. "Bridges of words."

Childress puzzled out the riddle. For it was indeed a riddle, however he phrased his words. "A course of study is a bridge of words," she said slowly. "Learning built one text at a time. While gold . . . gold is the highest of metals, emperor among the elements. So the Golden Bridge is perhaps the Imperial Bridge. A course which can be trod only by the most elevated of feet. The path of the wise."

"All paths lead to wisdom, for those with eyes to see the way."

"Well, certainly." That sounded like an empty aphorism, but Childress was trying neither to bait the man nor argue with him. "Even so, there's some specific piece of wisdom for which you are hunting here." Her conversation with Leung, about the bridge being more of a tunnel, came back to her. "A path that leads through the Wall would be a special kind of wisdom."

He tilted his chin slightly toward her.

"But a path which led through the heart of the world . . ." She stopped, staring at him with speculation roiling in her mind. "It's not just the Wall, is it? You could fly over it if you wanted to badly enough. So I'm told. And flight is not among the secrets of the ancients."

"You are indeed a Mask," said Wang. "Even if you are not who was appointed to come, and you do not bear what was appointed to be brought."

"I am who you have been given," she said sternly, all Poinsard for a moment. "The Wall is there for a reason. God's plan, in the European view. Part of the order of Heaven and earth in the Chinese view. That you seek to overpass it is foolishness bordering on suicide. There is more danger and terror in the Southern Earth than you would ever wish to know."

"Have you crossed the Wall to see these things for yourself?"

"No, of course not. But in six millennia of human history, no one has kept open a way across the Wall."

"Chersonesus Aurea did," said Wang. "And we shall again."

"Look around you. There is nothing here but parrots and monkeys and salt water. Did the men of this city found or topple empires? Create new sciences for the glory of God and the benefit of man? No, they dug a hole and crawled into it, hiding amid their books until the ocean came to sweep them away. How will this benefit your Celestial Emperor?"

"Not here." Wang smiled. "There are other centers of scholarship." He leaned forward, gave her a significant look. "Phu Ket, and the temple of learning there."

She didn't know anything about Phu Ket, but admitting ignorance wasn't what had gotten her this far. "There is no point in the effort there, either." Her voice was low and serious.

"You of all people deny the pursuit of knowledge?"

"I am the last to deny the pursuit of knowledge. But knowledge has a purpose. Here . . . you build a bridge to nowhere."

"You mistake our destination, Mask." He reached forward, his fingers brushing her abandoned teacup. "I have read your power. You are not come to bring us to ruin. Go among the library and see what you can learn. We will see what we can learn from you in turn."

"So you release me to the texts, and to my contemplation of your destination?"

"*Dwei le,*" he said. *Affirmative.* Wang favored her with one last nod.

Childress returned the nod, then rose and returned to the gallery beyond. There she went to look for Leung.

"I don't know what they are doing here," she told him. "But it is not what Admiral Shang believed."

"There is no bridge, of course," the captain said.

They were at the far end of the pier where the launch was tied up. The only people nearby were Leung's sailors. *Five Lucky Winds* sat peacefully at anchor in the little bay. Something called intermittently in the night, a croaking argument with the rising stars.

"You are correct about there being no bridge. I never saw how it could be literal. I don't believe that Wang and the rest are trying to pass through the Wall in any case. They have another destination in mind. He said as much to me."

"What destination could that be?"

Whether it was a poverty of imagination or some failing of vision, she could not say what destination would matter more to the Celestial Empire than passing beyond the Wall.

What greater game was there to hunt in God's Creation?

EIGHTEEN

PAOLINA

She was ashamed. Ashamed and afraid. She had cried on al-Wazir's chest like a girl in her mother's arms, while the old sailor was probably dying.

Paolina sat up and wiped her face. He stank. A relic of his fight to save her. She looked at al-Wazir, whose eyes were closed. His breathing was regular. She couldn't tell if he'd passed out or was merely asleep.

Either way, he needed to rest.

They were in a small cabin with woven mats upon the floor and no furnishing nor windows. A wan electrick glowed in the ceiling, keeping them in dim light. She could not tell if there had been furniture before, and it was removed, or if their captors favored empty cabins. Surely this tiny room had another purpose.

The damned Chinese! They were as bad as the British. Worse, maybe. She'd had a clear view of the chaos in Mogadishu as their ship had risen out across the Indian Ocean. One of the Royal Navy airships had exploded at mast, and a second was damaged. The third pursued, though she lost sight of the action when the Chinese officers finally thought to force her belowdecks. The lack of running and shouting overhead suggested that the chase had fallen astern.

Paolina wondered if that was all there would be to her life—written out of history as a footnote to a battle in the skies above an obscure African port. Surely these Chinese no more had her interests to heart than did the Silent Order back in Strasbourg. Less, for while the Silent Order had worked by subterfuge and the application of social leverage, this airship had fallen upon Mogadishu as a raider, spreading death and destruction.

No differently from I with the gleam in my hand. She'd brought one of these very ships down herself, after all. The world would end in jealousy and hatred if people could kill with a thought.

Paolina gripped al-Wazir's remaining hand and studied the bulkheads. This ship varied so much from *Notus*. It was as if one empire had seen the other's work from afar, then returned home to re-create it from memory. Chinese airships had a different shape to their gasbags—she'd observed that while fleeing north from *a Muralha*.

Here beneath the decks it was clear that construction proceeded from a different philosophy of design. They used some lightweight wood laid down in thin, flexible strips. The whole vessel creaked like a house in a storm. *Notus* had been primarily built of maple and willow, with oak beams and knees. More stout, and tougher.

A trade-off that made sense to her. She could see the wisdom of both options. It depended on how much premium you placed on speed, how efficient your engines were, and how much hydrogen you wanted to carry and manage in order to maintain buoyancy.

Al-Wazir groaned, bringing her back to the moment. Paolina felt a flush of shame at how her thoughts had wandered from the fate that lay before them.

"I'm very sorry about your hand." She gripped his right even tighter.

He groaned again. "Hae they tarred the wrist?"

She forced herself to look at the silk rags wrapping the stump. The gray cloth was soaked almost black with fluid. "I can't tell, Chief. All I see is a covering, thick with something. Blood?"

"'T hurts like the fire piss a dozen times over." He struggled to his elbows, successfully this time. "Well, and how are we planning to get out o' this one, lassie?"

She had to smile at that. "I don't suppose there's any out to get. We're here till they set us down somewhere."

"No, no, there's always a way out. Especially on an airship. Down's favorite. Nothing between you and the ground but empty air. No fences, no guards, no howling dogs. Believe you me, missy, there's much worse things than being aboard ship."

"Even a Chinese airship?"

"Aye. Even a Chinee."

He was pale and shaking. The lost hand was affecting him badly.

If she'd had the gleam, she might have been able to do more, but here, now, there was nothing but her and al-Wazir and a ship full of belligerent Chinese.

She remembered the men left behind on the ground and corrected herself: A *flimsy* ship, *partially* full of belligerent Chinese. Surely a plucky girl of parts and an experienced sailor like al-Wazir could find some way to free themselves. If the Chinese carried those parachutes that Davies the loblolly boy had spoken of back in Praia Nova, perhaps they could escape to whatever lay below them.

Thousands of miles of ocean, she realized. Their only problems there would be thirst, starvation, and shark attacks. Even that would constitute an improvement over their current chances of reclaiming their freedom.

Later a plump man came to see her and al-Wazir. He was bespectacled, and wore blue silk with no rank or insignia. When he entered their little cabin without knocking, the first thing he did was bow and make that strange little bird sign. Lachance had shown it to her several times back in Strasbourg. The steward on *Star of Gambia* had made it as well.

Not the Silent Order then, but something else reaching from England to China and back that was just as large. *A marvelous but frightening prospect,* Paolina thought.

"I physician," he said, his accent thick. "See big man wound."

Paolina nodded and stepped back from al-Wazir, who had slipped into deep sleep and now snored lustily.

The doctor squatted on his heels and took the Scotsman's good hand by the wrist for a moment. He then ran his fingers slowly over al-Wazir's face. Both men's eyes were closed, until Paolina had the strange idea that the doctor had fallen asleep as well.

He finally took hold of al-Wazir's left forearm and studied the wrist stump. The doctor did not remove the bandages, nor probe the wound, just held it for some time. His eyes fluttered shut repeatedly.

"Fire in blood." The doctor stared at her seriously. "You England know fire in blood?"

"Infection?" she hazarded. Paolina turned her own forearm toward him, slipped her sleeve back and traced the line of a vein. "Like here?"

"Ah." He patted al-Wazir's forearm, then laid the limb down. "Yes. No have here."

"Good." She was baffled as to what should come next.

"He make smell, he make fire in blood, you say for me, ah?"

"Of course." She wondered how a large middle-aged sailor *couldn't* smell. Flatulence and wine breath seemed to be the perpetual lot of men past their boyhoods. The doctor presumably meant something newer and nastier. Skin rot setting in, for example.

"Ah." He stood, bowed. "Welcome to *Heaven's Deer*, la." Then he stared at Paolina as if willing her to do something.

"Thank you . . ." She felt the fool. Paolina moved her hands in imitation of the sign he'd made. "What are you?"

His face grew very still. "I doctor."

"You are helping us. Why?"

The hand sign again. "Birds watch over you."

"Like Lachance."

The doctor looked blank. "White birds fly in sky over you. Never silent, never in order."

"The other side," she breathed. Her sense of how the world was ordered shifted. "You stand against the Silent Order. Against England."

"No, not the thrones. Different. Earth and heaven." He looked unhappy.

She tried a different tack. "Where are we bound, then?"

"Phu Ket," the doctor whispered, hands fluttering now. His face had become a study in agony. "The captain no orders, ah . . . Silent Order?" He turned and fled.

It took her several moments to realize the door hadn't been latched from the outside. At least, there had been no snick or click.

The Silent Order, she thought. *The same that Sayeed had taken her to at Strasbourg.* Their reach was everywhere. Almost everywhere.

The white birds flew against them, though, and bore her on their wings. She wondered why, how that would be.

In any case, she could not go to Phu Ket. Must not. They needed an escape.

Paolina turned back to al-Wazir, eyeing him speculatively. An airship was an airship. He must help the two of them to freedom. She could be his left hand.

She sat back to some serious thinking while she watched the big man sleep off his pain.

When al-Wazir awoke, Paolina scooted close so they could talk quietly. "How do you feel?" she asked. "Can you understand me? Do you have your strength?"

He sighed, gripping his left wrist with his right hand. "Lassie, I feel as though all the hounds of Hell have been coursing through me bones."

That was the most cogent answer he'd given her yet. The fever had broken! She felt a burst of glee, followed by a wash of guilt that she was celebrating his return to conscious pain.

"I'm glad you're back," Paolina said. "Those hounds are going to be coursing a lot harder through your bones when we get to wherever we're going." She sighed. "I don't think we have much time left."

"For what?"

"You asked how we're going to find our way out of this. We're going to take over the airship."

Al-Wazir began to wheeze with laughter, then immediately stopped, his face transfixed with agony. "Och," he said after a moment, then took a deep breath. "You're having some cruel fun with a dying man."

"You're *not* dying!" She wanted to slap him. "Listen to me. This ship, it's built of wood so light, it might almost be paper."

"Bamboo. That would be bamboo."

Whatever that *was,* she thought. "Thank you. The ship is built with bamboo. You are strong enough to tear the walls open."

He pushed his stump toward her. "No more, no more."

"Listen." She set her hand on his arm, below the bandaged wrist. "Your Queen is not my friend. These Chinese are even less so, I am certain of it. They take me to my greatest enemies, with no thought to help us. Anything we can do to be away would benefit us both.

"Even with one hand, you are twice the strength of any other man on this vessel. They left a portion of their crew behind in Mogadishu when the ship lifted. The Chinese are shorthanded, possibly with a British airship in chase. If we can move quickly, find where they store their parachutes and weapons, then tear a hole the hull, we can be gone."

"Into the Indian Ocean?"

"If there's one of yours back there, they'll investigate us. Shorthanded, the Chinese will not fight well. Do you think our chances are better once we've been carried all the way to Asia?"

"No, no . . ." Al-Wazir grinned, his smile crooked. She could smell the sweat of pain and fear on him. "Though you seem to forget that I am also shorthanded. Most like they'll cut us down. Even if we make it safely over the rail, the ocean will swallow us."

"You don't know that," she said. "The Wall is close. There are fishing boats and islands in every sea of the Northern Earth, and we are probably pursued by one of your airships. All possibilities, compared to the certainty of our vanishing into Chinese prisons."

Al-Wazir plucked at his shirt a moment. "They pissed upon me," he said as he struggled to his feet. "What is the first step o' your plan, lassie?"

"Getting you to stand up."

"What is your next step?"

"We open the door, strike down whoever stands without, and find the locker where their expeditionary gear is stowed."

"If the Chinese run their airships in any fashion similar to Her Imperial Majesty's Navy, those should be amidships."

"I trust your intuition, sir."

"More fool the both of us."

They took positions by the door. Paolina ready to throw it open and launch into the corridor, al-Wazir close behind her. She recalled it as a short passageway leading to a ladder in the waist of the ship, but she had been dragged belowdecks in the heat of the ship's escape from Mogadishu and had not been diligent in noting details.

With a deep, shuddering breath, she stepped out.

The sailor on duty turned, mouth agape. Paolina smacked her fist right between his teeth. She tore open her knuckles as she gagged him. He stepped back and tried to swing a pole, but al-Wazir followed her close, crowding all three of them into the opposite wall of the corridor. He jammed his thumb into one of the sailor's eyes, pressing his handless forearm into the man's neck until the Chinese collapsed with blood running down his face.

Paolina dropped to her knees and retched. Al-Wazir kicked the collapsed sailor in the side of the head twice, hard.

"Come on, chit," he growled. "This is your plan. We must follow through."

Shuddering back tears, she stood again to see a series of wooden doors and more walls paneled with narrow strips. There was a ladder to their right. She refused to look at the man they'd just blinded. Or killed.

Paolina couldn't decide which was worse.

Al-Wazir leaned close—the height of the ceiling forced him to bend. "Where?" he whispered. "Do we start cracking open doors?"

"No." She could barely control her voice. "Look." *Think. See.* Paolina pointed to the door across from the one they'd exited. "The w-wooden handle. It's been l-lacquered." Her mind raced. "This one's worn. L-l-let's see if some of them are not so worn. They can't use parachutes every day on this ship."

They peered at handles for a few minutes. Just past the ladder, as Paolina was looking over the last door, someone opened the hatch above. A blinding glare of light stabbed down. She hissed and stepped back into shadow.

She couldn't see al-Wazir. He must be on the other side of the ladder.

A small man came almost sliding down. He landed lightly on his feet and looked into her eyes, surprised.

Paolina punched him in the gut. Even as he fell, al-Wazir's great rock of a fist caught the sailor in the side of the head with a crack. Someone above called out in Chinese, then laughed.

She felt a rush of panic. They were about to be spotted. "Quickly!"

Al-Wazir wrenched open the nearest door. The room beyond was a rope and tool locker. He stepped in. She grabbed the fallen man by the collar and tugged him after the chief. The smear of blood on the deck churned her stomach anew. The reek of offal only made it worse.

"I'm sorry," she whispered.

"Get hold of yourself, lassie." al-Wazir took two hanks of rope and a large grappling hook. "This'll do."

"No parachutes in here?"

"Maybe. But I'm more in a mood to have my way."

"No." Paolina caught at his arm. "We must get off this airship."

"And we will, lassie. After we've spiked a few guns."

She saw that he was swaying. His face seemed to glow as well, with fever or exhaustion. "Chief al-Wazir, we have a plan. Please, help me keep it."

"They trapped your Brass friend away from us both," he rumbled. "They killed at least one of the airships in port. I'm nae letting these Chinee bastards get away so free. You'd best find something sharp and heavy, at least till we learn where the guns are."

He stepped back out as someone called down the ladder. Al-Wazir roared back, "Aye, and I'll feed you to your dogs, you black-eyed bastard!"

There was a shriek, and a meaty thump; then the shouting and running began in earnest abovedecks as the big man swarmed up the ladder one-armed.

Paolina worked her way down the short hall, bashing open doors with an ax she'd found in the ropes room. Whatever havoc al-Wazir raised abovedecks would only last a minute or two. Rampage or no, he was a one-handed man with a hook in his shaky grip, not an invading force under arms.

The third door proved to be the weapons locker. Firearms were racked along one wall, while red canisters stood at the other. Paolina didn't know the first thing about guns, so she studied the canisters a moment.

Each had a metal clip at the top, with a little wooden rod through a hole in the clip to keep it down. A very simple lock to retard the action of the clip, she realized. So if one tugged the rod free, the clip would pull back. *No,* she corrected herself, spring back.

And something bad would happen.

There must be a time delay as well, otherwise it would be fatal to the user.

That was good enough for Paolina. She didn't have to aim or fire anything. The chief would be dead in moments if she did not act. She used her ax to hack off the bar that held the canisters in their rack. Some were already gone. Discharged back at Mogadishu, then.

She pulled five, barely fitting them in her arms. At the door of the weapons locker, she set one down and tugged the locking rod free. The click popped back. Paolina then turned and ran to the ladder, climbing with arms full of the four remaining canisters.

As she cleared the ladder into the sunlight, there was a loud explosion, which knocked her forward onto the deck. Wooden splinters spun through the air as someone shouted very loudly in Chinese. She got back to her feet with her canisters still in hand—one had spun loose—pulled the next rod free. She held that canister over her head, keeping the clip down only by the pressure of her fingers.

"Stop it right now!" she screamed.

Al-Wazir was farther aft, apparently fighting toward to the poop. Two men clung to his back, while a third faced him off a long pole. Half a dozen more were laid on the deck. A crowd was close around the chief. Almost all of them now stared at her, or at the smoking hole in the deck just aft of the hatch.

A few looked up at the gasbag, which smoldered above the shattered gap she'd blown open.

"Do you know what that is in your hand, lassie?" al-Wazir asked quietly. "All these lads certainly do."

"It's something you don't want me to let go of." Paolina tried to keep her voice from spiraling into a shriek.

"Aye." He shook the men off his back. Most of the crew scuttled to the far rail.

She saw that al-Wazir was bleeding from a handful of new wounds. He still burned with that fevered intensity as well, but paradoxically seemed steadier on his feet.

"Who speaks English here?" she called. "English. Now!" She waved the canister again.

The chief stumbled over to her. "I hope your plan has another step, lassie." His breath heaved.

"I've got three of these."

"And any one of them will set the gasbag to blowing up. 'Tis a miracle your first did not already do so."

"Oh." She hadn't thought that through.

A short man in the ubiquitous blue pajamas stepped forward from the poop. "You are fools," he said.

"Dead fools," Paolina told him. "All of us. I want your parachutes on the deck, now."

"Parachutes?"

"Yes, or you'll be jumping overboard without them."

She hadn't even looked yet, but she was confident that it was a long way down to the sea.

Without taking his eyes off her, the officer barked something in Chinese. The men by the far rail muttered, but none of them stepped away. He turned and pointed out three men.

"Follow them, Chief," Paolina said.

She had no idea what to do next, but she was certain she had to do it quickly and purposefully.

Al-Wazir stumbled to the ladderway to meet the men who were sidling around Paolina as best they could. He growled, slapping his grappling hook against his thigh. They dropped downward quickly.

"I cannot go below," he told her with a tired sigh.

"Then watch the hatch. If they come back in some wrong fashion, I will release this handle."

"You will not," said the officer calmly.

Paolina shifted her grip and the handle popped up. He yelped and started to jump toward her. She counted three seconds, then turned and tossed the canister over the rail. As she did, Paolina noted that the ocean was indeed far below.

There was a loud crack. Smoke billowed behind the ship.

She turned back and slid the next rod free. It clattered to the deck. Using her toe, Paolina pushed it toward the officer, whose face was now sheened with sweat. "If you tell me I am going to die, you must be prepared for me to believe you."

"Fools." The officer stepped back a pace.

Behind her now, al-Wazir called out, "They're coming."

Moments later the three sailors had deposited a dozen backpacks on the deck.

"All right." She held the canister high. "Every officer on this ship takes a parachute and jumps."

"Lassie . . . ," rumbled al-Wazir.

"Starting with you." She jabbed the canister at the English-speaking officer.

"I will die before doing so."

Her mood was wild, fey, full of fire and fury. "Fine. I'm ready to go."

"Lassie . . ."

She popped the handle on this canister and tossed the explosive to the protesting officer.

AL-WAZIR

He was on his feet only through sheer panic. His missing hand burned, while the one that still remained to him ached. He wasn't sure any of his ribs were intact. Every breath felt as if it had been strained through a net full of shattered glass.

But when Paolina threw the grenado, he knew his life was over.

The Chinese officer grabbed the tumbling canister, taking a few steps back toward the starboard rail as he did so. *Sheer reflex*, al-Wazir thought, wondering how few seconds he had left to live.

The girl shot past him. She screamed as she slammed her shoulder into the officer's belly. He stumbled backwards, shouting something as she slugged him in the wedding tackle. Over the rail the officer went, taking the grenado with him in a shriek that ended in another blast.

Paolina turned, brandishing her next grenado. How many of those fewking things did she *have*?

"Get off my ship!" she screeched, advancing on the gaggle of sailors backing toward the poop. She reached up and slipped a little wooden peg from the top. "Get off, *now*!"

Three of them broke from the crowd to sprint for the packs on the deck. Al-Wazir held back a wheezing chuckle, staving off the pain. She had more nerve than he might have expected from any man.

The first sailors jumped over the rail as Paolina stalked the deck, shouting in a language he didn't understand. Another bunch charged for the parachutes. She was emptying the ship.

Al-Wazir started to think he might live out the day. Or at least the hour. In which case, he realized, the rest of the ship's officers needed to be dealt with. No one carried firearms on ordinary duty aboard an airship—the dangers were too great—but if they had an arms locker in the poop, there would be pistols out at any moment.

He scrambled for the grenado Paolina had dropped. Once it was retrieved, al-Wazir skirted the smoking hole in the deck and headed toward the poop.

The stern was laid out much as a British airship. There were five or six sailors clustered near the wheel, and two men with the look of officers. Al-Wazir broke into a run, brandishing the grenado much as Paolina was doing and hoping they'd panic as well.

Surely enough, there were two men climbing up out of a hatch there with pistols in hand. He leapt the pair of steps from the main deck to the poop and ran them down, kicking one in the head while the other ducked. Al-Wazir turned and swung a fist, remembering only as his stump drove into the other man's face that there was no longer a hand at the end of that arm.

The agony nearly blacked him out. He dropped to his knees, the grenado rolling away from his grip. Two of the sailors jumped on him, but al-Wazir managed to grab a loose pistol that was spun on the deck.

He was down flat then, being punched by two shouting men who each probably weighed half of what he did. Al-Wazir got the pistol up and shot one in the face. The other jumped back, cursing.

Looking up he saw the second officer aiming another pistol down at his chest. The Chinese was smiling as they pointed their weapons at each other.

"Think you have yourself a standoff, do yer now, laddie?" Al-Wazir smiled back. "Me, I already figured on dying today." He pulled the trigger.

The punch that should have drilled him to the deck and claimed his life never came. Instead his opponent toppled backwards. Al-Wazir lurched up, tucking the burning hot barrel of his weapon under his left arm, and grabbed the second pistol.

Where is the damned grenado?

The poop had emptied of all but the two dead men. Stumbling back to the low drop to the main deck, he saw there were a dozen men kneeling or lying on the boards. Paolina stalked among them, still shouting incomprehensibly, grenado in hand.

Everything else was quiet.

"What do we do now?" he tried to ask, but his voice was a strange and distant croak.

She turned toward him and burst into tears.

"Heading?" al-Wazir demanded a few minutes later.

Paolina shook with the aftermath of her battle lust, her last grenado lodged between her feet. "The Wall."

He looked to the south. *Heaven's Deer* had made a course north of east out of Mogadishu, bound for Phu Ket. A group of islands lay in the distance along their course. The Wall was still well in sight.

"If we make east of south, we'll keep a fair wind at this altitude. Easier sailing."

He was more concerned about clouds to the north and west, out over the empty desert of the Indian Ocean, but he didn't say anything. There was too much to worry about already. Fourteen of the ordinary crew remained aboard *Heaven's Deer*, along with the doctor.

Al-Wazir and Paolina were forced to occupy the poop. They'd demanded that the sailors stay on the maindeck. This would work until they ran into foul weather. Then . . . what? How could they stop the remaining men from plotting?

How could they sail the ship alone?

It took only one hand at the wheel, when everything was in proper trim. But as soon as an engine began to run rough or a cell in the gasbag lost pressure, they would be at the mercy of the men. He wouldn't have cared to sail *Bassett* shorthanded, and he knew that ship as well as he knew his own boots.

This ship was something else again. An unknown vessel with the remnants of a hostile crew, unwilling to follow his orders or set his course. Assuming they even understood what it was he wanted.

There was nothing for it but to run toward the Wall and pray they reached their destination before any of a dozen disasters caught up with them.

"I bleed," he told Paolina.

"Then see the doctor."

He handed her the pistol he'd been holding and walked on down among the resentful, blue-clad men.

The doctor bound al-Wazir's ribs, then tended to various wounds.

"Why did you help us?" al-Wazir asked once the pain had subsided.

"You Europe. You bastards, make fight, take fight." There was a moment of silence as the physician concentrated on a stitch. "That is way of thrones, ah?"

"Well, yes." Al-Wazir looked around the deck. His effort at distraction didn't help when the doctor's needle dug into a thigh wound al-Wazir didn't recall sustaining.

"Silent Order . . ." The doctor's voice trailed off. "Not serve Celestial Empire. Not serve Europe Empire. Serve self, against order of world."

"Aye, laddie." Al-Wazir closed his eyes against a wave of pain-induced nausea. "So much is against the order of the world, I'm afraid."

The doctor looked up at him, eyes old, bright, and wise in his fleshy, pale face. "China live forever, ah. Silent Order have different idea. Girl, she too much. Golden Bridge burn world down. She Golden Bridge."

"Golden Bridge?"

But the doctor would not say more.

When he returned to the poop, Paolina took her chance to leave. "I'm going below."

He didn't ask what she intended. Their shared violence seemed to have changed something between them, in a way that he'd never felt on his own. He concentrated on keeping their heading and wondered what to do when night fell.

The doctor might be an ally. At least he was not so much of an enemy. What would they do with the crew, though? Tie them up? A dozen men, bound for the night, didn't seem wise to al-Wazir. Their discomfort and resentment would spark an uprising faster than anything else he could think for them do.

Two days' sail to the Wall. If he were in decent health, he could stay awake that long. With his current injuries, that didn't seem reasonable.

Several hours passed with no sign of Paolina. The men on the deck had settled into some game of tiles. Hands moved and faint clacks carried back to him at the wheel. The sunlight slanted low across the deck.

When darkness came, he would be hard-pressed not to fall asleep.

Al-Wazir tried to catch the doctor's eye. The old man rested against the rails, apparently sleeping himself. That would not be of any help.

The chief twisted to look down the deck hatch where Paolina had descended. Unless someone was hiding—and they'd been unable to make an effective search, unfortunately—she should have had belowdecks to herself.

Where had she gone?

He would need Paolina to stand watch tonight. All night, probably. His body had the heavy feeling it got after a fight.

Right now he missed Boaz very much. The Brass man's presence would have shifted this problem right smartly.

The worst was that he could not leave the wheel and go search for her. Having neither of them on deck watching the remaining crew was the height of madness.

Let them get used to us, he prayed. When need came, they would do their jobs simply in order to survive. Of course, he had no idea which divisions these men came from. If every jack among them was a deck idler, they were in trouble.

Al-Wazir amused himself by watching the clouds pile in the west as the sun descended. A real corker of a storm was brewing. His weather sense didn't apply here—different winds over this ocean—but he'd lay money they'd feel the lash of wind and rain before making their destination.

That would be enough to end it all, if the crew did not cooperate.

Paolina reappeared at dusk, climbing up out of the hull.

"Where the fewk have you been, lassie?" al-Wazir demanded. He was so exhausted, he could barely think.

She gave him a hard, tired look. Her dress was stained with blood, her face still smudged from their morning's uprising. "Making sure there were no more grenadoes to be used against us, nor guns."

"What did you do?"

"Threw them overboard. There are ports in the hull below." She smiled weakly. "I didn't want the crew to see me doing it."

"Fair enough."

"I found a machine shop."

"Did you now?" He was already slipping into a tunnel of blinded sight and blinkered thought.

"I cut some gears."

"Aye." Al-Wazir slumped to a sitting position. "Keep us pointed at the Wall, lassie, and don't fight the wind." His body was so damned *heavy*. How had that happened? As if his limbs were fashioned from lead. "Trust that old doctor if you must trust someone."

"What about when that storm hits?"

"Wake me. If I'm nae dead, I'll answer t'call."

"Please stay with me, Chief."

The note of pleading in her voice got his attention.

"I can't do this alone." She stared down at him with watering eyes. "I shouldn't have done it all. I just won't . . . won't . . . be a *thing* for them to use. The *fidalgos,* these Chinese are just like the *fidalgos.* No different from your English either."

"Hush, lassie." He tried to lift his hand, but it was fastened to the deck by gravity and fatigue. "There's no more of that. Yon Wall is your home. You'll be there soon."

"I don't want to kill these men." She sounded miserable. "I never wanted to do anything like that. I am not one of them."

He reached for words lost deep inside himself. "Would you give up to them?"

"No, no."

"Then you do what you must so you are not taken, lass." The stars came rushing in on him then, echoes of old dreams as the fingers of his lost left hand reached out to grab at the lights of heaven.

His face was wet when he was shaken awake. Al-Wazir blinked past dreams of Brass men falling from the orbital tracks on ropes as long as the world was wide. Rain blew across the deck, which was pitching slowly.

The doctor leaned over him. Paolina was barely visible in the shadows beyond.

"You not sleep more now, ah. Demons in head take thoughts."

"The sleep of wounds?" He hated how muzzy his voice was. He'd seen men lie down after an accident or fight, and never awaken.

"Demons in head."

"Where's the storm?" He staggered to his feet.

"Almost upon us," Paolina told him. "The clouds are piled as high as the stars."

Wall storm. With that, al-Wazir realized he'd been stupid. They should have driven north, gaining altitude and distance to survive the battering to come.

Lightning cracked among the clouds, casting a swift, blinding glare across the deck.

"I'm going below," she said as al-Wazir blinked away the sudden flash. "I must."

"What?" he asked, but she was gone. The wheel spun until he lurched forward to catch it with a bone-wrenching crack in his good hand—his only hand.

Just another hurt, that.

The doctor shouted over a wind gust. "Crew not attack me."

Al-Wazir looked. They certainly weren't huddled on the maindeck anymore. He should have checked that first—a possibly fatal mistake. "Where are the men?"

The old man leaned close. "Motors, bag!"

Al-Wazir braced his stump into the wheel and fought the wind. He had little choice of heading, save a need to keep the ship from spinning beyond control. Lightning passed within the clouds around him, setting the textures of the sky glowing in fitful contrast. It might have been beautiful had it not meant his life.

He wondered if they could lift above this storm, but it was too late. He wasn't even sure how they controlled altitude on this vessel. So hand and stump, al-Wazir kept the ship turned away from the wind and let it be driven east and south while the weather raged around him and the object of this bitter quest remained belowdecks on some mysterious errand of her own.

CHILDRESS

"Whatever the Golden Bridge is, they are not building it here," Captain Leung said.

A storm moved in from the west as the evening fell—they could see the clouds on the horizon. The harbor at Chersonesus Aurea was still very pleasant but for the excruciating heat.

"No. They are here mining the bones of this old library." She thought about that some more. "Whoever came before didn't use this knowledge the way Wang and the others want to, either."

"Where do they build it, then?"

"There is no Golden Bridge, Captain. These people are looking for something more. Something different. They seek to undermine the order of the world."

Something in those words . . .

"All the world is order," he said.

"No . . . I mean, yes. There's something about the order." She thought through her conversation with William of Ghent, with Admiral Shang, with Leung himself. And what the Malaya Chinthé agent had told her about a panic in Europe.

Gleam, that was the word. The mysterious European girl had somehow been the key to overturning the order of the world. And now the Silent Order were looking for her.

Here, the Chinese worked both for and against the *avebianco*. Which was another way of saying they were working both for and against the Silent Order.

"Your people play both sides against one another," she said. It began to make a certain awful sense. "You overreach. It is not the Golden Bridge at stake, except in the loosest sense. There is a girl who burned down half of Strasbourg with some magic. Or science. I don't know which. The Celestial Empire has been trying to build that same power here. She has entered their plans. Or perhaps the Silent Order is pursuing this project, using the Celestial Empire as a stalking horse. "

"Phu Ket," said Leung. "The great house of the Silent Order is at Phu Ket."

"Wang mentioned Phu Ket. Why? Does the Celestial Empire have a university there?"

"Nothing is there." Leung's voice was slow and thoughtful. "A small fishing port, and the Silent Order. No more."

"The Silent Order . . ." She took a walk through her house of memory. This kept coming back to the Silent Order, from the very beginning. The Mask Poinsard had summoned her forth from the library for the sake of the Silent Order's vengeance. The devilry that the Malaya Chinthé agent had mentioned was the Silent Order's doing. Now Wang had brought them up again, as if expecting her to know the significance of Phu Ket.

Even though she was a Mask—or at least claimed to be.

Does Wang even see a difference?

A second, quieter thought crept in. *What if there is no difference?*

She came to a conclusion. "It is the Silent Order to which we must turn for an accounting of this. Not the Celestial Empire. You yourself explained how being exiled to Tainan placed the Beiyang admiralty outside the bounds of the Imperial Court. How much further from the Celestial Throne is a project which abides here at the waist of the world? This has been arranged for the convenience and ambitions of the Silent Order, not China." She stared at Leung in the pale light of evening. It didn't matter why, in whose behalf, only *what.*

"Through this Golden Bridge, they seek control of the very engines of creation. The girl who destroyed Strasbourg must be a great clue to them. That is the sort of power which will shatter the world." Her voice became more urgent as her thoughts raced ahead. "We must go to Phu Ket, now. It may be a fool's errand, but I would see what can be done to convince the Silent Order of the dangers of their pursuit."

Childress knew the Silent Order spoke with the Feathered Masks. She would carry her deception into the heart of the enemy. "How soon can *Five Lucky Winds* sail?"

"*Five Lucky Winds* sails at *my* command."

She stifled the surge of anger that roiled through her. "Certainly, Captain Leung. I should think no less." She leaned close, almost touching noses. "How soon can *you* command *Five Lucky Winds* to sail?"

"My orders have great latitude, but the waters of the Indian Ocean are beyond the purview of the Beiy—"

She cut him off. "So are the waters of the Atlantic Ocean, yet you found me there. You owe me lives, Captain, the life of a ship and everyone aboard her. For better or worse I *am* the Mask now. You helped make me so. And everything you and I and Admiral Shang spoke about that might be happening here at Chersonesus Aurea is doubly true of the machinations of the Silent Order at Phu Ket." Childress paused, trying to find the right words. "They are *godless,* sir. They know no order, no naming of things, save that which they impose themselves. An affront to the Celestial Empire and the British Empire alike."

"So what if we go?"

Cataloger Wang loomed out of the darkness. He spoke in Chinese, but Childress followed him well enough. *"If you go, you will bring disaster on yourself and everyone you touch."*

She looked beyond him. Leung's sailors were in the hands of four big men from the library staff.

Leung began to speak urgently, an admonition that slid into argument too rapid for her to follow. Childress stepped back, then gathered a great breath and shrieked as if her life depended on it.

Wang and Leung stopped arguing and stared at her. Someone called out from the tower of *Five Lucky Winds*. The deck watch, of course. What she had been playing for.

The two constrained sailors lurched into motion, fighting their captors. Another sailor popped up the jetty from down inside the launch. Wang threw an ineffectual blow at Leung. The sailor shouted and vaulted to the top of the ladder to wade into the fight.

Childress sat down and covered her face and neck. She had no place amid fisticuffs. At least there was a fight, rather than the endless chaffering the Chinese seemed to prefer as they sought to save face for themselves and one another.

She knew that they should sail now for Phu Ket, ahead of the storm and whatever came next. Waiting here in the shadow of the Wall for rounds of negotiations and wireless messages was pointless.

She didn't even glance up as someone gave a shout that cut off with a hard thump. There was a splash of a body falling in water, then two more splashes.

"Please hurry," said Leung, touching her arm. "More will be here."

Childress looked up from her crouch. "Are we sailing, Captain?"

"We are now." His face and tone were grim, but his decision was in favor of her thinking.

"Then I come."

By the time the launch reached the submarine, there were shouts and bright lights on the jetty. Childress thought she heard the crack of a gun, but Captain Leung acted as if he had noticed nothing.

He certainly made no effort to return fire.

Then the hatches were closed, the bells ringing, and the engines humming to life. For the first time, she was allowed on the bridge.

It was as close and tight as any other area of the submarine. The electricks had bloodred lenses over their lighting elements, which lent everything a strange Dantean aspect. Great brass wheels were arrayed along three bulkheads, some of which had men already working to spin them. Leung sat on a tall stool next to a pillar in the middle of the space, staring at the array of gauges and dials above the control wheels.

She could make little of it. How did they navigate from here? How did they know anything of their sailing at all?

The pilot called orders through an electrick box, which crackled and spat and hissed as it brought his voice down from the tower above. The vessel must be moving slowly into the winding channel out of the harbor.

Childress stayed back by the hatch as Leung put his face against a pair of goggles set against the pipe before him. He spoke quietly to the pilot. No one else talked, save to murmur a response to Leung's occasional orders.

They were moving. The librarians of Chersonesus Aurea had no forces with which to pursue *Five Lucky Winds*. The submarine could sail below the stormy seas to come.

Why did she feel a sense of panic?

More murmured conversation. Slowly they walked out. Leung would not rush this. She knew that. Even if they had been under fire, he would not have pushed his ship through that winding, strange channel.

When the pitch of the engines changed and the pilot stopped speaking almost continuously, she knew they'd reached the open, shallow waters of the Kepualuan Riau islands. Leung snapped shut a cover on his goggles. Without turning about he said, "Mask Childress, I believe the bridge is off-limits to you, on the terms of your parole."

"My apologies, Captain."

She left the bridge. Childress knew she should go back to her own cabin. Or the wardroom, perhaps. Not wander the vessel.

Instead she climbed the tower ladder. They would not dive among the reefs and shoals of these islands, not until they'd cleared the Strait of Malacca.

Opening a hatch in the outer hull was a gross violation of orders. No officer or crewman of *Five Lucky Winds* would do such without a direct instruction from the bridge. The pilot would require permission to come below when time came. No one went up without the captain's explicit assent.

She was the Mask Childress. She would go where she willed.

Undogging the hatch and spinning back the great brass wheel, she climbed into the little chamber at the bottom of the tower. Childress shut the hatch again, spinning it closed from the outside, then climbing the rest of the way. The tower was bare, nothing more than an observation stand with a small cluster of plugs and dials normally closed by a waterproof cover.

Ming seemed unsurprised to see her. He nodded as she greeted him in Chinese. *"Good evening. Are you well?"*

"I am well, yes."

It was a full night. Singapore glowed to the north and east of them, while the Wall glowered close by to the south. The prow of the submarine coursed through waters that glowed as they broke across the hull. Ahead, the western horizon was dark with clouds limned by flashes of lightning. The night reeked of salt and distant jungle and the smell of weather.

"We sail well," Ming said.

"Yes."

After that, they both fell silent. From time to time he picked up a small speaking horn he'd plugged into the panel and murmured some comment as they slid through the night-dark islands. Childress watched the sky, picking out the threads of brass.

When the stars began moving, she wondered what it was she saw. She tugged at Ming's arm and pointed. He turned and looked. After that he began speaking more urgently into the horn. She caught some of it— *airships, Singapore, Navy.*

"Do they chase us?" she asked, forgetting herself to speak in English.

Ming glanced at her.

"Are they for us?" was the best she could do in Chinese.

"Yes." He seemed calm.

She did not worry yet, but she watched lights move, then wink out.

Had they lifted with lanterns lit? Why? To warn *Five Lucky Winds*? Or possibly to send a message to the people of Singapore. Malaya Chinthé would certainly be watching.

She began to be afraid. The maps were clear enough—the Strait of Malacca was a long, narrow body of water. It was shallow as well. She was fairly certain that airships could move faster than submarines.

Though not through the coming storm.

Childress smiled. She began to understand Ming's apparent lack of worry. She stayed in the hot night, watching them sail into the storm and away from pursuit, convinced that there was nothing more they could have done.

Nothing more she could have done.

Her journey from New Haven would make sense if they found their way to Phu Ket and brought reason to the Silent Order. Or better yet, stopped the project entirely. She had no idea how she would do that, but if they could sail into the teeth of this storm and make their goal ahead of their pursuit, anything was possible.

Lightning danced in the sky before them, a bright bonfire to illuminate their way.

NINETEEN

PAOLINA

The machine shop tucked within the lower decks of *Heaven's Deer* was small, even by the cramped standards of an airship. The storm was not making matters easy either. The ship rolled and bucked while the bamboo walls vibrated to the point of thrumming. They sweat stormwater as well, but Paolina decided after brief thought that this was probably a desirable feature rather than a defect in the ship's construction.

Whoever had designed the shop had anticipated the need for repairs under fire or storm. She was thankful for that. Every flat surface had vises, mounting hooks, or braces. Many of the tools were gimballed. Some were electrick as well, something she'd never seen or really even considered.

It made sense—an electrick cutter could do so much more than a hand with a file, if everything were properly braced.

Her greatest challenge was that the shop had been equipped for engine and weapons repairs. Many of the tools were simply too large a scale to support what she was attempting.

Paolina was building another gleam.

Even now, cutting gears to fit into the crude casing she'd adapted from the base of a large caliber shell, she was having trouble justifying it to herself. The death of Lachance, even of those venal fools back in the Strasbourg Cathedral, had been a very high price for her last such effort. But she was heading for *a Muralha* now, passing beyond the reach of the Silent Order. Their greed for her fabrication would mean nothing once she'd regained safety.

Her largest worry now was that if she built the thing, or at least enough of it, the gleam might fall into Chinese hands. Events in Strasbourg made it perfectly clear that these people were capable of anything once they got a gleam into their hands. All the more so if it came to Phu Ket and the control of the Silent Order for a second time.

Her second largest worry now was that she might not be able to build another.

The original stemwinder had come to her in the fevered dark, from parts and tools that had traveled down *a Muralha* to her. Her memories of its design and construction were incomplete. On the other hand, her sense of its purpose and function was much better.

The gleam was a miracle waiting to happen, potentiality trapped in the gears and energy of the clockwork. A sort of magic, written in the same clockwork that underlay the order of the world.

Why *she* could build it, and others could not, was a question that begged an answer Paolina was not prepared to think on. Especially at that moment, with *Heaven's Deer* shuddering at the force of the wind. This was a Wall storm, piled so high, nothing but an angel could fly above the violence of wind and rain. It could only be ridden out, with hopes of not being driven down or forced so far south that the airship impacted *a Muralha*.

Al-Wazir knew his business. The chief's experience and their reluctant crew should bring the airship through. Her hope was to finish the gleam in time to help them survive, if possible.

The cutter she was using whined and spat as the electricks flickered. *Lightning strike?* Up here away from the earth the power in the bolt would move on harmlessly. She hoped.

Paolina was building an escapement now. It would translate the power of her mainspring to the hands. She had no jewels for the movements, no method to set the hair-fine axles solid and secure in their courses, but she would find a way. For all that the shop was cramped, it was equipped with a multitude of drawers like a giant puzzle box. There seemed to be half a dozen of everything a craftsman might wish to have, if only she knew where to look.

The hardest part was building without a plan. She had done so once before, but she hadn't understood her own purposes as she did now. Knowing too much was almost as bad as not knowing enough.

Still, she set to her work, bracing her body against the swaying of the little room.

When lightning finally did strike the hull, she understood the difference between weather and a Wall storm, at least from aboard an airship. The electrick over her head flared, died, then sputtered back to fitful orange life. The bamboo walls crackled as the water rolling down them puffed to steam. Her teeth ached, her skin prickled, and her hair felt just *wrong*.

For a moment, Paolina thought the pick and file in her hand were hot. She nearly dropped them, but held on as she was trying to set a gear train into her case.

The work was so crude that she nearly despaired of it. The storm was growing worse as well, the airship pitching forward more and more. Was the gasbag in trouble?

She wondered how far down the ocean was. Then she wondered how close the ocean was. She set both thoughts aside and kept the task at hand close.

Her mechanism. A way to address the order of the world. It wasn't just her, either, for the Silent Order had made a horrid mess of things back in Strasbourg with the first gleam.

Paolina prayed that only she could build one. The world didn't need *more* of these devices—one was enough to rewrite history, in the wrong hands.

With that thought, she felt a renewed surge of guilt at building this one. Was it fair to protect herself with such a creation? This was no different from a man making himself a more powerful gun.

All the while, her hands kept moving, following a plan she didn't fully understand. Distraction was good, Paolina realized. She prayed for more distraction.

The storm kept shaking the airship, her work progressed, and she tried not to think about the waves surging below them, the rain pouring around them, the wind pounding *Heaven's Deer* apart while the airship could neither fight nor rise above the weather.

The next time she noticed a strike was when the hull began to smoke. Paolina looked up to see water pouring down the inside wall. Was there flooding in the corridor? That shouldn't be possible, not on an airship.

Then she remembered the gaping hole she'd blown in the deck above the arms locker.

She looked down at her new gleam. It was larger, cruder, and simpler than the old one, but it was of a type with the first—a mechanical incantation written in springs and gears that moved in sympathetic echo with the hidden order of the world. Creation was nothing more than a complex dance of belief and mechanism, a design worded in the dreaming mind of God. All man could do was attempt to read the Divine intent and apply what could be perceived.

At the moment Divine intent was sluicing an inch or more of water past her ankles.

Working quickly, Paolina clipped a face to her gleam. This one more resembled a clock than a pocket watch, but it had the same four hands. She'd set them to the same tempi, too—the beat of the hours, the rhythm of her own heart, the time that counted at the heart of the world, and the fourth hand freewheeling to match whatever she could match.

She clutched it close and stepped to the hatch. The door was stiff and would not open at her tug. Paolina put her weight into it, yanking the door harder. It popped open just as the ship flexed with another great groan and a blast of wet wind.

Heaven's Deer was coming apart, shaking itself like a wet dog in the face of the storm.

Paolina stumbled into the passageway as the ship rolled violently. She slipped across the floor and collapsed against the far bulkhead. More water flowed across her, soaking her shoulder and side. Wind and rain tore through the passageway from the gaping hatch to the maindeck.

She fought to her feet, holding the gleam above her head to keep it out of the flow of the water. There was no help for the streaming rain. She made it to the ladder before the airship lurched again, and kept her feet this time by grabbing on to the ladderway. Once the ship settled a little more, Paolina climbed one-handed. She kept the gleam close.

There was no question that *Heaven's Deer* was dying in the air. If the gleam could find the rhythms that drove this storm, she might be able to at least bring them down safely. Otherwise their survival would be up to al-Wazir and his reluctant crew.

The ship yawed again as she made the deck, giving a gaping view of darkness. Cloud banks below them were illuminated by jags of lightning. Paolina's stomach lurched—it was a more disorienting sight than anything she'd ever seen from *a Muralha*—before *Heaven's Deer* heeled the other way and the rain closed in again in thick curtains.

A frightened Chinese face loomed out of the storm's gloom, waving a rope. She jumped away, but he caught her waist.

A safety line, Paolina thought. She tried to thank him, but her voice was captured by the wind, and her ears were still ringing.

She stepped close and let him knot it around her. The crewman then led her to the poop, walking hand-over-hand along another line strung along the deck. He had to stop twice and reset her safety line, and once more as the airship pitched hard. She realized she could hear something besides the storm's rage—the gasbag was booming.

That couldn't be good.

Al-Wazir was lashed to the wheel like some hero out of ancient legend. The Chinese doctor huddled beside him, tied to ropes staked to the deck and stretching to the aft rail, clutching a little storm lantern. Her escort dropped back as she stumbled up the steps to the poop. Her rope caught on something, then popped free.

She finally reached the wheel.

She screamed at al-Wazir, "Are we dying?"

Another lighting strike sizzled, flaring across the lines and midmasts on the deck. It was a wonder that the gasbag had not caught fire.

He stared at her. She could see little more than a silhouette, a shape in the darkness, but the man was practically glowing with effort. His eyes were red, either bloody with effort or glowing in the fitful light of the doctor's storm lantern.

Al-Wazir opened his mouth and roared. The words were nothing but fragments to her. ". . . ocean . . . nae . . . Almighty . . ."

She turned her hand and showed him the gleam.

This time his eyes practically bulged. "You . . . a clock . . . fewking . . ."

Another swirl of rain blew by, a horizontal flood that choked Paolina so hard, she wondered if she were drowning.

The next lightning strike showed her something far more fearsome—the ocean heaving at a high angle of view. *Heaven's Deer* was diving for the water.

She was too late, far too late.

Al-Wazir was trying to tell her something more. ". . . nae . . . crew . . . few . . ."

Paolina tucked her head down and focused on the gleam. The three hands beat as they should. She pulled her crude stem—a large brass key, in truth—to the fourth stop and began to set the hand. Could she find the storm's beat long enough to steal calm from the enormous forces driving them to the waves?

This time she had a better sense of how to set and drive the hand. The problem was the overwhelming fury of the weather. It was like trying to tune in to the key of all life at once, find each of God's creatures amid a cry or shout or shriek. A Wall storm was an explosion of water and wind, an epic eruption of force fit to rewrite the face of lands.

In that moment, she would have traded all of this for one of the great waves that had ravaged *a Muralha* two years earlier. At least those came, cleared their paths, and moved onward.

Paolina tried to slip inside the rhythms of wind and water, lightning and thunder. The ocean below their keel was nothing but another place, the clear air high above the storm clouds nothing but another time. Here, now, *Heaven's Deer* was in the heart of the storm.

How would God have done it? He would not have parted the waters of the air and stilled the winds with His hand; she knew that. The Divine would instead have turned one from the other, as water tumbling from a cliff will fold past a quiet place. Or how a swirl of drainage always had clear air at the middle, pointing down into the depths.

Order from chaos, in keeping with the same laws and movements that generated that chaos in the first place.

The gleam clicked as it found the movement of the storm. She was inside now, but the forces were too complex, the scope and scale of the thing too large. Still, Paolina thought she could deflect the worst, perhaps make a blade of air to shield the last of *Heaven's Deer*'s fall.

She had one glimpse of al-Wazir, his mouth in a rounded *O* of surprise or shock; then she was lifting the storm like draperies away from a statue. Something swung her gut from hips to teeth and back again, and she choked on her own bile, but she held open the way.

The ocean hit her in all its tons with the slap of the world's gleam. Someone grabbed her while Paolina clutched the new gleam as close as she could, curling her body into nearly a ball. Water battered her first against a wooden beam, then an enormous soft surface.

The gasbag, she thought, before she was yanked about again. She rolled over and broke free of the water a moment to find herself at the top of a sliding mountain of ocean, the fabric billowing in a trough below her. Paolina took a deep breath just before she was pulled under once more.

The next time she came up, al-Wazir was dragging her onto a matted mass of ropes and deck lumber. Paolina loosened her grip on the gleam long enough to hook one hand into the ropes, then clutched her treasure tight again. The wreckage shifted, tugging her along as it rose up the next mountainous wave to clear the crest. Somehow they didn't turn turtle or spin out of control as the mass began to slide down the far side.

She found her blade of air again in that brief respite and banished the rain from the raft. That did nothing to stop their wild slide across the angles of the ocean, but at least they could breathe.

Al-Wazir looked at her and growled, "Now what, lassie?"

Paolina hitched herself higher up on the matted mass. "We make ourselves fast. When I release the storm, we shall have to survive the worst."

"Aye," he growled, with a look that made clear how much he doubted that eventuality. "And what will ye be doin' when ye releases the storm, lassie?"

"Calling to whoever will hear us," she said calmly.

Her stomach lurched again as the raft topped another crest to again slide rapidly down into the dark pit of the waters.

He stared at her. "Who would hear us now, lassie?"

"God, if no one else," she answered primly.

"You're crazed beyond measure, girl."

Paolina folded herself close around the gleam. "Crazed I may be, Chief, but I'm the one that calmed the storm over our heads."

He made a show of looking up from the trough through which they were sliding, where lighting danced across the sky and rain moved like Heaven's rivers. "Aye, that."

His remaining hand slid free of the ropes and gripped her arms. "Bless ye, lassie. God bless you."

"God bless us both," she said, then turned her attention to the device ticking in her hand, and the world ticking around her.

AL-WAZIR

He looked at the girl huddled on their makeshift raft and wondered when the storm would close over them again. She'd as much as said it would. Right now he believed anything she told him. Without Paolina, there'd be nothing left to believe in save the crabs picking at his waterlogged body.

Al-Wazir had written Paolina off to panic before she'd finally reappeared in the last, desperate moments of their descent. She'd literally glowed as the ship had come down. Once again, he had seen his death tumbling from the air. Once again it had been denied to him. Denied, or at least postponed a short while.

His luck almost made him sick.

Whatever magic the girl thought she was up to with the little clock-box, the great magic that had gotten her into so much trouble, well . . . he couldn't imagine it helping them much once the storm fell back upon their heads. The very air would drown them then, stealing life from their lungs as quickly as they could suck it in.

He tried to make his peace with God, fumbling at half-remembered prayer. God wasn't having any of Threadgill Angus al-Wazir. At least there was no sign of acceptance or contentment in whatever served him as a soul.

"To hell with God." He'd always put more faith in sheer human cussedness anyway. And damn him if Paolina Barthes was not easily the most cussed girl he'd ever had the misfortune to meet. She'd struck him as something between a beloved daughter and a dread termagant, though right now she more resembled an Old Testament prophet gone wrong.

She looked at him and said, "Breathe deep."

He sucked in air as the water collapsed around his head like a rock fall.

Without the protection of her magic watch, the storm had them fully in its grip. Water raced in white-foamed hillocks whipped by wind and rain until the boundary between ocean and air was little more than a laughable notion. It was pit-dark as well within the bowels of the storm. They might have been beneath the soil, but for the forks of lighting riving the sky. One moment al-Wazir's eyes were full of stinging salt; the next they were blinded by a stab from the heavens.

When the strokes began skipping from one wave crest to another, he worried. Then he laughed—what was the point in fearing electrick death from the heavens when the next surge of the sea could easily fold them to their graves?

He tried to focus on Paolina. She'd coiled herself inside a mat of rope a foot or two away from him, still in a protective ball around her device. As a practical matter, if their little raft of junk didn't flip or get dragged under, they might be able to survive awhile. Every time they rode over the folded top of a wave, that was put to the test. Each yawning valley was another death-gate through which they must pass. Some were black as Acheron's bed; others glowed with sparking lightning.

He tried to close his eyes. That made the furious pitching and tossing all the worse.

Al-Wazir's other concern was whether they were close to land. Should they live, he did not want to be lost amid a thousand knots of ocean. On the other hand, being driven onto a beach now would be more deadly than riding out the worst of the tempest on the open sea.

A saltwater fist caught him in the face, lifting him bodily from the makeshift raft until only the ropes tangled around his legs kept him from being torn completely away. The wind cut through his clothing like cold glass knives while he tried to cough out the brine that had been forced down his throat.

I am a fool, al-Wazir thought. *Moments from death, I worry about tomorrow's landfall.* "I am sorry," he screamed into the wind, still choking on the salt. "I am sorry we will die."

If Paolina heard him, she made no answer. Another round of lightning lit her body, wet and curled tight beneath her mass of ropes. He could not tell if she were shivering or fighting or struggling. He wondered if the sea had already taken her.

A sharp lurch in his gut told him they were racing up another wave, heading for another crest. White foam gleamed around him as it rose to a steeper and steeper angle. Was this one nigh vertical?

He looked up into another lightning strike as something large flapped across the sky. Part of the gasbag from *Heaven's Deer*. Or maybe a demon out of Hell, in this storm.

The raft spun once, twice, three times, then lost all support. They tumbled in the air, al-Wazir finally giving in to the scream that had been clawing up his throat. He realized the mass of bamboo and ropes was *above* him. Something caught, the raft lurched, and they landed flat at the bottom of the next trough even as a combination of rain and spray closed in once more.

Paolina grabbed his arm, startling another scream from al-Wazir. Her face was little more than a pale blur. He could see the dark oval of her mouth flexing.

He had no idea what she was saying, but he closed his hand over hers. Their grip held a moment before each slipped back to their rope nest.

The next lightning strike caused his legs to flex so tight, he kicked himself in the buttocks. Something tore within each knee. The water burned, too, crackling and glowing. Al-Wazir's throat closed so tightly that nothing could have forced more screams from him. That was just as well when another wall of water collapsed over him.

He opened his eyes—a second later? Minutes? How much longer could he survive in this wet and bitter hell? A wall of wet metal passed close by.

That makes no sense.

Al-Wazir closed his eyes and took a deep breath.

That makes no sense either.

Where was the storm?

She's brought back the calm.

He opened his eyes once more. A vessel riding far too low in the water slid by them. A pale face peered over the top of the metal wall.

Al-Wazir pulled himself up on one hand and bellowed as he'd never bellowed before. "Halloo!"

Then the ship was gone, slipping into the curtain of howling rain that surrounded their narrow island of calm. Not ship, *submarine*. What in blazes would such a thing be doing in such killing weather? They could slide below the chaos of air and wave and wait it out, or cruise for better seas.

The raft spun in the bottom of a wave trough, neither rising nor falling.

There was little more than mist in that moment. The wind and rain had been calmed by Paolina and her magic.

"Can you hear me, lassie?"

She groaned as she turned to face him. The movement made her cough up seawater in plenitude just as the raft began to lift up the face of the next wave.

"You done good," al-Wazir told her.

They joined hands again as the raft rose into the wet night, carrying their little blade of calm with them.

Much to al-Wazir's surprise, the submarine returned. The raft was spinning along the flank of a wave rather than sliding straight down when the vessel rose in the trough below them. The tower, what he'd previously mistaken for a wall of metal, heeled over as the ship rolled. Her side rudders lifted out of the water, twisting to gain purchase. Three pale faces appeared at the side of the tower as a light flared above them. One of them raised a weapon and fired it at him.

Al-Wazir was too exhausted to wonder why they'd risk their lives to ensure his death. Something streaked overhead, sizzling as it passed, and a cable splashed in the water near the raft. A white float was dragged backwards past him.

There was no more time to think. He tugged Paolina with him as he tried to pull himself from the ropes that tangled his legs to the raft. Trapped, he was trapped, and the damned float was skimming away.

"Grab on t'it, girl!" he shouted.

She lunged without breaking her grip on his wrist, but fell short.

"The gleam," she called back. "I cannot lose it."

Al-Wazir clawed toward Paolina. "Give the damnable thing to me!"

There was a look of pure panic on her face in the sputtering glare of the flare.

"I've but one hand, lass. I cannot hold on and also grab the float if they try again!"

She shoved the magic clock at him with her free hand, then began plucking at the ropes. He tucked it tight between his arm and body before renewing his good-handed grip upon her.

The wave was threatening to overtake both raft and submarine when they fired their line once more. This time it soared high over al-Wazir to splash into the water above them. The calm was wavering, too, as the flare hit the sea and spluttered out.

Paolina grabbed at the line, shrieked, then grabbed at the float as it slithered into her arms. Line and float pulled her free of the raft so that she was connected to al-Wazir only by the grip of their hands on one another's wrists.

"No . . . ," she screamed as their fingers slipped.

The wave lifted farther above the raft, forcing it toward the submarine. For a moment his grip was secure in Paolina's. Then she was jerked away as the raft slammed into the iron hull.

I am undone, he thought amid the flying splinters and flapping ends of broken line.

Something—no, someone—plucked at his shoulders. Al-Wazir looked into a Chinese face. It was a man in a puffy vest and harness, who in turn glanced up at the wave forcing the submarine to roll further and further away from vertical.

The Chinese smiled, said something, then they all slipped beneath the water once more.

This time he forgot to breathe.

There was a dark indigo moment of cold air, a bubble like transparent steel. A surprised sailor tugged al-Wazir into a metal deck. A hatch stood open in the tower before them. The ocean roiled all around, above, below, held back by a sphere of crackling air.

Al-Wazir stumbled, following the sailor and one of his fellows into the tower. They slammed it shut as water coursed around them with a clap like another lightning strike.

They were thrown so hard against the metal of the inside of the tower that the wind was smashed from his chest and into the eager salt water. It drained away fast, even as al-Wazir's lungs felt fit to burst. One of the sailors banged sharply on a hatch in the floor. The wheel spun, and the first sailor dropped down below the deck. The second looked at al-Wazir and said something urgent.

Anything was better than this storm. He climbed one-handed, clumsy with cold and exhaustion, desperate to clear the deck before water folded over them again. The second sailor followed so close, he kicked al-Wazir in the head, and tugged the hatch shut behind them. They passed through a second hatch to alight in a narrow passageway. He had to bend low while half a dozen more Chinese sailors stood close with knives, shouting.

Al-Wazir chose the better part of valor and collapsed to the deck, coughing up seawater with the last of his panic. He wondered where Paolina was.

CHILDRESS

"Get down the ladder, now!" She didn't know how to make herself heard over the storm that had closed back in after a few moments of unnatural calm. The girl had come *up* instead of going below.

Childress still had no idea how they'd gotten here—one moment *Five Lucky Winds* had been heading toward the distant storm, land visible on both flanks of the ship. The next they were deep in a horrendous torment of the sea. That she and Ming had survived the few minutes that followed was a testament far more to luck, and Ming's quick thinking, than any merit of hers.

They had seen that raft with the two people clinging to it. Ming had argued on the speaking horn briefly, then more intently, until she'd grabbed it and shouted, "Turn the damned ship!"

Now they had one castaway gone below after a lunatic rescue involving a line fired from a gun. The other was here in the tower with them as *Five Lucky Winds* slid toward another dunking.

They could drown right now. They should have already.

The girl looked at her calmly. "I can hold back the ocean until we go below."

And then she did.

Ming, Childress, the girl, and Fat Cheung with his line gun scrambled down the ladder even while the waters roiled around a ball of air centered on them. Cheung rapped on the hatch in the dark damp at the base of the tower, then dropped in as it was opened from below.

"Go," said Childress to the girl.

"The air will follow me," she warned.

Childress nodded, then scrambled down the ladder, wet as she'd ever been. Her eyes and ears and throat stung with seawater. Bells were ringing alarms all over the ship.

Above her, the girl and Ming crammed into the lock together—something that would not have been possible if they were not both of small stature. Ming closed the outer hatch as Childress found the deck.

She heard them pass the inner hatch, but her attention was taken by the two cooks bending over that giant European that had been pulled from the same raft as the girl.

He was a massive redheaded brute, and he'd produced an astonishing quantity of salt water. One of the cooks pounded his back while the other held his head up above the water and vomitus pooling the deck.

"I see you have taken us fishing," said Captain Leung from behind her.

The girl stepped off the ladder and screamed at the cooks, "Get away from him!"

"Wait," Childress called.

She whirled, anger and panic clear in her face. "What?"

"They're trying to save his life."

"These are *Chinese*!" In the cold silence that followed, she added with an edge of fury, "They're almost as bad as the English."

"Enough," said Leung. He rattled off some rapid Chinese, which sent most of the sailors scattering. He then turned to Ming with a question. Childress caught the phrase "All men" in Ming's answer. *All men,* whatever that meant.

"We dive now," Leung said. "As soon as we know how deep and where we are." He looked at the girl. "Where *are* we?"

"I don't know," she gasped. Her anger drained away from her as fast as the water from the man on the floor.

Leung stepped back into the bridge, where alarms continued to ring. In the silence that followed, Childress was very aware of the hull groaning and popping.

"*Take him forward when you can,*" she told the cooks. "And my profound gratitude." Then, to the girl, in English, "Let us repair to the wardroom. We'll be out of the way. If the ship survives this storm, there will be many questions."

"The questions are there whether or not the ship survives the storm," the girl said more calmly. "I won't leave al-Wazir."

"The wardroom is a few steps aft," she said. "You can see him from there."

She picked her way past the groaning giant. The girl followed her with an anxious glance backward.

"You'll forgive me if I do not make tea," Childress said as the submarine rolled again. The hull continued to groan. The noise of water was more loud than she'd ever heard before.

The girl shivered under the blankets Childress had given her, and kept glancing at the open hatch.

She leaned forward. "You're the girl with the gleam, aren't you?"

"If you know that, you know everything." Her voice was sullen.

Childress felt a surge of sympathy. She kept her voice level and calm. "You've nearly drowned, my dear, and been chased across half the Northern Earth if I don't miss my guess. But that's nearly all I can say. I don't even know your name."

"We nearly drowned after crashing an airship. And worse, along the way." After a moment, she added, "I am Paolina Barthes, of Praia Nova, along the Atlantic extents of *a Muralha*."

"Well, Paolina Barthes, I am the Mask Childress, also known as Emily McHenry Childress, sometime librarian in New Haven, Connecticut."

"Mask?"

"Of the Feathered Masks. The *avebianco*. Spiritualists searching for man's path in God's world."

Paolina stiffened. "I have had enough of searchers. Your Silent Order has been the death of many in their quest to abuse me."

"Not my Silent Order," Childress said carefully. "They have a writ against my life."

"So why are *you* aboard this ship?"

"Looking for you, I think. To stop the Silent Order from taking you to finish building their Golden Bridge."

"You must be the other ones, the birds."

"Yes." Childress wasn't certain whether to be pleased or concerned at what this girl knew. "The white birds, as I said."

"And what are *your* plans for me?" The anger was building once again.

"For you?" Childress was surprised at the question. "Nothing. To offer you aid, if possible, and somehow ensure your freedom. Our aim was to stop another project in which you and your device seem to have come to play a critical role. If you find a way to escape the Silent Order, we may have succeeded in a single stroke." Phu Ket could wait, if this Paolina somehow left the chase behind.

"If you want a single stroke, best cut off my head now and be done with it."

"No, I do not think so." Childress gathered Paolina's hands in hers. The girl did not resist. "We do not do things that way. *I* do not do things that way."

"Do you command this ship?"

"No, of course not. But I am the Mask here. And your fate is most properly my concern, far more so than Captain Leung's."

Paolina fell silent. She did not pull her hands away from Childress' grip. The ship shuddered again, rolling with some motion of the waves as they found their depth.

"Listen," Childress finally said. "You must have had a direction, a goal when you were forced down by the storm. Where were you bound?"

"We had t-t-taken *Heaven's Deer*."

"You stole an airship?"

"No. We took her wheel from her captain."

Childress turned that over. "Who? You had a crew."

"Just me and al-Wazir," Paolina whispered.

"Two of you took on an airship?" She was impressed and alarmed. This girl was very powerful. No wonder the Silent Order and the Chinese were both after her. That Paolina might be the Golden Bridge brought to life seemed very possible.

"Yes we did."

"Bound where? What was your plan?"

"We f-f-forced most of the crew off. We were headed for *a-a-a Muralha*—the Wall. If the storm had not taken us, we would have made our d-d-destination in another day or so."

"So you want to go to the Wall."

"I was born on the Wall. If I am to die soon, I would prefer to die on the Wall. If I am to live, I would p-p-prefer to live there. As you v-v-value me, take me there."

"Then we sail to the Wall," Childress said, her tone firm.

"Not until I know what caused *Five Lucky Winds* to move two hundred nautical miles in a moment," Leung said from the hatch. He slipped into the wardroom and sat at the table with them. "I am Captain Leung."

Paolina just stared at him. "B-b-but you're Ch-ch-chinese."

"Yes, he is," Childress said, stepping into the argument before it erupted. "He is master of this vessel, and it is his ship and crew that have saved you from certain drowning. Captain Leung, this is Paolina Barthes, late of the Wall. *A Muralha*, she calls it."

"Miss Barthes, it is a pleasure to make your acquaintance." His voice grew hard. "What happened to my ship?"

The girl tugged a brass disk from the folds of her blanket. It glinted with recent dunking. "The gleam," she said softly. "I called you to me."

"Called me? Called my ship? How did you know to find us?"

"I did not." She looked up, met his eyes, then Childress'. The Mask saw misery in the girl's gaze. "I arranged the world so that rescue might come to me."

Leung was incredulous. "You moved a vessel of over three hundred tons with the power of your *arrangements*?"

"This is the strength of the Golden Bridge," Childress snapped. "The missing keystone to their arch lies in what this poor girl can do. She *is* the Bridge, in a very real way. She already carries what they seek to build. The Silent Order and your government have pursued this girl across Northern Earth. You can see what such power would mean in the wrong hands."

"My last gleam destroyed half of Strasbourg," Paolina muttered.

The captain stared at her. "A bomb? Aboard my vessel, you have brought a bomb?"

"More like . . . a spell." Paolina showed them what looked like a clockface. "A windup spell."

"There have always been wizards in Northern Earth." Childress wasn't sure which of the three of the them she was speaking to. "William of Ghent, for example." The stakes for which this game were being played had grown immense. "This thing that you have wrought is a grave danger, Miss Barthes."

"People have died," she muttered. "Too many."

Childress led her to the horrifying conclusion. "Because it might make any man a wizard."

"That seems true. Though I built the one which damaged Strasbourg, I did not wield it."

"I should dump both you and that device in the ocean," said Leung. "You are the most dangerous person to walk this Northern Earth since K'ung-fu-tzu."

Paolina turned to Childress. "I told you."

"Let him think, child," she said in her calmest voice, the one usually reserved for an angry professor. *Childress* knew better. Leung was not planning to dump this poor girl into the sea. Still, his reaction echoed her own. This was exactly the sort of disruptive, destructive force that she feared in the Golden Bridge project. Leveling cities, indeed.

"Where were you bound with it?" the captain asked.

"As a prisoner aboard one of your airships." Sullen, resentful, angry. "Reportedly to Phu Ket. Al-Wazir and I had turned it south toward the Wall."

Leung sounded amazed. "You suborned the crew of one of the Celestial Emperor's airships?"

"We took it from the crew, cast the officers overboard." Her voice was filled with a fearsome, fragile pride. "We would be at the Wall now except that the storm forced us down."

"You captured an airship of the Celestial Empire, then crashed it into the sea. This is not the power to level cities, but some other glamour. That makes you all the more dangerous, girl. I do not believe that one-handed monster lying in my passage could have done so on his own."

"Then dump me into the ocean," she said fiercely.

"No." Childress had her best Mask Poinsard voice on now. "We shall put you ashore at the Wall. From there, you must carry on as best you can." She turned to Leung. "In the meantime, we will let her rest. In my cabin, undisturbed, as her sailor still lies in the passageway."

Leung nodded, but remained seated. Childress took that as a hint, and escorted Paolina out of the wardroom and the few steps forward to her cabin. Casting eyes on the snoring, snorting British sailor, the girl refused further aid once they'd reached the entrance.

Childress returned to the wardroom to sit with Leung once more. "How did you discover our position?"

"We still are not certain," he told her. "There are, ah . . . wheels that turn and keep their orientation? Very strong, small wheels?"

"Gyroscopes?"

"Yes. Gyroscopes. In our compasses. I believe we are about a hundred nautical miles west and north of Sumatra. I am not certain, and thus we must be very, very cautious as to our depth and heading until the storm reduces and we can take a reliable position from the sky."

"The gleam." Childress tried to imagine how the *avebianco* or the British Crown would react to the presence of such power in the world. Much as the Silent Order already had, she assumed.

"An accursed device if ever there was one." He looked at his hands. "I will make a heading toward the Wall, if you will work to find a way to assure me that once ashore she and her device will trouble us no more."

"How could I make that assurance?"

"You are the Mask here. I rely on your discernment and discretion."

"Indeed." *Discernment and discretion are all well and fine,* she thought. What she needed was a flash of genius.

More than a flash.

TWENTY

PAOLINA

She awoke shivering violently. *A fever*. She felt neither burning nor chilled, though. She was unclothed, wrapped in layers of blankets, lying in a narrow bed in a tiny metal-walled room. She distinctly remembered it pitching and rolling when she'd lain down. The deck seemed level now.

Metal meant she was no longer on the airship. *No, the submarine.* She'd fought with the captain. A panic overwhelmed Paolina as she cast about for the gleam, but it was under her covers with her. She must have slept with it wrapped in her hands.

Holding the thing calmed her. She rose and pulled on her damp, tattered dress. There was nothing else to wear. When she opened the hatch a sailor stationed there turned and smiled at her, then called out.

That old woman—Childless?—appeared from down the corridor. "Good day, young lady."

Paolina couldn't decide whether to be appalled or pleased that there was an Englishwoman aboard a Chinese vessel. It made no sense to her at all, yet here *she* was. "How is Chief al-Wazir?"

"Your great lummox of a Scotsman? He has a dreadful fever, but seems in no danger of passing away. He has twice asked for you."

"Where is he?"

"The forward torpedo room. With you in my cabin, it's the only place on *Five Lucky Winds* to put him."

"I would like to see the chief."

"Not before Captain Leung says so, dear. Besides, we are coming to a shore. There will be distractions."

Her heart leapt. "*A Muralha*?"

"No, no. I am afraid only a small harbor along the southwest coast of

Sumatra. We lost most of our fresh water in the storm. The captain would prefer to take on further supply. Once that is sorted, we are perhaps a day's sail from the Wall."

"Oh." There was only delay, disappointment, more kinds of trouble ahead. That was all she could see, ever and again.

"Do not despair," the old woman said kindly. She picked up a bowl and pair of the Chinese sticks. "Here, you should eat. It will improve your mood."

They breakfasted on cold rice with some slippery, naked beans in brownish sauce. To her surprise, Paolina did feel a bit better. A sailor stepped in and whispered to Childress, who nodded and murmured her thanks.

"We can go see your angry giant now, Miss Barthes. Then if you'd like to come up into the tower, we might look upon the shore of Sumatra."

"How is Chief al-Wazir?"

"I can assure you he's well cared for." Childress rose. "Come with me."

They headed for a hatch at the end of the short passageway. A sailor swung it open at their approach and waved them in.

The room beyond was very narrow, lined with long cylinders and two round hatches at the front. A set of winches was stowed above, and the cleared space on the floor where the cylinders—torpedoes?—could be handled was currently occupied by one Threadgill Angus al-Wazir.

He in turn was surrounded by half a dozen sailors in their blue pajamas. They seemed to be fascinated by the towering redheaded man. It had been somewhat the same aboard *Heaven's Deer*, though with far more anger and weapons. Al-Wazir and the airship had met fighting, after all. Still, he'd exerted a certain strange attraction to the Chinese.

"Lassie," al-Wazir mumbled. His voice was thick as mud.

"Chief," she answered.

"They're feeding me crap, lassie. Stewed crap what tastes like the worst of last winter's oats."

He sounded so pathetic, so small. It made her want to cry.

"We're safe," she lied. "Safe for now in this place."

"They'll not take ye to Phu Ket?"

"No, Chief, not to Phu Ket." She took his remaining hand in hers. "We're going to the Wall, soon as we bring on supplies."

"Aye, the Wall." He looked at her with some strain of desperation in his eyes. *Is he drugged?* These sailors had risked all to save her and al-Wazir. Surely they would not trouble to kill him now.

"We're safe." She squeezed his hand.

"Come above, girl," the old woman told her. "Come above."

Paolina stumbled back to the door.

"Lassie," he said as she was about to step out.

"Yes?" She stared back, still wondering how truly ill he was.

"You brought this ship from far away. Could you send us to the Bight of Benin? Or all the way to Lanarkshire?"

"Perhaps I could."

She climbed the ladder with tears stinging her eyes. It was very different when the storm and threat of tons of water were not hanging over her head. Still damp and stinking of the sea, but at the top there was sunlight and the scent of shore—green and deep, soil crossed with perfume and old fruit. Birds circled overhead.

Five Lucky Winds was anchored a quarter mile offshore. A launch pulled from the beach with oars flashing. A small group of men were on land with a pile of barrels next to a stream. Some were in blue pajamas; others were dark-skinned with pale brown skirts. Sailors and locals. Fuzzy wuzzies, al-Wazir would call them.

People, Paolina would call them.

The land was beautiful, lined with a dense jungle that put her in mind of the western African shore. The color here was brighter, more emerald, and the scent was different. Mountains rose behind, with clouds wreathing the peaks. She turned the other way and tilted her head back to face the rising immensity of *a Muralha*. The Wall was so close, she thought she could have reached out to touch it.

Why did they need to take on supplies for such a brief trip?

The launch tied up. Shouting men wrestled the heavy barrels aboard. The water was no lie, that was certain—there was too much effort in those to be anything else here so far from oil or wine. Paolina heard a long conversation in Chinese at the base of the ladder as she stood quietly with Childress and another sailor in the tower. "There's peace up here," she finally said, talking over the discussion below.

"Yes." Childress touched her arm. "It's why I asked to bring you up. You went from airship to storm-tossed sea to these iron decks. You needed a measure of peace."

"I am sorry if I have been rude."

"You have faced great pressures, young lady. And you carry a strange burden in your hands and in your heart."

A burden which threatens the very order of the world, Paolina thought. "Yes. Even if I destroyed this one, I could make another. This is the second. The people who want it . . . me . . . know this."

"The Wall is endless. Lose yourself upon the face of it. No one will find you, especially if you carry the gleam for your protection."

"Why . . . why do your White Birds not seek to grasp this?"

Childress look a long, slow breath. "Perhaps some among the *avebianco* do. But I am the Mask here, and for me it is enough to let the world turn as God intended it, without attempting to remake Creation wholesale."

"You work to preserve balance and order in the world."

"Yes. At least the best of us do."

That explains Lachance, Paolina thought. And the purser aboard of *Star of Gambia*. That there might yet be good people in the world, some of them men, seemed a distant surprise. Still welcome, though.

Footsteps echoed up the ladder. Paolina and Childress edged back from the open hole in the floor of the tower's top. It would be crowded with four up here.

Leung came up.

"Captain," said Childress, with a smile and nod.

"Captain," Paolina added grudgingly.

"Mask," he replied. "Good day. You as well, Miss Barthes." He glanced toward shore. "I have news of serious import."

"What sort of news?" Paolina asked, a new stab of fear in her heart. She was so close. It was almost as if she could *swim* to the Wall.

"Last night, during the Wall storm at about the time you, ah . . . translocated . . . *Five Lucky Winds*, there was an earthquake in the Strait of Malacca. Somewhere near our prior position."

"*They* know that?"

Childress touched her arm. "Hush, girl. The Chinese have wireless stations in many places."

"Whatever you did with that gleam. It killed many to move us." His eyes narrowed as he stared hard at her. "This device is dangerous."

"I *know* that," she almost shouted. "Dangerous to everyone, most of all me. It makes of me a weapon. I will not be so used!"

"No one will use you," said Childress.

"We killed people to move you a hundred miles. Al-Wazir wants to go to Scotland aboard your vessel. How many would die for us to leap ten thousand miles?"

Captain Leung gave her a long, steady stare. "I pray we never find out."

"No." Paolina nodded. "You are right. I will not do such a thing, even though he asks it."

"You and the Mask Childress owe me an answer soon," Leung reminded them.

Paolina glanced between the pair. "About what?"

Childress tightened her grip on Paolina's arm. "We have not spoken yet."

"I go back to my crew." Leung nodded at them both. "I suggest you consider the costs we incur here, simply with every minute we do nothing while such power is loose in the world."

"We are," said Childress.

"What do you think I am running from?" Paolina asked.

Leung did not answer, but climbed down quickly to rejoin his launch before it pulled for shore once more.

Paolina turned to Childress. "Of what are we speaking?"

Childress met her gaze, the old woman's brown eyes glittering. "How to put you ashore with surety that the danger will not again walk the Northern Earth."

"Indeed." Paolina stared at the glinting water. The sea here was so clear, she could see the submarine's hull and the pale sand below it. Fish moved across the bottom, flickering in shoals, larger ones stalking in predatory solitude. The jungle beyond was quiet. Birds continued to circle overhead.

If she could fly away with them, she would, but the gleam's powers didn't seem to extend to transformation.

"I . . . I thought to learn from the wizards when I left *a Muralha*. The English were to be my guides. So I believed. Instead I have found myself both too strong and too foolish for them. I wanted a purpose, to meet the future with full knowledge."

"No one but God has full knowledge," Childress told her. "That is more than any person can expect, child."

"No, no one can. But I have already learned too much on my own. Surely there are greater philosophers in Europe or China? If so, I do not know where to find them. All have betrayed me."

"The world stands against you because you hold power over it in your hands. Your mechanism is too great. It is as if the hand of God had come among us once more. We cannot live in the direct presence of the Divine, not when the world can be unmade and remade at the stroke of one person's will. This is the power too many have pursued of late. The danger is that they might succeed through you."

Paolina stared at Childress a moment. "You do not serve China or England, do you?"

"I am a Mask. I serve the *avebianco,* and through the *avebianco,* the interests of humanity in the world."

"I know nothing of Masks," Paolina said. "All I know are people who find power within service, greed within sacrifice, and see me as the key to more of what they desire."

"You do not need to know of Masks. You merely need to know of your own heart."

"My heart is silent," Paolina said, miserable.

The Mask Childress seemed sincere. Still, she'd had enough of the British, the Chinese, their machinations. She owed nothing to anyone in Northern Earth. Only to keep herself separate from whatever poisonous intrigue they took up among themselves. The world was never so simple, even when it seemed little more than a giant version of Praia Nova with the pettiness and power of the *fidalgos* writ large across the hemisphere.

"You go to the Wall, but how? The captain's question is an excellent one. How shall we put you ashore in safety? Should it be enough to cast the thing into the sea?"

"I . . . I would still know how to make another."

"You cannot undo that knowledge," Childress said sadly.

"Perhaps," Paolina told her. "Perhaps." An idea stirred in the back of her mind.

AL-WAZIR

When he finally woke with a clear head, his lungs ached. Fiercely. He was also surrounded by Chinese sailors. This seemed like a problem.

Al-Wazir sat up on his hands. The cascade of blinding red pain reminded him he was missing one. An even bigger problem.

He fell back to the deck, swallowing curses and renewing a headache he'd managed to forget. Two of the sailors helped him up again, bracing his elbows and chattering at him in Chinese. Someone else stroked his hair. The compartment smelled strongly of machine oil and the Chinese as well as salt-logged al-Wazir.

"Air," he said, gasping. "Might I have fresh air?"

They led him stumbling down a passageway to a ladder. Pistols appeared in a few fists. *These men are not fools,* he thought. In his current state, al-Wazir couldn't take over a rowboat. Still, he was easily twice their size, and not fit at all for this little vessel.

They chivvied him up the ladder. One-handed, exhausted, al-Wazir didn't think he could make the climb. Only the smell of fresh sea air drew him onward.

He stumbled out onto the deck of the submarine. Clear water the color of blown glass lapped close by. Breeze plucked at him. A green-wrapped coast was close by, with a small crowd of men along the shore.

Al-Wazir shuddered in the sunlight, then collapsed to a sitting position with his back against the cold, damp iron of the submarine's tower.

Where am I?

The sailors who'd brought him spread out across the deck, leaving him to his thoughts. Two of their number armed with pistols remained crouched close by, grinning at him. Despite the weapons, al-Wazir did not feel threatened. It was like a man showing his fist in a bar . . . a promise of what might come, if things went awry, but no intent of violence in that moment.

"Chief?"

He glanced around. That had been in English.

"Chief al-Wazir!?"

"Paolina?" Al-Wazir looked up. Someone peered over the edge of the top of the tower, but it didn't look like the girl. He couldn't easily tell—the person's head was silhouetted by the sunlight.

Feet on a ladder within the tower echoed behind him; then Paolina burst out onto the deck. She hurled herself at al-Wazir's chest, hugging him. "You're better! You're walking."

"Aye, and waking, lassie. Ah, lassie, I thought I'd lost you, too. That would be a foul hard blow after leaving John Brass in Africa." He stroked her hair a moment. "Now get up before yon Chinee gossip about us."

"I hope Boaz found a way to slip free of the violence." She sighed a moment. "You remember asking me to take this ship to Lanarkshire?"

He frowned, thinking back into the confusion of recent hours. "Ah . . . no."

"Your fever was breaking." Paolina's expression sagged oddly. "Oh, Chief, I'm so sorry."

He didn't like the sound of that at all. "For what, lassie?"

"When we were drowning, in the storm, I used the gleam. To improve our chances of surviving. This ship, *Five Lucky Winds,* moved a hundred miles in a moment. In your fever, you asked if I could move the ship to Lanarkshire. P-probably I could. But we caused an earthquake here. People d-d-died."

"Lassie, lassie, never you mind that." He wished that he hadn't pushed her away. Her misery was writ large upon her face.

"The Mask Childress w-w-wants to put me ashore on the Wall. I want that as well. But the gleam. It's too powerful."

"You'll know what to do, lassie." He prayed that was true. Her toy was a terrible invention, one that could make any man a wizard with deadly will.

"I do now."

"And what is that?" al-Wazir asked softly.

But she wouldn't tell him. Instead she just shook her head and stared out at the horizon.

———

An Englishwoman joined them shortly thereafter. Older, slight of build, gray-haired.

"I am the Mask Childress." Her accent was colonial. She stared down at him.

He tried to get up, but his legs trembled too much. Instead he made a clumsy salute from where he sat. "Chief Petty Officer Threadgill Angus al-Wazir, of Her Imperial Majesty's Royal Navy airship service." He wondered what a Mask was, but he was too tired to ask.

"Pleased to make your acquaintance." Childress nodded. "You brought this girl and her mechanism across the Indian Ocean, I see."

"No. She brought herself. I merely followed."

"We were taken," Paolina said. "In Mogadishu. Where we lost Boaz."

"It does not matter." The Mask looked at them both, with something like pity in her eyes. "You are here. You have hard choices now."

"I have a plan," Paolina announced. "How to stop the threat of the gleam. It touches people as well as the world." She took a deep breath. "I w-w-will use it to erase my own knowledge of how to build another one."

"No!" Childress seemed shocked.

"Aye," al-Wazir said.

The Mask met his eyes. "We cannot do that to her," she said.

"'Tis not we who do aught to her. She kens the danger even if you do not."

"Neither of you shall do anything to me," Paolina said. "The gleam is deadly dangerous. I made this thing. It is for me to take it from the world."

"You cannot." Childress was gaping and waving for words. "To destroy a known thing, to remove knowledge from the world . . . it is wrong."

"This knowledge is evil," al-Wazir said. "There's them as kills and dies for what this girl knows."

Paolina nodded. "*I* have killed for it. I have nearly died for it, over and over. Two empires pursue this. It must be removed."

Childress seemed to have control of her voice now. "I disagree. A thing done once will be a thing done again. Much like the path the Silent Order seeks to reopen under the guise of the Golden Bridge and their efforts to pass beyond the Wall. This thing of yours is in the world. To damage your mind, your soul, is too high a price to pay for something which cannot be hidden anyway."

"No, no, 'tis her that does it," Al-Wazir finally got to his feet, though the horizon swayed as he stood. "If she removed herself and her infernal device from the world, no man would find the manner of doin' it again."

"It would be best if I did not know," said Paolina. "Should the Silent Order ever again take me somehow, they cannot force me to make another. For your Golden Bridge or any other purpose."

Childress shook her head. "Not *my* Golden Bridge. Regardless, you owe yourself your best strength, your highest effort. Not cutting off the fingers of your mind."

Al-Wazir found enough strength to step away from the support of the tower. The two sailors with their pistols waddled back as well, keeping their distance, but they did not seem worried. "Paolina . . ."

She met his eye.

"What would Boaz have you do?"

"Boaz would have me do what was best." She sighed. "He was not a moral actor, Chief. He was a Brass man of Ophir, a creature of *a Muralha.*"

"The Wall is neither moral nor immoral, woman. It swallowed me ship, it swallowed me da's soul, it swallowed up the Roman Empire, and it may yet swallow up the British Empire. I do not know whether a man o' the Wall can be any more than a man o' the Wall, but he can show you the way."

"I am a woman of the Wall."

"And a woman of Northern Earth," Childress said softly.

The launch returned with the water barrels as they spoke. The deck was suddenly aswarm with Chinese sailors, tuns of water, and two puzzled Sumatrans in straw skirts with painted faces.

Leung rejoined them as the water was pumped into a connection inset in the deck.

"The girl has a plan, Captain." There was a catch in Childress' voice.

"Aye, and she has the right of it," al-Wazir added.

"This is for me to decide," Paolina snapped.

Leung shook his head. "It is for *me* to decide. I command here."

Paolina drew herself up and squared her shoulders. "You do not command me."

One of the Sumatrans called out, pointing. Al-Wazir looked, following the line of the man's arm.

A trio of Chinese airships rose over the line of mountains behind the shore.

Leung shouted up to the tower. The lookout shouted back down.

"Ship smoke to the northwest," he said. "The pursuit out of Singapore has located us."

"What now?" asked al-Wazir, suddenly very tired of fighting.

The captain looked at the airships a moment. "We bind ourselves over.

Five Lucky Winds cannot flee an entire fleet. Not in these waters, in clear weather and broad daylight."

"Then I must do this thing now," said Paolina. "Put me to sea in your boat, so that the gleam will not affect the submarine."

"No," said Childress.

"Aye," said al-Wazir.

Leung barked orders in Chinese, then offered Paolina his hand.

CHILDRESS

She watched Paolina step down into the launch. Ming and Fat Cheung went with her to man the oars and lend her aid. Leung had the crew dump the barrels they had not yet pumped and pass the empties back down the hatch.

"They cannot move the full ones down the ladder," al-Wazir said. "Too heavy."

Childress nodded. "In port they open larger hatches and use cranes."

Both of them watched Paolina as they spoke.

The girl looked up from her seat in the small boat. It rocked slightly on the water. Ropes coiled around her feet, and the sunlight caught Paolina's hair like polished oak.

Ming, just aft of Paolina, smiled up at Childress. "*Zai jien,*" he said. *Good-bye*. He and Fat Cheung then put their backs into the oars, pulling away from *Five Lucky Winds*.

Childress watched them go as the deck cleared around her. "How far?"

"I'd make it a thousand yards, me," said al-Wazir. "If I was them. Did you hear their captain giving them orders?"

She thought about that a moment. "No. Actually, I did not."

"Nor did I."

"What does that mean?"

"They's gone without orders, is what it means. That Ming, he's kind of a Chinee petty officer. He has an understanding with the captain here. Since there's seven kinds of admiralty hell about to land on this here deck, the captain's used the chief to send his biggest problem away."

She had to laugh. "You are also a large problem for Captain Leung, Chief al-Wazir."

"Not so large as yon poppet and her device. I'm a big man, she has the killing of the world in her hand."

"Paolina will erase part of herself, and perhaps cast that thing into the sea. It won't be such a problem then."

Meanwhile a series of whistles and bells caused the crew of *Five Lucky Winds* to pour out onto the deck. A few sailors were stringing flags to the tower, while others mounted the staves at the bow and stern.

Al-Wazir snorted. "Yon captain's making a show if it. He'll go down in full kit, I reckon. He seems something of a gentleman for a Chinee."

Childress bit back a cold retort. "Captain Leung is indeed a gentlemen. You would do well to remember that, Chief."

The airships approached over the jungle. A Sumatran canoe slid up to the hull to take the two local warriors off. One of them turned and gave al-Wazir a long, solemn look.

She noted that the chief's guards had disappeared.

"Ye want off for yon island?" al-Wazir asked Childress. "Methinks the captain is letting all his biggest problems slip overboard."

"No." She didn't have to consider it. "I will stay with the ship. I am the Mask Childress. The Celestial Empire holds no fear for me. But please, take yourself ashore."

"The Celestial Empire holds plenty of fear for me, ma'am, and begging your pardon." He sighed and raised his bandaged stump. "I've run too far, and without me southern paw I'm not the fighter I was. Besides, I will not leave an Englishwoman behind in heathen clutches."

Childress took his remaining hand in hers. "You're a better man than you believe yourself to be, Chief al-Wazir."

Al-Wazir let her hold on to him for a moment. He nodded at the Sumatran, who grinned and shoved off in his canoe. Childress scanned the water, watching Paolina's launch pull farther and farther away. She could hear the engines of the approaching airships growling in the sky.

Within minutes the crew of *Five Lucky Winds* was assembled on the deck. Most were in better uniforms than the usual blue service cotton she'd become accustomed to seeing them in. Three flags snapped from a staff rigged on the tower, while a series of smaller banners hung on the forward line.

It was ceremonious, even pretty, in the light of an equatorial morning. She felt like she was attending an execution. All that was lacking was a drum beating the measure at the end of a man's life.

Two of the airships closed to pass overhead. The third split eastward toward where Paolina bobbed in the launch with Ming and Fat Cheung. She looked to the north and west. The ships steaming toward them were visible to the casual eye now. As she watched, a wisp of smoke rose from the oncoming hull as a single gun boomed to send a ripple of sound across the restless water.

Each of the airships passing overhead dropped a smoke pot into the water near *Five Lucky Winds*. One burned red on the starboard side, the other burned white on the port.

Al-Wazir leaned over and rumbled in her ear. "Bracketing their shots, they is. Showing your captain what's what. Airships is the best thing for fighting these blasted submarines."

"I would expect that they don't generally fight their own side."

"No, no." He added contemplatively a moment later, "Not so as you'd think, at any rate."

The airships circled overhead, engines whining. She watched each vessel drop a set of lines over the side. Preparing to lower men to take over *Five Lucky Winds*. Though it was obvious even to Childress that the true threat would come from the approaching surface ships.

The airships could destroy the submarine, but they could not force Leung to surrender. Whatever angry admiral rode aboard the approaching line of armored ships held all power over them now. She wondered if Admiral Shang had some influence to the good over what would come next.

A gunboat approached *Five Lucky Winds*. Its rail was crowded with armed sailors. Leung had four of his men take lines that were cast from the surface vessel and make them fast to the submarine. The two floated close, only a set of narrow cylindrical bumpers keeping the hulls from battering together.

A trio of aging mandarins stepped across a narrow gangplank, disdaining any escort. They wore formal robes, layers of red and black and gold over creamy underrobes, much more stylized than even the cheongsams of the librarians at Chersonesus Aurea. Each also had a small square hat with a colored stone atop. A very old man led them, who moved as smoothly as any dancer. Childress marked that he had something of the same presence as William of Ghent. He was a wizard, almost certainly.

The mandarin did not look to Leung, but rather stepped straight toward Childress. His hands closed one fist over the other, then made the gesture in reverse.

The Silent Order. She offered him a small smile and the bird sign of the *avebianco* in return.

"You have strayed far from what was agreed, Mask."

Childress realized that this man must think her to be Poinsard. *"As it may be,"* she responded. Whatever Admiral Shang knew, or thought, the chief of the Beiyang Navy had not communicated it with these gentlemen of the Imperial Court. She added in English: "You stray too far toward what should not be."

"You will not judge. You cannot. *Woman, devil.*" He added a third word, also in Chinese, which she did not follow, but Leung's breath hissed.

There was a ripping noise as the ropes dangling from the circling airships reached the submarine. One flier had held a position above *Five Lucky Winds* to drop air sailors down to the deck. Leung barked a quick order for his men to stand and hold. They were quickly swarmed by a dozen fighters armed with short rifles and long knives.

In moments all the crew of *Five Lucky Winds* was facedown on the deck, save for Leung himself, along with Childress and al-Wazir. The mandarin never even turned to look at the commotion behind him.

The mandarin smiled, his lips thin. "I believe you will find our hospitality more convivial than the company of mutineers and English revanchists."

Childress wished she possessed the courage to cast herself into the sea in that moment. Instead she continued to play the part of Poinsard. "Where should this hospitality be found? In Phu Ket or Nanking?"

"Do not be a fool, Mask." A flash of distaste crossed his face, as if he'd eaten of something foul. "In the end we have far more in common than that which separates us."

How much have the Silent Order and the Feathered Masks been in collaboration? she wondered. *Enough to sell me to the star chamber.* Or more to the point, to be drowned in the Atlantic along with the rest of *Mute Swan*'s crew, just so Poinsard could go on to China without there being a hue and cry behind her. "I wish to be clear which way the wind blew here."

She glanced northwestward. The rest of the mandarin's fleet was approaching. All in service of the Silent Order. She wondered if *Five Lucky Winds* would be posted missing, as *Mute Swan* must have been, lost at sea without ever word of her true fate coming back.

Surely these crews would talk more than that.

"The wind blows as it always has, toward the Middle Kingdom." He turned and shouted something in Chinese.

The invaders on the deck began shooting the prone sailors in the head. They moved quickly even as some of Leung's men rose to their knees in shouted protest. The captain screamed and strained against invisible bonds.

Beside her, al-Wazir lurched into motion with a vasty roar.

TWENTY-ONE

PAOLINA

Out in the gently rocking launch, Paolina had studied the gleam as the airships approached. There had been little enough she could do except to remove herself from the board as a playing piece. Not that the Silent Order would ever believe that of her. Still, she could only fight one struggle at a time.

If only Boaz had come with them. She prayed he had survived the carnage and chaos back in Mogadishu.

Here, now, her problems were far more immediate.

She'd spent time fiddling with the hand that corresponded to the time that beat inside her. How to touch the shadow of one thought within her own head?

It was a problem that frightened her deeply.

Ming muttered something. Painfully aware she was out of time, Paolina looked up. Ropes descended from the airship over *Five Lucky Winds*. The airship circling over their launch was losing altitude, also dangling ropes now.

Then gunfire echoed across the water.

"They're killing the crew," she whispered.

Paolina had no love for the Chinese, especially not the airshipmen, but Childress' submariners had saved both her life and al-Wazir's. And been decent about things afterwards. Most important, the chief was still with them.

In a surge of anger, she tugged the stem to the fourth position, away from her focus on herself into the focus on the world. She moved quickly, without thinking, much as she had during the storm when she'd drawn *Five Lucky Winds* to her position.

The attacking fleet came into sharp relief. The hand quivered as it found their wavelength. Bound by a skein of duty, of orders and shared obligation, they were as much one entity as all the wind and waves and falling water that made up a storm.

She'd been touching the edges of her own mind, exploring the forests of forgetting. Now she reached into theirs.

It was like skimming cream from milk, like winnowing wheat from dross. Reaching in, she used the gleam to twist them just *so*, creating an absence of memory, of purpose, of thought.

There was a pop, and a flare of light unseen except at the corners of vision. Ming and Fat Cheung both swore quietly as something rippled away from the launch. She heard a faint clattering, clockwork moving everywhere around her.

The airship circling over the launch broke out of its maneuver on a heading south of east. The descending sailors dropped into the water and began to flounder. The airship above *Five Lucky Winds* also broke position to drag its landing ropes away south. The other airship straightened out of a stationkeeping arc and moved off west of north.

More important, the men with guns on the deck of *Five Lucky Winds* left off their shooting and began to look around. Leung's surviving sailors rose in a body and drove their invaders overboard. There was no struggle that Paolina could see, just bodies falling into the water as if they were men asleep.

She felt a cold chill down her spine.

"Great God in His brass heaven," she muttered. "What have I wrought?" It was the same thing she'd done to Boaz, back at the bottom of the Wall, writ across a mighty force of men.

With the stemwinder, the Silent Order really could kill the world.

Ming touched her elbow. There was a deep, passionate sympathy in his eyes. "We go ship now."

The only thing that staved off her rush of guilt was the knowledge that these same men had been intent on her own death mere moments earlier. Still, the sight of them bobbing quietly in the water was horrifying.

"Go ship now." She nodded.

Ming and Fat Cheung put their backs into rowing, covering the distance toward *Five Lucky Winds* as quickly as they could, even as the silhouettes of the ships on the horizon widened. The naval units each turned in one direction or another without respect to the rest of their fleet. The men in the water trod water or swam slowly, but didn't seem to understand their situation. Not a one looked to the launch for aid, or to resume the attack. Neither did they head for shore.

They just waited there for someone or something to tell them what to do. A few had already sunk into drowning.

Have I made them into idiots?

Bells echoed over the water, followed by a horrendous rending noise as two of the ships collided.

Fat Cheung said something quietly to Ming.

Ahead, the deck of *Five Lucky Winds* was already clearing in a mad scramble. The wounded and the dead were being taken below, while the colors were struck. A larger weapon had appeared on the tower. A sailor trained it on her.

Al-Wazir and Childress stood, watching her approach.

Paolina knew there was no turning back from what had taken place. She kept one hand firmly on the gleam. The power of forgetting was on display even now, as men about them faded ever further from their duty.

"Hold your position," al-Wazir bellowed as they came within twenty or so yards of the submarine. Leung shouted in Chinese from his position atop the tower, where he was surveying the damage and directing the submarine's departure.

After backing water to slow them down, Ming and Fat Cheung shipped their oars. Ming called something out in Chinese. The launch continued to drift slowly toward the submarine.

"You cannot come aboard," Leung called down. "You are too dangerous."

Al-Wazir gave Leung a long, hard look that Paolina could interpret even from her position. The gun on the tower still tracked her.

"I saved you all," she said, not even bothering to shout.

The boat had slipped to ten yards' distance. Close enough to swim in a few strokes. Close enough for that weapon next to Leung to cover in the pull of a man's finger.

"Our thanks, lassie," bellowed al-Wazir, "and more than. But what will ye be doing now, eh?"

Paolina stood in the boat, her balance uncertain but trusting to the moment. She raised the gleam above her head. The words came. "I am too much for this Northern Earth. Even if I were to wipe my own memory clean, they will never believe me incapable of this power they crave so badly.

"Instead I will sail to the Wall and find my own Golden Bridge to pass beyond. There are wizards in the Southern Earth, and Great Relics, and people with no care for London or Peking. Bid me farewell as I will pass from this life, taking the gleam with me."

Al-Wazir gave Leung another long, hard glare. Leung stared back down at the chief, at the Mask Childress, then locked gazes with Paolina. Even as the two of them looked into one another's eyes, the launch bumped against the hull.

"Go," he said. Leung then called to Ming in Chinese.

Their boat bumped the submarine's hull. Paolina sat down as Ming argued. Fat Cheung climbed out of the launch with a crooked smile for her. He ran for the hatch at the base of the tower, while Ming remained in the launch.

Leung shouted down at him, but Ming pushed them off with his oar. "We go," he said to Paolina, and pointed her to Fat Cheung's abandoned seat by the port oarlock.

She slipped over to the warm seat, placed the gleam between her feet, and began to row. They faced backwards, as the fishermen did, and so they watched *Five Lucky Winds* awhile, until a horn blasted above the submarine and she began to make way, passing beneath the waves as she did so. She only wished Boaz were with her now.

There was nothing left but the bobbing heads of the airshipmen, who slipped beneath the waves one by one. Some went silently, others in bloody shouts as the sharks of these waters came to take them.

They rowed south in silence, toward *a Muralha*, which towered behind her sure as any man leaning over her shoulder. This she would conquer, surpass, and pass beyond; that she knew.

When Ming began to sing, she listened awhile. Though Paolina was no singer of any skill, she made a wordless harmony to go along with him. It was like a little prayer, except that the two of them spoke to the noontime of the world. Their oars dipped in the bounteous salt ocean as they rowed.

AL-WAZIR

He'd not spent time wondering about the girl, nor staring after her as Childress had done. Rather, al-Wazir lent his strength, prodigious compared with these busy little men even while working one-handed, to getting the wounded and the dead below. The sailors of *Five Lucky Winds* were not leaving their own behind to share this bit of ocean with those who had attacked them.

It was a feeling he could understand.

Leung came down from the tower finally. "She is out of range. We must go."

"Aye." Al-Wazir looked at the Sumatran shore a moment, recalling the recent invitation. Surely they were being watched intently from there now. Unless the mechanical spell invoked by Paolina had overwhelmed the fuzzy wuzzies as well. "And where are we heading now, sir?"

"I have a mind to sail west, Chief al-Wazir. There is no choice for me here. I could attempt to make my home port while being hunted for a traitor and a mutineer, but *Five Lucky Winds* would be broken on the bottom of the Strait of Malacca within the day, I believe."

Al-Wazir had to laugh. "Too far west and you will be hunted for a Chinee invader. I trow the bottom of the Indian Ocean is little more pleasant than the bottom of some Asian strait."

"I have two English passengers to discharge. Perhaps an arrangement can be made."

"Oh, you *are* an optimist, Captain. But as it happens, I have the ear of the Prime Minister, if we can find a way to send a message without immediate fatal consequence. I owe him a report at the least and should like to hear his thoughts. In that same duty, there must be a rescue for some men I left along the Wall on the eastern edge of Africa. This is something else the PM will want very much to hear of. Most importantly, I've unfinished business in Mogadishu. I left a friend behind."

"In a British port? Surely this is not a problem."

"A friend of Miss Barthes'. A man from off the Wall."

"Ah." Leung added something in Chinese.

"You'll need to be teaching me that cat's yowl, I think, if I'm to ship aboard your vessel."

The captain seemed surprised. "How's that?"

"Your just put one of your best petty officers asea in a boat, Captain. And yon heathens did for nigh half your men. *Five Lucky Winds* sails short-handed, with no friendly port in the Northern Earth, not as things stand today. I'll stand watch if you'll have me."

Leung laughed, short and bitter. "Let us go below," he said, "and speak to the Mask Childress. I believe she is with the cooks, doing what can be done for the wounded and the dead."

Al-Wazir took one last look south. The launch was lost to him, invisible in the complex texture of the water and the looming mass of the Wall beyond.

"Farewell, lassie. I'm off to find your Brass man, and see that's he's free and hale."

Then he went to look for the Englishwoman.

CHILDRESS

She looked up to see there was no one left to wash. The dead deserved to go into the sea clean. She had put their faces in her *ars memoriae*, to honor them in the privacy of her heart.

The passageway was filled with bodies, fourteen of them like giant cocoons. Two more in her cabin, Yao and Sweet Lu. She thought them unlikely to live to see another dawn.

Childress realized that *Five Lucky Winds* had gotten under way sometime back as well. One of the cooks, Ping, gave her a crooked smile and a hot cloth with which to clean herself.

"She's away, Mask," said al-Wazir, surprising Childress. It amazed her that a man so large and loud could make a quiet entrance, especially in a place as cramped as the interior of this submarine.

"Emily," she said, who had not offered her given name to a man in over thirty years. "You may refer to me as Emily."

He smiled and squatted down on the bloody deck. "Aye, and I'm Threadgill to me ma and me first and last priest back home. I'll not know who 'tis you're talking to if you say the name. In any case . . . Emily . . . the lassie's on her way. No calling her back nor stopping her now."

"Where are we bound?" she asked. The question should have meant everything, but right now all she could feel was relief for Paolina and exhaustion for herself. There was still the matter of Phu Ket, but with Paolina away from the clutches of the Silent Order, they could take the time to plan their action.

"Africa, to help a friend. Then wherever we can find a peaceable port."

Childress considered that. "The captain is confident."

"The captain is no such thing," Leung said from behind al-Wazir. "But he is still the captain, and so must set a course."

"I've never been to Africa." Childress wondered if that benighted land were any closer to God.

Al-Wazir growled. "Well, 'tis a pit of Wall monsters and Englishmen in my experience."

"Peace be with us all," Childress said.

"Peace, indeed," said the chief.

Over his shoulder, Leung nodded. "Everything in the order of the world has a name, Mask Childress. To name someone is to become them."

"Then I name you friend," she told him softly. "You and Ming and the cooks and everyone aboard this ship."

They turned west toward the sunset, preparing for a mass funeral as *Five Lucky Winds* slipped beneath the waves.

EPILOGUE

Paolina walked slowly through the freezing mists. There was a huge drop ahead, one she didn't mean to find the hard way. This area had been formal gardens once—that much was clear from the broken stones and sweeping paths. Ming had found some fruit, too, remnants of an orchard, but they'd steered clear of the sagging building covered with frost-burned vines and the thorny canes of bushes. It smelled like old stone and little else up here now. Whoever had built and lived in this place was long, long gone.

At least they were on the south side of *a Muralha*. Beyond even the most distant clutches of the Silent Order, the Feathered Masks, or the competing empires through which both intertwined.

She wasn't sure where Ming was at the moment. Exploring a little to the west, she thought. Paolina couldn't imagine what he was finding—she could barely see from one tree trunk to the next herself.

When she came upon the angel, she nearly shrieked with surprise until she realized it was a statue.

When the angel turned its brass head and nodded, she was too surprised to shriek.

"Welcome to the Southern Earth," it said in Portuguese, the language at the bottom of her thoughts. *"Fetch your friend. There is someone you should meet."*